In praise of Diane Duane's works

On *Deep Wizardry*

"Diane Duane is a skilled master of the genre."
—*The Philadelphia Enquirer*

". . . the author has remarkable and original imaginative powers."

—*Horn Book*

"Duane's ocean setting and her non-human characters are captivating, her human characters believable and likeable."
—*Science Fiction Chronicle*

On *High Wizardry*

"Duane is tops in the high adventure business . . ."
—*Publishers Weekly*

"Duane writes about people you can really care about, with lots of quirks and endearing traits that feel real in a way that most people don't manage."

—Tom Whitmore, *Locus*

THE HARBINGER TRILOGY

DIANE DUANE

STAR★DRIVE

NIGHTFALL AT ALGEMRON

Volume Three of the HARBINGER TRILOGY

Diane Duane

Wizards
OF THE COAST

For Alison Hopkins

NIGHTFALL AT ALGEMRON
©2000 Wizards of the Coast, Inc.
All Rights Reserved.

Cover art by rk post
First Printing: April 2000
Library of Congress Catalog Card Number: 99-65620

9 8 7 6 5 4 3 2 1

ISBN: 0-7869-1563-3
620-T21563

U.S., CANADA, ASIA,
PACIFIC, & LATIN AMERICA
Wizards of the Coast, Inc.
P.O. Box 707
Renton, WA 98057-0707
+1-800-324-6496

EUROPEAN HEADQUARTERS
Wizards of the Coast, Belgium
P.B. 2031
2600 Berchem
Belgium
Tel. +32-70-23-32-77

Visit our web-site at **www.wizards.com**

Yet how shall we judge the battle by blood,
by counting the lives, mere columns of numbers?
By the size of the field? By the ships there to-gathered?
All these are but symbols: true reckoning runs deeper.
The desperate deed in hot haste enacted,
the blaze of blasters, the swift ship's firing,
are ever held up as the warrior's meed.
Yet all axework still must give pride of place
to the courage that stirs in uncertain silence,
slowly facing the fears of war's desolation
and the great awful dark of unknown inner spaces,
the cold empty realms uncharted, unhearted,
till the hero comes and with his will conquers,
inhabiting darkness, and owning the silence.
Uncertain that battle: all unknown its ending:
and known least of all by him who has triumphed—
for breath's a deceiver, and mocks its own victories:
life's nightfall alone tells the truth of the battle.

Helm's Saga, song iii, staves 480-498, Grawl.

Chapter One

GABRIEL CONNOR STOOD in bright sunshine on the little hill, looking down the dusty single lane road that led down to the center of Tisane Island.

You've come this far, he thought. Get it over with.

He felt guilty about his own reluctance. He had been avoiding this visit for long enough. He shouldn't have to feel that going to see his family was a chore. Except this was his father, and Gabriel had not heard from his father in more than a year . . . and he was scared.

In the days before his exile from the Concord, Gabriel would normally have taken a public transport—landed at Hughes Island, taken a Blue Sea Lines hopper to Stricken, and then a small "subsidized" hopper from Stricken across the straits to Tisane. But something about such a routing, enjoyable as Gabriel would have found it, made him nervous. There were too many things that could happen, too many chances that someone would query his ID and discover that he should not have been there at all . . . that the ID was a fake, hiding the identity of a wanted criminal. He finally had opted to simply file for a landing permit for *Sunshine* with Bluefall Control—under the identity that Delde Sota had crafted for him—and control had granted the permit. As an infotrader's vessel, no one was going to subject *Sunshine* to too much in the way of customs formalities without reason.

Then Gabriel had taken her down. It had been a casual landing, one partially handled by ship's navigation systems so that he had not needed to call Enda to help. Still, as

Gabriel kept an eye on the progress of the landing, she had come along in the middle of the approach, looking through the door from the main hallway at the great, glowing blue curve of the world that filled the front viewports.

"Shall I come with you?" was all she had said.

Gabriel had thought about that. Her presence would certainly have been welcome. There was something about Enda that always made him feel more confident. It was not specifically that she was a fraal—slight and slim and pearl-complected—that made him feel large and strong around her. It was not her age, though she was old enough to be his grandmother several times over. *She just has the gift,* Gabriel thought, *of bringing out the best in people.*

But not today, not right now. Bringing her along would seem too much like an admission that he needed her around to help him handle his fears.

"No . . . thank you, though," he'd replied.

"All right," she had said. "How long will we be down?"

"Probably not very long, an hour or so."

She had gone back down the hallway and said nothing more. The rest of the landing went without incident, and *Sunshine* had more or less landed herself at the little field down at the far end of Tisane, shutting her engines down to standby.

Gabriel had gone to the airlock door, called the lift, and stood there a moment brushing himself off. His cream-colored smartfabric jumpsuit meant he was slightly over-dressed for the climate—they kept the ship at about 20 C, and it was closer to 30 outside—but he was not going to spend more time temporizing over his clothes. He was nervous enough as it was.

One more thought had occurred to Gabriel, and he had almost been ashamed of it, but his life was no longer the predictable thing it once had been. He had gone down to the arms cabinet and come back with his little flechette pistol, a present from Helm. He had pocketed it, ashamed even to be thinking that he might need it in this place of all places.

"Back shortly," he had said to Enda. He had been surprised by the strangled sound of the words as they came out.

"All right," she had said as the door opened for him.

Gabriel had entered the lift and ridden it down. The door slid open—

The fragrance of the air . . . he had completely forgotten it. That peculiar and specific mix of salt, water, sun on water, ozone, flowers, dried or rotting seaweed down at the shore, just at the bottom of the cliff where the landing pad was positioned . . . and the light, the constantly shifting light nearby, of water moving and glittering in the sunlight, and the more distant, hazy blue-white glow of cloud and haze and showers trailing against the horizon. It all came together and took Gabriel by the throat, the sudden light and scent of childhood lost. For many long moments, he had only been able to stand by *Sunshine* and wonder if this was really what he had named his ship after: this memory, this most basic of his experiences.

He had started to walk, mostly to have something to do besides stand next to *Sunshine* like someone lost. Decidedly, Gabriel was not lost. If he knew anything, he knew this road back to his house from the landing pad. How often had he come here as a kid to watch the hoppers jump off, carrying local people about their business or visitors back to their ships and off to the stars? There hadn't been that many visitors. Tisane was not a place to which people tended to come back once they had managed to get away from it.

It wasn't that way with the rest of the planet, of course. Bluefall was one of the most beautiful planets in the Verge, possibly one of the most beautiful worlds anywhere on which humans and their associate species lived. It had received its share of tragedies and difficulties over its history, but the friendly climatic range, the buoyant economy, and the fact that the place was at peace kept bringing more colonists to take advantage of the world's bounty.

It had become a rather crowded place, of course. There were something like four hundred and thirty million people from all species here now, and every stellar nation had at least one island here. Beyond those, though, away from the big, long-settled islands like Hughes, maybe three thousand islands lay scattered in small chains or long ones, as accessible or inaccessible as their settlers chose to make them. Tisane, near Stricken, was one of the more accessible islands that nonetheless was known by almost no one but its immediate neighbors. This was emphatically one of the uncrowded places. There were a few other small ships and hoppers parked on the pad, but that was all.

Pushing the memories aside for now, Gabriel walked down the single paved road that connected Tisane's landing pad to the rest of the island. He looked at the houses as he went. Almost all of them were the same, built and shingled in local woods and composites. Here and there a lot was empty, the house that had stood there most likely fallen victim to one of the vicious hurricanes that came through here every decade or so—the price you paid for living in a place so casual, so relatively unregulated. Stricken had been settled by Hatire people, and some of them had come over this way, but only a few of them remained here now. Most of the population was human, but there were a few fraal scattered here and there as well. The island had a school, to which Gabriel had gone until he hit the secondary level, and then he had to catch a hopper over to Stricken and back every day. Now he found himself wondering how many children were left here, or whether there were any at all.

Gabriel walked through the shade of the big tropical alaith trees, which towered up on either side of the dusty main road with their pale peeling bark and big blue-green fronds edged with red. The place was very quiet. This was the hot part of the day, and many people rested or worked inside until the sun became a little more tolerable.

Gabriel walked. He was shocked by how different everything seemed even though it was all the same. Everything looks . . . *wrong* somehow, he thought.

When he had been here last, he had been young and innocent. Now it amazed him just how innocent he had been, and how certain that the world was going to go well for him now that he was a Concord Marine. None of that certainty clung to him now. The Marines had shaken him out as a criminal, and the world had proved more complex and nasty than he had ever suspected. *Probably nastier than I suspect even now,* Gabriel thought. The uncaring forces that moved people around like gaming pieces, him in particular, were doing it more aggressively than ever. His increased consciousness of being so moved had not improved matters. The world that once had been clean and cheerful and exciting now looked to him like just another beautiful untruth laid over a substrate of intricate motion and countermotion, interwoven plots, inadequately understood motivations, and endless traps set by those who were in on the secret for those who weren't.

Gabriel stopped in the sunlight and took a few deep breaths to try to calm his nerves. He was at the top of the little rise that divided the island in two, the hump over which the road crossed. From here he could look down to see the little house, still all by itself down at the very end of their town's street, with more of the alaith trees all around it, and up in those trees the whitetails singing "beewee," "beewee," "beewee," interminably as always.

Nothing had really changed. Nothing . . .

I have, though, Gabriel thought. It was very strange to stand here, being where he had been and who he had been for the last year and more—and yet see everything else here exactly as it had been when he left, as if time had stood still. Down in the cove, the blue water glittered. The fronds and leaves of the trees moved gently in the wind, and everything was very quiet, but the disconnected feeling, as if everything was somehow out of joint, would not go away.

Gabriel walked down to that little house with its broad roof and low eaves. He went up the front steps, carefully, and touched the door signal set into the wood of the shut door.

He waited.

No answer.

He pressed the signal again, not wanting to seem too urgent. Then it occurred to him. Of course he's not going to be here, Gabriel thought, starting to become annoyed at himself and at his own obtuseness. It's the middle of the day. He's off at work.

He turned away from the door, grimacing at his own stupidity. I can't believe I did this, he thought. Nice move, Connor. Just admit it to yourself, you don't want to see him, not really, and you set it up for yourself so that you wouldn't. You didn't even—

The door opened.

Rorke Connor, his father, stood there looking at him, looking hard, and with an expression of puzzlement—the look you give a stranger on your doorstep for the first time.

He doesn't want me to be here; he's pretending not to know me, was the first thought to flash through Gabriel's mind, followed by another: he doesn't really know me. I'm too changed—

Gabriel's insides squeezed painfully. He had been gutshot in his time, but to his shock, he found that this hurt worse.

And then his father rushed at him. Oh, gods, he's really angry, Gabriel thought in desperation. He doesn't want me here—

Gabriel actually backed away a step, but his father's arms were thrown around him in a fierce grip, and the old man was saying in a broken, ragged voice, "Where have you been, you idiot, where have you been?"

His father was actually shaking him, whether more in rage or relief, Gabriel had trouble telling. "What have they done to you?" his father cried, holding Gabriel away from him and staring at him. "What did they. . . ?"

Gabriel could only blink and had to do it a lot for a few moments. "No," he said finally, "it's nothing they did, Papa, it's just . . . They didn't make the hair go white. That's not their fault."

All around them, the whitetails were singing their two notes with insane conviction. His father was holding him away, looking at him. "You're older," he said, bemused, as if this should somehow be news.

"Not that much older," Gabriel said. "Papa, can we go in? The neighbors are going to stare."

"Let them stare," his father said fiercely. "Had enough of them, this last year. Would have moved, except it would have given them something they wanted, the—" He shut his mouth on numerous things he plainly wanted to call them. "Come on, son, come in."

They went in from the porch through the narrow front hallway and into the living room. It was all the same, except that somehow it looked bigger than it had when he'd left. I would have thought it'd be the other way around, Gabriel thought, but then he had been spending so much time in enclosed spaces over the last few years— first his Marine carrier, then jail on Phorcys, then *Sunshine*—that a normal house looked ridiculously roomy. His father pointed him at the big four-person lounger, which hadn't changed since he left. Everything—the artwork on the walls, the light fixtures, the place where the wall-surfacing was cracking a little over the door to the kitchen—looked almost *too* familiar, too prosaic, like a room where someone used to live, which is being kept for them just as it was when they were last there, against all hope that they might return.

Gabriel sat down. His father, looking at him intently, took the chair across from him and pulled it closer to the lounger. "Where *have* you been, exactly?" he said softly. "How did you get here without—"

"Without the authorities picking me up?" Gabriel grinned, though not with good cheer. "Papa, maybe you don't want to know too many of the details. I won't be staying long. It could be dangerous for you."

His father snorted, and Gabriel had to blink again at the dear familiarity of the sound. "They've made it as dangerous for me as they can already," he said. "Investigators and military types dropping in at all hours of the day and night, all last year. Quizzing the neighbors, too, and the neighbors ate it up. Damned gossips." He frowned. "If any of them did see you, they're probably on the comm to the police right now. Fortunately, it'll take them a while to get here."

It was one of the island's advantages, Gabriel had to agree. "I won't be here that long, I promise."

"As if I care about them!" his father shouted. "You stay as long as you have a mind."

Gabriel swallowed and held himself quiet. He had forgotten, almost, how intense his father could be when he was annoyed.

"No, I know, son," Rorke Connor said. "Sorry. It's just"—he scrubbed at his eyes for a moment—"I hate the thought that I'm going to have to lose you again shortly. I thought I'd lost you once when I heard about the trial."

"How much did you hear?"

His father rubbed his hands together and stared at the floor. "About the ambassador and all of them being killed," he said, "about the conspiracy—you and 'persons unknown.' I didn't believe a word of it." His father was getting angry again. "And then you were released . . . and vanished. They said it was proof that you were guilty."

" 'They'?"

"All the stuffed shirts who came around here afterward to interrogate me. They were sure you would come here to hide. I told them they were out of their minds. My son would never do such a thing. I told them so."

"Papa—"

"And then the neighbors started in on me. The ignorant—" He stopped himself again. "They believe everything they see on the Grid, the idiots. I told them you were innocent. I told them all."

Gabriel looked up at his father, at that hard and indignant face, and had trouble opening his mouth.

"I might not be," he said.

His father looked at Gabriel in shock.

"Papa, I did not murder anyone," Gabriel said, "that much is true, but I was tricked into doing things that resulted in people dying. That's too true, and there's no getting away from it."

His father just looked at him.

"I'm going to have to face trial eventually," Gabriel said, "by the Concord rather than by the planetary government where it happened. The Marines are convinced I did it on purpose, that I was part of some kind of plot. I think I was—but not the kind they're going to accuse me of. I'm getting close, I think, to getting the evidence that will help me prove that to them."

"And clear your name."

Gabriel breathed in, breathed out. It had been hard enough telling himself this next part. Telling it to his father would be more bitter still.

"As far as it can be cleared," he said. "I may have committed manslaughter. I may have to do time for that, if I'm ever to be able to come home or go anywhere else in Concord space and stay free. But I'm not going to go anywhere near Marine justice until I have enough evidence to prove that I'm not a murderer. So I'll probably have to keep running for a while . . . and I won't be back here for a long time, one way or the other." He paused for more breath. His throat felt very tight. "We're going to be heading off soon to keep looking for that evidence. I wanted to see you first. And there are other things going on . . ." He trailed off. How do you tell someone that you're deeply involved with some kind of alien artifact that may or may not be trying to kill you—or worse yet, may be trying to make you less than human . . . or more?

No time for that explanation, Gabriel thought, not now. Things are complicated enough as they are.

" 'Do time,' " his father said, very softly. "You mean more jail time."

Gabriel had no way to tell what this particular tone of voice meant. He did the only thing he could think of. He kept still.

"What kept you so long, son?" his father said softly, at last. "A long time since they let you leave Phorcys. Why didn't you write?"

"I did," Gabriel said. "You didn't get the messages?"

His father shook his head.

Gabriel hardly knew what to think. Someone must have been intercepting his father's messaging, certain that Gabriel would try to get in touch with him and try to arrange a meeting. They must have trashed the messages when they indicated that Gabriel had no such intent. *It was just as well I didn't comm him first,* Gabriel thought. *But who's at the bottom of this? Regency security? The Concord? Kharls?*

That last thought brought him up short for a moment. *Lorand Kharls. No, though I do want to have words with him at some point. . . .*

"I did write to you," Gabriel said. "Someone must have been stopping the mail."

"Sons of bitches," said Rorke Connor softly.

"When I didn't hear back from you," Gabriel said, as softly, "I stopped writing. I thought maybe you didn't want to . . ." He trailed off.

It was fear that made him stop, the sudden realization that, whatever and whoever his father might have been when Gabriel had seen him last, he was not that person any more.

"I wrote to you, too," his father said. "They must have stopped the messages, intercepted them. Bastards!"

The two of them sat quiet for a few breaths. "Tell me one thing," his father said. "Has it been worth it?"

Gabriel blinked.

"Before you . . . I mean, before it went . . ." his father struggled for the words. "Before you left, you were always

sure that everything was going to go well for you. A great
adventure . . ."

Gabriel sighed. The constant wonder of starrise and starfall, the sight of new planets, strange people, aliens, danger
and sudden unexpected delight . . . He wished he could find
words, or time, to tell his father all about them. But crowd-
ing them out came images of fire in space, the briefest millisecond of screams before death took his friends, the walls
of that jail cell on Phorcys, the cruel set of Elinke Dareyev's
face the last time he saw her . . . Rejection, pain, loss,
betrayed expectations . . .

"Worth it?" he finally said and wasn't sure what else to
say. How did you put worth on a life? Was it fair to judge it
merely by whether things had gone well, gone according to
plan or not? "I guess so. Things haven't been all bad."

Gabriel thought of the luckstone. Whatever else might
be happening to him, boredom wasn't part of it. Uncertainty, yes, but life *was* uncertainty to some extent. "They'll
get better," he said. He put all the conviction he could find
into the statement, hoping his father would believe him.

He looked up again, met the elder Connor's eyes, and
was not quite sure he'd carried it off.

"They've been bad enough, though," his father said.
"You're going to have to go to jail again, you think."

"People are dead," Gabriel said with a great effort, "and
whether I intended it or not, I was partly responsible. Yes, I
don't see how it can be avoided."

His father was quiet for a while.

"People are going to hear about that, then," he said, "and
our family's name is going to be in trouble again. I never
brought it to any such place. I never expected you to,
either."

Gabriel held still.

"And it's all going happen again," his father said very,
very quietly. "The people staring. The damned neighbors
whispering. I'd hoped I could tell them it was all going to
be over soon. Settled, finally. Our name cleared."

Gabriel kept holding still. "Our name . . ."

"When it's all over," his father said, "when it's done, when our name is cleared, come home. Until then, you'd better not."

Gabriel felt himself start to go numb inside. He had expected acceptance or rejection, not this ambivalence. He didn't know how to take it.

"I was afraid for you," his father said. "I'm glad to know you're well." He got up, pushing himself up out of the chair as if he were somehow afraid to move. "But, son, I'm—" He broke off, and a brief choked laugh broke out of him. "I was going to say, 'I'm getting old,' but look at you! How can I say that now?"

He was clearly fighting tears, and it came to Gabriel that the best thing he could do, the wisest thing for both of them, was to get out of there before those tears had a chance to break loose. "Papa," he said, "I'll be all right, so please take care of yourself. I'll be back. I promise."

He turned and went out the way he had come. The door slammed behind him—harder than he had meant, much too hard. Its hydraulics were not what they had been.

Without looking left or right, Gabriel went back up the road again. He heard the creak of the door, but he would not look back. Even looking straight ahead of him as he passed the neighbor's houses, he saw the occasional blind or drape twitch just a little as he went by. He cursed them softly under his breath, words that other Marines would definitely have approved and that his father would once unquestionably have switched him for.

At the top of the little hill in the road, Gabriel stopped, almost against his will, and turned.

The front porch of his father's house was empty. The man who had stood there was gone now.

Gabriel turned and headed back toward *Sunshine*.

It had all gone wrong. Everything had gone differently from what he had imagined. He wanted to turn around, go back, try to do it all over again . . . but there was no point.

He stopped again and looked back toward the house. The porch remained empty.

He turned again and started back up the road. There was someone coming down toward him from the general direction of the pad. No, not from the pad proper, but out of the field that led down to the rocky beach on the far side of the pad. It was a man, dressed in the loose bright clothing that people in this climactic belt tended to favor. Good protection against the sun, comfortable when a breeze came up. The man had a net and a surfcasting reel over his shoulder. He had probably been down there doing exactly what Gabriel had done often enough as a kid: casting for gillies and sunfish. They favored that side of the island because of the prevailing westerlies.

Gabriel's first urge was to avoid the man, but then it occurred to him that this might be one of the neighbors, and he didn't want to look any guiltier around them than he already did.

Though if their minds are already made up, why should I bother caring one way or another?

Gabriel kept walking up the road and studied the man's face as he drew nearer. He didn't look familiar, but then any number of neighbors could have moved in and out since Gabriel had last been here. His heart ached a little at that. Once upon a time, he had known every soul on this island, and the sense of belonging had practically been a palpable thing. One more of the changes, he thought, as the man approached. *Nothing is the same. It's true what they say, you can't go home again . . .*

The man was smiling slightly as he got within calling range of Gabriel. *So I can be rude, a total boor, and ignore him, or*—Gabriel shook his head at himself and set his face into a smile as well. "Good morning," he said. "How're they biting?"

"Better than I thought," said the man. His smile fell, he dropped the rod and the net, and came up with a gun.

The blast went by Gabriel's ear as he flung himself aside

just in time. That could have been my head! he thought somewhat belatedly as he rolled, got up, then dived and rolled again, for the man was still firing at him, peppering the road with projectiles.

Keep moving, they had told him in his hand-to-hand classes. Whatever you do, keep moving until the enemy is disarmed.

Armed! Gabriel thought. The two concepts "being home on Tisane" and "carrying a weapon" were so far apart in his mind that he had forgotten what he had put in his pocket. Nonetheless, for the moment he kept moving, kept diving and rolling, trying to work his way closer to the man. Then he got his hands on his own pistol, brought it up, and squeezed the trigger.

Clean miss. He swore, dived, rolled again, choking on dust as he went down. A slug impacted the ground no more than three inches from his head. Gabriel bounced to his feet much faster than he would have thought he could, impelled by another close call, *much* too close—

This time, he and the man swung their weapons toward each other at the same instant, but Gabriel fired first.

The other's shot went wild. When Gabriel got up again, he could see why. Gabriel's flechettes had neatly torn the side of the man's head off.

Gabriel stood there, shocked, for again this scenario completely disagreed with his images of home, the feel of the place . . . Then he bent down hurriedly and began to go through the man's pockets. It took several minutes, and he felt distinctly creepy during the whole process. What if one of the neighbors comes along? What if—but that was not troubling him half so much as the strange feeling that had begun to creep along his nerves as soon as he got close enough to the man to touch him.

Something stroking, sliding, in his mind. Something warm . . . and loathsome.

Gabriel froze for a moment. He shuddered and set the feeling aside. He didn't know what it was, except that his brain had been put through some major changes recently, and as a result, he often found himself feeling things he couldn't identify. If he was lucky, sometimes he found out later what they meant, but there were no guarantees. In any case, this particular feeling was one he wasn't sure he wanted to know much more about.

There was a lump inside the man's shirt that didn't have a corresponding pocket to go with it. Gabriel pulled the shirt open, felt for hidden seams, then finally, in an agony of haste, simply ripped the shirt apart, tearing the fabric and spilling the contents onto the blood-spattered body.

He poked cautiously through the things. A little sheaf of Bluefall currency. A notepad, empty, but he took it anyway. One last thing that he used a corner of the man's big loose shirt to pick up and hold in a gingerly manner: VoidCorp Employee identification, GK004 967KY. Gabriel turned it over to see if there was any indication of what department of VoidCorp this man had been with. There was none that he could find, but he was more than willing to believe that it was Intel. They had been after him for long enough.

And if they know I'm here, who else knows I'm here?

Time to go.

Gabriel was sweating and dirty, and he brushed himself off as best he could as he hurriedly made his way back toward *Sunshine*. He didn't care who might see him at this point.

Was this guy alone? Gabriel wondered. *Did he have an accomplice, or was he just here on the off chance that I would turn up? How long might he have been waiting here?*

Well, his waiting's over, but as for me . . . I can't come back here now. So much for promises to my father. Now I've left another corpse behind me.

He felt more bitter as he got back to *Sunshine*. *This one part of my life,* he thought, *this one place in my universe, was untouched by what's happened to me. Now look at it. It's contaminated now, too, and not just by gunfire and a new murder. That strange, sliding, considering warmth . . .*

like something wet and nasty and alive. What had that been? Whatever it is, I want away from it!

Gabriel got into *Sunshine*'s lift, slapped the close and lock control, and then rode up to the cabin level, urging the lift to go faster all the while. When the door opened again in the upper level hallway, he stepped out, locked it, and headed for the pilot's cabin.

Enda looked out of their little lounge on that level as he passed. "How did it go?" she asked, sounding rather concerned.

"Let's get off the planet first," Gabriel said.

"That bad?"

"I'll explain on the way."

A few moments later, *Sunshine* lifted up and away from Tisane, up through the blue day again, gleaming. If one curtain down at the very end of the road twitched, suggesting that someone watched her go, it was much too late for Gabriel to notice.

* * * * *

A few hours later, well away from Bluefall and well toward the edge of the Aegis system, *Sunshine* rendezvoused with *Longshot*, one of the two ships presently traveling with them.

Across from Gabriel in the other pilot's couch, Enda let out a small sigh and reached into the holographic display that hung between them, touching to life the controls that would let their infotrading system speak to the Aegis drive-sat relay. As she did, the comms alert cheeped, and she gave Gabriel an amused look.

"Punctual as always."

Gabriel reached into the display and touched the comms slider. "*Sunshine.*"

"You're early," Helm Ragnarsson's gravelly voice announced. "Makes a change."

"You are cruel to tease us, Helm," Enda said, undoing

the straps and getting up from her pilot's couch. "And unwise, since next time we have dinner, it will be my turn to cook."

"What do you mean next time? I thought you were cooking today."

Enda glanced over at Gabriel. "I would have been," she said, "but something has come up."

"What?"

"I just got back from Bluefall," Gabriel said, "where I just shot somebody."

Helm's eyes widened a little. "Boy, you and your father *really* don't get along, do you?"

"Helm!" Gabriel said. "I did not shoot my father! I shot a VoidCorp Employee."

"Making a corpse out of a Corpse, huh?" Helm said. "Redundant, but I have to appreciate the sentiment. He started it, I take it."

"He was waiting for me, Helm. They plainly knew we were coming, and it can't be long, even on Bluefall, before the police show up and want to know who left this guy's brains all over the one road on the island. I think we should give dinner a miss this time and get into drivespace before they come after me. We can have dinner when we come out somewhere else."

"Such as?"

"I want to conference briefly," Gabriel said. "Have you heard from Angela?"

"About twenty minutes ago. She's inbound on system drive. Going to be late. She miscalculated the distance to the rendezvous point or something."

Gabriel rolled his eyes but smiled as he did it. He liked Angela Valiz well enough, but he was very unsure about her piloting ability . . . at least compared to Helm's. But then *I've had a long time to get used to Helm*, Gabriel thought, *nearly a year now. Maybe I'm doing her a disservice.*

Naaaah.

"Well, I'll shoot her a note to hurry up," Gabriel said,

"and when she gets here, we can conference on Delde Sota's 'special' comms and not have to broadcast our business—or the fact that we're here—all over local space. Your drive charged up?"

"Ready to go."

"Good," Gabriel said and shut down comms for the moment.

He sent the message to Angela on *Lalique* and then just sat for a moment, watching the front console as it displayed the text heralds that said the ship's infotrading system was doing a routine hourly check with the Aegis drivesat relay, waiting to see if there was any inbound traffic for *Sunshine*. The computer "shook hands" with the frequency for the Aegis drivesat relay, exchanged passwords, and then confirmed that it had no new data to go out. They had dumped their load to the Aegis Grid immediately on coming in-system four days ago. The drivesat, ducking in and out of drivespace two or three times a second, was apparently not too overloaded with traffic at the moment and was handing their system data back immediately rather than putting them in a queue.

It was a convenience, because they would not be here much longer. Again, Gabriel felt a pang of guilt at putting his friends through the inconveniences they had been suffering recently as a side effect of his being on the run. They were entirely too good natured about it for so oddly assorted and casually organized a group, a loose association of travelers in an unusual assortment of sizes, all possessed of wildly varying motives and, in some cases, slightly murky histories.

There was Helm, a mutant and occasional arms dealer with his overengined, overgunned ship *Longshot* and his much-scarred armor, sporting weapons that showed signs of serious use, though it was rare that you could get him to talk about exactly what they had been used for.

There was Delde Sota, mechalus doctor and Gridrunner on sabbatical—at least she described this long peripatetic run as passenger for Helm as a sabbatical, which (considering what they had all been through recently) sometimes made Gabriel wonder what her idea of work would look like.

There was Angela Valiz, in her ship *Lalique,* a family vessel being run more or less at pleasure while Angela proved that she could make a living moving light cargo around the Verge. A tall, big-shouldered blonde with large, soft eyes, Angela possessed the slightly feckless air of someone gadding around without too much in the way of money worries.

There was Angela's companion Grawl, two meters and two hundred kilograms of weren poetess, clawed and fanged, with a nasty sense of humor and an excellent aim with the weapon of her choice. Bodyguard, satirist, and general eyes-behind for Angela, Grawl had taken the opportunity to escape her own clan on Kurg to see something of the universe.

And there was Enda, who had dropped out of nowhere into Gabriel's life, picking him up when he was cast adrift on the Thalaassan planet Phorcys and heading out into a new life with him as naturally and calmly as if she had been planning it for months. Gabriel knew Enda well enough by now to understand that she was utterly trustworthy, but at the same time there were mysteries about her, areas of her life that she did not discuss. Nothing strange about that, Gabriel thought. When you've been alive as long as she has, there may be big patches you just don't want to think about because they're so boring.

Then there was Gabriel himself. I don't know what business I have thinking the *rest* of them are odd, he thought. There are enough chips out on me in enough systems that I'm the one most likely to stand out in a crowd.

Or a lineup of suspects for a murder, said something at the back of his mind.

He sighed and looked at the general comms display, which had hooked into the system Grid as soon as the info-trading system had come offline. Now it was showing the standard hourly update screen from the Aegis Grid—news flashes from in-system, from the rest of the Verge, and from back beyond the Stellar Ring; inbound and outbound ship information; drivespace relay usage stats; the present transit schedule for the *Lighthouse* . . . Then came the system's main weather report. Gabriel paid less attention to the downward-scrolling text, full of letters and numbers in several different alphabets, than he did to the big red-flaring sphere of the local sun. Aegis was in an unusually bad temper at the moment. Huge gossamer-scarlet plumes and fans of fire, the program's rendering of the highest energy particle streams, were splashing up out of the star's photosphere and irritating an already overexcited corona. The text part of the report suggested that the big chain of sunspot colonies presently marching their way around the surface would be doing so for another week or so, playing havoc with the entertainment schedules of those who got their Grid feed from the Aegis system's commsats. It was a bizarre state of affairs for what was normally so placid a star. It would have been a matter of some concern to Gabriel if he weren't sure that every available solar expert in the system was watching Aegis day and night, ready to send out warnings should the star become dangerously cranky.

In case the commsats went down, Gabriel had something else to keep him busy: an armful of starship catalogues. He had been looking forward to sitting down with them soon. It seemed he would have the opportunity sooner than he had expected. They would be in drivespace shortly, with a hundred and twenty-one hours to kill.

"Have you had any results with those?" Enda asked.

Gabriel blinked. "Are you hearing me think again?" he asked softly and with a little unease.

A pause. Enda gazed at him thoughtfully from those huge, hot-blue eyes. "I would not have to," she said, "since you have had your nose in those things nonstop since we left Coulomb. In fact, well before then."

Gabriel smiled just slightly at the way that Enda could fail to answer a question if it suited her. She was, however, correct. The thought of a new ship, a bigger ship, had been on Gabriel's mind for a while now . . . especially after the recent events at Danwell, which had left them with a tidy discoverer's royalty attached to the exploration contract that Angela had sold them.

The problem was the expense of a new ship, even with trade-in allowances and the possibility of finding a more understanding banker than their last one. A new ship would certainly make a big difference in their lives in terms of room to live and work and being able to travel more quickly—say, fifteen light-years in a starfall/starrise cycle rather than their present eight. The change would also return his and Enda's financial health from fairly comfortable to precarious. Gabriel was conscious of how little in the way of finance he had brought to their partnership, and he was chary of spending what he still considered mostly Enda's money too freely.

At the same time she was insistent that "her" money was his, that their present slightly flush status was mostly Gabriel's fault and that he should examine his options carefully, for the goals he sought were, for the foreseeable future, hers.

Gabriel had not felt like pushing the issue much further than that. For one thing, he was never entirely sure what Enda might be able to foresee. For another, he had been foreseeing things a lot more clearly than humans normally did. It made him nervous and eager to spend what he had in order to get to the bottom of the changes happening to him: the strange dreams of darkness and fire, still not completely explained, and not exorcised either, after their experiences at Danwell. And there were other changes, physical ones, mental ones . . . all of which seemed to be pointing him toward something yet undiscovered, something out in the darker spaces of the Verge, the unfrequented places. A faster, bigger ship—and ideally one that was also better armed—would be a big advantage as Gabriel went hunting the causes of the mysteries that were now haunting his life.

And other things . . .

"In fact, now that I think of it," Enda added, as the update dump from Aegis finished itself and the infotrading system closed down, "I would correct myself and say that you have been immersed in that material since Mantebron."

"Oh, come on. I was not."

"You were indeed. It does seem like a long time ago, though."

"No argument there," Gabriel said. As usual, when things became hectic, time seemed to telescope. When things had blown up at Danwell, *Sunshine* had been carrying a load of data for delivery at Coulomb, and at the time Gabriel had not been sure that they were going to be able to deliver it this side of the grave. They had made the delivery within their original schedule after all, and after some brief consultations, he and Enda had decided to pick up a load destined for Aegis and head over that way again. It was partly business—the Coulomb-Aegis data run was somewhat under subscribed, and you got a good premium for such haulage—but also partly personal. Gabriel had unfinished business on Aegis.

For the moment, that particular business was at the back of his mind. Instead, he concentrated on what he had picked up at Coulomb before they moved on: catalogues from all the major ship manufacturers and from various second-sales outlets and distributors scattered around the Verge—particularly in the Aegis system. Gabriel was looking through printouts for the three strongest candidates at the moment, two on Bluefall and one back at Mantebron, and was deep in currency conversions and calculations of local tax and handling and prep charges. *Although maybe now we won't be buying on Bluefall. . . .*

"Far be it from me to distract you from an enjoyable pastime," Enda said. "You do love a bargain, don't you?"

"One of the few things worth hunting for in this sorry world," Gabriel muttered. "Trouble is that there don't seem to be that many of them here."

Enda sighed. "Ship-buying is never cheap, or if it is, you usually wind up paying for a bargain in some other way. Having to replace the whole drive, for example, the day after the limited guarantee runs out."

Gabriel sighed. "Have you given any thought to that?"

"To what?"

"Replacing *Sunshine*'s drive."

"With another mass reactor, you mean?" Enda looked thoughtful. "I suspect that would turn out to be a false economy, Gabriel. We would lose at least half our cargo space, perhaps more. Then how would we make a living? The present data tanks would have to be torn out and replaced with smaller, much higher-density ones. More expense . . ."

"We could shift closer to one of the busier routes and carry higher-priority data."

"And less of it, yes, I see your point, but that would remove what I would have thought was one of your chief goals: freedom to head out into the more distant parts of the Verge after . . ." She would not say it. "You know."

Gabriel nodded, not caring to take up that particular subject just at the moment. Meantime he was still doing sums in his head. None of them were coming out the way he wanted, but then that was more or less the story of his life at the moment.

"Upgrading wouldn't be enough," Gabriel said after a few seconds. "It would need to be a new ship, if we're really going to exploit the ability of a higher-powered drive to give us more light-years per starfall."

"The expense would be considerable," Enda said, "but Gabriel, if I have learned nothing else in nearly three hundred years, it is that money is intended for spending, and that when the correct thing to spend it on comes along, only a miser hangs onto it. Money is about promoting growth and the free flow of the things that produce that growth. It must flow, not go stagnant because of the old habits of penury. Not that we have not occasionally been a little on the penurious side, but that is not our problem right now."

Gabriel grunted noncommitally.

Enda sighed. "A bigger ship makes possible a bigger engine and longer starfalls, but what will those get us, if we are so busy maintaining the ship that we have no energy to pursue our goals once we make starrise in their neighborhoods?"

"Longer starfalls," Gabriel said, "make those neighborhoods a lot more accessible—a lot fewer days spent getting where we're going."

"Yes, but one of us would have to stand down from piloting and from everything else to become a full-time engineer, if you are going to start pushing that kind of power into the stardrive. Engines developing that kind of power have a way of taking over your life, and believe me, as someone who has ridden city ships in my time, I know about this firsthand."

Gabriel didn't much like the idea of losing Enda from the "up front" seats, especially in cases where fighting was concerned. His expertise with the ship's weaponry had been increasing over time—a good thing, considering how much fighting they'd had to do in the last year—but Enda had a natural gift with the guns that Gabriel had no realistic hope of approaching any time soon. There had been enough times lately when it had taken everything both of them had to stay alive. If Enda was stuck in the bowels of the ship nursing her engines and they ran into another such situation, it would only happen once, and after that they would not be greatly concerned about anything else.

Gabriel knew where all this was taking him. "If we got the right AI," he said, "we would be able to manage."

"If we paid enough for it," Enda said, tilting her head sideways in a nod, "which would come to a considerable amount of credit—more expense added to that already applied to the new ship. We are talking about a hefty chunk of debt, Gabriel. Not that we have done so badly with servicing our present debt, but it would take some doing to find a financial institution out this way that would be willing to hold escrow for us when the amount has *this* many zeroes after it. And then there are the security concerns. . . ."

She glanced forward toward the pilot's compartment where *Sunshine*'s registry lay. Gabriel knew what she was thinking. *Sunshine*'s registry information had been most expertly tampered with some months back by Delde Sota in order to conceal the altered nature of *Sunshine's* weaponry so that they could hitch a ride with the *Lighthouse*. Such forgeries and alterations were done pretty routinely, it was true, but do them repeatedly and the odds of being caught began to increase at an unhealthy rate. Gabriel was already in enough trouble with the Concord. Adding fraud to the accusations of manslaughter and murder wouldn't help him.

Gabriel glanced up toward the pilot's compartment. Up there, hidden very discreetly in a place where it had been assumed he would not think to look, were a couple of broad-band listening devices hooked into ship's comms and her Grid access system—in simple terms, "bugs." Gabriel had not removed them for reasons of his own. There were times when allowing such listening to occur was to his advantage. There were other reasons more obscure, having to do with figures fairly high up in the Concord hierarchy, figures with which his relationship was ambivalent at best but—to Gabriel's way of thinking— useful.

He had had a word with Delde Sota about those tapping devices while she had been doing other work designed to conceal *Sunshine*'s identity. Delde Sota had been a Grid pilot before she was a doctor, and she was unusually adept at the delicate art of subverting complex computer equipment into doing something for which it was not designed, or making it think it was doing what it had been designed for while it was in fact doing something else entirely.

"Yes," Gabriel said. "I had been thinking about that as well."

"There would be one other problem," Enda said, "the delay. It would take a month perhaps? Maybe even two to get transferred to the new ship and get everything sorted out. Once that was done, at least one trail will have become colder than it is already."

Gabriel nodded. He was still hunting the man (or possibly a number of men) called Jacob Ricel, the man who had handed him the innocent-looking little chip that ignited the bomb aboard the shuttle that took the ambassador to her death, along with several of Gabriel's friends. Without that man himself—or one of the men identical to him—to provide evidence that something unusual had been going on, Gabriel had no chance of avoiding a conviction for murder when the Concord finally caught up with him.

"It's cold enough already," Gabriel said, "though not exactly frozen. I've been looking into his whereabouts over the last couple of months, though not on the open Grid connection." He smiled slightly. "Those who notice such things will be thinking that most of my researches have had to do with a new ship and with matters farther out."

Though whether some of them will be fooled by appearances, Gabriel wondered, remains to be seen. He personally doubted it and hoped that the rather obvious gap in his Grid investigations would suggest to at least one observer what he meant to suggest.

"What about Ricel himself then?" Enda asked. "Will we now go hunting him directly? I confess, I would much like to catch up with him." Her expression went, for Enda, surprisingly grim.

Gabriel had to suppress his grin, for though Enda might look as small and delicate as most fraal, underestimating her strength or her temper when she was angry was a mistake. "So would I, but . . . Enda, you're going to laugh at me."

"Often," Enda said, "but not for the reasons you fear. Tell me your thought."

"I think we have more urgent business on our plates at the moment," Gabriel said, "or about to spill onto the table anyway. These kroath we've been running into, now we know they're not an isolated manifestation. They're around, and they're taking people and turning them into these undead creatures. They've been doing it for a long time—at least as far back as the destruction of the Silver Bell colony, but still no one knows what they are or where they're coming from. Why do we keep running into them? We've had a lot more than what I would consider the statistically likely number of encounters."

She looked uncomfortable. "I would have to agree with you there."

Gabriel looked at the pile of printouts and catalogues. "I hate to say it," he said, "but I think my own personal business has to wait for the moment. I may have been a Marine, but I was a Verger first. If this keeps on, it won't be safe to live out this way for much longer—maybe not anywhere else, either."

This last cost him some effort to say. He was afraid to sound foolish, but Enda looked at him and nodded slowly.

Gabriel continued, "I'm going to put the whole ship buying thing on hold until we get some results in other areas. I don't say that it'll stay on hold for a long time, though."

"This is your choice," Enda said. "I trust you with it. I trust you to take it up again when you feel there is need."

Gabriel nodded. "What I don't understand," he said very softly, "is *why* you trust me."

Enda stood up and stretched. "Because when I do, you prove yourself trustworthy."

"But when you first trusted me," Gabriel said, "when you first found me, I hadn't yet proved anything."

"One must start somewhere," Enda said, "and if, as some

say, the One made a whole universe out of nothing, should we find it hard to do so with an item so small as trust?"

Enda got up from the pilot's seat and headed back toward the lavatory.

Gabriel sat there quiet, unable to find a response, especially in the wake of the memory of the dusty road on Tisane with a man's brains spattered all over it.

Chapter Two

I T TOOK ANGELA a while to reach the rendezvous point. Gabriel sat where he was, trying to relax, but he was twitchy. His eye fell on a particular spot on the deck plating—a little scorched pit, maybe five centimeters deep, a near-oval shape.

Gabriel frowned slightly, slipping his hand into his pocket. The ship had already been out of the manufacturer's warranty when we bought it, or I'd send them a letter about this. The deck plating was supposed to be proof against everything. Acid, abrasion, fire . . .

Not this, he thought, looking at the luckstone that lay in his hand: a little black oval pebble, matte-surfaced. Faintly, as if awakened by the heat of his hand, a dull dark-gold glow awoke in it.

A sudden stream of images jolted through him—

It had been happening more frequently of late, as if the events on Danwell had broken open some door inside him—or not precisely broken it open, but wedged it ajar so that images and sounds and experiences from some "other side" were coming through, more and more frequently. Sometimes they were benign or familiar. Some had to do with the edanweir people on Danwell and his contact there, Tlelai—images of day or evening, of his counterpart's working day as a hunter, a glimpse of greenery, some huge beast being carted home to the family lodges. More often those images would have to do with light and darkness, great gouts of fire being flung at a shadowy enemy. Increasingly those images were associated with a feeling of slightly desperate familiarity.

We have done this before. We are doing it again.

Will it work?

There never seemed to be any answer to that question.

One particular set of images had become a lot clearer lately. A large system, a populated system. Two, maybe three planets, swinging in the darkness around a fierce star. Something hidden on one of the planets. Something Gabriel was very interested in indeed . . .

He blinked. It took a moment to get rid of the image of the alien sun, the two worlds swinging around it, and on one of them, the secret.

The luckstone lay there in his hand, dark now. It was a Glassmaker artifact . . . he thought. The Glassmaker people had inhabited some of the worlds of this part of the Verge untold millennia ago. They had left a few artifacts behind in the ruins of their cities—objects usually inexplicable, most seemingly made of this glasslike material, some of them having energy trapped or sourced within them in ways no one understood. Some were thought, perhaps, to be weapons. Some were tools, though to do what jobs, no one knew. The species itself was long gone from these spaces, and no one knew anything more about them, not even what they looked like.

This little stone had come to him as a gift, part of a load-lightening exercise by another Marine going home. There were stones like it from some of the Stellar Ring worlds, natural electrically charged silicate-compound fragments that would glow sometimes, and so at first Gabriel had thought nothing of it. But slowly it had started to make plain that it was more than just some pebble picked up on some alien beach. Some of its behavior was simply peculiar—like melting that hole into the deck when it had been dropped there. Other things it did, though . . .

He shook his head, scuffing with one soft-booted toe at the little melted pit. The stone had become a key to the detection and use of other alien artifacts scattered around this part of space. One such facility had been hidden on

Danwell, revealed when Gabriel and Enda came there in company with Helm, Delde Sota, Angela, and Grawl. Other things had been revealed as well, as Gabriel found the stone opening parts of him that had been locked up, their presence hitherto unsuspected—especially a part of his mind that seemed increasingly likely to see the future as just a kind of past that hadn't yet happened and to remember what Gabriel hadn't yet personally experienced. That same part of his mind started experiencing all kinds of other traffic as well: he found himself participating in the edanweir's communal telepathy and being used by the alien facility on Danwell for its own purposes. Defending the planet, yes, but there had been something else going on as well.

One of the powers he had met on Danwell—then wearing the shape of a very small edanweir child, but as time went by Gabriel was less and less deceived by this—had told him that relatively nearby was a great hoard of the same kind of alien technology—very old, very powerful . . . waiting. She had not said so in so many words, but the implication had been *waiting for the right person to come along*. Someone carrying the right kind of key . . . or who, in contact with it, had *become* the right kind of key . . .

The comms chimed.

"Hey, *Sunshine*," Angela said, "*Longshot*, sorry for the delay."

Gabriel smiled slightly and reached into the control display to toggle the image-conference mode. There was Angela, blonde and cheerful as always, and Grawl beside her in their roomy cabin.

"It's all right," Gabriel said, as Enda came up the hall to sit down in the other pilot's seat. "Angela, we really ought to get out of here immediately. You didn't have any further business here?"

"What's the problem?" Angela asked.

"I had to shoot somebody."

She whistled softly. "Did they start it?"

"Did you ever know me to start anything?" Gabriel said.

"No, you've always been a perfect gentleman," said Angela. She smiled sweetly.

Grawl guffawed.

"I didn't mean that," Gabriel said.

Helm's image appeared in the tank, along with that of Delde Sota in her usual mechalus *rlin noch'i*, her hair bound back into a long braid all intertwined with cyberfiber and motile fibrils so that it wove and wavered gently in the air as she spoke or gestured. "Assessment: probably needed shooting, if you shot them. Concern: possible early exit from system advisable, though some will draw incorrect conclusions from same."

Helm looked across the table at Gabriel. "Before we go on to decisions about where to go next, what about this new ship you wanted to buy?"

Gabriel sighed. "There are a few possibilities sitting around in some of the showrooms on Bluefall, but the prices here are pretty inflated."

"The prices *everywhere* are inflated," Enda said, somewhat wearily. "This is, after all, the Verge. If we were within the Stellar Ring, the prices would be lower." She sighed and said nothing more.

Gabriel clearly heard her not saying it and was briefly both amused and annoyed. He couldn't go within the Ring because he would immediately be arrested. Still, there were times, like this one, when he was tempted to do it in order to get a price break, but that wouldn't work either. In the Ring, buying a ship with false ID was even harder than it was in the Verge.

Helm grunted and said, "Only thing the Ring has over the Verge is that the swindlers are packed that much closer together. The paperwork back there would kill you, not to mention the ancillary expenses. Registry fees, police inspection fees, planetary taxes, national taxes, city taxes, local squeeze . . . I'd sooner pay a little extra and have less attention from the snoopies to what I was doing."

"It's the paying a little extra I was trying to avoid," Gabriel muttered.

"No way to do that," Helm said. "One way or the other, they get you. I'd just prefer to pay people I *like,* but that removes one set of options. We won't be staying on here. So what do you have in mind for our next jump?"

"Well . . ." Gabriel knew what the response was going to be to this, without recourse to any luckstone-assisted visions, but that couldn't be helped. "I was thinking about Algemron."

The others looked at each other in surprise.

"Algemron?" Helm said. "Don't like a quiet life much, do you? Or a long one."

"What's the matter with Algemron?" asked Angela.

"They're shooting at each other," replied Helm.

"Again?" Grawl said.

"Not so much 'again' as 'still,' " Helm said. "That war's been going on, how many years now, fifteen, twenty? And it just doesn't seem able to stop."

"A good war," said Grawl, "can become traditional."

Delde Sota laughed, but the laughter had little humor about it. "Conjecture: can become part of business as usual," she said. "Result: participants decide they cannot do without it."

"Like Phorcys and Ino," Gabriel muttered. "All the same, I think that's where I'm headed."

"Can I ask what brought on this sudden attack of insanity?" Helm asked. He glanced at Enda.

She shook her head. "This is the first I have heard of it."

"Conjecture: Gabriel is running a hunch," said Delde Sota.

He nodded. "That's about as much as I can confirm at the moment."

"Okay." Helm sighed. "We're going to Algemron. Fine. You'd better brush up on your guns, and so will I." He started to get a thoughtful expression.

"Advice: no gunrunning on this run, Helm!" Delde Sota said immediately.

"No," Helm said almost sadly. "I suppose not."

Gabriel smiled a little. The governments of the two planets Alitar and Galvin were always hungry for new weapons, but usually they preferred to buy in bulk from the major arms companies. Private gunrunning was frowned upon, and both worlds' police vessels routinely stopped passing traffic to see whether it was carrying contraband. Their levels of enforcement in this regard varied wildly—in some moods, personal sidearms had been adjudged to be contraband, and the sidearms' carriers had been imprisoned for prolonged periods.

"We'll only be running data," Gabriel said. "There's no drivesat there, and there are too few infotraders coming in. Both planets are always complaining about it."

"Might the reason there are so few infotraders," said Angela, "be anything to do with the war, and the fact that it's dangerous to go anywhere near that system?"

"Especially when the two worlds go most eagerly to war," said Grawl, "when they draw close, once each year . . ."

"We wouldn't be anywhere near that time right now, would we?" Angela said.

Helm's eyes narrowed as he did math in his head. "Coming up on it now, I think."

"Beginning of 'close approach' season in ninety-four standard days," said Delde Sota. The end of her braid, presently looped around her whisky glass, twitched a little.

"Helm," Gabriel said, "what I mean to tell you is . . . this might actually be too dangerous. I wouldn't want you to—"

"Get in trouble?" Helm said and burst out laughing. "Gabe, you need your head felt if you think I'm going to let you go to Algemron by yourself, after not leaving you in places that should have theoretically been a lot less dangerous."

"I'm serious," Gabriel said. "When it comes to getting out of harm's way, we're not as quick as you are, and I don't like you having to wait up for us while we take an extra starfall or so to catch up. Leaving out the fact that it's dangerous, it's just not fair to you. The extra supplies you use up—"

"You let me worry about that," Helm said, narrowing his eyes at Gabriel a little in a way meant to suggest that

Gabriel should let it drop. "I don't mind."

"I just wish we had a more powerful engine for our drive," Gabriel said, "one big enough to keep up with you. How the heck did you get a ship with an engine like that, anyway?"

"Someone died and left it to me," Helm said, grinned, and narrowed his eyes harder.

Gabriel started to open his mouth, then thought better of it. There was no telling under what circumstances the "someone" had died, and possibly this was something Helm preferred left behind him. Helm had been good enough about believing Gabriel's protestations of innocence, no matter how unlikely they seemed. This seemed like a good time to return the favor.

"Look," Helm said. "Kid, you're into something here, you and your magic pebble. I don't know what's going on, exactly, but we were all at Danwell together, and I know the kind of results your hunches produce when you let them run. If you think you need to go to Algemron, I'd bet that it'll be worthwhile, if only in terms of how interesting things are going to get. I'd bet serious money that they'll get interesting enough for you to need some extra guns to back you up. So I'm in. I'll find a way to cover my expenses and have a good time, too." He turned to Delde Sota. "Doctor? You want to sit this dance out? Your choice. I can arrange reliable transport back to Iphus before we head out, if you like."

Delde Sota gave him a cool look, though it was an amused one. "Assessment: chivalry not yet dead. Professional assessment: unwise to allow this venture to proceed without adequate medical advice available. And other areas of expertise."

Gabriel cleared his throat, which felt oddly tight. "Angela, you don't—"

"If you think you're going to invite me out of this little venture," she said dryly, "think again. The past couple of months have been the most interesting that I've had in a long time."

"Maybe so," Gabriel said, "but look, your ship is a family venture. Taking *Lalique* into harm's way might—"

Angela tilted her head to one side and said, "For insurance purposes, title vests in whoever's piloting her at the time. Believe me, I've read the fine print in the contract. Mine is a private vessel. If I choose to travel with you to Algemron, and they try to interfere with me, I'll sic the Concord on them. The place may be hazardous, but the rule of law hasn't broken down entirely out that way. Otherwise there would be no infotraders going there. Or am I wrong?"

She was right, a situation that annoyed Gabriel considerably. There was a particular smug look she got at such times. "Grawl?"

"I am a poetess and a chronicler of my times," the weren said, ruffling her forearm fur idly with one claw, "and it would look ill should I opt out of a venture merely because fangs may here and there be shown. Let us therefore lay our plans."

Gabriel looked over at Enda.

"It is as I have said to you before," she said. "I will be three hundred in a decade or so, and there are many places I have not been. Algemron, I must admit, is one of them." Enda shrugged gracefully.

Gabriel breathed out. "All right."

"So let's go, then," Helm said. "The sooner the better, it sounds like."

"I will query the drivesat for traffic destined for Algemron," Enda said. "There should be some, but not so much that it will delay our departure by more than half an hour or so."

Helm got up to go do a weapons check somewhere else in his ship. "Okay," Angela said, "flash us when you're ready to go . . ." The connection from *Lalique* faded out.

Enda went back to the main infotrading console to start the business of picking up a load of data from the drivesat. Gabriel started to get up. "One moment," sad Delde Sota. "Professional requirement: put arm in display, please."

Gabriel blinked and put the arm that had his medical

chip embedded in it into the control display. The end of
Delde Sota's braid went out of sight of the pickup. A vague
tickling sensation started in the skin around the chip.

He glanced at the doctor with slight concern. That long,
high-cheekboned face was more than usually thoughtful.

"Any big changes?" Gabriel asked quietly.

"Corrected assessment: what else *but* big changes,"
Delde Sota said, more quietly still. Gabriel was rather
astonished by the look of concern in her eyes. Delde Sota
was a very managing type, both of her own emotions and
of situations in general. It was not usual to see her seeming
out of depth.

"How?" Gabriel said. "I haven't started to sprout toadstools yet. Or horns and batwings, either."

"Might be preferable," said the doctor. "Could suggest
interventions for those." She breathed out, a concerned hiss
of sound. "Systemic changes, shifts in microchemistry,
endocrinal balances, neurochemistry . . . here a molecule,
there a molecule; a bond breaks, another one fuses in a new
way . . . the implications are disquieting."

"We both know I've been changing," Gabriel said, "but
you said there was no physical engine for the changes. It's
not as if I'd been hardwired or anything."

"Hardwiring too could be dealt with," Delde Sota said. "At
least some chance of selectivity there, of personal choice, or
of putting it back the way you found it if you don't like the
way things have turned out. But who chooses what happens
to you now? Where are these decisions being made, and by
what instrumentality? Internal? External? Combination of
both by way of implanted suggestion?" She shook her head.
"Diagnosis: no sign of such, and hard enough to get you to
take a suggestion anyway, even *not* implanted. Molecular
engine? No sign of such. Reprogramming of DNA? No sign
of that either. Changes are coming out of nowhere. Going—"

"Nowhere, maybe," Gabriel said.

She looked at him with the expression of someone willing to humor a crazy person, but only so far. "Challenge:

tell me again that changes of such subtlety, so perfectly tailored to you, are happening accidentally. Have various bridges to sell you, if you believe that."

Gabriel looked at her slightly cockeyed. "Why would you want to sell me bridges?"

Delde Sota gave him an exasperated look. "Waste of good idiom. Gabriel, neurochemical changes alone suggest purpose. Careful phasing of neuropeptide sequences into ancillaria, concealed myelin restructuring strategies—"

"I can't feel those," Gabriel said. "Even if I did, I still wouldn't know what they meant. I'd sooner know why my hair's gone so white."

"Assessment: archaeotypically hominid-masculine response," Delde Sota said, flipping her braid in the air in an I-give-up gesture. "Follicular obsession. Opinion: only fortunate the perseveration does not concern iphyphallocointrinism." She rolled her eyes as she said this, and Gabriel tried hard to fix the last word in his mind so that he could look it up later. "Warning: more important things to be concerned about. Idiomatic description: your body is becoming less your own and more something else's." She paused. "Incorrect. Some*one* else's."

"As long as it's still mine," Gabriel said.

"Precisely the problem," Delde Sota said, "since the 'someone else' in question *is* you. Alert: mind/body is a spectrum, not a dichotomy! Shift one part, other parts shift as well. Physical affects mental as profoundly as mental/physical." She looked at him narrowly. "Example: rather odd events just now on Danwell. Alien machine acting as mind/body extension. Conjecture: unaffected?"

Gabriel kept quiet for a moment and thought about that. The strange dreams he had started having before Danwell had not stopped, though their emphasis had changed. Since then, he had been feeling . . . well, not exactly tired, not physically anyway, but as if he had overextended himself somehow. At least he had been feeling that way for the first few days after that last battle. The feeling had gone away. Now he was beginning to wonder whether it had done so too quickly.

"No," Gabriel said, "I don't think so."

Delde Sota let out another long breath and said, "Statement: remiss of me to leave client unsupervised during period of unpredictable change. Addendum: if toadstools do occur, would not like to lose chance to publish."

Gabriel gave her the driest look he could. "Ambulance chaser."

Delde Sota gave him that look right back, with interest. "Notification," she said, "skilled enough practitioner has no need to chase. Knows where to stand so that vehicle stops right in front of her."

Gabriel smiled too, though he had to force it a little, and closed down the display.

* * * * *

Much later that evening, after they had made their first starfall on their way to Algemron, Gabriel lay in the dimness of his little cabin, under the blanket, with the luckstone in one hand.

He had begun to feel it looking at him.

The feeling had first crept up on him when they arrived at Danwell, and it had been increasing since. It was not an unfriendly regard, particularly . . . just a sense of being thoughtfully, carefully watched.

It wanted something.

Yet the wanting was very cool, dispassionate. There were no emotions attached to it that Gabriel could sense, which was just as well.

He wished he knew what it wanted, so that he could get it out of his life.

Is that even possible any more? Gabriel thought. There were the physiological changes Delde Sota had spoken of . . .

In the dimness, he glanced across the room toward his mirror. He knew that if he got up and looked at himself, he would only see again what he had been trying not to see every morning: all the hair that was coming in silvery white, the hair of an old man. Though not entirely white yet, it would be soon.

What else in him was aging in ways he didn't know about? Was he just going to wrinkle up and die suddenly, without warning? Delde Sota felt his organs were in good enough order for a man in his mid-twenties, but would they stay that way for long, and if so, for how long?

He had no choice really but to pursue the course he was now committed to follow. The hints and visions, the dreams and hunches that were occurring to him now . . . following them had become Gabriel's life. Only that way would he be able to come to the end of the path they were drawing for him. Once the stone had what it wanted—or whatever the unseen power that lay behind it wanted— then he would be able to pick up his own life again, try to knot up the parted threads of it, and find his own way.

Probably into a cell, said that chilly voice at the back of his mind.

He lay there a moment more, then put the stone aside and turned over in the bed to try to get to sleep. It would be tomorrow all too soon, and he would have to embark on the one errand that held him to what now seemed the most distant part of his life, the part before the Marines. Tomorrow would either see that particular thread snapped or reinforced. After that, what would happen to him . . .

Only the stone knew. As the room light cycled down to complete darkness, the last thing Gabriel saw was the light dying out of the stone, leaving it black and dead.

* * * * *

After that, for a long time in his dream, dark-green thought stroked and tangled in and out through itself, incomprehensible, uncomprehending.

In his dream, Gabriel stirred and moaned.

Chapter Three

IN ONE OF the many white-on-white corridors of the Concord Cruiser *Schmetterling*, Commander Aleen Delonghi stood outside the closed door and hesitated, not entirely willing to go in. She could hear noises coming from inside.

Nonetheless, she raised her hand to knock. You did not keep a Concord Administrator waiting when he summoned you.

The door slipped silently open, and the slim dark-visaged young man she had been expecting to see was standing just inside it. "Yes? Oh, it's you, ma'am. Come in. The Administrator will see you."

She stepped in, rather out of her depth. She did not normally expect to see Lorand Kharls in the ship's gymnasium. He had an office, a perfectly nice one—if somewhat underfurnished for someone of his station—and she had never seen him out of it. In fact, there were people aboard *Schmetterling* who claimed he never left it at all. Apparently their information was in—

CRACK!

The sound brought her head around fast. The gym was mostly empty, the majority of the equipment folded away into the walls. The lights were dimmed, glinting somewhat brassily off the white walls and ceiling since the holography equipment was presently running. Off to one side, wearing nondescript dark blue sweat gear, Lorand Kharls was fighting with himself.

That would have been most people's first impression, anyway. Kharls held the tri-staff of his office crosswise in front of him, and he was circling warily around a holographic simulation of himself, also holding a duplicate of the staff. The hologram's imaging field was charged, so that when there was any physical incursion into it, a big spark and shock-noise was generated. As she watched, Delonghi saw it happen again, the administrator feinting, feinting once more, a fake high, another one low, and then a change of grip on the tri-staff and a big swinging blow at his twin, who danced back—but not far enough. *CRACK!* Kharls danced backward as the other plunged forward, the staff whirling in its hands. The hologram brought the staff around end-on to Kharls, held it poised just for a moment—

Something that looked entirely too much like lightning lanced from the end of it. Kharls leaped to one side, still holding the staff, hit the ground and rolled, came up out of the shoulder roll, lifted the staff as if to parry the other's next attack, and then flung it.

It left his hands like a spear, spitting lightning as it went, and flew straight through the center of his adversary's body. The shadowy Kharls dropped its own weapon, made as if to clutch at the tri-staff, and then lost coherence, shivering into interference-pattern insubstantiality, then into static snow, and then darkness.

Kharls let out a long breath, went over to pick up his staff, then looked over at Delonghi, leaning on the weapon.

"Would you care to dance, Commander?" he asked.

She swallowed. "I prefer the waltz," she said and went over to him, not so slowly as to suggest she was afraid.

"It's been a very full day," Kharls said, "and I would hope you would forgive me asking to see you just now, but there's no other time available for the next twenty-four hours or so, and I didn't want to wait."

"It's not a problem, sir," Delonghi replied, privately considering that no Concord Administrator did anything without a reason, no matter how random his or her motives might seem to the uneducated observer.

"Very well," he said. He stood there a moment wiping away sweat and getting his breath back.

"I've never seen one of those used," Delonghi said.

Kharls looked momentarily surprised then glanced at the tri-staff. "What? Oh, but this wasn't use."

"You could have fooled me," Delonghi said.

He threw her a wry look that suggested, without needing so many words, that in fact in the past he had certainly done so but was too courteous at the moment to pick up on her straight line directly. "No," Kharls said after a moment, "believe me, when *this* gets used, really used, then life and death are on the line." He looked at the staff with a certain amount of pleasure. "Of course you need practice in handling it . . . getting the moves right. There's never enough time for that, but I make what opportunities I can."

It was entirely too tempting to take him casually, this little bald man. He was not at all plump. Delonghi suspected that Concord Administrators' lives ran at too high a speed for them ever to put on much weight. The overt effect of the baldness and shortness together somehow suggested a jolly man, a cheerful soul. Then you saw the eyes and the rest of the face, and that impression went entirely out of your mind. The cheer was there all right, but there was a ferocious, cool intelligence behind it—a sense that this man might do anything at all in the course of his business, which, as the motto said, was peace. Still, Delonghi knew that Kharls was not above producing a fair amount of conflict and trouble along the way if he felt them required to produce the final result for a large enough group of people. In this he merely proved himself true to his kind, for Concord Administrators were no armchair politicians. They went where they were needed, from the inner worlds to the emptiest and most dangerous spaces of the Verge. They took action—sometimes quite brutal action—and took the responsibility without shirking it. The tri-staff was symbolic of their need to handle it personally, "getting their hands dirty," which, as judge, jury, and executioner, they often enough did.

"Meanwhile," Kharls said, "I've been waiting for some matters to come to a head, and they've finally done so, which is why I've sent for you." He lifted the staff again, executed a neat if large reverse moulinet with it. "Gabriel Connor."

Delonghi had expected as much and restrained herself from letting so much as a flicker of expression show. "Where is he now?"

"Surely you know," Kharls said, "being Intel and having something of an interest in the man's case."

I won't swear in front of him, Delonghi thought, I won't! "Aegis, at the moment," she said. "I think he's planning to change equipment. It's a good place to buy a new ship."

Kharls nodded slowly and for a few moments looked up into the air as if examining a distant landscape. "Other things he can be doing there as well," Kharls said. "I wonder . . ."

He fell silent.

"I don't see why you won't let us take him," Delonghi said. "The new identity—"

"Please," Kharls said, lifting a hand. "Commander, you must understand that I know there's some animus in Intel regarding this particular case. It's always annoying when someone produces results so wide-ranging without either funding or the appropriate clearances. Worse yet when they appear to be on the wrong side of the law."

"He *is* on the wrong side of the law," Delonghi said, "and when the Marines catch up with him—"

"You have been talking to Captain Dareyev, I see," Kharls said and smiled slightly. "Well, why wouldn't you? Cross-discipline messes are welcome enough on these long hauls away from home."

Once again, the thought struck Delonghi that there might be other reasons why the various forces aboard

Star Force ships were encouraged to mingle so freely in their off-duty hours. Star Force had its own Intel, but so did the Marines, and—

She choked off that thought for the moment, for Kharls was looking at her thoughtfully.

"You know of course that there is some animus between her and Connor as well," Kharls said, more quietly. "More than usual, under the circumstances. Not particularly surprising, since they were such good friends before, and when a death comes between friends this way, the results can be unexpectedly bitter. And there are other considerations as well."

He was looking, it seemed to Delonghi, straight through her. The expression made her want to shiver. "You wouldn't know about those, would you," said Kharls, "or have any little suspicions that the captain had more irons in the fire concerning Connor than she's entirely willing to let on?"

Delonghi was only able to shake her head numbly.

"Well," Kharls sighed. "I suspect some, but then I suspect so many things, and this isn't any more or less likely than the rest of them." Again that very disturbing look, as if he could see right into the bottom of her. "Well," Kharls said, "Aegis. What would you do, if you had your druthers?"

Delonghi swallowed, for this was exactly what she had been afraid he would ask her. "While it would make the Marines happy to send someone straight there and arrest him—"

"Doubtless it would. I take it they don't yet have Star Force Intel's information about his present alias?"

Delonghi shook her head again, hoping desperately that what she presently knew about this situation would not show.

"Well, if they ask, obviously interservice courtesy will have to be done, and the information shared."

"Will it? 'Obviously'?" Delonghi asked.

This time, when he looked at her, his eyes flashed. It was

an entirely approving expression, and Delonghi was not sure that being on the receiving end of it was any more comfortable than receiving one of his more censorious looks. "If they ask," said Kharls, "of course. Meantime, though, you had a further thought."

Delonghi swallowed and spoke. "Connor has been allowed to run for the value of what he's been turning up. Obviously Danwell and the events there are an example of the kind of thing he turns up. Not just Danwell itself, either."

"No, indeed," said Kharls. "Some odd things began happening in that system a short time after Connor arrived. Of course, you arrived then, too, and so did that VoidCorp security operative. There might be some who would find the waters muddied by the additional personnel. So much the better. Now he's off again looking for another ship, you say."

"We think he wants to extend his range so that he'll have less trouble hunting down whatever he's after now."

"And you think this is. . . ?"

Delonghi paused and shook her head. "We're not sure," she said. "It's unlikely to be anything having directly to do with the warrant out on him. If he were hunting evidence to back his claim that he's been framed or duped, he'd be looking toward more populated areas, not into the back end of the Verge. We've been able to track some of his Grid usage, and he's been paying a lot of attention to places like Mantebron and High Mojave. Nothing back this way."

Kharls nodded and turned away. "Well, that matches my thinking somewhat. Now, the crunch. Doubtless you would like to look further into this matter. Why should I send you?"

The next few moments stretched out unnaturally long for Delonghi, for she had not expected to be asked this question. She had botched her last mission involving Connor—botched it spectacularly. She had returned to her posting on *Schmetterling,* and to her continuing shock, for the next couple of months, nothing had happened. No review board, no loss of grade and pay. The uneventful quality of those months had been horrifying—all of them spent in the same job, all of them spent waiting for the axe to fall. Each time she had started to become a little numb, thinking that perhaps she would be let off the hook and allowed to continue her career from the point just before she screwed it up, there would come some small reminder that this was not to be the case. Kharls had not forgotten. Always, when her pay chip came in, there was a large number down at the bottom of the readout, the cost of the Star Force ship that Delonghi had signed for and (because of Gabriel Connor) had not returned. The number had many zeroes after it, too many zeroes ever to be paid for out of her pay in her lifetime, but also, there was always the note that appeared beside that awful number: DEFERRED.

Deferred for what? she would think. For how long? Until now?

Her mouth was very dry.

"Sir," she said, "you should send me because Connor knows me and knows me to be connected with you. He is therefore less likely to kill me than anyone else you might send."

Kharls stared at her and then burst out laughing. It went on for an embarrassingly long time, and he actually had to wipe his face at the end of it.

"Delonghi," he said, "oh my . . ." He was still chuckling. "You're worried about Connor killing you? I wouldn't waste too much concern over that. He has his own agendas that would militate against it. Besides, if a tool is likely to be all that deadly, I don't throw it out into the dark. I keep it in my hand, where I know what it's doing."

The look he gave her was openly merry now, and Delonghi did not care to read too much into it.

"Indeed," Kharls continued, "you are known to him, and that's an advantage. Connor has several things on his mind which he did not confide in me, and one matter that is fairly major, about which I have some curiosity. Oh, really, Delonghi, do you think I can't tell when people aren't telling me things?" That look was even more amused. "You think it's all about holding your face still? You're Intel, didn't your kinesics instructor tell you that the shoulders are—" He stopped himself. "Well, you'll find out. Anyway, Connor wouldn't have been such a fool as to go straight off after whatever it is he wants and about which he hasn't told me—not without taking a little time to recover from the Danwell experience first. I'd say he's about ready now, though. So get yourself another ship, and go after him. Find out where he's headed. You may need help to stop him from getting whatever he's after . . . or to slow him down until we can get there."

"What if he tries to make contact with other intelligence forces?" Delonghi asked, for this was one of the rocks on which her last mission had foundered, and she wanted to be very clear about her options.

"Yes, there is always that, isn't there?" Kharls replied. For several moments he was silent, gazing at the floor and turning the tri-staff gently around and around as he leaned on it again.

He looked up again. "How would you handle it?"

"I would watch," she said, "and see who made the first approach. If they were the ones who came after him . . ." She breathed in, breathed out, not sure if this was the right answer. "I might be concerned for his safety."

"After past experience, I'd say you would probably be right there," said Kharls. There was a slight soft edge in his voice all of a sudden, which made Delonghi even more nervous than she had been. "There may be others besides intelligence assets who come looking for him as well: others who are as determined not to have him find things as we are to let him get out there and turn over the rocks. If they come along, you'll do well to be more than concerned. Protect him and yourself. Make sure your armament is more than adequate." Kharls glanced at the tri-staff, fitted one thumbnail into a hardly visible recess at about the five foot level, and concentrated on the spot for a moment, tapping in some coded message.

"And when he finds . . . whatever it is?"

Kharls laughed softly. "You'll have to send word back with someone else or bring it yourself. I wouldn't quote you odds on there being a drivesat anywhere nearby, not in the spaces he's likely to be investigating. Be prepared for a speedy return to his location after that, since if I know Connor, he will be up to his neck in something unpleasant. Whether he'll be able to handle it or not . . ."

He shook his head, wearing that cool expression again, a man willing to throw the dice and wait to see how they fall, and not at all concerned about any opinions the dice might have on the matter.

"Go on, then," he said. "We'll be at your dropoff point five days from now. So good luck to you. Better luck than last time."

"Thank you, sir," she said, saluted him, and turned to go out.

Halfway to the door he spoke again. "One thing, Delonghi."

She paused, turned.

"Don't wait for him to buy a ship," Kharls said. "He won't bother. Not now."

"But his comms traffic—"

"Yes, I'm sure. Whatever he may have been doing, I think now he's sensing that one of the trails he's following may be going cold. He waited as long as he could, partly for tactical reasons, I feel, but he plays his hunches, too. Don't dawdle. Get after him."

"Yes, sir."

"And if you'd be so kind, when you go back updecks, ask Captain Dareyev to call on me at her earliest convenience."

Delonghi nodded and went out. Not that it would normally be my business to pass on such messages, she thought, but he wants her to know that I've seen him, and—since he knows she'd ask, and I'd tell her—he wants her to know something about what he's told me. Not all of it, of course.

Why?

For the time being, though, Delonghi knew there were likely to be no answers. All she could do was try to carry out this mission more effectively than she had carried out the last one. It was tough enough to come out of a session with Lorand Kharls with a sense that your head was still fastened on. Rather to her surprise, hers was.

He sees some use in me still, she thought. I wish I were entirely sure that this is a good thing.

* * * * *

Light-years away, a dark ship moved in the outer reaches of the Coulomb system. No one was positioned to be able to detect its presence, which was just as well, for if anyone had come across it, they might not have escaped again to tell the story.

Deep inside the ship, in the administrative center, a tall slender man in a dark coverall sat, looking at the little viewer built into the big shining desk before him and reading a file. He was in no hurry, for he had read the file before and was merely refreshing himself on some of the pertinent details.

Well, the last operative would make no more mistakes. The next one, though . . . what *she* would do was another question entirely.

Finally, the call he was waiting for came through.

"RS201 67LEK here," said the man at the other end of the connection. He looked paler than usual, which was an interesting effect in someone so blond to start with. Like the man he was calling, he wore a very plain dark one-piece suit, though in gray rather than black. Probably wise, for black would have made him look positively undead.

The man at the desk looked thoughtfully at the message

herald showing across the bottom of the screen. "Took you a while to get here."

"Couldn't be helped. I had other business that kept me closer to home, and I've already been away from Main Office a lot longer than planned. As soon as we recharge, we're off again."

"I must admit, I wasn't expecting to see *you*. I thought it would be SL223 98MFT."

"He couldn't make it," replied RS201 67LEK.

The man in the dark coverall said nothing. There had been many detentions recently, and the lateness implied by a number of them was more permanent than usual. Company politics was heating up somewhat.

"So," the man at the desk asked, "you'll be heading straight out again?"

"A few starfalls. No more, I'm glad to say. Have you heard anything to the point from Upstairs?"

"No more than I need to. As usual, they're being circumspect and covering their fundaments."

RS201 67LEK sighed in frustration. The man at the desk shared his frustration but was not going to express it, not in front of someone so close to his own grade. Be polite to your underlings on the way up, the saying went. You want to be sure they underestimate you if they meet you again on the way down. He was sure that RS201 67LEK had his own ideas of which each of them was. It was not his business to disabuse the other of those ideas, especially since they were erroneous.

"So what happened to RS881 34PRM?" asked the dark man before the other could bring the matter up and wring even that small satisfaction out of it.

"What do you think?" RS201 67LEK replied. "The Concord wrung her dry and chucked her out. We picked her up afterward, and . . ."

"Contract terminated, then?"

RS201 67LEK shrugged. "It's not like she didn't know it was going to happen. Apparently, they refused her request for asylum, though. That was something of a puzzle."

"They preferred her out of the way," said the man at the desk. "Unusually sensible of them. I'd half thought they'd lock her up to keep us from doing the merciful thing. Never mind. Did the pre-termination debriefing turn up anything interesting?"

"No. Whatever happened on Danwell, she was out of commission for the interesting parts."

"And that's the hot question of the moment, of course," said the dark man. "What *did* happen at Danwell?"

RS201 67LEK shook his head. The upper reaches of VoidCorp were still buzzing with the strange occurrence that had terminated there. Three VoidCorp vessels had been en route to that planet to take pre-emptive possession of certain alien technology discovered there, but something odd had happened in drivespace. Everybody knew that a starfall/starrise cycle lasted exactly a hundred and twenty-one hours, but those vessels had come out of such a cycle only to find that a Concord cruiser that had left at least two hours after they did had nonetheless arrived at Danwell *before* them and was now sitting there with its guns hot, spoiling what would otherwise have been a very advantageous and lucrative day.

When it suddenly appeared that natural laws were breaking themselves in favor of one side in a political dispute, naturally a great deal of interest was created, but there was more to this interest than the suspicion that somehow the Concord had found a way to bend the rules of physics in its own favor. Other business had been scheduled to happen near Danwell, and the Concord's presence had disrupted it. A favor in the act of being done for a potential business partner had been derailed, and the upper reaches of the company were now in a turmoil trying to put the situation right.

"Well," said the man at the desk. "We'll find out one way or the other. Meanwhile, the investigation is moving on, since the main suspect has moved on as well."

"Where now?"

"Probably High Mojave."

"Oh?" RS201 67LEK said. "Where does that intelligence come from?"

"You'd be surprised." The dark man laughed. "There's been a change in tactics. No more squabbling between factions, no more Intel against Operations. This comes from way up in the Vs somewhere, up in the rarified airs where they've decided that we're all supposed to be one big happy family." He made a face meant to suggest that this prospect was a less than rapturous one. "The target is to be picked up and 'made safe' by someone senior. No more minor ops are to be involved. People with more seniority, all up and down the line, are taking charge now."

"Oh?" asked RS201 67LEK. "People like you?"

The man in the dark coverall didn't quite laugh. "As if I wouldn't go, if I had time. The whole business is fascinating, but I have my own fires to put out back at the important end of things. The damned administrator has been turning the heat up, and I'm busy keeping the immediate superiors from panicking and turning everything over to Intel. They've been the source of our present troubles as it is. Division in the company isn't a good thing."

"I would have thought they'd be suggesting that the representative you sent was to blame," said RS201 67LEK.

"Spare me your helpful ideas. As for Intel, my branch has seen little enough useful product from any of them, high or low, in the last few months. Thought higher up is shifting in regard to their general usefulness. I'd keep well away from them. Anyone seen to be taking their part is likely to get splashed when the big reorganization happens."

RS201 67LEK laughed. *"That's* supposed to happen now, is it? What a laugh."

The man in the dark coverall didn't respond to that. Let poor RS201 think it's not going to happen, he thought. Getting splashed will be the least of his worries, and if he can't keep away from the splash, that'll be one less thing for me to worry about. "The company has business to tend to," he said, "and it's going to be tending to it with some vigor. In particular, we have word that the target is after something very valuable indeed, something we want first."

"For development purposes, I would suppose."

You just go on thinking that, thought the dark man. "Stars only know what the policy people will make of it once we've got it," he said. "All we have to do is keep out of sight and stay with the target until he leads us to what we're after."

"Sounds almost too easy."

It was another nasty little jab, for that was what RS881 34PRM was supposed to have been doing on Danwell, and it had all gone wrong. "Confirmation that the target's genuine came along from our big Concord contact. He's not as careful about who sees his communiqués as he might be."

"Really?" RS201 67LEK looked genuinely interested for the first time. "How did you manage to—" He stopped himself, and the man in the dark coverall was amused for a second or so, though carefully he did not smile. Even RS201 67LEK knew that it was unwise to ask your superiors how they had managed to get ahead in their work. Too much curiosity could lead to you having the techniques demonstrated to you personally, and your career could suffer.

"So we follow this guy?" RS201 67LEK asked.

"It won't be difficult. He's picked up another set of friends. They're a cozy little threesome of ships now. Some interesting possibilities there for a creative agent, should it be possible to split them up somehow."

RS201 67LEK waved a hand dismissively and said, "Administrivia. Fascinating in its place, I'm sure, but I prefer results. We follow him to High Mojave and then evaluate what he finds. Possibly with help."

That would be one way to think of it, thought the man in the dark coverall. He nodded and said, "There's no rush about it. We wait until we're sure the material the upper-ups are looking for is unearthed, then go in. We get to keep the target and wring him out. Then, if we feel like it, we can toss what's left back to the Concord people as a reminder of who's leading in this particular foxtrot." He smiled slightly.

"Surprised you plan for there to be anything left to toss," replied RS201 67LEK. "Don't want them to get the idea we're going soft."

"I don't think they'll get that idea," said the dark man, "not by the time we're done. In his case, anyway, he'll be done breathing."

"Some satisfaction in that," said RS201 67LEK, making a face, "after all the trouble he's caused us. Be a good thing to make an example of him."

"Oh, I think we'll manage that," said the man in the dark coverall. "What does your timing look like now?"

"Tempting to do an overshoot and meet him there," said RS201 67LEK, "but probably it's safer to follow at a safe distance and give him rope. Amusing if he hanged himself with it before we did anything."

"Follow him by all means. And good hunting."

"Anything else?"

"Not a thing."

RS201 67LEK nodded, and the viewer went dark.

The man in the dark coverall leaned back in his chair and smiled gently, for RS201 67LEK plainly had no idea of what the reorganization was going to involve. It was a good question whether he would survive it.

The man in the black coverall had seen some preliminary images. He knew that things were really about to start moving in these spaces. All hell would break loose while his people were seen to be having nothing to do with it. Until afterwards, he thought, when the situation that remains can be best exploited, but now there was little more to do than watch it unfold. The Concord and the nonaligned worlds would be screaming bloody murder within a few months. Let them scream. The Company had been waiting for this particular shift in the balance of power for a long time—had in fact done a great deal to start bringing it about. Now a lot of people, shirkers and scoffers, the less-than-fully-committed, were going to get the shock of their lives—not that those lives were likely to last long. After that, those people would be made *really* useful. The technique was enough to make your blood run cold, until you saw the potential of it.

He hoped to see that potential demonstrated on RS201 67LEK and numerous other people who had gotten in his way at one time or another. It was, after all, an ill wind that blew nobody any good.

Chapter Four

WHEN THEY MADE starrise at the end of the first of their five jumps to Algemron, Gabriel was still in no mood for one of the three ships' usual get-together dinners. The gathering was postponed, and all three crews went about doing what they usually did while waiting for their drives to recharge: maintenance, systems checks, and the hobbies that were the mainstays of private pilots who had learned the wisdom of structuring their idle time while in drivespace or recharge downtime. Gabriel had thought he would take another look at those ship catalogues, but his heart wasn't in it. He was still too upset by what had happened back at Bluefall. Now, when Enda had gone off to take a nap, Gabriel found himself sitting alone in the pilot's cabin, feeling very much at loose ends.

When the comms circuit chirped, it startled him. Gabriel looked at its control in the display, then stuck his finger in and activated it. "*Sunshine.*"

"Gabriel." It was Angela. "Is Enda available?"

"Napping, but I'll get her."

"No, it's not that important. It's just about a shopping list for Algemron." There was a pause. "You sound so bored. Why not take a break and come over?"

Bored had nothing to do with it, and normally he would have refused politely and gone to take a nap himself, but *Sunshine* was just too quiet at the moment. If he sat here, he would start hearing that voice saying, "When it's all over, when our name is cleared . . ." Also, there was a peculiar twanging noise in the background, and he wondered if something on Angela's ship was acting up again.

"Sure," Gabriel said. "Why not?"

"I'll put out the tube," Angela said.

A few minutes later he was climbing through *Lalique*'s airlock. That odd whanging sound was coming from down the hallway. Then it ceased, and Angela was coming up the hall toward him, carrying a large jug of some kind.

"New batch just finished," she said. "Want some kvass?"

"Uh," he said, glancing around him to get his bearings as Angela went by him with the jug. He had only been over here a few times, but every time he came, he more envied Angela the room she and Grawl had to roll around in inside *Lalique*. We are going to have a ship this size, he thought, and sooner rather than later. I swear we are. "Sorry. What's kvass?"

"It's mild booze."

"I'm up for that."

"Come on down here then."

Gabriel followed Angela down the hallway. "What the—" he said, suddenly hearing the strange noise again. "Have you got engine trouble?"

Angela laughed. "No, it's Grawl."

He stared at her. Angela pointed through a doorway, and Gabriel looked through it as he came up with her.

Grawl was sitting on a low couch, in what as apparently her quarters, plucking at a *rhin*. Suddenly Gabriel understood. He had heard the instrument in recordings but had never until now seen one. It was one of the several different styles of weren lap-harp, half a frame on which strings were strung for plucking, and half a voicebox with tuned metal prongs extending partway across it. The prongs produced the bass notes and rhythm, and the strings were for melody . . . if that was the word for it. They were tuned in a scale that Gabriel had never heard before, and which to his possibly untrained ears sounded profoundly dissonant, like wild animals having an argument in an enclosed space.

"She doesn't go in for the epic poetry," Angela said. "We should be grateful."

"Should we?"

"You have no idea. It goes on for hours, and the choruses would deafen you. Come on, Gabriel, don't hang over her," Angela said. "She gets self-conscious."

He shook his head and followed her away from the door. "Somehow I can't see her getting all shy and blushy," Gabriel said. "She always seems so self-possessed." As someone might, he thought, who outmasses nearly everyone else around here by a factor of two.

"Well, she's not."

Angela led him into the living space just behind *Lalique*'s piloting compartment. She put down the jug, took down a couple of glasses from a shelf, blew the dust out of one, filled both from the jug, and handed one to Gabriel. He sipped at the kvass and found that it was tart, fizzy, and not all that alcoholic.

"This is good," he said. "How do you make it?"

"Just yeast and fruit juice concentrate," she said. "Low-grade hooch for when you can't afford the high-grade stuff." She sprawled out on the sofa across from him, and Gabriel sat down on the other, looking around.

"Go on, put your feet up," Angela said. "We're not that houseproud. Besides, it's one of those smartfabrics. You'd have to set fire to it to get it to show dirt. Just as well around here."

Gabriel hitched his legs up to sit crosslegged and put his drink off to one side.

"You didn't have much to say about your trip to beautiful Bluefall," Angela said.

"No."

"Doubtless an indicator that your visit didn't go quite as planned."

"Uh, no," Gabriel said. "I guess it didn't."

Then, having said that much, he felt foolish not saying anything more. So he leaned back and slowly started to tell her about it, as much as he could bear to. The original pain was wearing off somewhat, but the memory twinged anew every time he touched it, and in some new place: the bright, brassy way the day had looked, some aspect of his father's expression that he had been too shocked to notice at the time. At the same time, he found himself increasingly able to view it all as if it had happened to someone else.

"The strain on him through all this has to have been horrible," Gabriel said softly when he had finished. "It's such a small place, Tisane. The neighbors are watching you all the time . . . everything you do. You can't avoid socializing with them. They're all there is, but if something embarrassing happens to someone, everybody knows about it in seconds."

He shook his head and turned away. "It has to have been like a prison for him," Gabriel said, "house arrest. He'll have been lonely, but there wasn't anyone to turn to, anyone to talk to. Even when things were all right with the neighbors, he was never the most social person. When they tried to be with him after my mother died, he never was able to take it the way it was meant. He always drew away."

"Sounds like he may have started doing it now," Angela said. "It'd be convenient, too, for him to blame you for it so he wouldn't be to blame at all."

Gabriel blinked at that.

She shook her head. "I don't know what to tell you," Angela said as she sat up, curling her legs underneath her and reaching out again for her kvass. "You're probably just going to have to let him get over it. I bet he was more upset than you were, just no good at showing it—not that it would have helped. You would almost certainly have made each other worse."

Gabriel nodded slowly, surprised how glad he was to hear this judgment. It made him feel less as if he had fled entirely in panic at the end. "You sound like you've been through this kind of thing."

She shook her head. "No. It's weird, but I had a wonderful childhood." Angela laughed. "I mean, 'it's weird' in the sense that it seems like no one else I know has had one or has a good relationship with their parents now. We always got along really well, our family, even my brother and me. Well, I had to thump him sometimes, but you assume you're going to have to do that with your brother so that he'll at least come out vaguely human." Angela grinned a little. "Since I went out on my own into the big world, I see the kind of things other people have gone through . . ." She shook her head. "I see how they suffer or suffered, and I say, 'God, I was lucky not to have that happen to me. How did I luck out? What did I do right?' It doesn't seem fair, somehow."

She sighed. "This looks like just more of the same, but even now, look at the group of us. Enda . . . well, you'd know more about her history than I would. Grawl, though. Chucked out from among her own people, almost without a thought, for being the runt. Helm . . ." She paused. "I get a feeling Helm's childhood wasn't exactly a joyous romp. Just say the words 'parent' or 'child' around him and watch him stiffen up. The doctor . . ." She shrugged. "Mechalus are kind of a mystery to me. Do they have children or send away for a kit?"

"A little bit of both, I think."

"Well, there's no telling how Delde Sota took the process. They keep retrofitting themselves until they get it right, the mechalus—isn't that the idea? No telling how much of her 'original engineering' is left then. She might just have done a valve and ring job on herself or a complete rebuild." Angela shrugged. "Anyway, in terms of human childhoods, I seem to have come off unusually well. I look at the people around me and wish I could patent the process somehow and sell it."

"You'd be rich pretty quick," Gabriel said.

"That's my guess."

They sat there quietly for a little while, sipping at their kvass. Down the hall, Grawl was twanging away at the *rhin* and producing astonishing dissonances that continued to sound more like drive malfunctions than anything else.

"How do you put up with that?" Gabriel said.

"Mostly I don't," Angela said. "Mostly she does it when I'm asleep."

"How could you *sleep* with that going on?"

Angela shrugged. "If she did it while I was going to sleep," she said, "I'd never get there. Afterwards, you could detonate a force grenade in here and I'd just sort of go 'uh' and turn over." She smiled, rather sheepishly. "It's one of the reasons I was glad she agreed to team up with me. You don't want to know the kind of volume levels I had to set my ship's alarms for when I was alone to wake me up if something happened during my downtime."

"I'll make a note to shout at you if you doze off," Gabriel said and fell silent for the moment.

You'd know more about her history than I would, Angela had said. Gabriel could have laughed at that but was in no mood. He still knew so little about Enda. She had her own privacies, which even after all this while he was unwilling to probe.

All this while, Gabriel thought. How long have I known her now? A year?

It's just been such a *busy* year . . . but once again Gabriel was left thinking of how many questions he had to ask her and wouldn't but still wished he had answers to.

He and Angela talked a good while more, mostly about inconsequential things, but Gabriel came back again, eventually, to his father. "The one thing I should have said to him," Gabriel said with something of an effort, "is that I loved him, and I didn't want him to worry, but I didn't say that. And I think he meant to say it to me, despite it all . . . and he didn't say it either."

"That's hardly your fault," said Angela. She shook her head and sighed. "Anyway, you can still drop him a note next time you shift some data."

Gabriel shook his head. "Anything I send him is going to be intercepted," he said. "He might never see it. He doesn't seem to have seen messages I sent him very early on."

"Well, what if it *is* intercepted?" Angela said. "So the snoopies discover that you secretly love your dad. If that information confuses them, so much the better. The hell with them, anyway."

Her belligerence surprised Gabriel a little. "They've been putting you through all kinds of grief," Angela said, seeming annoyed. "No harm for you to annoy them back a little. Maybe they need to be jolted into thinking of you as something besides some kind of inhuman murderer."

Gabriel thought about that. "I'd be more worried that they might try to use the information against me somehow, or against him."

"Sounds like they've already tried everything they could in that regard," Angela said. "From what you say your old man said, it didn't take. Look, it's your choice, Gabriel, but whatever happens, someday this is all going to be over, and you'll be able to come back again. You want to make sure you have someone to come back *to*." She stretched.

Gabriel nodded. "Your weapons in order?" he said.

"Grawl's checked everything out," Angela said. "I'm going to double-check in a while. We don't have anything that could remotely be considered contraband, and everything but personal arms is going to be locked up while we transit the system—except the ship's armament, of course, but it sounds like we won't be there that long."

"I want to do some provisioning there," Gabriel said, "things that could attract attention if I picked them up here. Long-life supplies, some exploration gear . . . we may be gone for a while."

She grinned a little. "You've caught the bug," she said. "Just as well I sold you that contract, I guess. You sure made it pay a lot better than I did."

Down the hall, a soft chirping noise began and started to escalate. "Comms," Angela said, and then raising her voice, said, "Communications, reroute to sitting room. Yes?"

"Angela, it is Enda. I was wondering if Gabriel was over with you."

"Hi, Enda. Yeah, he's here. Hey, I have that list for you. I'll send it back with Gabriel when he heads home."

"I'll be right back, Enda," Gabriel said to the air.

"All right."

Gabriel finished his drink then stood up and stretched. "Maybe I will," he said.

Angela blinked. "Will what?"

"Send that message." He looked thoughtfully at her. "As for the snoopies . . . maybe a little confusion will be a healthy thing."

Angela smiled slightly as he turned away. "Maybe so. See you later."

* * * * *

They lay bathed in light, and all the voices sang in the stillness there, and never an unharmonious note was heard.

They do not know.

They do not know, chorused the others.

It was not really a song, at least in terms of sound being involved, but sound was just another form of interaction which they understood well enough to use when the need arose. They preferred their own methods: silence and the interweave of thought and long lithe movement, however confined. All life was movement inside confinement, until that frightening time came when the walls of the world broke, and they went hunting another world to live in. Fortunately, such times rarely lasted long. The universe was full of worlds in which to live. Sometimes they resisted, but the resistance was never able to last long.

Right now, the warm light of this particular world bathed them all, and they lay luxuriating in it while they considered their business. It was leisurely work at the moment, though the wisest of them knew that soon there would be need to speed the pace a little. Things were changing outside. The plan was moving forward by indirect means, as they themselves moved—long slow strokings of body against body in the tangle, while thoughts wove and curled about one another, while ramifications slid forward through time and became manifest.

"Outside" was their great problem now.

They do not know.

They still do not know.

In that regard at least they were safe. The hosts who carried them about, the mobile worlds, were blissfully ignorant of what they carried. Oh, when they first took possession there might be some small difficulty, some little struggling of the stubborn parasitic "intelligence" that clung inside these creatures, but old habits were soon enough unlearned, and things settled down. The tangle grew in the glow of warmth, and the host discovered how not to struggle, discovered that everything was so much easier if it just gave up the troublesome habit of thought and will. There was so much *other* thought, so much *other* will, waiting to relieve it of the difficulty. Sooner or later, it always gave in.

There was always the hope that things could become simpler. There were those far away, great minds, huge knots and matrices of thought native to other tangles on the outside. They looked forward to the day when a host would be perfected that did not struggle at all, a little world even more perfect, one capable of swift movement, far travel outside, which did not put up the tiresome battle for its own autonomy. As if there was any such thing. As if any one creature by itself could lay any kind of claim to intelligence. Mind came in numbers, and the proof of it was the way that the poor pitiful spasms of thinking that the present "outside" worlds manifested were unable to resist the presence of genuine thought, genuine will, for very long.

They do not know. . . .

It was the tangle's eternal consolation. Their way of life, if anything, brought intelligence to those unfortunate wandering spasmodic shells, poor purposeless things lurching and staggering about the outside world in their little bodies and ships. Once a tangle took hold in one of those small worlds, brought it direction and purpose, then were they intelligent, then would they know. Someday they would all know. Someday the stroke and curl of thirty or fifty or a hundred bodies would enlighten them all, the twining of useful and purposeful thought as it bred inside them.

The Others, one thought came from some distance, from another tangle, *they come closer now to finding the way to bring that time when worlds no longer resist us . . .*

The time comes.

It comes. They have found the place where the secret is hidden.

They have found the one who will find the place.

Soon now.

Soon . . .

Thoughts stroked and writhed against one another in luxuriant pleasure. Soon the enablers, the ancient devices, would be found. For so long they had been thought to be only myth, random thought, erroneous imagination. Then an image had come drifting along the thoughtways, leaked from somewhere perhaps, cast away by some being that had seen such a thing and not recognized it for what it was, but the Others recognized it, the one true group intelligence that did live outside. They searched in that great dubious emptiness of "physical reality" and found what they sought: the truth of the image, the source of the enablers, the devices that would make all the outside safe for their kind, would turn all of it into an endless infinity of unresisting worlds, hosts that did not have to be subdued.

But the Others were delayed.

They were delayed.

Sorrowful commiseration that such a delay should have to happen. The first place that had held the enabling devices had been inadequate. Not as expected, not as predicted. The devices had been interfered with. The Others had not been able to make use of them. Many of the wild host-creatures, willful, destructive, uncooperative, had come to that place and made it impossible for the Others to be there, to take what they desired.

Agitation. Thought curled and writhed against itself, frustrated. From somewhere came a faint sound, unpleasant.

The sound repeated.

The tangle asserted itself.

The sound choked off.

They had all been angry, but the anger was unnecessary. There was another source for the enablers, the Others said.

Soon they would come there, be brought there. Soon the source would be revealed, and all would once again go to plan.

The thought came curling into their own, colder and clearer than one of the voices of their own tangle.

We will know soon where that place is. Prepare your hosts to set about our business.

A stirring, a sense of amusement. *They are always about your business, for we are always about your business. All are the same.*

See to it that what you say is true. Put your hosts to following these, to watching for them. Come to grips with them. Make hosts of them if you can, but be ever with them once you have found them.

Images: Three ships, and the wild hosts associated with the ships. A woman, a weren, a human mutant, and a mechalus. A fraal . . . and a human of sorts, though that was changing.

The tangle writhed and squirmed even at the distant thought-image-of-an-image. There was something about the last one, the light, unlike their light—but a sensitivity as well, a mind that was almost a mind like theirs, even though he was only one.

Impossibility.

The tangle writhed more violently. Agitation. From outside again came the unpleasant sound, the scream.

The tangle asserted itself.

Silence fell again, and all bathed in the warmth, the light, once more uninterrupted.

Find them, said the voice of the Other. *Follow them. Call us when you do. Tell us where they go, what they do. Make hosts of them, if you can. Great will be your reward, for what they seek and what you can force them to find will make our world what we wish it to be at last.*

And they will not know.

They will not know . . .

Satisfied, eager, thoughtful, ready, the tangle smoothed and preened and stroked against itself, bodies writhing among bodies in the warmth, thought knotting through thought.

Outside, unregarded, water ran down the face of the world, and great sobs shook it until the tangle finally asserted itself again and choked the air away.

Chapter Five

SEVERAL WEEKS LATER they prepared for their final starfall into Algemron. Everyone's nerves were on edge.

The first problem with this system was exactly where to arrive. Much of it was theoretically neutral territory, but there was a lot of that to police and only one force doing the policing: a little Concord task force based on Palshizon at the edge of the system. Gabriel and everyone else discussed this via comms before their final starfall.

"If we go in under escort from the Concord ships there, we won't have this problem," Angela said.

"We could," Enda replied and glanced at Gabriel.

Gabriel said nothing for the moment.

The problem was the war. In a way, it was an offshoot of the Second Galactic War, continuing even though the Thuldans and Austrins had long since ceased that particular conflict. Some of their client worlds, however, had been slower to give up the war, and the inhabitants of Galvin and Alitar had been slowest of all. Only the *Monitor* Mandate, some years back, had prevented the two planets' "parent" stellar nations from becoming directly involved in the conflict, but even the Mandate had not been able to stop the "children" quarreling and killing large numbers of one another at every possible turn. While the Concord might not approve of this, there was nothing it could do about it at the moment. It kept a Concord Administrator permanently in the system, a woman named Mara DeVrona, which to Gabriel's mind was a clear indication of how desperately intractable it considered the situation there. They kept the little base at Palshizon, which conducted an escort system for ships passing through the system, trying to bolster the economy and local stability by keeping trade moving. Still, there were problems with their presence as well.

"If we do report there," Enda offered, "and they decide to query Gabriel's records . . . Well, that would be bad."

"You have a talent for understatement," Gabriel said gently.

"I don't want them escorting me in any case," Helm said. "It gives people the wrong idea. Anyway, all our roles are straightforward enough. You two have business there. You're infotraders. *We're* your escort. The Concord force there has enough problems taking care of people who do need escort. We won't bother with them."

Gabriel's feelings about this were mixed. On one hand, he still felt loyalty to the Concord and felt like a Marine, like one of the good guys, despite the way he had been treated. He hated having to avoid them. On the other hand, he was in no mood to have the Concord grab him at this moment in time. The luckstone was increasingly on his mind, and not just in terms of certain odd dreams he had been having. Lately, he could feel the stone "leaning" away from him toward the more distant areas of the Verge. In its wordless way, it was becoming most insistent that it was important, very important, to get there soon.

"If we stay close together," Gabriel said, "and we're polite to the inspection ships when they come out to meet us, we'll be all right. I've had a look at the reports on the Grid for the past few months. There don't seem to have been any incidents."

"That got reported, you mean," Angela remarked.

Gabriel sighed. "So we go in, get searched if we have to, and land at Fort Drum. The shopping's pretty good there, to judge from the ads on the Grid."

It also was just about the only city into which the Federal State of Algemron was likely to allow an offworlder without going too deeply into his records—something

Gabriel was as nervous about from the Algemron side as from the Concord. The Concord at least had due process and believed in the assumption of the innocence of the accused and his right to prove himself guiltless. Gabriel was unsure of any desire on either the Galivinite or Alitarin side to do anything but prove their enemies dead, and they seemed a little hasty about deciding who their enemies were. Someone discovered by either side to be running under a false identity would probably not be assumed to be very innocent at all.

Helm folded his arms. "All right for you, but I don't particularly love the idea of landing myself in an armed camp."

"You mean one where they are better armed than you are," said Grawl.

He grunted. The implication that anyone could be better armed than Helm was never likely to sweeten his disposition.

"I would have thought you would have selected Alitar for our business," Enda said. "It is somewhat less repressive in its philosophy."

"I'd have preferred to go there myself," Gabriel said, "but the suppliers don't have the equipment I'm after, and if I'm right in my analysis"—he looked at Helm—"the Galvinites have the edge on the Alitarins at the moment, especially in terms of patrol ships. If we filed a plan for Alitar, the Galvinites would come down on us in a hurry, possibly impound the ships . . ."

Helm nodded and let out another grunt. "How long you think it'll take you to do your business?"

Gabriel had been studying their starfall schedule and the system times. "It'll be local morning when we land," he said, "assuming we're not delayed too much on our way in. Most of the day for the shopping, and then the end of the day for the export formalities." The Galvinites believed in stringently checking outgoing cargos to make sure that nothing left their planet that might be of any use to Alitar.

"Overnight there, since the port curfew means they won't let us move between end-of-business and local morning, then straight out and on to our next destination."

"Which is?" asked Enda.

"No system," Gabriel said. "Starfall in space, possibly several of them, one after another."

"You are hunting a directional trace, then?" Grawl asked.

Gabriel shook his head and said, "I don't know if it's directional in the normal sense, but what I'm after is several starfalls away, at least."

"Okay," Helm said. "Off we go, then."

So they made starfall together, in a flare of what Gabriel considered a very noisy pink. Five days later, in what for *Sunshine* was a ferocious bloom of white fire—much brighter than usual, Gabriel thought—they made starrise in the Algemron system and began broadcasting their flight and landing plans on the properly allotted frequencies. They had been concerned that they might come out too close to Galvin and Alitar, a bad idea at this time of year when the two planets were drawing into the annual close-approach configuration that usually meant an escalation of hostilities. Both sides tended to get trigger-happy during such periods.

Sitting in the pilots' compartment, strapped in next to Enda and with the weapons on standby, Gabriel found himself wishing heartily that the Algemron system had a drive-sat relay. It would have been nice to be able to file a destination plan early so that people wouldn't be surprised when you turned up.

Though it might not make a difference with these people, he thought.

He shrugged the JustWadeIn fighting field around him and looked around. In the darkness of the field, schematic indicators relayed the system even though the actual bodies weren't visible. The brassy G5-gold of Algemron itself dominated the field. All its satellite bodies—the barren

inner worlds Calderon and Ilmater, and beyond Galvin and
Alitar, the uninhabitable planets, the gas giant Dalius, the
small worlds Wreathe and Argolos, the ice-and-methane
world Reliance, two more gas giants, Havryn and Halo—
all of them did their slow dance around the star. Away back
there in the darkness of the field was the little flashing point
of light that marked Pariah Station on Palshizon. The whole
system, if history had gone a little differently, could have
been a busy, friendly place, full of gas miners and with two
lively, well-settled Class 1 worlds at its heart, but the great
powers had begun quarreling with ever-increasing intensity
after only a few decades, making it highly unlikely that
peace would ever break out here again short of everyone
dropping dead.

"Any answer yet?" Gabriel asked Enda, keeping an eye
out around him.

She tilted her head "no" and then went back to looking
around in the field.

He peered into the darkness. Close as they were to Alitar,
there was no seeing the planet as a disk yet, no glimpse of
the hole in the ground marking where half of the city of
Beronin had been once upon a time. Even when they got in
sight of Galvin, there would probably be no clear sign of
where the Red Rain had once fallen, killing a third of the
planet's population at that point. All very nasty, Gabriel
thought. You don't want to spend too much time where
people have been fighting so hard that the conflict leaves
marks on the planet that can be seen from space. . . .

In the middle of Gabriel's head, something began to itch
slightly. Oh, not now, he thought. This was a sensation he
had begun experiencing since Danwell, since the time his
telepathic contacts with his "counterpart" Tlelai started to
become both frequent and easy. The itch, the twitch, usually meant that the power trapped in the luckstone was
becoming active. Gabriel was often unclear about the reasons it did this. Sometimes it seemed to react to his stress
levels—and they're fairly high at the moment, he thought.

At other times the itch happened for no reason whatever, or none that he could detect. Delde Sota had been able to cast no light on the sensation, except to suggest that it was something similar to the "phantom pain" suffered by amputees, except in reverse: a sign of new neural connections being forged, rather than old destroyed ones still thinking they were active. It might be a reflection of one of the physical changes of which she had spoken. A molecule here, a molecule there . . . leading to what?

Gabriel wrinkled his nose a couple of times, but it made no difference to the feeling. Enda shifted a little in her seat and glanced at him.

"You feel anything?" Gabriel said.

She shook her head. "Your stone—"

"It's up to its tricks," Gabriel muttered, "but don't ask me why."

She turned her attention back to the field, and so did Gabriel, ignoring the itch as well as he could, while they made their way in closer to Galvin. There was no sign of anyone or anything in the neighborhood, no telltales of approaching vessels, no nothing. If you stumbled in here by accident—fortunately an unlikely occurrence—you would probably not realize that this was one of the most heavily militarized systems in the Verge.

"Quiet around he—" Gabriel said.

WHAM!

Sunshine pitched violently to one side, thrown that way by Enda to avoid the energy bolt that had just torn through the vacuum past them. Little auroral rainbows of ionized particles writhed and danced where the beam had passed, like dust in a sunbeam, but with much more energy. Back in *Sunshine*'s body, things finished falling off shelves, banging onto the floor, and rolling around.

"You never do put everything away before one of these exercises," Enda said, "no matter how many times I advise you to."

"Invading vessels," said an angry voice down comms, "this is FSA interdiction control. Cut power and prepare to be boarded. If you power up again, we will fire with intent."

"What was *that* supposed to be," Helm muttered down private comms, "an accident? Assholes."

"Understood, interdiction control," Enda said calmly. "Complying."

Gabriel was already reaching into the drive-control display, and he killed *Sunshine's* drive immediately. *Lalique* and *Longshot* did the same, and the three of them drifted along in careful formation while the other ships swooped out of the darkness and formed up around them.

There were six of them, all long smooth ovals in shape, and all of them had what Helm liked to call "chunky and exciting detail"—meaning guns and weapon ports made as obvious and nasty-looking as possible. Gabriel was aware that there was a science to it—the business of making a weapon look so aggressive and unfriendly that the person on the wrong end of it would never do anything to provoke you to use it—but he was not happy to see how very highly that particular science seemed to be esteemed in this part of the Verge. These ships looked even more aggressive than *Longshot,* which until now Gabriel wouldn't have thought was possible. They were positively warty with weapons; plasma cannons were glued all over them like growths.

The comms receiver bank of controls in the central display tank between Gabriel and Enda came alive. Before Gabriel could reach out to activate it, a face appeared there: a shining black helmet with the goggles pushed up, partly hiding the Galvinite emblem, and under the helmet a face with narrowed eyes, a long thin nose, and a mean thin mouth.

Gabriel opened his mouth to say hello.

"If you make any movement toward weapons, we will fire instantly," said the officer. "Identify yourselves."

We've been doing that for the past twenty minutes, Gabriel felt like growling, but instead he said, "Infotrading vessel *Sunshine*, registered out of Phorcys."

"*Longshot,*" Helm growled, "Grith registry."

"*Lalique,*" said Angela, "out of Richards."

"ID confirms that," said a voice from behind the officer.

"Oh, does it?" he said. "Well, infotraders we don't mind." He sounded somewhat as if he personally preferred they didn't come anywhere near him. "What are you two here for?"

"Armed escort," Helm said.

"Same here," said Angela.

The officer glanced slightly to one side and guffawed. "Him, maybe, or so scan indicates, but *you?*"

"I carry a modicum of useful weapons," Angela said. "Look, if it makes you more comfortable, just consider me to be social services." Her voice curled in a naughty way around the last two words.

Oh wonderful! Gabriel thought, and began to sweat.

The officer snickered. "We'll see about that. Two, three, five, board 'em."

Gabriel tried not to swallow. If they boarded *Sunshine* and nosed around sufficiently, they would be likely to find that her gunports concealed weaponry rather larger and deadlier than they seemed to. That might lead them to other searches—

"Don't much care for boarders," Helm said, sounding unusually casual.

"I don't care what you care for," said the officer, starting to sound rather nastier than he had to begin with. "I don't care much for your tone, either, now that you mention it. Maybe boarding isn't called for. Impoundment and ground search might be more to the point."

Enda looked thoughtfully at Gabriel and the control panel. He could not precisely hear her thinking, but he knew that there was a starfall setting laid into the panel, and he strongly suspected that she wished she could activate it.

Fraal could be mindwalkers, and Enda had said often enough that she had some slight talent that way but no training. I wish we could starfall too, but we're not charged and we won't budge. Anyway, even if we could, I wouldn't want to leave the other two here. I got them into this, I have to get them out—

"I have little experience of being boarded," Enda said mildly. "Do we send the tube out to you, or does your vessel call it?"

"What the—? Sir!"

It was a shout from one of the other ships, which had been holding comm silence until now. Gabriel looked up in the field, which was still around him, trying to see what had made the other Galvinite officer react.

The new ship was coming in at considerable speed. It was a rather small ship, but not the kind that Gabriel would normally have thought of under that title. It was in fact bigger than *Lalique*, which was saying something. It looked like a long stun-baton, slender, with flaring fins at the end, jutting out of a broader area that apparently held the drive. It was armed, as discreetly and handsomely as the Galvinite ships were armed noisily and tastelessly. There was money in that ship, and better—or worse—access to very expensive weaponry, the kind of thing that only the Concord military could get its hands on.

In the field, Gabriel could see several of the ships surrounding them turn to angle themselves better toward the incoming vessel.

"Ready to fire," someone said from one of the ships.

"Belay that!"

It was the officer in the display tank, presently looking off to one side as if seeing something that seriously upset him.

"Commander Aronsen," said a female voice, "thank you kindly for delaying."

Gabriel started. That voice was familiar.

Enda glanced at him. "It would appear that more interesting things are to happen to us than mere boarding today."

Gabriel gulped.

Another face appeared in the tank, which subdivided itself to handle the image and Gabriel found himself looking at

Aleen Delonghi. "Is there a problem with these vessels?" she asked.

He cursed softly under his breath. *After what I did to her last ship,* he thought, *she gets this one instead. Is she related to somebody?*

"They're unauthorized," said the officer leading the interdiction control. "Didn't come in with escort—"

"While I will grant you that vessels doing so enter these spaces at their own risk," Delonghi said, "registered and recognized infotraders with escort might be allowed to do their business without undue interference, I would think."

Gabriel watched the officer bristle. Amazing how it managed to show even though he had a helmet on.

"Your ID says Concord, lady, but I—"

"It says more than just that," Delonghi said. "I'm attached to the Neutrality Patrol, just in with the new cruiser doing relief duty for Pariah Station. I sent my IDs and clearances ahead of me. They should be in front of you at the moment."

A few seconds' silence followed. "They're genuine," said someone from out of range of the pickup.

"They look genuine, but I've never seen this ship before," growled the commander of the holding force. "Get it confirmed from the base at Palshizon."

Another few moments' silence. "They confirm."

"This ship and her crew, and the companion ships and crews, are known to the Concord," Delonghi said, "and are cleared to go about their business as far as we're concerned."

Gabriel wondered if it was accidental that she did not say that they had a clean criminal record.

"Why would they be so all-fired interesting to *you*, Commander?" asked the holding force commander. He looked like his teeth hurt, and Delonghi's title came out as reluctantly as if he had to push it out.

"I'm afraid I couldn't discuss that with you, sir," Delonghi replied. She actually smiled as she said it, a pity-

ing sort of smile, one suggesting that she didn't usually talk
about such matters with mere system-based small fry. "We
would appreciate them being given your full cooperation
while they're discharging their business here."

The holding force's commander was quiet for a long,
furious moment. He turned back to pickup again and glow-
ered at Gabriel. "Lucky they came in and pulled you out of
the fire," he muttered. "I'd prefer to have toasted you
myself. Too many smart boys like you wandering in here,
little space lawyers with too many friends . . ." He trailed
off, looking at a display off to one side. "Proceed to the port
clearance facility at Erhardt Field. Do not delay. You're
expected."

The display went blank. Gabriel had rarely been more
glad to see anyone's ugly face disappear. Unfortunately, his
tone had suggested that their clearance procedure through
Fort Drum was going to be less than pleasant. *Just what we
needed.* There was still one face left in the display tank:
Delonghi's.

"What are *you* doing here?" Gabriel asked.

"Just passing through, Connor," Delonghi replied.

"Oh, please!"

She grinned. It was the first time he had seen her produce such an expression without it looking actively nasty.
"All right. Obviously I'm keeping an eye on you."

"I bet," Gabriel said.

The last time he had seen Aleen Delonghi, he had not
felt terribly well disposed toward her. She had been prepared to blow up *Sunshine* with very little reason and had
been doing other unsociable things as well. Now here she
was, apparently expecting to see him, and worse, Gabriel
was beholden to her for the moment. He disliked that
intensely.

"I suppose you expect me to be grateful for this," he
said.

"Gratitude?" she said, and the grin scaled back to a more
familiar wicked expression. "From you?"

That stung, but he wasn't going to let her see it. "You won't be surprised, then," he said, "when I vanish suddenly."

"It seems to be your specialty," she said. "You won't be surprised, then, when I find you regardless. This time I'm better equipped. You will not be shoving me into any more teddy bears' meat lockers."

He glanced out the front viewports at her new ship and thought that perhaps she was speaking of more than just personal preparedness. That new ship of hers could be equipped with anything.

"Delonghi," he said, "I wouldn't do a thing like that to you twice." I'd find something else. Possibly more permanent, if you get between me and—

No.

He pushed the image aside, satisfying as it was at the moment. She was only doing her job, no matter how energetically she got in his way. All I have to do now, Gabriel thought, is lose her and go about my business.

"Nice to hear it," Delonghi said. "Meanwhile, you people had better get going. I don't think your escort will take it kindly if you make them wait for you too long."

Indeed the Galvinite ships were all finishing turns that oriented them toward home, plainly waiting to kick in their system drives.

"We will no doubt find you waiting here for us when we leave," Gabriel said.

Delonghi looked at him with amusement. "I could be useful to you, Connor."

"Only as a doorstop," Gabriel said gently and shut comms down.

Enda was already swinging *Sunshine*'s nose in the direction of Galvin. Very neatly she maneuvered the ship into the center of the formation of Galvinite vessels, leaving a little way on her at the end of the maneuver so that she drifted gently forward.

The Galvinites kicked in their system drives, and *Sunshine* went after them.

* * * * *

Gabriel followed them down in an oddly reflective mood. It would not be the first time he had had the feeling that the stone was not just alive, but sentient and capable of somehow managing affairs—not just its own affairs, but his and those of anyone who got in the way. He had occasionally sat with it in his hand and felt an odd sort of vertigo sourced in the idea or sensation that only the stone was actually still, and that everything else around it—him, *Sunshine*, sometimes even the planet on which he might be sitting—all of it was being invisibly moved by the stone, moved around it into some pattern that suited its needs. Whatever those might be . . .

Now he was wondering about the stone again and wondering exactly how the hell Aleen Delonghi had found him here. Had she figured Gabriel's path out by herself, or had someone told her?

He bet someone had.

He bet he knew who.

Delonghi's Concord Intel, Gabriel thought, but hardly an experienced old hand. Why did Lorand Kharls keep sending her after him? Was he trying to give Gabriel a fighting chance to get away, or was he trying to train his new young officer in the art of chasing rogues?

Gabriel sighed. Working out what was going on in Lorand Kharls's head was a full time job, and right now he had several of those.

All this time he was aware of the stone in his pocket, moving things to its own preference, calling the tune. Gabriel wished he could hear the tune. Hard to know how to dance, under these circumstances.

The control ships pulled in a little tighter as they came closer to Galvin. Off to one side Gabriel caught a gleam of light, a point of it, moving: real sunlight on metal, not an indicator in the fighting field.

"The Defense Net, I would imagine," Enda said, looking out the viewport on her side.

Gabriel nodded as they dropped farther toward the planet and the fringes of atmosphere. There were several hundred satellites in orbit around the planet—that was the published number, though Gabriel wouldn't have been surprised if there were more, the Galvinites being masters of disinformation when it suited them—and three big orbital facilities running the whole show. Nothing came or went through that net unnoticed. Nothing unwelcome got through. The satellites themselves were armed with missiles tipped with nukes and other hardware, including anti-radiation devices. Every bit of the local space was covered by at least three of them. If the other two were occupied with something else, that third one would still get you.

Gabriel looked grimly at the closest of the satellites they passed and could understand the Galvinites' need for such things. One bright and sunny day the FSA ship *Ajax* had landed in the middle of the city of Beronin on Alitar and detonated a fusion bomb that leveled half the place. The Galvinites were very eager not to have the same kind of tactic used on them, and it was likely enough that someone might try it. The attack had been one more reason for the Alitarins to scream "Never forget! Never forgive!" The Galvinites knew their enemy well enough to know that they weren't merely grandstanding. The war had been going on "quietly" for a long time, too long. Each side had begun to believe that the other one was due to do something spectacular in vengeance for old wrongs. It was one of the reasons why this system was no longer the hub of commerce it had started to be in more controlled times. No one wanted to be here when the shin-kicking started in earnest, and it might start again at any time. . . .

They dropped past the gleaming satellites and into atmosphere. Gabriel looked down and was slightly surprised by what a green world Galvin was. It was actually rather attractive, with numerous inland seas trapped in a net of green that varied from the tropical swamps of the equatorial area to the drier, paler greens of the steppes and plains near each of the polar caps. All the time he looked at it, all the while they descended, Gabriel could not shake the feeling of guns being pointed at them, guns with the safeties off.

Control, Gabriel thought.

They landed at Erhardt Field in the port clearance facility. The port proper was situated about twenty kilometers from Fort Drum in a bowl-shaped valley of the Verdant Mountains. Gabriel was used to seeing spaceports with moderate security around them, but this one looked, well, like an armed camp. The rim of the "bowl" was an almost solid line of air defense batteries. As *Sunshine*, *Lalique,* and *Longshot* came in over them with their escort all around, the mobile launchers whipped around to target them, locked on, and followed them longingly down toward the ground. It was not, Gabriel thought, a place to surrender to a sudden urge to perform aerobatics. You would be dust a few moments later.

He cut the system drive back hard and let *Sunshine* come down slow behind the lead ships, which started to drift off to one side of the scattering of buildings and hangars. Around the designated landing area itself, high blast fences were erected in a huge oval. At intervals around the oval and at the foci of the oval were watchtowers bristling with weapons. This was just another smaller example of the mindset displayed by the presence of the Defense Net. The whole world was, as Helm had said, an armed camp—and better armed than they were.

They landed the ships on three parking pads that had plainly been left empty for them. The little oblong gunships that had escorted them in now hovered overhead to make sure they went where they were told. Gabriel was obscurely relieved when he felt the small bump and settle of *Sunshine*'s landing skids coming down on the ground. He killed the system drive and looked over at Enda.

She was looking out the front ports at the armed men who were hurrying out of the nearest building, a long low dingy-looking structure that was probably the "arrivals-security" facility.

"There must be twenty of them," she said in mild interest. "What kind of dangerous characters do they think we are?"

"I wouldn't answer that question until we are safely out of the system," Gabriel replied. They unstrapped themselves, got up, and went to the lift door. "What's it like out there?"

"Twenty C, give or take a degree," Enda said as they stepped into the lift and the door closed on them. "Nice."

When the door opened, the bottom of the lift column was entirely surrounded by men in dark uniforms pointing guns at them.

"This is a definition of 'nice' I haven't encountered before," Gabriel said softly, as the security people closed in around them. They were Galvinite Army troops, as far as he could tell from the insignia, and two of them stepped forward and searched him and Enda roughly before signaling to the others to take them into the arrivals facility. Gabriel glanced around as they were taken away. He was only able to get a quick glimpse of *Lalique* and *Longshot,* which were now parked not far from *Sunshine.* They were so surrounded with Galvinite Army people that it was impossible to see anything at the moment of Helm and Delde Sota, or of Grawl and Angela—if they were even out of their ships yet, not that Gabriel was going to be given leisure for much looking. A weapon's muzzle poked him pointedly in the back as he paused. He sighed and walked toward the arrivals facility.

The place was built in a style of architecture that Gabriel was beginning to recognize as "generic government": very plain, a little worn at the edges, not always as clean as it might be, the walls inevitably finished in a shade of pale beige calculated to show as little dirt as possible with as little care as possible. He and Enda were hauled off down a long hallway studded with doors, but no other features, and then one of their escort went a little ahead of them and opened one of the doors.

"No," came a voice from inside, "not in here. Norrik."

"Huh?" said the man who had been leading them down the hall.

"You heard me," said the unseen source of the voice inside the office. "Norrik wants these two first."

"Typical," said the soldier in front of them. He shut the door and led them farther down the hall, muttering, "Nobody ever tells *us* anything." At the end of the hallway he turned left and opened another door, then stood aside and waved them through.

Gabriel went in and paused inside the doorway, looking around while Enda slipped in and did the same. The room contained several tall cabinets for solid-data storage and a large metal desk with several small piles of carts stacked on it, very neat. A couple of simple chairs were stationed in front of the desk. Behind it in an identical chair, another Galvinite Army officer was looking up at them. His uniform had that too-pressed look that says officer, and Gabriel straightened a little, looking at him. Reflex, he thought a moment later, and considered slumping a little again, except that there would have been no point. This man had a very noticing look about him.

"Please sit down," the officer said and reached out a hand to take from the escorting officer the two ID chips that they had taken from Gabriel and Enda during the search. He dropped them on the display patch on his desk as the escorting officer closed the door behind them. Gabriel got a glimpse of the name over the man's breast pocket: MAJ. GARTH NORRIK.

The man was tall, good-looking, and keen-eyed, the kind of person who can look at you and immediately make you feel guilty, whether you have done something wrong or not. For someone in Gabriel's situation, with good excuse to feel guilty about this and that, this seemed likely to prove a very uncomfortable situation, but rather to his own surprise, Gabriel was not uncomfortable at all.

Inside his head, something itched. He restrained himself

from wrinkling his nose up, partly because it wouldn't do any good and partly to keep himself from looking more foolish than he already did.

"Thank you for coming to see me," said the major, "Mister . . . Calvin, is it?" That was the name of the false identity on the chip that Delde Sota had crafted for him.

As if I had the slightest choice, Gabriel felt like saying, but didn't. For the moment he merely lapsed back into standard military good behavior and said, "My pleasure, sir."

"What brings you to Galvin?"

"Shopping," Gabriel replied.

The major looked at him and broke into a very unexpected grin. "I've heard a lot of funny reasons lately," he said, "but not that one. Not for too long to remember it, anyway."

Curl, something went in the back of Gabriel's head—so suddenly and so bizarrely that he nearly flinched, but something else cautioned him to hold very still, not to show anything, not to move suddenly. A great deal depended on it.

I've felt this before, Gabriel thought. On Bluefall!

"Shopping for what, exactly?"

"General supplies."

The major blinked then looked thoughtfully at Gabriel. "An odd place to do your routine shopping, surely? I don't know if you've heard, but there's a war going on."

"I had heard," Gabriel said, "but I hadn't heard that there were unreasonable people involved in it—at least at this end of things. I'm getting into some exploratory work. A member of my party has had some experience with that in the past. We're looking to get a contract from the CCC and go off into the wild black for a while. We'll be doing data runs in between times to make our nut, but meanwhile, we need long-life victuals, high-reliability outdoor gear, and so on. The suppliers' prices here very competitive, and it was on our way. We'll be heading out to Mantebron and then beyond."

All these things were true. The major nodded, looking over Gabriel's forged ID chip.

"You were vouched for by an unusual source on your way in," said the major and looked up, directing a hard look at Gabriel.

Gabriel swore. "That gods-damned woman has been turning up places where I've been turning up for months. She's got it into her head that I'm some kind of asset. Trouble is, it's not an asset she's after, it's my—" He broke off. "She propositioned me once, and I turned her down. Ever since then she's been following me around and making people suspicious about me. I tell you"—he turned to Enda, not having to feign his annoyance—"if I'd known what kind of a nuisance she was going to be when she first asked me, I would have taken her back to that little cubbyhole of hers on Iphus and—"

"Spare me the sordid details," said Norrik, "thank you." All the same, he was smiling slightly, which told Gabriel that the man didn't know enough about what was really going on to detect where Gabriel was bending the truth—at the moment, almost everywhere. "She is indeed new to this system, so for the moment we'll let the matter pass, inasmuch as *we* run things here, not the Concord, no matter how much it would like to pretend otherwise."

Gabriel allowed himself the slightest twist of smile, though he thought that the behavior of the interdiction crews did not exactly bear that statement out. The *Monitor* Mandate still held here, and it was the Concord's weight that had imposed it and continued to hold it in place. Doubtless the Galvinites enjoyed baiting the Concord forces in the system when they thought they could get away with it, but they would not antagonize them too openly. If the Concord pulled out, there would have to be a full-fledged war between them and Alitar, and Galvin was not ready to win that war . . . not just yet.

Norrik looked down again at his data reader and picked up Gabriel's chip. *Curl*, said that strange taste/movement/thought in the back of Gabriel's mind. It was not his own thought. It came from somewhere outside. It was definitely what he had felt about the man he killed on Bluefall, but also familiar in some other way.

Don't explore that too closely, said the feeling inside his head. Gabriel looked casually at his chip in the major's hand.

What is that that I'm hearing? Gabriel thought. Could it be the stone? It's never spoken before. Or is it something else? He tried to stay calm, not to break out into a sweat at the thought. Life had been strange enough recently. He wasn't sure he needed the stone itself to start talking to him now.

The major handed Gabriel back the chip, looking at him again. "And you, madam?" he said to Enda.

"I would not normally come so far for a shopping trip myself," Enda said, "but as my companion says, this facility is on our way. I much fear he is still young enough to hunt bargains as if he did not know that, sooner or later, the universe averages everything out." She gave Gabriel a slightly reproachful look.

"Well," said the major. "This time I am inclined to overlook the fact that you came in without the usual escort. I understand you might have thought that as infotraders, you didn't need to bother, but I warn you not to try it again. If you do, I will not be able to avoid arresting and prosecuting you for suspicion of espionage . . . and in these parts, we shoot spies."

About twenty different replies surfaced in Gabriel's brain. *Don't,* said whatever was suddenly so vocal inside his head.

"Yes, sir," he said.

The man's eyes dropped again to the display on which Enda's chip still rested. "So where are you shopping? Hansen's?" As he looked down, there was a change of expression, a flicker, a sudden impression of layer underlying layer of thought and intent—several layers belonging to the man himself, and another layer belonging to—

Careful!

—*tangle*. Things stroked and writhed against one another, warm in the darkness, a warmth that seemed like light to them. They looked out through eyes that were being held at the moment but could be very empty if they let them. For a flash, a terrible second, Gabriel saw what the presence that looked through him saw: the layer that had been a man once, a personality, and still thought it was. Such was the dreadful persistence of this particular personality: self-assured, fierce, clever—so much so that it could not tell that it had been gnawed hollow as a bug-ridden tree on the inside, and that there was nothing left inside it but tinder and air. Below that layer was another, the deeper personality, the one hidden from most people and from the man who owned it: quite cold, quite fierce, a killer's heart, an assassin's heart, waiting for the right moment to be let out and do its work. But this layer too had been gnawed to a mere shell of itself, fragile, brittle, all too likely to break if any pressure were put on it—not that it would be. The people around this man feared him.

Under that layer, under the oldest layers of personality—a furious child, a consoling but despised parent, a chilly adult that spent its life reckoning the odds and balancing politics and violence against each other—should have been the inside.

But there *was* no inside, or no human one.

Tangle. The stroking, slithering warmth in the darkness—eyeless, soundless, mouthless, voiceless . . . except that Gabriel could hear their voices speaking to one another, looking at him through the major's eyes. The major did not know they were there. They found this amusing. They looked at Gabriel and saw nothing but another human, not a threat. They did not feel the presence that rode inside Gabriel, but that presence recognized them, knew them from some ways back.

Gabriel held very still and did not stare or shudder or get up and run screaming out of the room or do any of various other things that he would have liked to.

Something else, said the advising voice inside his head, silently, so as not to be overheard—for the creatures writhing in the darkness were sharp at this kind of hearing, this inner kind. Not anything human . . . something much older.

Gabriel very carefully did not look at the man's chest, half expecting to see some sign of squirm or writhe through skin and bone.

It all happened so fast. He had had experiences like this on Danwell, where half a life went by in a split second, the way it was supposed to when you were about to die. To have it happen this way in the middle of life had been very unsettling at first. Now he was beginning to get used to it, but for that first second or so after the return to "real time" Gabriel always blinked and found the resumption of life at one-second-per-second very bemusing. Now he blinked and didn't try to hide it. He rubbed his eyes and said, "Sorry. I had a late night."

"Starrise syndrome?"

It was common enough, the inability to get to sleep the night before an arrival. Gabriel shook his head and laughed a little ruefully. "No, just too much chai, I'm afraid. That last cup before bed is always so tempting. I never learn. But no, not Hansen's. I didn't care much for their stock, and their prices looked inflated. Lalain's Sundries was the store I had in mind."

The major laughed. "Yes, I see you've done your research. After that you'll be moving right along again." It was not a suggestion.

"We'll be dumping our data to the local Grid after I finish with you, sir," Gabriel said, "and then doing our shopping. After that, on to the next destination. If we can find a load to take with us, so much the better."

"You'll have to help yourself there, I'm afraid," the major said. "Unfortunately government contracts are something I'm not allowed to get involved with. Thank you, Mr. Calvin, Madam Enda."

They were escorted into a holding area with some plain chairs but nothing to read or do. Gabriel, quite certain that they were being observed there, talked absently to Enda about the difference between the prices at Hansen's and Lalain's establishments, wondered out loud when the others would clear customs, and then trailed off. He was still trying hard to make sense of what he had experienced.

It occurred to Gabriel that since Danwell, he had come by some form of protection—or rather, a protector. He thought of the little edanweir child that he had picked up so casually, in big-friendly-uncle mode—only to find that the child was the one who was in charge, the conduit or perhaps the hiding place of some old power that had been waiting inside one or another of the edanwe people for a long time, waiting for the right combination of circumstances and people. Had she passed something or someone to Gabriel in turn? For a month or so after leaving Danwell, after the strangeness of his experiences there had a little time to wear off, Gabriel had felt that he had left the influence or attention of that power behind. It had, he thought, only been interested in the stone. Now, though, he wondered if it was the other way around? Was it the stone that was interested in that ancient intelligence on Danwell? Did I just stumble into some old association that had been broken for a while—a few tens of millennia or so—and was now reforging itself?

He had no answers. I need to talk to Enda about this, Gabriel thought, but definitely not right this minute. This was not a place to discuss your troubles. It had a pressured feeling, like a cooker with the top bolted on, slowly getting ready to blow.

After a while Helm came in, looking very sour indeed, along with Delde Sota. Helm sat down and folded his arms and would not say a word. Doctor Sota sat down beside him, leaning back in one of the much-used chairs with as much apparent ease as if she were sitting in her own lounge.

She smiled at Gabriel and said, "Assessment: our party most interesting thing to pass through these parts in a while."

Then Angela and Grawl came in. Angela looked pale and annoyed. Grawl was narrow-eyed with anger and growling after every breath.

"You okay?" Gabriel asked Angela under his breath.

She gave him a sidelong look and replied, "Yeah." She would say nothing else.

A few moments later a Galvinite soldier came in and said, "All right, you people can go. Your ships are in impound until you're ready to leave."

"But we have data to dump—" said Enda.

"Guess you won't be lingering in town, then," said the soldier and grinned a most unsympathetic grin. "You said you were going shopping?"

"Lalain's," Gabriel said.

"Go out the front door here and pick up a transport. They'll drop you at the access/exit facility in Fort Drum. Walk west half a kilometer—you can't miss the place. They'll ship the stuff back here for you, so it can be searched and packed."

A few minutes later they had been bundled into a small transport flyer and were taken to the exit facility in town, a blockhouse-like building also surrounded by high blast walls and weapons emplacements. Here each of the six travelers was given a chip embedded with his or her picture and ID details, each one covered with the repetitive statement PROPERTY OF FSA.

"Show that to anyone who requires you to," said the bored officer who made the IDs. "Do not attempt to purchase anything without showing this ID. Do not discuss local politics. Do not enter any premises that show a representative of this ID with a negation sign over it. Do not attempt to leave the city without authorization. Be back by 1700 local time if you wish access to your vessel before tomorrow at 0800. Enjoy your stay in Fort Drum."

They went out into the street, a long stretch of concrete with mostly military traffic parked along it.

"You know," Enda said softly, "I think that the tourist board here has its job cut out for it."

"You don't know the half of it," Helm growled. "Did you know what that—"

"Advisory," said Delde Sota. She paused. They all looked at her, for such pauses were unusual. "Can it. Invitation: go shopping."

They went.

Chapter Six

IT WAS WITHOUT question the single most unpleasant city Gabriel had ever been in, and as a Marine, he had seen a lot of unpleasant cities.

It was not that the place was physically unattractive. Fort Drum was actually extremely handsome. Wide swathes of parkland and arboretum, patches of what looked like native forest, and pools and grasslands alternated with broad avenues and clusters of handsome buildings. The place looked much less populated than it was.

But Gabriel knew what the field sites concealed: vast hardened bunkers containing power plants and hospitals, comms facilities and computer centers, transport junctions, storage caverns and armories, all built to the orders of Galvin's Supreme Commanders. Down those wide airy avenues, Gabriel kept hearing the menacing rumble of armored weapons carriers. Uniformed and helmeted men came out of every street, stopping them and asking for their identification and looking at them as if they were almost certainly an enemy in disguise. For Gabriel, who for the moment felt like no more than an innocent shopper with Concord dollars to spend, it was all extremely wearing.

The thing that made it most annoying was not the soldiers and the weapons—he had dealt with enough of those in his time—but people's faces, just the ordinary faces of citizens in the street. There was a peculiar look to them, not the "planetary look," famous among Marines and other service people, who claim they can tell the inhabitants of a given world from some attribute particular to that planet among all others. No, the faces of people here had a pinched quality, a hard look. People's eyes were narrowed, and their faces seemed very constrained. They always seemed to be looking sidelong at things and at each other, as if afraid to be caught looking . . . as if afraid of something they might see. The hard look was set deep in everyone over the age of fifteen, as if long years of never letting it go, even during sleep, had stamped it there indelibly.

Gabriel found himself wondering what you had to do to people to make them look this way. Numerous possibilities suggested themselves to him, and he liked none of them. The most likely one was, "Have a hundred-odd years of war." Another was, "Make sure that no one knows whether or not the person walking down the street behind him is in the secret police." Gabriel knew that the Galvinite Internal Security Directorate had thousands of uniformed and plainclothes officers watching and listening to their people, making sure that they adequately supported the war effort—meaning that they never spoke against it. For his own part, he was determined to keep his mouth very shut indeed until it was time for them to go.

The store they were hunting was close to the access/exit facility. Lalain's called itself, perhaps due to some obscure family tradition, a "Sundries Supplier." It was in fact a hardware store and ship's chandlery of magnificent, even florid proportions. Nearly two acres of space was filled with every kind of supply for people who lived and worked in space. Gabriel could have happily spent their entire day—hell, he thought, two or three or four!—ranging around and examining the merchandise: the mining and exploration gear, the beautiful range of pressure suits, the ships' equipment and ancillary vehicles, the clothes, the furnishings, the accessories, but every time he turned into a new and interesting aisle, he came up against someone wearing that same guarded, hard, uneasy face. After a while it took all the enjoyment out of what he had come to do.

Gabriel sighed and got on with putting together his order. By the time an hour had passed, he had two large induction palettes and the better part of a third packed with low volume staples and a very mixed assortment of "specialty" single-pack foods, the kind of thing that would serve to break the monotony if they were out for an unusually long time.

Enda, walking along with him, looked at the big pile of staples and sighed, rather ruefully. "I remember telling you that you were going to have to stop eating like a Marine," she said. "I did not expect you ever to take my advice quite so much to heart."

"You never do anyway," Gabriel said, slightly amused.

Enda clucked her tongue in mild annoyance and looked ruefully at the industrial-sized vacuum bricks of starch staples. "I am going to have to start exercising more," she said and strolled a little ways off.

They met Helm and Delde Sota by the checkouts with a small fleet of supplies, and Angela and Grawl with two palettes of their own.

"Better go to separate staff for this," Gabriel said. "Last thing we need is to have someone mix the orders up."

Grawl grinned at that. Angela looked amused, for several of the larger packages on their float were entire irradiated carcasses of gurnet and whilom, two quadripedal herbivores apparently much favored by weren when they could get them.

"Sure you don't want these, Gabriel?" Angela asked.

"Please, don't tempt me," he said. He headed over to one of the checkout podiums, and the palettes came after him, Enda bringing up the rear to make sure nothing fell off.

It took another half hour or so to see the purchases paid for, wrapped, and labeled, then the whole massive lot was trundled away out into the back area to be loaded on the transport for Erhardt Field. Gabriel sighed to see it go, partly because of the money he had just dropped. The others gathered around.

"Now what?" Helm asked, glancing around him.

"We could go find somewhere to eat," said Angela.

"Opinion: welcome change of pace," Delde Sota said. "Query: any good restaurants in this city?"

"There are supposed to be several," Enda said, "but we are on the wrong side of town for them, I believe. If we can find a public transport, we might head over that way."

They waved good-bye to the Lalain's front-of-house clerks and headed out into the street. A large convoy of armored personnel carriers was presently making its way down the avenue. Gabriel paused to watch it go by. From the tops of the carriers, an assortment of hard, frowning stares lingered on him.

Angela said softly, "Is 'looking hard at the hardware' an offense here?"

"Let's go get lunch before we find out the hard way," Helm said. It was so unusually pacific a suggestion from him that everyone immediately began looking for a transport stop.

"Uh-oh," said Angela after a moment. Down the street, they could see a young woman in Galvinite Army uniform coming in their direction and making straight for them.

"Do we try to escape," Helm muttered, "or flip a coin to see who gets to take her?"

"Helm, hush," Enda said.

The young woman came up and greeted them courteously enough. "What's your destination in the city today?" she inquired.

"You might tell us how you know we're not heading back to Erhardt Field," said Helm.

The young officer smiled. "Because you can't get there from here," she said, "but more to the point, you didn't tell the people in Lalain's that that was where you wanted to go. When you went out the way you came in, the assumption was that you'd be going into the city. For that, you need an escort. Rina Welsh, Department of Hospitality."

Whether you like it or not, Gabriel thought. "We didn't have an escort getting here," he said.

She grinned at him. "Maybe not one that you saw, Mr. Calvin, but you were in a hurry, and you were on your way to take care of specified business. The staff in there said you had been mentioning lunch. Anything specific in mind?"

"There was a restaurant called Elmo's," said Enda, "over by the big hotel, I believe."

"The Interstellar Arms," said Welsh. "It's about a block away. I'll take you there. Come on. The tram stop is down here."

She led them about half a block down the avenue from Lalain's, and as they came up to the stop, a transport came along, a roofed-over floater with poles to hang onto, presently inhabited by about ten of the hard-faced city people.

Welsh invited Gabriel and the rest of the group aboard and said to the driver, "Near side of Central Square."

As they went, Welsh pointed out various parks and lakes to them, a handsome building here, a spire there. Enda, Angela, Delde Sota, and even Helm and Grawl all nodded and made various vaguely complimentary noises. Gabriel had to smile slightly. He had never seen such a planet for making people either very polite conversationalists or shutting them up entirely. When they finally pulled up in Central Square among the tall clean-lined buildings, all done in white stone, Gabriel found himself wishing that someone would do something unusual here, shout, swear, scream or collapse—except that the police would almost certainly come along in short order and throw everyone involved in jail. No, he thought, save the noise and collapsing for later.

They all got off the tram and made their way around the green expanse of the Square.

"No walking on the grass," Welsh said cheerfully. "The Supreme Commander wouldn't like it!"

Past the imposing facade of the Interstellar Arms, all gleaming in white marble, she turned the corner after the hotel and led them down a little street.

"Elmo's is down this way a few hundred meters," she said.

The group followed, looking into shop windows as they went. Next to Gabriel, Enda made a small weary sound as they walked.

"Long day?" Gabriel said.

Enda tilted her head to one side. "If it were only that," she said, "I would not be so troubled."

"What, then?"

"I dislike to speak of it here," she said.

Unusual as that was for Enda, who was nearly always talkative, Gabriel understood. No question, he thought, that this planet definitely makes you want to whisper. He sensed that everyone was listening and that any innocent word could be misunderstood and probably would be. Some uneasy shopkeeper would get on the comm to the authorities, and seconds later he would be in front of a firing squad for some unsuspected but deadly infringement of the local laws.

Certainly the shop people in Lalain's had been listening. It probably would have been as much as their jobs were worth to let us out of there without calling the Hospitality Department. Who'll be listening in the restaurant? It was an annoyance, for Gabriel had about twenty things he wanted to discuss with Enda. Now he wasn't about to broach any of them until they were somewhere safe—meaning off planet and possibly entirely out of this system. The whatever-it-was inside Major Norrik completely horrified Gabriel. He had never heard of such a thing before, yet whatever had briefly spoken up inside him plainly knew something about what it was.

Gabriel looked in a store window at some cool weather clothes draped over a clutch of stylishly minimal mannequins and suddenly remembered a dream he had had not too long ago, one which had been gone upon waking. That same perception of heat as light, that same sense of things writhing, wreathing, stroking . . . He shuddered. It was awful but familiar, especially after that terrible morning on Tisane.

Dreaming it only makes things worse, he thought. That particular kind of dream had a habit of coming true. The last time something similar had happened, in those dreams of flinging light into darkness, the reality had come to find him within a matter of months. He was still having those dreams, too, but they were more definite than they had been.

It was all disturbing, but not disturbing enough for Gabriel to lose his appetite. They came up to Elmo's within a few more steps.

"I hope you weren't expecting it to be pricey," Welsh said. "It isn't."

"That is always good news in a strange city," Enda said, pausing outside the restaurant's smoked glass and chrome facade to study the menu display. "Hmm. Not a bad selection. There is caulia, prassith, and . . . goodness, look at the mixed grill."

Gabriel had to admit there was nothing wrong with the choice of food, which was considerable. His stomach was growling, but he was as eager to lose Welsh as to have something to eat. "This looks good," he said. "Helm?"

"They have steak," Helm said. "No indication what kind of animal or vegetable it comes from, but I don't care. If it won't run off the plate screaming when I stick it, it's mine."

"Rrrr," said Grawl and simply smiled.

Angela and Delde Sota looked at each other. "It'll do," Angela said.

Delde Sota's braid reached out from behind her, wrapped itself around the restaurant door's handle, and tugged at it suggestively.

Welsh laughed and pulled the door open. They went in. A small dark-haired woman with big dark eyes and a simple black dress greeted them effusively and took them to a table. As the hostess made her way back up to the bar at the front, Gabriel saw Welsh have a few smiling words with her before turning, waving, and heading out the door again.

"She'll be back to pick us up," Gabriel said softly, "about the time we're having our chai. Bets?"

"The Department of Hospitality," said Helm, "is a division of the Internal Security Directorate."

"The snoopies," said Grawl. She had picked up the word recently from Helm and had been using it on every kind of bureaucratic official.

"True," Angela said, "and the hell with them. Let's order."

"Won't be any problem with service," Helm said, looking around at the place. Its interior was ornate in contrast to the plain exterior, but it was also nearly empty.

"So much the better," Grawl said. She was looking around in such a way as to suggest that she might eat the table covering if something better didn't come along soon.

Fortunately it did. The menus, when they arrived, had three times as many dishes on them as the one outside had. Finally everyone managed to pick something, and within about twenty minutes—during which the better part of a bottle of kalwine had already been killed—the food started arriving. Chandni steak in red sauce, awarathein mince with sweet green cabbage on a coulis of sharp Grith broadbean purée, an entire haunch of whilom for Grawl—the range of dishes and the expertise with which they had been prepared was astonishing.

Gabriel ate about half his whitemeat in vanilla eau-de-vie sauce before having time even to whisper to Enda, "This may be a totalitarian dictatorship, but they know how to eat."

They must have been there for nearly three hours. Afternoon was going brassy and the shadows were starting to lengthen on the far side of the smoked-glass window.

"If we don't get out of here soon," Angela said, "we're not going to get back to that—whatchamacallit?—exit facility in time to get back to our ships today."

Gabriel agreed, but at the same time, something in his head was saying, *Don't leave just yet.*

That made him start to worry. On one hand, he had been starting to discover that these hunches could eventually be useful. On the other hand, he had noted that they tended to get him in trouble first. He had just had a nice meal and some nice kalwine, and his insides were saying to him, Trouble? Are you kidding? Why would you want to spoil this? Additionally, the idea of getting in trouble on this planet, above all others, didn't attract him.

At the same time, the inside of his head kept itching . . .

"Let's pay our scot," Gabriel said, "and walk around a little. We can make up our minds then."

Helm, who was closest to the hostess's station, gestured her over, and everyone produced their credit chips. The hostess took them away to feed all their respective meal charges into them.

"How long, do you figure?" Helm asked softly, leaning across the table toward Gabriel.

"I think about three minutes," Gabriel whispered back.

Despite the fact that the hostess did not make a move toward any form of comms apparatus, as the party had their chips returned to them and the hostess was thanking them and telling them how glad she was that they had enjoyed the meal, the front door swung open. Rina Welsh slipped in.

"Four," Helm muttered.

"So I owe you a fiver," Gabriel muttered back.

They all greeted Welsh with a bonhomme that was not entirely faked. It was hard to feel hostile even to a sort of junior secret policeman after a meal like that.

"So," Welsh said as she came over to them, "what's the story? Will you be heading back to your ships now?"

Inside Gabriel's head, something went itch again, more urgently.

"Well, we were hoping to walk around and window-shop a while," Gabriel said, "if it's all right with you." He looked at her intently and tried very hard to have her get the idea that a while spent in his company would be pleasant.

The genuineness of her smile rather surprised him and made him feel guilty. "Certainly," Welsh said, "why shouldn't you? There's some spare time. Come on. I'll show you around the main shopping district. It's not far."

The company got up, said good-bye to their hostess, and then headed out after Welsh. As they went out, Helm nudged Gabriel with one massive elbow and grinned half of one of his face-splitting grins on the side of his face that was away from Angela.

"Pushing your luck a little, aren't you?" he said.

Gabriel looked sideways at Helm, uncertain what he meant.

Helm just chuckled and went after Welsh.

A slight cool edge was coming into the air as the afternoon wore on, and the short walk to the shopping precinct was pleasant. For the first part of it, Gabriel walked with Welsh, chatting about inconsequentia with her and trying to seem fairly casual about it. When they got to the precinct, a large pedestrians-only area arranged on either side of an avenue of tall evergreen trees and dotted with little mini-parks, Gabriel let others take on the business of keeping Welsh busy. Delde Sota immediately moved into this role, with the merest glance at Gabriel, and started looking in store windows.

There were plenty of them, with a considerable spread of imported goods. Gabriel had not seen such a comprehensive shopping area since Diamond Point on Grith. There was also more to the area than just this one avenue. Other smaller streets crisscrossed it at hundred-meter intervals.

As the group scattered around her, looking in the windows of various stores, Welsh called to them, "Don't get lost now!"

Gabriel smiled slightly, knowing that if any of them did, this area would very likely be crawling with police in not much more than a few minutes. Indeed Welsh was starting to look just a little worried, but the others kept coming back to touch base with her, and eventually the worried expression began to fade.

The six of them wandered gently down the shopping precinct, calling each other over to look at something:

jewelry, more exploratory or outdoor supplies, and after that came a gourmet foodshop, a data-and-book store . . .

Gabriel was looking in the window of this last when he felt the tickle again, so hard that he wanted to sneeze, more emphatic than the itch, more specific. He strolled on to look at the next window, that of a wineshop, while trying to work out the source of the sensation. What *is* it? he said to the inside of his mind. Come on, give me some help here!

Nothing.

With the others a little behind him, he wandered on with his hands in his pockets, passing by the store windows and crossing one of the small streets and looking again, sorrowfully, at the passersby. Even those who were fairly young, barely out of their childhoods, had that uncomfortable, watchful, hard look to their faces. There were a few children being pushed along in hoverprams or being led by the hand, and some of them smiled. But Gabriel looked at those faces, too, and saw the shadows of where that hard look would eventually engrave itself. It was profoundly saddening.

He sighed and looked in the window of the next shop. More clothes. I have enough clothes, he thought, not sharing Delde Sota and Helm's fondness for such things. They were stuck several shops ahead of him, exclaiming over more of the same while Welsh watched. Gabriel smiled slightly. Helm bought all kinds of good planetside wear, but you hardly ever saw him in anything but a smartsuit or armor. Habit is a terrible thing, Gabriel thought.

He glanced toward the end of the window and caught a reflection of someone approaching close, as if to pass between him and the window, then angling away again. Gabriel turned to move out of the way and got a glimpse of a face even more pinched than many he had seen so far today, very tired, very clenched, a face holding itself like a fist. Feeling absently sorry for the man, Gabriel turned his attention away and looked up the street toward where Welsh and the others were continuing on—

—and recognition went right up his spine like a hot wire.

Jacob Ricel!

He turned.

The man was gone.

A moment's incredulous uncertainty went through Gabriel. Did I hallucinate? he thought. Did I just see someone who looked like him?

Itch. From the luckstone in his pocket, a sudden twinge of heat and power surged that he felt right through his hand.

No, dammit! Gabriel thought. Just a few doors behind him was the cross street, and he had glimpsed an alleyway leading from it between two buildings on the nearer side. Probably a service or delivery access. If he had gone that way . . .

Rina Welsh was maybe ten meters ahead, walking between Helm and Angela and talking animatedly to them. Grawl's broad back was briefly between her and Gabriel.

He immediately turned in his tracks, and trying not to hurry in this city full of armed people, this city where every move you made was noticed, he headed back the way he had come, feeling in his pocket and looking down at the ground like someone who had lost something. Gabriel retraced his steps—keeping them small steps, resisting the urge to let them lengthen into strides.

At the corner he paused, looked down the cross street along the ground. Two doors down he saw a shadow slip hurriedly into the alleyway.

Gabriel turned the corner and made for the alleyway. Behind him, in the main street, he could suddenly feel Enda look up in confusion and not see him there. Looking around for him—

He tried to draw in his attention like a tortoise hiding its head, tried to keep her from feeling where he had gone. At this moment of all moments, he did not want her to get involved. Gabriel walked casually and quietly into the alleyway, while inside he tried hard to bring to bear the

half-unwanted talent that had been creeping up on him
since Danwell and was getting stronger all the time. *Come
on,* he said to that silent presence that was more or less
inside him. *I help you do what* you're *trying to. You help
me, now.*

A pause. A wash of sudden confusion from that interior
core of thought and feeling that was not his own.

Come on, he thought again as he went quietly down the
alley. It seemed blind, but there was no telling whether
there were surveillance devices of some kind down here.
He tried hard to look like a briefly confused tourist.
*Where's he gone? I need him. I need him alive. I've got
questions for him, and I must have answers.* Where is he?

Possibly confused by the sudden intensity, that interior
presence gave no answer.

Then out of a little doorway that at first glance had
seemed empty, Ricel jumped him.

Gabriel grappled with the man, intent on not hurting him
and not allowing Ricel to hurt him back. They lurched
back and forth in the alleyway.

That Ricel seemed unarmed heartened Gabriel. Then
again, no one was allowed to go armed on Galvin. Where's
his escort? Gabriel wondered. He must have slipped them
somehow. There was little time to spend wondering how
Ricel had managed to fool the Galvinite authorities into
letting him pass.

What's *he* doing here?

Silly question. *I'm* here.

Whether I'm going to be able to find anything out from
him . . .

They struggled, both hampered by their need not to be
noticed and by the tight quarters in which they were fighting. Ricel was more interested in getting away, as he had
been on the *Lighthouse,* but Gabriel was not going to allow
that, not this time. He blocked Ricel's hands as they clawed
at his face and tried to hammer into his head. Then he did
a leg sweep and took one of Ricel's legs out from under

him. Ricel went down. Gabriel threw himself on top of him, and this time, unlike at the *Lighthouse,* he did not miss.

They wrestled futilely on the ground for a few moments. Gabriel had already had this kind of encounter with the man once and had come off the worse. This time, though, he was not going to let that happen. He rolled, got a good grip on Ricel, turned over, came down on top—

"Gotcha!" he said softly.

Here it was, the moment he had been looking for, waiting for, for the better part of a year and a half . . . no, more like two years. Here under his hands was the man who had tricked him into killing one of his best friends and an ambassador he served with pleasure, a woman he respected above almost everyone else he had met in the service. This was not just someone who looked like him or was disguised as him either. This was the man himself, with the right wrinkles in the right places, the man he had served with on *Falada.* Here was the man who had destroyed his friendship with Elinke Dareyev—a loss he still felt profoundly, partly because he wasn't sure what might have come of it some day, partly because he also missed Elinke's friend and lover who died in the same accident, that mad spirit Lem, one of life's nice people who did not deserve such a sudden and terrible end. The terrible urge to kill Ricel, just *kill* him and be done with it came up, but Gabriel instantly crushed it down and away. Dead men make poor witnesses.

If I can ever get him off this planet to a proper trial, Gabriel thought desperately. He could just hear Norrik saying, "We shoot spies." Whatever else he might be, Ricel was certainly a spy. Gabriel could see himself in the weird position of trying to save Ricel's life . . . and failing. It would be too damned much irony for one day.

He didn't even have the freedom to simply beat the man into a pulp. Gabriel was getting into a very bad mood.

"I want some answers out of you right now," he said softly to Ricel. "They'll be here in a few moments. *Why did you do what you did to me?*"

Ricel's eyes focused briefly on him.

Gabriel shook him. "Come on, talk," he hissed. "Why did you do it? Why did you set me up?!"

Ricel struggled one last time. Gabriel's hand clamped on his throat. Ricel tried to resist, but Gabriel squeezed harder and did something that had worked with the VoidCorp agent on Danwell: he "bore down" with his mind, trying to create a sense of pressure and inevitability. All his anger weighed in behind it, making the pressure real.

Ricel's head twisted from side to side, as if he was trying to avoid a gaze he couldn't escape. "You had to," Ricel gasped, "they said you had to be split away. Discredited. She—"

He fell silent. That listening presence inside Gabriel "heard" something else: a sudden internal cry, desperate and horrified, as some kind of trigger snapped . . .

. . . and the body struggling with Gabriel began to spasm.

Gabriel gulped. Suddenly he knew what the trouble was. No, it's not fair!

Implanted suggestion. What it had been implanted to do was hard to tell. Gabriel suspected that somewhere inside Ricel, a blood vessel had just blown itself out. The brain was beginning to die . . .

Not fast enough, Gabriel thought.

He pushed himself upright and closed his eyes. He had done this once with a healthy brain, and with help, on Danwell. Now there was no help, but he had no choice. He remembered how it was done. No nonsense about "reading" a mind as if it were text, but more a business of listening, sealing everything else away, listening for the whisper in the darkness, and looking for the light that the buzz and business of your own mind would drown out otherwise. Four minutes to work in, no more. So make it happen. Darkness, silence, *listen.* . . .

Dying. Not dead yet, but soon. Last time, on *Lighthouse*, the danger had not been equivalent. This time his masters could not afford to let him be captured and questioned. This time . . .

Gabriel brushed past the narration for the moment. It would wait. He concentrated on the small fleeting images, burning bright up out of the darkness and fading again. One of them was central.

A slide . . .

* * * * *

He had been one of six. One had died when they were "young"—if that was the word you used when all of you were cloned to become conscious for the first time when the body they had grown was already the equivalent of twenty-five standard years old.

Their childhood had lasted about three years. The people who took care of them made sure it was a good one, not for any concern about the individual "children" involved, but because the psychologists among them knew that this was the best way to produce a stable and reliable product. This one had various vague happy memories of that time, including a slide that he was particularly fond of. He would climb up its ladder and hurtle down it again and again, while behind the glass wall of their playroom he could hear, clearly enough, the amused laughter. The watchers had liked it, too. That made Jake happy.

They all had longer names—Jake's was DW003 43FER—but they didn't use those with each other. He was simply Jake Three, or Threefer for short. Those, the psyches told them, were their grown-up names, the names they would bear proudly when they went out to work for the Company, but meantime they had to earn them. Right now they had to do that by studying hard. Later, there would be other ways.

Their adolescence—what they were allowed to have of one—lasted about three years. They were only allowed to leave the growth facility under carefully controlled conditions, which meant with about ten staff members around them. There was sex, but only with other clones, and that was also carefully supervised. The figures behind the glass walls might have been absolutely silent and the far side soundproofed, but you knew they were there, because after all, it was sex, wasn't it?

There was a certain amount of rebellion, but it was carefully channeled into their training. Their training was the most important thing in their lives: the game that kept them together, that made them something important, the purpose for which they had been bred (as they were constantly reminded).

They were trained in weapons first, which delighted them. They became expert with everything from chainswords to laser rifles, and they continued that training right through until their time in the facility was over and they were adjudged to be adult. They were trained in hand to hand combat, various kinds of small-craft flight, and checked out on various "positions" on bigger craft.

They were taught all kinds of ways to conceal information, both physically and virtually. They were taught bare-brain encryption and every known non-machine cipher. They learned quick recognition, "fast memory," brain printing, and many of the other techniques that turn a human brain into a recording device for audio or visual input without needing any kind of hardwiring. There had been several sessions—none of them knew how many—of deep sleep work and hypnotherapy to help them cope. All of them suspected that they were having deep triggers implanted, including the one which would make sure that if they fell into the hands of a sufficiently competent enemy, they would never reveal the secrets of the force that had trained them. They even joked about it.

"Now that we're ready to die," Jacob One said one night, "they'll let us out to *live*. . . ."

They knew that they had been bred and trained for the really dangerous work, missions too perilous to send less talented or committed Employees on. They were eager to get on with it.

At last had come the time when they all graduated. The clones were split up. They had all gone through counseling to help them handle that, the usual conditioning to help them see it as a graduation exercise rather than a tragedy, but it was still a wrench, and it took some months before any of them were really able to do anything without looking over their shoulders to see what the others thought. Nonetheless, proud to be Employees at last of the greatest force in the known worlds, they went out to do their jobs and repay the kindness of the Company that had raised them.

They had all been put "where they would do the most good," some of them working for VoidCorp Intel, some of them slipped into other Intelligence services among the stellar nations. In the case of Jacob Three and one of his brothers, they had entered Concord Intel, the heart of the Company's deadliest enemy.

It was exciting work, dangerous, uplifting—for Jacob at least—that sense of winning the Game, putting one over on everybody. That sense of "gotcha" overcame the staggering boredom. In some cases he might stay in one place, one job, doing nothing for months, a year, two years. Then the word would come through: cause this person to vanish. Steal this document. Pass on this message. He would do it and then quietly settle up his affairs to leave. It was the Game to do everything so that no one ever noticed, so that no trail was left, no betrayal. It was very important for Jacob and his brothers not to be noticed, for their work was increasingly becoming the removal of other Intel assets, sometimes the Company's own, who had become too dangerous to leave running.

But there came a time when someone did notice. After that, everything changed.

Jake Three had been given an assignment on a Star Force vessel. "Stay there," they told him. "Hold down this job.

You're going to pretend to be from Star Force Intel. Someone there will approach you, or we'll identify him for you to
contact. Either way, jolly him along. Once or twice you'll be
asked to have him get you some minor piece of information.
The third time, it will be less minor. You will use him to
carry out an intervention, and he will take the fall afterward.
He's getting too close to one of our assets aboard, and we
want him away from her. After he goes down, you'll be
withdrawn, so just sit tight."

It was just one more job, and Jake had carried it out
exactly as instructed, but when he was withdrawn, it hadn't
been VoidCorp that did it. The Company's protection failed
him or was somehow subverted. He refused to believe that
they might have abandoned him. He woke up to find himself not in a safe house or protected facility but strapped on
a floater with a man's thoughtful face looking down on him.

That face belonged to a bald man, small and quiet, who
simply said, "I have some questions for you. You will
answer them for me now."

That had been a little more than a year ago. Jake Three
had not believed in hell until then. He believed in it now
and knew for a fact that it was run by Lorand Kharls.

He had finally escaped it only by offering the single
thing Kharls wanted: that he should change sides. His body
itself rebelled against the idea. No surprise there. His conditioning had been arranged that way, but there were drugs
and more conditioning and much "sleep work," after which
Jacob would wake up hardly knowing his own name. The
final solution triggers had been subverted or removed—he
didn't know which. Kharls finally offered him the choice to
do what Jacob had been ordered to do next anyway, but to
do it for Kharls's side. Jacob had resisted this as long as he
could, but when it finally became plain that Kharls would
simply have him put to sleep like some kind of damaged
animal if he didn't cooperate, Jacob agreed.

He went out to space again, feeling damaged inside . . .
but alive. He always hoped against hope that his own

people would find him, rescue him, and put him back the way he had been.

But it never happened. He was alone, a "tainted asset." He knew the phrase all too well and knew what it meant. His own people would be far more likely to kill him than help him. His own clone-brothers, if they met him, would be bound to do the same.

Finally, the word had come from Kharls's people. He was to come here and investigate certain matters. One of them would be a familiar one. When Jacob had heard that, he had gone along with it all meekly enough. Concord Intel had its competencies. They had managed to set him up in a solid identity here. But he waited, and once he was here he made a few other quiet contacts, activating assets he knew were here—his Company's assets. He had received a new set of instructions from a quiet, husky woman's voice over the comms in his apartment one night. They would get him out after it was all over.

He never realized that there might have been a pattern in the words she spoke to him over the comm. There had been no obvious code words, but there had been one trigger left, one last failsafe, the one which the Concord people had not found and disabled.

Fool, he thought. I was a fool.

It was going dark quickly now.

Behind him, in the alley, Gabriel could hear footsteps, heavy ones. Helm, he thought. For all his bulk, Helm moved faster than any of them in light gravity like this.

"Gabe!"

"Not now," Gabriel whispered, keeping his eyes closed, diving into the darkness.

Ricel was struggling now, arms flailing as the seizure locked his lungs and his nerves in spasm. Gabriel shut his eyes and thought hard. There was something there in the background, lurking.

The conditioning, he thought, from the Concord side. He could see it, like the inside of one of the irradiated onions

Enda sometimes made him peel, though this structure was not nearly as tidy. Here was layer after layer of quarreling instructions and interdictions, big parts of Ricel's mind that other parts were not permitted to look at, areas fenced off by chemical or attributional barbed wire, blocked away except at certain times or under certain circumstances, waiting for key words or triggers to be issued. It was a terrible patchwork of a mind. It had been a wobbly enough place when it started, but now it looked like a building that had experienced an earthquake and been partly rebuilt, then had suffered another, and another, and had been reconstructed each time by people intent on removing or entirely subverting earlier structures. The original structure was still in there somewhere, but it had been terribly compromised. The loadbearing members had been cut into, and now, now . . .

Now it was all crumbling. Here on this damned grim world it had all gone to pieces finally. So let it end now. It was going to anyhow . . .

Gabriel tried to push his way in, tried to shoulder his way underneath the collapsing beams as the dust and detritus of a disintegrating mind came sifting down all around him. They came down illuminated in a growing darkness, as if fire lived in the debris, glimmering a little as it fell and went out. Pieces of memory, pieces of mind, fell down all around Gabriel, and the observing presence in the back of his mind warned him, *You had better get out of here. It will take you down with it. Unwise to stay in a dying mind—*

They had told him that at Epsedra, too, when he stayed with his buddy, who had been shot, and pulled him out. *Crazy to stay! You can't help him! Leave him with the medics!* Then later on he was shot himself, but Gabriel couldn't make himself care because he knew he had done the right thing. He would do it now. He stayed there, stayed while Ricel's mind came fully undone and cast itself loose from the moorings that held it into the body. All over now. All done. Now it began, the long coast down into the darkness, down one last time . . .

The slide, Gabriel thought sadly.

Half lost in terror, the other seized on the image from a time when there was no fear. *The slide.* Climb the ladder, laughing. Pause at the top, teetering. Look down to the bottom, but there the bottom was only darkness, and there was no telling what was down there or who might be there to catch him.

Sorrow. A pause. It was all over.

Bye, Threefer, Gabriel said.

Jake Three jumped and went down the slide into the darkness . . .

Gabriel squeezed his eyes shut so as not to see what Threefer saw as he went down, down into the darkness, out the other side . . .

* * * * *

"Gabriel."

It was too dark to see. There was no telling who was calling him.

"Gabriel."

He could find no voice with which to answer. He could find no direction in which to turn. It was dark. Light sifted down through the darkness, unperturbed. A great distance away, someone said, *the darkness comprehendeth it not . . .*

"Gabriel!"

His eyes snapped open. His back hurt wretchedly. He was kneeling over what he held in his arms, the cooling body of a man. Strange how quickly you became aware of the wrongness of the temperature . . .

There was a clatter of footsteps at the end of the alley. Gabriel looked up after a few moments and found Welsh and a number of men in dark uniforms and goggled helmets staring down at him from all sides. Helm and Delde Sota and Grawl and Angela crowded against the sides of the alleyway.

"It must have been heart failure," Gabriel said, as if every death was not heart failure to some extent. "I heard him . . ." He looked down at the very still face, the eyes still open and looking up past him, the hands clutching him so that Gabriel had to pry them away. It took some effort.

"Just like that," Gabriel said. "Just like that. After—"

"Gabriel," Enda said.

The sorrow with which she spoke the word was also part warning. Gabriel did not need it. He knew where they were and who surrounded them, but the irony of it, after all this while, was terrible. It's all over now, Gabriel thought, and who can I tell? What evidence is there? What evidence will there ever be that can stand up in a court?

He let go of Jacob Ricel and stood up.

* * * * *

It led to questioning, a lot of it, as Gabriel had thought it would. He and the others spent several long hours in the nearest police station, all of them being questioned first by the police and then by the army. Finally, last in a long line of questioners, Gabriel was not at all surprised to see Major Norrik turn up.

He sat down across the table from Gabriel, dismissed the guard, and waited for the door to close.

"So tell me what happened," he said.

Gabriel knew better than to protest that he had already told about thirty people. "I thought I had lost something out of my pocket back there at the cross street. This." He brought out the luckstone and put it on the table.

Norrik looked at it blankly. "It's a rock."

"It's some kind of silicate mineral, a composite," Gabriel said. "Some planets have beaches full of them. A friend gave it to me as a souvenir a while back. I'm kind of attached to it." He was studiedly telling the truth, not knowing what kind of voice analyzer they might have working on him right now. "At the time I thought maybe it had fallen out and gotten kicked into the alley. I went down there a little way to look, and then I heard this noise like something grunting. This man was down there having some kind of fit." Gabriel shook his head.

"It wasn't anyone you knew or recognized?"

Here it came. "No," Gabriel said.

Norrik looked at him. "Why did you leave your guide?"

Gabriel shrugged. "I just wanted to find the stone, that's all. It's a keepsake, a luckpiece." He made a face. "Turns out I'd forgotten that I put it in one of the top pockets. I didn't realize that until after all this was over, with this poor guy . . ."

Norrik simply looked at him for several moments. *Some of these people have implants,* Gabriel thought. *Who's he listening to, and what are they reporting on me?*

Or is he listening to something else entirely? The thought was awful. It reminded him of that sensation that he did not want to feel at all—

At last Norrik nodded. "Mr. Calvin," he said, "your stay here is starting to prove inconvenient. We'd appreciate it if you'd leave the planet immediately and move on to your next destination without delay."

"Our drives won't be charged yet—"

"You will be confined in your ships until they're charged, then you'll depart immediately."

"Uh, fine," Gabriel said, "no problem with that." He paused a moment then said, "What will happen to that poor man?"

"Reaction mass," said Norrik. "The parasitic heat from handling his remains will go to help our war effort. Not a hero's death, possibly, but a fate that all good Galvinites approve."

Gabriel nodded.

There followed a prolonged silence, then Major Norrik stood up. "The transport will be waiting to take you to your ships," he said, "and when your drives are charged, an escort will see you up to space and out to your starfall point."

Gabriel nodded to him again, trying to look suitably abashed for having caused trouble. Inside him, so many feelings were roiling that he hardly dared try to focus on any one of them.

"I should mention," Norrik said as Gabriel turned to the door, "that you should not return to this system. You are now classified as a person under suspicion to be detained by any of our forces that come in contact with you. Understood?"

"Yes, sir," Gabriel said.

"That will be all."

Gabriel went out of the room.

Inside his head, faintly, he could feel something writhing, stroking against itself in the warm green darkness, watching him in a thoughtful way.

* * * * *

The others were standing around in a windowless holding area, while two armed Galvinite Army staff watched them. Gabriel was put into this room with them.

Enda came to him, looked at him closely, and asked, "Are you all right?"

Gabriel nodded. "A long day," he replied, knowing she would understand.

After a moment another officer, a policeman, came through the door and looked around at them. "All right," he said, "there's a shuttle waiting for you people." He glanced up briefly at the humming sound of the covered stretcher with Ricel's body on it as it passed the door. He looked over at Gabriel. "Was it quick?" the policeman asked. "Did that guy suffer much?"

"It was pretty quick," Gabriel said softly. As regarded the suffering, he preferred not to go too deeply into it. No one here would understand. He barely understood himself.

"Right. Come on. The shuttle's waiting for you."

They were herded out to it and sealed in—the back of the shuttle being a windowless affair of the kind that the Marines would have used to transport prisoners or corpses. For all of that, the return was less stressful for Gabriel than the outward journey, partly due to having other things to think about. Once out on the landing pad again, Gabriel walked toward *Sunshine* with the greatest relief, practically ignoring the Galvinite soldiers that flanked him and Enda.

A couple of bored soldiers were standing by *Sunshine*'s lift column. They looked at Gabriel and Enda's ID chips, exchanged a few words with the armed escort, and then nodded unconcernedly as they stepped aside for Gabriel to hit the lift control. It came down, and he and Enda stepped in and let the door close behind him.

When they were on *Sunshine*'s deck again, Gabriel merely turned to Enda and said, "Let's dump our data."

Enda got the transfer going, and Gabriel called Helm.

"Gonna be fun sitting here cooling our heels for two days," Helm said. "They won't even let us socialize ship to ship."

"We'll cope," Gabriel said. "Doctor Sota around?"

"Identification: present," her voice said.

"Handling comms at the moment?"

It was a quiet way of telling *Longshot* that Gabriel was about to encrypt transmissions at his end, using the algorithms that the mechalus had installed in *Sunshine* and later in *Lalique*.

"Affirm," Delde Sota replied.

Gabriel reached into the display and shifted intership comms into encrypted mode. "Change of plans," he said. "When we leave, we're still headed for Coulomb, but we need to make one stop on the way. Crow."

"Crow?" Helm said. "What the devil's at Crow that we need to go that far out of our way?"

"Lighthouse," Gabriel answered, "as I see from the schedule we picked up passing through Aegis. It's getting there next week, and it'll still be there when we turn up in three weeks. We won't be hitching or staying longer than it takes to recharge our drives, but there'll be stuff I very much need to drop off."

Gabriel could hear Helm shrugging. From *Lalique*, Angela said, "Always wanted to see that thing, even if there's no time to stop and shop. You're on."

Chapter Seven

TWO DAYS LATER, *Sunshine*, *Lalique*, and *Longshot* lifted with ten small FSA ships surrounding them. Together, the three ships made starfall, *Lalique* in a blaze of blue, and *Longshot* all flowing with crimson. *Sunshine* went into drivespace in a rush and flow of a deep purple almost ranging into the ultraviolet—the fabled lucky "black starfall."

That first night in drivespace, Gabriel was desperately weary, but there was something he felt he had to do before he slept. He stayed up into the wee hours, making a recording of absolutely everything he could recall from his prolonged, final brush with Ricel's mind. He was terrified that he would forget it, but more, he was terrified that if he did not immediately report his version of what had happened to someone in a position to do something about it, he would be lost. It was all just too convenient that Ricel should die here and now before Gabriel was about to embark on business during which Kharls certainly knew Gabriel wanted no tails or trails on him. If explanations weren't made now, the ones required later might take forever . . . or prove fatal. The last thing Gabriel needed was another murder rap hung on him by a Concord Marine prosecutor already suspicious of Gabriel's semi-acquittal on Phorcys and unwilling to accept the assessment of the police on Galvin.

Gabriel had originally thought the task would take him only a couple of hours. He was mistaken. Every time he would start unravelling a particular memory of Ricel's to detail it fully, other buried or unexpected details associated with it would come rushing back. Again and again this startled and frightened him, so he would have to stop, get his breath back, and start again. If there was one thing he didn't want, it was Jacob Ricel's memories stuck in his head.

What if they *are*, now? he wondered. What can I do about it? His memory, he had noticed, was already a lot better than it used to be—one of those changes Delde Sota had told him about, a kind of side-present from the stone. Useful enough for everyday things . . . but this, this was another story.

Please let these memories fade, he pleaded inside him, on the off chance that some passing spacer's deity might be listening. Please let it go away like a normal memory, go vague . . .

About four in the morning, he was finally finished—or rather, he couldn't bear to continue—and his voice was faint and hoarse.

He canned the message into *Sunshine*'s data tanks as an encrypted mail addressed to Lorand Kharls. It would go out to the drivesat relay aboard *Lighthouse*, and once that was done, Gabriel could continue on his original course out into the dark. A last fling, he thought. For when he next returned to the more populated parts of the Verge, he was going to have to face up to the Marines at last.

I'm so tired of running, Gabriel thought.

After a little while, Enda appeared from her quarters, to which she had retreated after their takeoff and starfall to have a nap. Carrying the little squeeze bottle she used to water her ondothwait plant, she looked into the living area and said, "I would have thought you'd have taken some rest by now."

Gabriel shook his head slowly and replied, "I won't be able to sleep for a while, but I'm glad you're up. I have to tell you what happened down there."

Enda blinked. "But I was with you, for all but the questioning anyway."

"That's what I mean, partly. You were with me for this part, too, but not the part I saw—if 'saw' is even the word . . ."

He told her about the creatures he had heard inside the major. She listened with the rapt and concerned look of someone attending to a sleeper newly wakened from nightmare. "Horrible," she said at last. "Where would such a thing have come from? Did that man know it was—*they* were—inside him?"

"I don't think so," Gabriel said. "I got a sense that it was controlling him very delicately, but it won't always be doing that. It will slowly get stronger and stronger, and he will become weaker and weaker until finally he will be no use to what is inside. Then it will—" He rubbed his head, for it was beginning to ache a little. "I think it will move on and find another host somehow, or breed, or both."

She shuddered. Gabriel could completely understand the reaction.

"There was more to it than that," he said.

Gabriel fell silent for a moment, turning the stone in his pocket over and over. He probed in a gingerly manner at the memory of his encounter with the creature's thoughts—no, *their* thoughts—as if it had been Ricel's memories that he had just now been turning over. In a way, he was half afraid to do it, for the things with which he had been in contact were still alive, and Ricel was dead. *That* Ricel, anyway . . .

"There were many more of them," he said, "many more . . . *tangles*, I guess that would be the word. Many colonies, living inside various people, various hosts. I don't think the hosts necessarily have to be human. . . . It doesn't matter. They can communicate, I think, over long distances—if communication is even really the word for it."

"What are they doing?" Enda whispered.

"Controlling people," Gabriel said. "It's all about control."

"To what purpose?"

Gabriel probed the memory again but got nothing back. "I'm not sure," he said slowly. "There wasn't a lot of that, but there does have to be a purpose."

He closed his eyes and looked into his mind again, trying to bear more weight on the images. Very slowly, with difficulty, they began to resolve in places. The paradigm seemed to be hologrammatic. Even the most fragmented part of one thought or image-in-thought seemed to preserve parts of others, many others.

What Gabriel got this time was not so much an image as a concept. *Others.* There are more like us, not like us in terms of species, but in motivations, intentions. They want what we want. We want what they want, what they will have.

More. More like us.

He opened his eyes, shook his head, then decided not to do that again, for the headache was becoming blinding.

"There are a lot more of them," he said softly, "a big group of some kind"—he searched for the proper word—"an association. Different creatures meeting for a common purpose."

"What purpose?"

He held his head quite still. "I didn't get enough," he said, "or I can't get more now. For all I know, they get together to play cards."

"Gabriel," Enda said, "this is most terrible. Someone must be told about these creatures."

"Who?" Gabriel said.

"Your friend Lorand Kharls at least," Enda said.

Gabriel had been thinking about that. "I don't know," he said. "I have a few days to decide about that yet. Just . . ." He leaned forward, rubbing his head. "It's hard to interfere with communications in transit, I know that once a message goes into a relay, those conduits are pretty much watertight, yet at the same time I'm not sure that they're completely safe from tampering. I would really hate for someone to decrypt this information and start spreading it around. People are paranoid enough as it is, but more to the point, if it got out, and someone or something associated with these things worked out that the information had come from *me* . . ." He shook his head. "Life for the two of us is dangerous enough at the moment. I don't want it getting more so. If I become a target for some secret society of unknown aliens, then so do all of you."

"If you do not pass this information on to someone able to make the most of it, and quickly," Enda said, "you put more people than just us in danger as well. What if something should happen to us after we leave Crow? It would be unethical to leave this plane of existence without having passed on this information."

Something about the turn of phrase was amusing, and Gabriel cracked just a slight smile. "I'll endeavor not to do that," he said.

"If you are going to play the situational ethics game at this elevated a level, Gabriel," Enda said, "you must play it fairly and from both sides at once, which is, at any rate, the requirement for any truly talented player. We are all in a position to make our own choices about how to face this new danger, but you, I think, have a responsibility to protect those who are not able to make the choice for themselves by making sure the data that defines the necessary choices is in the hands of those who must have it. If you are uncertain about passing this information to Lorand Kharls via transmission, you must consider whether it is now time for you to do so in person."

"The only way I could do that," Gabriel said, "would be if Concord forces took me to him, and you know what that would mean."

"Of course I do," Enda said. "I did not say the consideration would be a simple matter or necessarily pleasant, except insofar as any ethical act is pleasant in and of itself."

Rather to Gabriel's horror, he could see her point. "No," he said, "pleasant probably wouldn't be the word I would choose, especially not after Ricel . . ." He shuddered.

"What did happen to him?" Enda said.

Gabriel let out a long angry breath. "There are two possibilities," he said, "and both of them might be true. One is that coming face to face with me and having that little contretemps so compromised what he was doing there that he had to suicide immediately, knowing that the Galvinite police would be on him within a few minutes. The other is that somehow *I* killed him."

Enda looked at him in shock. "Gabriel, you would never—"

"Oh, wouldn't I?" Gabriel said. He was angry at himself, partly because until yesterday he would have agreed with her. "Did I set off one of his conditioning triggers by being in his mind and wanting to kill him? Did his own mind misread that as an instruction to die, right then because that was what I *wanted* him to do?"

Enda opened her mouth and closed it again.

"I don't know," Gabriel said. "I might have killed him." He turned away. "I told Kharls as much in my report. That will go out via the drivespace relay at the *Lighthouse*."

"I take it you did not care to return to Aegis to use the relay there?"

"No," Gabriel said. "I want a little while to recover from what happened, and when I finally go back into Concord space again, I might as well surrender myself because there's no chance of finding any further evidence to clear me. The one man who might have done that is dead."

"Delde Sota wondered," Enda said, "whether you were being made over in some other image." *A harder one,* Gabriel suddenly "heard" her think. There were no words as such, but he got a quick image of reactions, emotions, edges being sharpened, tempered. *To hone,* Enda thought, *or to shatter against the rocks. . . ?*

Gabriel blinked and said, "Maybe." He was unwilling to respond in speech to the intercepted thought, not being sure what kind of protocol there might be among fraal for such things. "Whether I am or not, they're waiting for me, and it might look better if I go to meet them willingly rather than having to be dragged."

Enda nodded. "Your choice."

"What will *you* do?" Gabriel asked.

Enda gave him a thoughtful look. "If you have a while

to make your larger choices," she said, "so do I, but I think it is safe to say that you will not be alone to make them. Meanwhile, there are less fraught choices before us. Sugar in your chai or black?"

"Black," Gabriel replied.

Enda headed off to the galley.

Gabriel sat and looked at the image on the sitting room display of the great blocks of text that he had dictated for Lorand Kharls, and then he shifted the view back to Enda's green fields. There would be time enough for the dry words and what would come of them in the weeks to come. All the same . . .

He reached into his pocket and fingered the luckstone there. When luck won't assist you outright, Gabriel thought, you do your best to make your own.

* * * * *

Three more starfalls and twenty-five days later they arrived at Crow. The primary itself was a weary little orange K-class star with only a few planets—all rocky airless globes except for the middle one, simply called Crow II. That world was mostly steppe and sand with a sparsely settled colony in its northern temperate region, built around an old terraforming project that, though much scaled back in recent years, had still met with some success. Breather gear was necessary for those who went out of the colony domes under the dark violet sky, but it was thought that in perhaps another fifty years there might be enough oxygen in the atmosphere to start active addition of the nitrogen necessary to make the mixture safely breathable. The population was tiny—maybe ten or twelve thousand humans and fraal.

"Which is why I don't understand what *that's* doing here," Helm muttered to Gabriel over comms, when they came out of drivespace.

It was a convenient starfall, for the *Lighthouse* hung there gleaming in orange light from Crow. Gabriel looked at it a little longingly from the pilot's compartment where he was watching the data heralds come up on the main display as the infotrading system synched with the *Lighthouse*'s drivesat relay.

"I did some research," he said. "They had some kind of attack here thirteen years ago. Nearly wiped out the whole colony."

" 'Some kind of attack'?"

Gabriel looked idly toward *Longshot* and *Lalique*, which had come out of drivespace slightly before *Sunshine* had. "A pattern you might recognize," Gabriel said, rather grimly. "Little round ships came out of nowhere and killed half the population apparently. Then they just vanished. So did a lot of the rest of the population. The place has been building itself back up, but only very slowly. The Concord, needless to say, is in and out of here all the time. I had a look at the *Lighthouse*'s schedule for the past couple of years. For a place with no huge political importance, it comes to Crow an awful lot . . ."

"Huh," Helm said from *Longshot*. "Someone thinks it's a good idea to have a drivesat relay here pretty regularly, even if it's only a temporary one."

Gabriel nodded.

Angela's voice came in over comms. "Your offloading going all right, Gabriel?"

"No complaints," Gabriel said. They hadn't had that much to offload in any case, and that one message was away now. No recalling it. He sighed. "We've applied to see what they've got for us that's going in the direction of Coulomb."

Angela laughed. "Oh, no, another 'Will we ever get to Coulomb after all?' run."

"Don't tease," Gabriel said. "It's a big responsibility, infotrading. People depend on you to get their data where it's going on time."

"Which, as I remember, is why you went for the slow stuff, last time," Helm said.

"Well, yes."

"Gabriel just likes to worry out loud," said Angela.

He had to laugh at that. "As for you, Miss Social Services . . . don't push your luck."

She laughed. "You don't scare me. Besides, it's Grawl's turn to cook tonight, and if you're not nice to me, I'll bribe her to burn it."

There was a rumbling sound somewhere in the background of the pickup from *Lalique*.

"What?" Angela yelled over her shoulder.

A confused noise echoed in *Lalique*'s background.

"Uh-oh," Helm said.

Gabriel chuckled and watched the infotrading system finish passing its information to the *Lighthouse*'s drivesat relay. As the inbound part of the cycle started, he found his hands clenching on the arms of the pilot's couch. Nothing came in but the usual infotrading system maintenance information, news of new node-assignments, changes of system addresses, addition of new traders in the network, deletion of old or defunct ones . . .

Nothing from my father.

The expectation that there would be something so soon was unrealistic anyway. Gabriel berated himself for having willingly opened that wound of uncertainty again. You brought it on yourself, he thought.

A moment later he could hear the shouting again from *Lalique*.

"What's going on over there?" he called.

Grawl's voice came on, snarling with annoyance. "They have lost my whilom!"

"What?"

"Half our big stuff isn't in the cargo hold," Angela said from the background.

"Those miscreants!" Grawl shouted, "I shall make such a satire on them that they will all break out in blotches and their mates will snatch them bald! Their young will grow no claws and their friends will see the error of their ways! Their—"

"She has broken meter," Enda said from the doorway of the cabin. "I missed the beginning of that. What is this about?"

Gabriel shook his head and said, "I have a hunch, Angela. Just hang on and keep her from cursing anyone else for a few minutes. You wouldn't want her to waste the energy."

He got up and made his way back to *Sunshine*'s cargo hold. A glance inside told him what he needed to know. He went back uplevel and paused in the living area, waking up the display there and tapping it into comms, showing both *Lalique* and *Longshot*'s pilot cabins.

"Grawl, relax," he said. "Stand down the heavy weaponry. We've got it over here. Two whilom carcasses, it looks like."

"What's half our meat doing in *Sunshine*, for pity's sake?" Angela said.

"They must have misloaded it at Erhardt Field," Gabriel said. "Possibly a genuine clerical error. We knew they were going to take the shipments apart and look for—oh, whatever Galvinite security people look for when they're being congenitally nosey. So they did it, and then they repacked it incorrectly."

Coming toward him from the pilot's cabin, Enda sniffed. "Fraal eat meat," she said, "but we are not quite *that* carnivorous. I do not know if I like the statement implicit in their redistribution of the cargo."

Helm laughed. "That's the crankiest I've ever heard you," he said. "They even got under your skin, huh, Enda?"

She looked at him in mild shock. "It is something of an overreaction, is it not?" she said. "My apologies."

"Oh, no, Enda, it was funny!" Helm said. Then he realized he was talking to the air. Enda had gone past Gabriel back to her quarters, and the door gently shut behind her.

"What did I say?" Helm said. "I didn't mean to make her mad."

"I don't think she is," Gabriel said. "Helm, don't worry

about it. Suit up and come over to help me get this meat sorted out."

All the same, while he was suiting up himself, Gabriel wondered about the little incident. Enda was normally the most inoffensive of them all, and Gabriel would have thought, until now, almost impossible to offend. It was a little strange.

He snorted at himself as he donned his helmet and touched the seals closed. *I'm* complaining about someone being a little strange? he thought. After what's been going on with the stone lately?

If I was worried about becoming less human than I used to be, I guess *that* part of my behavior is still human enough.

For the moment . . .

* * * * *

"Another forty-five hours for recharge," Helm said, "then we jump. Coulomb, still?"

"Not for the star itself," Gabriel said, "but in that general direction. In terms of exact coordinates, I'm not sure exactly where we're headed."

They were halfway through dinner in *Lalique*'s sitting room—a pleasant place for it. All the space made it possible to eat without getting your elbows in your neighbor's plate.

"Well, five light-years at a time," Helm said, "and we'll be in no danger of overrunning whatever you're looking for. Now, if you could do ten at a time like us . . ."

"I get the feeling you're beginning to enjoy rubbing this in," Gabriel said. "I'm beginning to wish we'd gone ahead and bought that new ship or that I could get someone to die and leave *me* one."

Helm snickered. "Don't get your hopes up."

Enda rolled those expressive eyes of hers and turned away with a slight smile to pour herself some fruit juice. Grawl had cooked this evening, doing an entire half-side of whilom. She was expert at the more carnivorous kind of cooking, and seconds and thirds had been happily dispensed to the participants.

"It is good to see you frail creatures exhibiting some kind of appetite," she said, sawing off another rib steak for herself.

"I've got the coordinates sorted out, anyway," Gabriel said and felt around in his pocket for the chips on which he was carrying the data. "You can lay them in when you get back." He handed one to Angela and one to Helm.

"Query: method of determination?" asked Delde Sota.

Gabriel looked sheepish. "I hold the stone and turn myself until it feels right," he said, "then the fighting field programs an equivalent and isolates the coordinates."

Helm guffawed. "Better hope we don't wind up at Aegis again," he said. "What if that thing's homing in on where you were born or something? Maybe it thinks you want to go home to spawn."

"Spawning is fairly low on my list of things to do at the moment," Gabriel said. He poured another glass of kalwine for himself then handed Enda the bottle. "It's not my home the thing's looking for. *Its* home, possibly . . . or one place it identifies as such."

"You hear it thinking?" Grawl said, looking up from the last bite of the ribs she was holding daintily in her claws.

Gabriel shook his head. " 'Thinking' isn't the word."

"Feeling?" Angela asked.

"I don't know about that either," Gabriel said, then he laughed. "Sorry. It's frustrating. There aren't a lot of words for the things it does, but when I make the image in my mind of what I'm after—the big 'facility' that the little edanwe on Danwell told me was 'not too far off'—the directional quality in the stone's response is really noticeable. The correlation's clear in the heads-up display for the navigational system. It worked well enough at just seat-of-the-pants stuff on Danwell. We'll see if it works out here."

Delde Sota looked somewhat mischievously at Gabriel. "Commitment: and if you *do* spawn, we get to watch."

He laughed and said, "No promises . . . about spawning or otherwise. You want to write *that* kind of scientific paper, you're going to have to make the details up."

Dinner went on as long and cheerfully as usual, and about the time the cook began to fall asleep, the separate ships' companies went back to their ships. Their first jump out into the darkness in search of Gabriel's unknown "facility" would be in forty-three hours, though there was no need to hasten out of the Crow system with the *Lighthouse* hanging there, silently benevolent and extremely well armed.

When they got back to *Sunshine*, Gabriel was ready to turn in immediately, but Enda sat down in the living area and stared at her display of the green field rippling in the wind. Her expression was a little troubled.

"Indigestion?" Gabriel asked, knowing this was not the case.

She glanced at him with some amusement, but the emotion was edged with discomfort. "Gabriel," she said, "I fear I am not myself at the moment."

"What? Because of the way you answered Helm earlier?"

"Not at all." She looked rather guilty. "I believe it is the stone."

"What?"

She laced her pale hands together as Gabriel sat down opposite her. "Gabriel," she said, "I feel it looking at me, and I am not sure the look is a friendly one. Do you understand what I mean?"

"About the looking," he said, "yes, but not about the unfriendliness."

"It . . ." She shook her head, gazed at the display, which was showing green fields wavering in a silken wind, a favorite display of hers. "It is keyed to you, that stone, or it *is* a key, and you are the lock for which it was made—or which it is remaking to fit it. That is what Delde Sota warned you of, is it not?"

"It wasn't so much a warning," Gabriel said, "as an advisory."

"Yes. The problem, I believe, is that it is keying itself to you and to you alone—and becoming less tolerant of others nearby, especially lifeforms that have the ability to mindwalk." She sighed. "If I read the situation aright, it began turning you into a mindwalker on Danwell. You had a great deal of help: a group of communal telepaths, and a considerable incentive to communicate with them. Friend-ship, support, danger . . ."

"You had that, too," Gabriel said.

"Yes, but not the stone. It took you through that particu-lar challenge and out the far side. Now it has another chal-lenge for you—a larger one. You do not yet know entirely what this one entails, and neither do I. You will find out, but the stone does not easily tolerate the presence of others whom it fears may interfere with its business."

"You speak of it fearing, making things happen . . . as if it were sentient. Is it?" Gabriel asked, for this was the one question that had been taxing him most lately.

Enda tilted her head halfway over in a gesture of uncer-tainty. "I would not know how to say. Sentience is such a slippery subject to define, even when you have it . . . nearly as bad as consciousness. I mean, you and I know we are conscious, but *how* do we know?"

Gabriel blinked. That was high on a list of questions that had *not* been bothering him.

"Let it lie," Enda said. "The point of all this is that I am not you, and the stone does not entirely trust anyone or any-thing that is not you. It has begun turning its attention to me with increasing intensity more and more often. I feel it as a physical discomfort at the moment. I can bear it. The stone has offered me no violence, mentally or psychically speak-ing. Should it attack me, I do not have the training or the power to stop it. If it should take a dislike to me . . . I would have to leave, Gabriel. I could not bear to stay with it in such a confined space."

Gabriel swallowed. "How long has this been going on?"

"Since Danwell," Enda said. "It was always on the borders of my consciousness before then, but at Danwell, something happened. I was judged, as you were, by whatever force or presence was lying hidden in the edanweir group unconscious. Both of us, fortunately, were not found wanting—otherwise we would not now be alive, but the stone itself was also . . . perhaps not judged, but . . . upgraded? Reprogrammed perhaps? Or maybe it had new programming added. It is becoming increasingly vigilant about protecting you, I believe, though its definition of protection may look odd to you."

"I think it made Jacob Ricel turn up," Gabriel said. This was a thought that had been lurking fairly unformed in the back of his mind and turned up again now.

Enda looked thoughtful at that. "Maybe," she said. "I do not know *how* it could do such a thing, but I suspect that it could. It does not seem to hold cause and effect the same way we do, and sometimes I think I can feel things twisting around it."

Gabriel nodded. "I feel something like that too," he said. He reached into his pocket.

"No, please," Enda said, "not right now. Seeing it makes me uncomfortable." She sighed. "I just felt I had to tell you that these feelings were growing on me, Gabriel. If I do have to leave you, it will be most against my will. We are good friends, and you have a great work that you are doing, for which you will need all possible friends around you, all the help you can get. If it comes to a choice between dying and leaving in hopes that the situation may improve, I think I will choose the second option."

"Well, of course," Gabriel said. He was trying hard, though, not to reveal how shaky he felt. The thought of being without Enda—

"I fear we are both too much mindwalkers now," Enda

said, "to be able to conceal such feelings from each other—
not without considerable effort, which you have not yet
learned to focus properly. It is always the danger of that
particular art, one of the reasons why I put it aside when—
" She broke off. "No, later for that as well. I think I will
have some chai."

"Don't worry about losing your temper," Gabriel said.
"You lose it less obviously than anyone I know. You barely
register on the tiff scale."

She smiled at him, the dry look of someone who does
not entirely believe a compliment. "Perhaps someday you
will see me really angry," she said, "and see how many tiffs
it registers. Meanwhile . . ."

She got up and went down to the galley.

Chapter Eight

SOME FORTY HOURS later they set out from Crow. Gabriel checked the *Lighthouse* one more time for any messages that might have come for him. One more time he found nothing and cursed himself quietly. If Enda noticed this, she said nothing of it.

The next several starfalls and the days between them were routine . . . insofar as any jump made not to a specific star, station, or facility can be considered routine. At the end of it, nearly two months after leaving Crow, *Sunshine*, *Lalique*, and *Longshot* came out into empty space with all their weapons hot, looking around with concern. This was by far the most dangerous kind of starrise to make, but there was no one here as far as they could tell. For his own part, Gabriel would have given a great deal for a starrise detector, but such equipment was far beyond his means. He also wished that he had some clear idea of what they were look-ing for.

"So where is it?" Angela asked, only partly teasing.

Gabriel sighed. "Not here."

"You can tell already?" said Helm.

"I can tell that the reading is stronger than it was, but not *that* much stronger," Gabriel confessed. "Definitely I know that it's not anywhere nearby, not anywhere we could use system drive to reach anyway. We need to keep going in the same general direction as the last starfall. I'll give you another set of coordinates when the drives have finished charging."

They met again for dinner in *Longshot* this time. It

turned out to be one of Helm's "I did it with a handlaser" dinners, a one-pot dish of the kind in which he so excelled.

Gabriel took a lot of good-natured chaffing during the meal about his stone not having produced the goods. "It might take a lot more jumps," Gabriel said. "I'm warning you."

"That means there might be some wisdom in not eating all the meat right away." Angela threw Grawl a look. "This means *you.*"

"I will try some other forms of protein for a while," Grawl said, "especially if Helm is cooking them with his handlaser, but I expect to come out at some civilized world within, say, the next month or so . . ."

"No guarantees," Gabriel said.

Angela gave him a look that he had trouble reading, and for the moment, not a whisper could he hear from the inside of her head.

That, Gabriel thought later when they had all parted for the evening, was something that was beginning to bother him. It was getting to the point where he could habitually hear not people's thoughts as such, but a kind of background noise made by their thinking and their emotions. It was like the faint rumble through a ship's system drive, except that it came in a slightly different flavor and timbre for each person. Sometimes it went away, but not often. Lately, he had awakened to think that the stardrive was malfunctioning in some new and interesting way, because he could hear and feel that vibration . . . except that it was no vibration. It was Enda.

The stone knew about fraal. It had known about them for a long time. That familiarity was plain, and also—strange to Gabriel—it had some obscure trouble with fraal, some problem. It seemed not to like them very much.

That made Gabriel wonder. Maybe Enda is right, he thought, and the stone sees her as some kind of rival or potential interference with its business. How do I tell it that it doesn't have anything to worry about? Its business is mine, for the moment.

Lying in his bed in the dark with the stone in his hand, he wondered if even that was open to question occasionally. There were moments when the fine hairs stood up all over him at the thought of what he was becoming. Some of his memories, Gabriel found, were becoming hazy. He had to concentrate to see them clearly. Some of them, quite old memories from his childhood, were becoming hazy enough that he had to look hard to remember whether they had really happened or whether they were dreams. In some cases he could no longer tell.

His mind was being altered. Compressed, Gabriel thought, to make room for something else? *What* else? There was no telling.

Delde Sota's warnings were beginning to seem more urgent to him now. When the changes had been merely physical and external—the hair going white, even the beard silvering rapidly now—those had seemed less threatening, but when things started happening in the inside of his head . . .

Still, Gabriel thought, this is the path I've chosen.

Or so I like to think. Has there been any choice in this? Has the stone been calling the shots ever since it got itself into my hand? What's it looking for when I use it to hunt down this old trove of alien science that the little edanwe— or what was hiding inside her—told me about? Granted, the Concord can use these things. In fact, he suspected that the Concord was going to need to have these things to protect its people, the civilization they'd managed to build so far, but that's not the stone's concern. It doesn't mind.

At least he didn't think it minded. He was almost afraid to try to look into that further.

But what does it really want?

Long silence. No answers came. In his hand, the stone declined even to glow.

Fine, Gabriel thought and put it off to one side on the shelf, turning over to go to sleep.

You just be that way, he said to the stone. *I'll find out myself, eventually, and when I do, we'll see which of us is* really *running this show.*

* * * * *

After recharging their drives, they jumped again. Again, five days passed during which Gabriel mostly avoided the stone and went back to studying the starship catalogues. Enda teased him mildly about this and occupied herself with her own routine, cooking, reading, listening to the fraal choral music that she favored, looking at "canned" entertainments and news programs downloaded from the Grid at Aegis or from the much bigger Grid that the *Lighthouse* carried with it.

When starrise came again, Gabriel had been awake for nearly twelve hours already, unable to bear the excitement, the thought that there might actually be something there this time, but they came out again in empty space, all the stars distant, not even an uninhabited one nearby. Gabriel nearly did not need the stone, or his slowly burgeoning ability, to hear Helm thinking, *Now what? There's nothing here . . .*

The three ships drew together in the darkness and linked up by comms.

"Everybody okay over there?" Helm asked.

"No problems," Gabriel said, looking at the mass detector. "Except one."

"There's nothing here," said Angela from *Lalique.*

Gabriel sighed and wished she wouldn't belabor the obvious.

"Gabe," Helm said, "this is really beginning to seem like a waste of fuel."

Gabriel flushed hot with embarrassment. "Look," he said, "I warned you that it might. The stone—"

"That thing might be *wrong,* you know," Helm said. "Has that occurred to you?"

"Yes, it has, but—"

"Well, when are you going to start acting on the idea?" Helm growled. "It's all very well to blow your own food and fuel and funds chasing all over the black backend of nowhere, but when you—"

"Helm, I didn't—"

"Oh, what's the use of trying to talk sense to you? The hell with it." Helm chopped off his comms.

Gabriel sat there torn between frustration and anger, for he could understand Helm's viewpoint all too well. From *Lalique* there was nothing but silence.

Gabriel swallowed. "Well," he said, "we'll charge up again and head out. Who's cooking tonight?"

"Opinion: my turn," Delde Sota said as *Longshot*'s comms crackled to life again.

It meant dinner in *Longshot*, which right now did not seem to be such a great idea. "What are you going to feed me?" Gabriel muttered. "Crow?"

"Assessment: cooking area here large," said Delde Sota dryly, "but not large enough to take a whole planet."

"Huh," Gabriel said, not sure how hard his leg was being pulled. Still, he reluctantly agreed that he and Enda would come over.

Normally, visiting *Longshot* amused Gabriel somewhat, for Helm's ship reflected a rather spartan lifestyle that was only slowly changing. One whole cabin of that fairly ample space was allotted to "things I don't know where to put"— a farrago of packed-up mining equipment, old entertainment chips, and a surprising amount of souvenirs and clothes, all pushed into that cabin and tied down. Every now and then, having acquired some new hobby or interest in his travels and then gotten bored with it, Helm would bundle up everything and stuff it into that cabin. "Adding a new layer," as he put it. When the three ships connected their tubes—*Longshot* having two airlocks made this their normal configuration when laying over for a recharge— Gabriel came over and found Helm engaged in this, while shouting suggestions over his shoulder at Delde Sota. The doctor was in the galley halfway down *Longshot*'s long central hallway.

Angela and Grawl looked over his shoulder in a mixture of curiosity and bemusement. "You ask me," Angela said to Helm, who was lashing a plastic box full of chips down onto the top layer, "you're the one who should be looking for a new ship, not Gabriel. You're a pack rat."

"What's all this stuff?" Gabriel said.

"More music," Helm said. "Delde Sota keeps saying I should broaden my horizons."

"Opinion: only thing about him which is not already broad enough," Delde Sota said from the galley.

"Huh." Helm snorted. "Gabe, you want some new music for your system, take a look through here later. Lots of stuff."

He sounded gruff but no longer actively angry, which relieved Gabriel somewhat. As regarded "looking through" the cabin, Gabriel had half been hoping Helm would offer. There were always interesting things to be found there. Last time, he had been going through a small box of anonymous looking datacarts and had found one that was an examination of "The Market's Best Small Arms." The holo showed fine small weapons of all kinds being test fired by good-looking, scantily clad women of various species. He had found it fairly educational, though perhaps less so about the small arms than about the women.

"What exactly is a pack rat?" asked Grawl as they made their way down toward the dining room. "Is it a creature of the Stellar Ring?"

"It never occurred to me to ask," Gabriel said. "Though my mother used to talk about them."

"Mine, too," Angela said. "I think I remember her telling me that it's this kind of bird that looks for shiny things and hides them away."

Enda came out of the galley carrying tongs and glasses. "Like a peewit perhaps?" she said.

"What's a peewit?" Angela asked.

Helm laughed and brought up the display installed on the far wall, and they called up a "bestiary" resource stored in *Longshot*'s computers, finding neither peewits nor pack rats, but coming across much other interesting information on creatures such as sirens, scraaghek, and Minshore crystals.

"Wouldn't have thought you'd be much interested in xenobiology, Helm," Angela said.

"Man's got to know what he's shooting," Helm said mildly.

"Or shooting at," Enda said, coming in again with the bottles of wine and reconned fruit juice.

"Exactly," Helm said as Delde Sota brought in the entrée, a huge pot of brown wailenta.

They all picked up their tongs and dug in. The conversation wandered off among the usual wild tangle of topics, but all the while Gabriel could hear everyone avoiding the one topic that he knew was most on their minds: yet another starfall, no results. This is while we're still in space that's not too far off the beaten track, he thought. What happens if we have to go somewhere genuinely out in the middle of nowhere?

I may have to go alone . . .

Though Enda will come.

Assuming she can bear it, said the back of Gabriel's mind. If the presence of the stone became too much for her to bear—and she was already showing stress from it—she would part company with him.

Dinner went on through dessert. Eventually Gabriel got up for a stretch and to go down to the end of the hallway to visit the head. When he came out, Angela was halfway down the hall, looking into the "junk" cabin.

"Uh, sorry, didn't mean to keep you waiting."

"I wasn't waiting for that," she said quietly.

"Huh? Oh," Gabriel said. While he could hear the faint under-rumble of her mind, on a note that suggested something out of the ordinary was going on, he didn't have a clue what it might be.

Angela looked at him. "I have to ask you," she said. "I really hate to, but I have to. Are you all right?"

"All right how?"

"In your head. You know . . . the stone."

Gabriel laughed briefly. "I'm sane, if that's what you mean."

"Are you sure?"

The look she gave him made him plain that she wasn't.

"Look," Gabriel said, "Delde Sota seems to think I'm all right. She would have said something if she wasn't certain."

"She *has* said things to you," Angela replied, "several times."

"In a general way," Gabriel said, "yes. She says there are some changes happening inside me, and she's not sure where they're going."

"That's mostly the problem at the moment," Angela said, "being sure where we're going. Are you?"

"If you mean do I know *where* we're going, no. That's the whole point. If you mean can I feel that there's somewhere specific that we're going to, then yes. No question."

Angela leaned against the bulkhead wall, her arms folded. "Are you sure," she said, "that the stone isn't just making you . . . I don't know . . . making you think that, feel that, for some reason of its own?"

That struck a little too close to home. "I don't have any reason to think so," Gabriel said. "It didn't act that way at Danwell."

"It might now."

"Just why exactly would it?" Gabriel said. "Do you know more about it than I do? It sounds like you think you do."

Angela's eyes widened for an instant then narrowed into the beginnings of genuine anger. "Gabriel, if you can't get it through your head that we're concerned about you," she said, "that might by itself be an indicator that something's going on in your head that wants looking at. We just don't want to see this thing dragging you halfway across the galaxy for no reason."

"It's not for no reason, believe me," Gabriel said, turning away. "There's something big going on here . . . really big."

"But you would have to believe that, wouldn't you?" Angela said. "Haven't you given any consideration at all to the idea that—"

"That what? That this whole thing is some kind of delusion? Look, Angela, you don't have to come along, if you're so concerned. I wouldn't want to waste your time and Grawl's."

"That's not the point! Idiot! As if we've been doing anything all that important with our time until we sold you that contract." She swallowed. "Gabriel, you're just . . . you've just stopped listening to people, to what other people think. All the time it's 'the stone' this and 'the stone' that. Sometimes it looks like that thing is all you're really concerned about in the world, and if people are going to go along with you out into the middle of nowhere because of that . . ."

He looked up at her slowly and said, very softly, "Maybe that *is* all I'm concerned about these days. What else have I got? If I go back to Concord space, they'll just sling me in jail. I have no new evidence to bring to my trial, even though I now know for sure what Ricel and his buddies were up to—a lot of it, anyway. They're just going to chuck me in a cell if I go back. What else is left but to go out and go away, if you can't go back? So I'm going out to see if I can find what the stone says is out there, and whatever it was living inside that little edanwe back on Danwell. If people are going to start leaving now—Enda might have to—then I understand that you might feel you need to as well. So you go right ahead. Helm's got business of his own. Maybe he'll take off, too."

She stared at him. Then she suddenly took a few steps forward and put her face quite close to his.

"You just listen to me," she said, even more quietly. "You are such a stubborn cuss. You just don't know how to

let anyone tell you they're *worried* about you, do you?
Goddamned Marines, all thick skin and thick heads. I don't
know how you ever got a medal for being shot, because I
can't imagine how anything ever got through that hide of
yours. It's like Helm's armor—confused armor, though,
because it bounces the friendly stuff off as well as the
enemy slugs. I don't know what Enda's problem is. You'll
have to sort that out with her, but as for me and Grawl, do
you think we care about being all the way out here,
wherever we are? That's not the issue. It's your big echoing
empty head that's the issue, Gabriel! We've seen that there
are plenty of people after your butt. You seriously think
we'd leave you here to cope with them by yourself? We
may not have been together long, but you plainly don't
know us real well if you think so. We just want to make
sure that you're genuinely running this show, whatever it is,
that your admittedly tiny mind is more or less in one piece,
though I imagine that just finding it must have been a real
piece of work for the Marine psychs, and even Delde Sota
must have to get out a magnifier."

She glared at him.

Gabriel opened his mouth and closed it again. Then he
said, "I really am running this show, and I'm sure I'll be able
to tell if it stops being that way. Satisfied? But why should
my telling you that resolve anything? There's been no
change in the situation between when I first told you so five
minutes ago and now, when you've spent most of the
five minutes belittling my mental capacity, except that now
I know you think I'm an idiot."

The opinion was certainly mutual, which made him grin
suddenly and then try to get rid of the grin with only partial
success. What helped the grin loosen and fall off, finally,
was the flash of thought. *Maybe I was wrong. Something
has changed after all.*

Gabriel's only problem was that he couldn't tell whether
that was her thought or his.

Angela looked at him with some annoyance. "And a

weird one," she said. She paused, as if looking for something to add to this, and then brushed past him and made for the head.

Gabriel made his way back down to the dining area. Everyone was talking animatedly about a picture of an Alitarin drexen on the display, and Helm was making some unlikely suggestions about how it might have sex. It was all entirely too casual for Gabriel, who was not fooled. The rumble of mind-noise got considerably louder as he came in, though as usual he could catch no whiff of content. He sat down and poured himself a glass of wine and joined the conversation.

Much later, when he and Enda were making their way back to *Sunshine* to prepare for the next jump, Gabriel said, "Well?"

Enda gave him a large, blue-eyed, innocent look.

"You must have heard it," he said.

They slipped in through the airlock, and it shut behind them. Enda touched the control to start the tube retracting. "A fairly quiet fight as such things go," she said. "Surely very low on the tiff scale."

Gabriel had to laugh a little, even though he was still feeling uncomfortable and embarrassed. "It would have been nice if it had resolved anything, but you guys knew what it was about."

"We knew."

"And?"

"We are with you, Gabriel," Enda said. "All of us. It is business as usual."

He really wanted to believe her. He sighed and went to bed.

* * * * *

Their next starfall turned out exactly like the last one: empty space, no worlds, no moonlets, nothing but the usual amount of dust. Gabriel let Enda make the routine contacts with the other ships and let her arrange dinner, but he didn't attend. He just couldn't face the others.

During that quiet time he sat in his cabin with the stone in his hands, trying to wring some kind of concrete results out of it, some definite kind of directional information about what he was hunting . . . or *any* information at all.

It was rather like trying to wring blood out of, well, out of a stone. There were no results, though Gabriel sat and listened with all his might. He queried the stone in words and images and generally hammered on it with his mind like someone using a sledgehammer on a pebble. The pebble resisted him with the nonchalance of an object on which entirely the wrong tactics were being used.

He sighed. Maybe they're right, he thought. Maybe I am crazy. This kind of travel's crazy enough, anyway . . .

Gabriel had a vague memory of reading about some ancient explorer on Earth who sailed west to find land that was supposed to be in the east, the idea being revolutionary at the time because his people had lost (in one of those cultural hiccups that happen sometimes) the information that the world was round. He had sailed to the very edge of his exploration envelope—well beyond it, in fact, so that his crew was apparently thinking seriously of throwing him overboard—when land finally appeared. The situation had exercised its own ironies, of course. The man had not reached the place to which he had originally been heading, but someplace else entirely, and the journey that had been planned to make him rich and famous instead wound up bankrupting him. The phrase, "Sail on! And on!" kept recurring in Gabriel's memory. Now he knew how the poor guy had felt.

He went back to his labors with the stone. An hour went by, then two, and still nothing happened. Finally he just lay back, let out a long exasperated breath, and then shouted silently into that maddening interior silence.

COME ON! he yelled inside his head. *Can't you give me something more concrete than just this vague "thataway" feeling? Don't you believe in star maps? You may have belonged to some species umpty-thousand years old, incredibly ancient and advanced and all that crap, but you must have had* maps!

Nothing.

Then came a slow sense of something looking at him from a great depth of time . . .

The hair stood up all over Gabriel. It was that silent presence that sometimes spoke in the back of his mind, but he had never had a contact quite like this before. Rather than the stone demanding his attention, he had summoned it. It was answering . . . slowly, patiently, as if he had awakened it hours earlier than expected, and it was restraining itself from what otherwise could have been a very intemperate response.

An image of stars drifting in huge currents washed past his point of view like sand in water—thousands of years' worth of movement in a few seconds, endless eddies and currents of motion, tumbling the stars and their systems among one another, out again, and onward through this arm of the galaxy. The movement was slow and graceful, but Gabriel knew that it had been sped up by a factor of millions for his sake. Millennia of movement were happening every second, as the myriad relationships among the stars shifted, shifted, and shifted again by tens and hundreds of light-years . . .

How much good, the image seemed to say, *do you think our maps are going to do you* now? *You must go looking. Were we with you, we could not do better ourselves . . .*

Darkness fell—*wham!*—with the contact cut off as suddenly as a door being shut.

Gabriel sat there and blinked. Suddenly his stomach turned over, a queasy flip, and he hurried into the head and had a prolonged discussion with the waste reclamation utensil. Possibly his body was outraged on some very elementary level by being forced to experience so much time, even indirectly, and it retaliated by attempting to throw up everything Gabriel had eaten since he first went on solid food.

When Enda came back a few hours later, Gabriel was in the pilots' compartment, sorting out the coordinates for the next jump. "Everybody okay?" he asked.

"They are fine," Enda said. She slipped out of the big silken shawl she had been wearing over her vest and kilt and laid it aside over the back of the left-side pilot's couch. "Are *you* all right? You look pale."

He nodded, trying not to think about how he had gotten that way lest the recollection trigger a repeat performance. "As soon as we're recharged, we can go." Gabriel said.

Enda sighed. "Four days yet. More uncertainty . . ."

Gabriel glanced back at the console to see if it had finished digesting the coordinates. It had, and it was blinking in a manner that at first scared him, until he suddenly realized what it was. It had been too long since he had seen this reaction. He began to grin.

"What is it?"

Gabriel grinned harder. *"Look—!"*

Enda leaned in toward the console. Gabriel hit the comms control and said, *"Longshot, Lalique,* we have our coordinates for the next jump."

"What's the rush?" Helm's voice came back, faintly annoyed.

"I just thought you'd like to know," Gabriel said. "The coordinates I've worked out from the stone . . . they match a previous set."

"And?"

"It's Coulomb."

Helm whooped, and Gabriel felt entirely better, stomach or not.

* * * * *

Four days later, they jumped. Five days after that, they made starrise in an extravagance of white fire such as

Gabriel had not seen for some while. Sitting in the pilots' couch with Enda across from him, he watched the blazing whiteness wash down the front viewports and caught the first glimpse of the little, weary, orange-red star about twenty million kilometers away.

In Gabriel's pocket, the stone flared with brief, definite warmth and went quiet again. Enda flinched.

It seems, Gabriel thought, that what we're looking for is here.

Chapter Nine

"STILL CAN'T believe it," Helm said over visual comms a few minutes later. *"We could have come straight here weeks ago!"*

"If we'd known that this was where we were coming," Gabriel said.

Lalique was online as well, and Angela's face replaced Grawl's broad, striped visage after a few minutes.

"We were here months ago!" Helm said. "Why didn't that thing act up *then?* Why didn't it lead you here then?"

"Maybe because I wasn't trying to make it lead me anywhere?" Gabriel said. "We came in after the craziness at Eldala with not much on our minds but dumping our data, picking up some more, and going straight back to Aegis. Frankly, I was so wrecked at that point," he added, "that this thing could have been jumping up and down holding a sign, and I wouldn't have noticed."

Angela snickered.

Helm gave Gabriel a wry look and said, "Okay, I take your point. You had a bad time of it. We shouldn't give you a bad time too." He sighed and looked at the weary red-orange star. "Well, you don't have any data to dump this run, but now what?"

"Opinion: do tourist things," Delde Sota said.

Gabriel grinned and said, "I think the doctor's idea is excellent. We'll go see the Glassmaker sites."

"Aren't you carrying something a little unusual in the way of admission tickets?" Angela asked.

Gabriel nodded to her. "This planet isn't that carefully policed," he said. "It's nothing like Algemron."

"Thank God," Angela muttered.

"Anyway," Gabriel said, "we shouldn't have any trouble making our way just about anywhere on the planet we care to go, and then we'll see what we find."

"Query," Delde Sota said: "stone indicating more strongly?"

Gabriel glanced over at Enda, who was looking rather uncomfortable. For her, the question would have been unnecessary. He gave Delde Sota a wry look. "It's practically shouting in my ear. The source of whatever energy it's been tracking—if it even *is* energy—is definitely Ohmel. Even now, I think I can tell that the source is on the side turned away from us. The 'signal' has oscillated a couple of times now from loud, to louder, to just loud again."

"Rotation," Grawl said.

"I think so, yes."

They made contact with Ohmel control at Charlotte, found out where they could land at the port, and made their way down into atmosphere. They had spent little time here on the last passage through the system, Gabriel having been too weary after the events at Danwell to care about staying, but now they would have a little while to get more familiar with the place. Last time there had been scant opportunity to notice much except that the port facilities were in astonishingly good shape for a world so far out at the end of things.

Ohmel itself was an old world, cold and dry, with only the occasional lake here and there to break the red-brown surface. Coulomb was a very elderly star, perhaps not as far along as Mantebron, but (as Grawl put it) "well stricken in years," with maybe another couple of hundred thousand years to run before it finally died. Meanwhile, its inhabitants did not seem to be much concerning themselves with far-future occurrences. They were getting on with their lives. Lights were twinkling down there as Ohmel's broad terminator drew itself across Charlotte Port and night slipped in behind. The town attached to the port was small

and prosperous and a good place to start a business as long
as one of your names was Ngongwe.

The three ships made for the same landing spots they
had used the last time over on the transient side of the port.
There were a good number of cargo ships on the non-
transient side. That came as no surprise, for the Ngongwe
family, one of the ruling houses of the old vanished Leodal
stellar nation, had parlayed their foothold here over a
number of generations into a small but flourishing trading
organization, the proceeds of which had enabled them to
essentially buy the planet. Most of their trade was done
around Aegis, Algemron, and Lucullus, but sooner or later
most of the ships came back here for service, retrofit, or (if
they had gone that far down the road) breaking. The
Ngongwes had not become as rich as they were now by letting anyone else profit from their salvage.

Sunshine's skids touched down on the cracked concrete
of the landing pad, and Gabriel glanced around in the dusk
at the surrounding low buildings.

"What's the temperature out there now?" he asked.

"Three degrees below zero C," Enda said and reached
into the central holodisplay to wake up the infotrading
system. "A lovely spring evening on Ohmel."

The infotrading system automatically came online and
started hunting in the local ether for the frequency that the
planet's Grid used. After a few moments, it found the
ingress/access nodes, and the Ohmel system and *Sunshine*'s
infotrading system went into synch with one another and
began exchanging ID and security codes.

From the voice comms, a cheerful rich voice belonging
to a man named Tabin Ngongwe, the port infotrading officer, said, "*Sunshine*, you back again so soon? We don't normally see a trader twice in the same six months."

Gabriel was slightly surprised at being remembered.
"We came back for the tourist season."

Tabin laughed. "What you got for us? You hauling
inbound or just passing through?"

"We're empty at the moment; the systems are just gossiping to confirm status," Gabriel said. "Anything outbound?"

"Depends, *Sunshine*. Where you headed?"

Gabriel suddenly found himself feeling cautious, but he couldn't say why. "Not clear about that just yet," he replied. "We thought we'd just stay a few days and see the sights."

There was a roar of laughter at the other end. "Here? There's nothing here!"

It was a comment that Gabriel had heard before from natives of other planets, sometimes with even less reason than someone on Ohmel.

"We'll take a look at the outbound list early next week," Gabriel said.

"I'll have it ready for you."

He closed down comms as the infotrading system finished its business and displayed the NO DATA TRANSFER . . . BEGINNING PURGE CYCLE heralds.

"It is kind of funny," Gabriel said, "to come straight back here."

"Maybe," Enda said. After a moment she added, "You are thinking that you know perfectly well why the stone did not bring you here the last time?"

"Mmm, partly, I was too tired, and I think I was still in shock. Can you go into shock after being telepathically wrung out?"

"You saw me do it on Danwell," Enda said. "For a human new to mindwalking, it strikes me as entirely likely." She looked out the front ports at the dark. "For my own part it was such a strange experience, that contact, and then the interfacing with the great machine down there in the old facility . . . I am not sure that I came away from it entirely unchanged, either."

"It wasn't so much that I was thinking of," Gabriel said. "After the little edanweir looked into me . . ."

"If 'after' is the word we are seeking," Enda said. "Causality took some bending that morning, as did my perception of the flow of time—yours, too, I think. We were both sifted, both examined, by whatever that presence was that looked at you through the child." She got up, stretched, and looked at Gabriel speculatively. "Otherwise I am not sure that I could have done what I did with the device that spoke so forcefully to me regarding its use. What it was bending—time or space or both—I am not sure, but I was permitted its use because we two were linked. Or rather"—she headed down the hall—"because I was linked to you and therefore permitted access."

Gabriel turned that over in his mind. "Are you all right?" he said. "The stone—"

"Believe me," Enda said, "I know. Its pressure against me is increasing all the time. I am maintaining, for the moment, mostly by trying to be very quiet of mind, but we are moving among uncertainties here. I do not know what will happen if the stone becomes much more active." Enda went down to her quarters to change into warmer clothes. "I would say this. You should be careful with yourself, for any attempt by the rest of us to investigate these places without you and the stone is likely to be disastrous. Just a feeling I have. The excitement of exploration is heady stuff, and I would not attempt to deprive you of it, but do not get yourself killed in the exploration we are about to undertake. If you do, we are all likely to experience something similar."

Gabriel swallowed hard and went for his coat and breather gear.

* * * * *

They met up with the other four, all of them wearing heavy coats and the breathers, which were sufficient for Ohmel's springtime. Together, they all went out to dinner at a place not nearly as good or as fancy as the one on Algemron—rough stone walls, a textured composite stone floor, rustic chairs and tables and a limited menu—but the atmosphere was much better.

"Actually," said Helm, "if you came here in the winter, you could say that it didn't have *any* atmosphere."

There were groans. "Terrible," Enda said. "Helm, you should be ashamed."

"Factual correction," Delde Sota said: "does have atmosphere in winter, but mostly lying on the ground."

More groans. "Better poor meal in comfort than stalled ox in military dictatorship," Delde Sota said.

"Sssh," said Enda, for "dictatorship" was not a word one used too loudly on Ohmel. There were many who would take offense at its use since it was an accurate description of the present regime. Lady Kfira Ngongwe was a true daughter of her house, meaning that as far as she was concerned she owned Ohmel and had no intention of simply letting the Concord waltz in here and liberate the place.

"Why is the ox stalled?" Grawl said. "I thought it was an animal. Is it a some kind of biomachine?"

This devolved into a long discussion of Standard idiom and many more bad puns, which Helm and Enda both considered a high form of humor. When the meal was done and they were nursing the last of their drinks, they began making quiet plans for the next day.

"It is good to have a guide with a 'detector' of sorts," Enda said. "At least we will not be going into this blindly, not knowing what trouble to expect."

"No," Gabriel muttered. "We're going to get into trouble right away, which will be worse."

Helm looked at him sharply. "You didn't mention trouble."

Gabriel laughed. "I didn't think I'd have to. You've got the bestiary. You know what kinds of things live here."

They had all spent some time after that dinner at Helm's running copies of the bestiary through its paces. There were numerous lifeforms known to be associated with Glassmaker sites, some of them believed to be directly associated with the Glassmakers themselves—creatures they either created or altered from others extant elsewhere.

The arachnons were the ones Helm had been most concerned about. Anything that could either rip you apart with synthodiamond claws or spit nitric acid at you if it couldn't reach you was worth taking more than passing note of.

"Yeah, well, I'll be wearing my armor," Helm said, "and I suggest everyone else does the same. Those of us who don't have any, we're going to have to fake something up. Meantime, that's just generalized trouble. Anybody could have that. Anybody sent you any postcards about what to expect?" He glanced at the stone.

Gabriel let out a long breath and replied, "Nothing specific, but Helm, this place is alive. It's like the place on Danwell but bigger. I can tell that from even here, and it's more dangerous. The Danwell site was an untended facility."

"Opinion: could have fooled me," Delde Sota said.

"The machines were somewhat alive, as we reckon things," Gabriel said, "but there was no one there to tend them, no caretakers. This place has those—the stone can tell—and we're going to have to deal with them."

"Will not the stone make that road open to you?" Grawl asked. "What use giving it to you, otherwise?"

"I don't know," Gabriel said. "It worked that way at Danwell." He glanced at Angela. "No telling if it's going to do any such thing here."

She gave him a look.

"Does the stone give any indication of exactly what those caretakers are?" Enda asked.

"If it does," Gabriel said, "it doesn't know how to tell me." Or, he thought, it's refusing to. He shook his head. "I may have to improvise when we get there. Meantime, the best we can do is arm ourselves sensibly, go in carefully, and have the ships handy so we can make a quick getaway if we have to." He looked over at Delde Sota. "One thing, though: the werewisps. I don't think the weather here gets quite as bad as it does on High Mojave, but the nights are still going to get very cold. Are they going to get cold enough to bring the werewisps out in strength? Those things could suck all the power out of a ship in a hurry."

"Assessment: even one or two are strength enough for me," Delde Sota said. "Initial response: borderline situation, as planet is on inward swing, approaching perihelion four months twenty-nine days approximately. Orbital 'spring' indicates nighttime temperatures plus-minus negative thirty degrees C, but no colder."

Helm shivered. "Remind me to get out the woolies."

Grawl looked at him. "What is a 'woolie'?"

"They're in the Awful Cabin, I bet," Angela said.

Helm threw her a look. "As a matter of fact—"

"Ahem," said Delde Sota. "Assessment continues. Temperature may be rather milder in central areas, but worst-case suggests no lower than negative thirty. More realistic suggestion negative fifteen degrees C."

"You won't even notice," Angela said to Grawl.

"I would prefer not to spend nights on the planet surface anyway," Enda said, "if that can be avoided."

"Well, let's see how it goes," Helm said. "No use tying ourselves into arrangements that may seem unnecessary. If the temperature starts dropping suddenly, though . . . we're out of there."

"No problem with that," Gabriel said. "Tomorrow morning?"

"Sounds good. After we find unbearable amounts of the unknown riches of the ages, we can come back and do the town again."

It seemed like a good plan. They finished their dinner and paid the bill, then walked back along the cold, quiet, narrow streets to the port parking area. Charlotte was more a town than a planetary capital, home to no more than fifteen thousand souls, and "downtown" was no more than a square mile of shops, retailers and restaurants—almost all of which had "Ngongwe" somewhere in their names. It was not very long before they came to a place low in a small dip in the local landscape of gentle hills. Here nestled an area

of lights, service buildings, and landing lights now down to
half-illumination for the evening.

Gabriel was strolling along looking at the lights and
noticed Angela walking along beside him, giving him a
thoughtful look. "Mmm?" he said.

"Was that an apology back there?" she said very quietly.

Gabriel thought about that and then said, "maybe."

She smiled slightly. "Well, then this might have been
one too."

They nodded at one another in agreement.

"I was worried is all," Angela said.

"Oh?" Gabriel said. "I thought it was mostly Grawl who
was worried."

"Absolutely," said Angela. "In fact, in the future I'll let
her do all my worrying for me." She glanced up ahead of
them where Grawl and Helm were walking side by side and
discussing the virtues and vices of flechettes.

"Seems wise," Gabriel said. "She's built for it."

"Seriously—"

"Don't mention it," Gabriel interrupted. "You had your
reasons. Can't blame you for that."

"Even the part about your tiny brain?" Her voice
sounded smaller.

"I haven't had it weighed recently," Gabriel said.
"There might be some truth in it, who knows?" He grinned
at her.

Angela nodded and wandered along to gradually catch
up with Grawl. Gabriel went after, his hands deep in his
coat pockets, fingering the stone.

Halfway down that dark road, a little ahead of Gabriel,
Delde Sota suddenly stopped and looked up into the night,
which was cold, but not yet seriously so, now no more than
negative ten C or so.

"What?" Gabriel asked, looking up, and then saw what
she saw.

Stretched right across the starry sky was a huge black
splotch. Only a very few stars were sprinkled across it,

compared with the more normal starfield scattered across the rest of the heavens.

"Identification: the Great Dark," Delde Sota replied.

"The galactic rift, isn't it?" Gabriel said.

Delde Sota nodded, and together they stood for a moment while the others walked on.

"It calls," Delde Sota said.

Gabriel looked at her in slight surprise. It was not often that she broke into sheerly human speech or forgot her initial modifier, and she never did so by accident.

"Yes," Gabriel said. "It does."

The more he looked up into that darkness, the more true he found the statement. He was briefly transfixed, and the stone in his pocket, which he had been turning over habitually in his fingers, reacted—not in the usual way, but by going cool, then cooler, and finally actually cold.

Gone, something inside him said, looking up at that great darkness. In his head, his point of view swung bizarrely so that he was not looking up into the sky but sideways or down over the edge of a great chasm, a huge gap in things. It was more than a merely physical emptiness. It seemed more the symbol of a greater one, a lack, a loss, a defeat. *Long ago,* said that silent presence in his head, somehow sad, and that sorrow awakened and stung briefly. *Long gone . . .*

Then the world resumed its rightful position, and Gabriel was standing on the ground again, not clinging like a fly on a wall to a precarious foothold with millennia of darkness lying beneath him, waiting for him to fall in silently and be lost. A long way down, said the human side of him, trying to make light of the image or impression he had just received. Irremediable loss, ages old. Something had happened, something that had not worked. Defeat, retreat, an ending . . . and the answer or solution or end of it all, far away into that seemingly bottomless darkness, far away on the other side of the night that never ends. . . .

"What're you two looking at?" Helm's shout came back.

Gabriel glanced over at Delde Sota, who gazed back, uncommunicative for the moment, and that, too, was strange for her. For a moment the soft amber light from the landing area reflected in her eyes, making her seem strange and otherworldly.

Helm came along and looked up at the sky. "What was it? A ship?"

Gabriel wondered how he could explain, and finally shrugged and said, "Look at it up there. No stars."

Helm glanced up and said, "Yeah, just the good clean darkness, something that our kind can't mess up." He elbowed Gabriel genially and went after the others.

Gabriel followed, wondering how true that was likely to remain.

Chapter Ten

H E WENT TO sleep more quickly than he had in a long time. It seemed to have something to do with being on a planet and the perceived stability of such a place. However, he got little rest, for immediately he began to dream—something else that had been happening all too frequently of late.

The dreams were innocuous at first, and even in the midst of them he began to relax. Stars made up the background at first, great panoramas of them, slowly changing—not the kind of thing you would normally see from a driveship, where the stars stayed the same, alternating with the dead black of drivespace.

Then his viewpoint drew back somewhat, and another shape got between Gabriel and the stars: a great darkness. It took him a while to realize that this was not some natural phenomenon like the darkness of the rift beyond Coulomb but something made, a ship—if ship was even the right word for it. There was what seemed a large base, under which huge structures had been built—the stardrives, Gabriel guessed. Above it all was a mighty complex of supports and some clear building material. Inside, all the lights twinkled, and Gabriel realized that he was looking at one of the great traveling city ships of the fraal. Inside that clear structure—a huge elongated dome—he could see what looked like buildings, tall spires with arched pathways between them. Tiny lights, small and faint as stars, glittered in them everywhere. A city of hundreds of thousands, all caught in glass like some rare plant, protected from the cold and dark outside . . .

In space there should have been no sound, and there was none, but he heard it nonetheless, the soft buzzing susurrus of many minds—thousands of them, tens of thousands— passing by in this empty place in the night. Fraal, he thought, coming from where? Going where?

Away, he realized, away from humanity and the human worlds, leaving it all behind and heading out into the darkness to try to find their homeworld. Strange that any species should be able to travel so far and for so long that it could no longer remember for sure where it came from. Many of those minds looked into the darkness and inwardly cried, *How long must we travel? How may we ever we come home when we have lost the way? Where is home? Are we the ones who left, or have we become so different that there is no home for us any more?*

We have wandered too long. We are not what we were. Take us back!

But one voice among the many cried out, *No! I will not be what we were. I cannot be what is gone and well gone, and I would not have the rest of us be so, either. We must be what these present times allow us to be, what our own selves make us.*

An image of some great meeting, under that domed sky. The fraal made no attempt to light that sky to look like day under some atmosphere, under some sun. The oldest night shone down through the dome, and outside it the slow stars went by. Here that single voice had been lifted and was heard without much concern by the others gathered in their thousands and tens of thousands. They had heard her voice before, and nothing had come of it.

You may go your way, if you feel so, the answer came in chorus, the many agreeing, all speaking together in the favorite way of fraal, almost in song. *Many others have done so, gone the way you wish. You will be happy among those others, the humans and their like, but when you have been there a while, young as you are, having lived among them and learned their ways, will you be fraal any more?*

Fear stirred inside her, but she said to them regardless, *I would sooner not be fraal than I would go through this life always saying,* This is not what I am looking for, *or* That is not what we once had! *None of us have ever lived in this ancient past we seek so fruitlessly, and it keeps us from living here and now the only lives we have!*

They laughed at her. It was not unkindly laughter, but it was infuriating, and Gabriel had heard its like before: from his father occasionally, or from others who knew that eventually you would get over this craziness of yours, that eventually you would see reason and come around to their way of thinking. It was the kind of laughter that made you, perhaps irrationally, turn your back on what you had and strike out into the darkness, though you shook with fear as you did it.

She faced them down, that great assembly that she had called, as any one fraal may. The single voice, though valued among fraal, was also feared as something that might be used as a weapon. Safe speech, among the fraal, lay in numbers, and "the lone voice in the dark" was how they characterized madness.

You, she cried, *you all have heard the voice whose words I speak now, the one that does not look back with joy on the old world but fears it and what it will make of us if we return. Does an adult climb back into its cradle or the sling in which its mother carried it? Is that the best thing to do with the rest of our lives? The uneasy dreams that make us all stir and cry out once or twice in a life are there for a purpose. They warn us of what happens if we succeed in returning to our childhood. It was in search of adulthood as a species that we went out into the night. Will we reject it now, when it is just beginning to come within our grasp?*

The violences and strifes of the humans and the weren, the sesheyans and the t'sa and all the others, said the chief of the voices that strove against her, *these are nothing to do with us. Their passions are not ours. Their fears, their hatreds are not ours. By drawing too close to them, by*

*remaining among them and sharing in their wars and
migrations and seeking after power, we endanger ourselves.*

Is life merely about being safe, then? she cried. *It was
not for safety that we undertook this long journey, but for
difficulty, heroism, pain, and passing through pain into triumph, for courage, danger and deliverance from danger!
All of them seek these same things, though the details may
vary. They hunt truth and justice as we do. They seek meaning, and where they do not find it, they seek to make it and
so become godlike, for meaning, like matter, is made out of
nothing! If you will leave them now to their fates, having
judged them too dangerous, too untidy, then when the equal
and opposite reaction occurs, and the universe judges you
in your turn, you will be right to be afraid! No other voice
will speak for you then. No one will say,* Evil beset me, and
you did not stand by idle but were our help. We were
trapped, and you helped us find a way out. We were alone
and hungry, and you fed us and bore us company!

It is easy, said several of the chief voices together then, *to
speak ancient sentiments in meeting and seem bold and com-
passionate, but it is harder to enact them without consensus.
You have had none before, and you have none now. Perhaps
it is time that there should be an end to your incitements.*

She was silent then for several breaths. All that great
assembly grew silent as well to see whether she would join
her voice to theirs again.

Finally she spoke. *We shall see how easy it is,* she said,
*to act instead of merely speaking, and to act by commission
instead of omission. You shall see me no more. You may
hear of me and may speak of me in chorus if you like, but
at the last, each of you will have to think of me alone and
hear me, alone, in your minds. Will you dare?*

She left them.

Astonished, they watched her go. She took with her, as
was her right, one seed from the city's gardens. No one
understood why she took that particular one, the slowest
growing plant of all, the least likely to come to flower

away from the conditions for which it was designed. Some saw it as a challenge, as her words had been, and they were glad to see her go. All around her, afterward, the silence fell, the silence that she had been trying to break ever since, with what success they would never know.

In the dream, Gabriel could hear the chorus of fraal voices raised to drown her and her memory out. He could see the little island of light and minds and voices drift away into the darkness, hunting an old dream . . .

. . . and that was when it began to shift. The voices all changed, grew ragged around the edges, and the light and the colors died, and that black blotch where there were no stars started slowly to creep across the sky, eating the stars that were there, blotting them out. The dream started to become nightmare as Gabriel started to feel, much too clearly, the many forms that nightmare was now learning to take. The writhing, stroking, strangling curl of the creatures living inside those like Major Norrik, and the acid pain and fury trapped inside the bioengineered skin of the kroath. Other anguishes, some that cut and some that burned, but all together, all working for the one cause now, not to conjoin voices, but to blot out and strangle all voices that were not theirs. A terrible low roar of hating mind out of the night, and the darkness ate all the stars, and as the last star went out, it screamed—

* * * * *

Gabriel jerked upright in bed, sweating. The stone, across from him in its customary place on the shelf, was glowing softly, pulsing in time with his heart.

Gabriel wiped his head and grabbed the stone as if it was some kind of anchor or lifeline. It was somehow cause to all these effects. He was terrified of it, but avoiding the fear would get him nowhere now. He waited until his breathing calmed and the stone's pulsing slowed, and then he lay down again, but it was a long while before he could get to sleep. He did finally manage it; and he dreamed again, but this time he was less frightened to see the darkness come creeping against the stars. In the dream, he stood watching and said, irrationally, *Now we begin to be warned against you. Now we are prepared. Come do your worst.*

Silent, the dark tide washed over him, but this time Gabriel laughed.

Chapter Eleven

THE NEXT MORNING Gabriel was the first one up. He got dressed in a slightly heavier than usual singlesuit and boots and made chai, drinking it black. Helm called from *Longshot* to discuss a schedule for the day's flying, and then Angela called to see if Gabriel wanted anything from the provisioners in town. They were assembling a shopping list when he heard the door open down the hallway and saw Enda in one of her long silky morning robes with all her long silver hair down her back come out to see about some chai herself.

The shopping list took a few more minutes, and Gabriel did not rush Angela. When Grawl's roars of "Hurry up!" from behind her finally encouraged her to finish, Gabriel got up from his seat at the dining table and went across to the galley for more chai. Enda slipped away as he came out, but by her door, she paused and looked at him.

Gabriel was still very uncertain about the protocol for these things. Finally, he simply said, "I had a dream last night."

"So did I," Enda said. She looked abashed and distressed. "It is one I have not had for a long time. I am sorry to have troubled you with it."

Gabriel shook his head. "I'm sorrier to have seen it."

She sighed. "Well, I was angry at first. We all have our privacies, and that was mine, but then I realized that it was not your fault. It comes, perhaps, from sleeping on a planet again. The mind relaxes, lets barriers slip. I would have told you eventually anyway, and—" She broke off. "Well . . ."

Gabriel shook his head. " 'They asked me to leave,' you said. You didn't tell me that it was a *City Administrator* that they asked to leave!"

She sipped at her chai and made a face. "Gabriel, how in the name of physics can this still be so hot after you made it such a while ago? You missed your career. You should have been an engineer of some kind. The heavens only know how far a starfall would take us now, the way you bend the rules."

He sat down with his cup. "I'm not going to bother you about this," Gabriel said. "I'm sorry I trespassed. I wouldn't have known how to stop, though. I get into one of these and it just sort of carries me along."

"Never try to direct vision," Enda said. "If you do so, it stops being a vision and starts being about control. There is enough of that about."

She sat down and pulled her hair back, starting to braid it. "A long life," she said softly, "but still that moment comes back to haunt me, every now and then."

"How old were you?" Gabriel said.

Enda sighed, pulling the braid around to watch what she was doing. "Just past a hundred, a youngster telling my elders what to do. I had worked my way up to the posts just below that position, and the council of elders and speakers elected me to the administration. They merely got what they had asked for."

"So did you, though," Gabriel said, and the suddenness with which this thought occurred to him surprised him.

She looked at him a little sharply, then leaned back with that small curl of rueful smile that he had seen often enough before. "To have the gauntlet thrown down before me, to be forced to take up the challenge, yes, perhaps I did. So I went out into the night and started to become someone else, a Builder rather than a Wanderer. The city went on without me, as it knew well how to do, being thousands of years older than I, but it caused talk. No fraal quite so high in Wanderer society had defected before or has done since. As for me, I only spoke what others were thinking but mostly had not yet dared to do. It is so often thus with the universe. A hundred people think something, and as the pressure of the thought grows, one of them, standing at a convenient moment in space and time, suddenly utters it. Months later, years maybe, it is as if everyone had the same idea at once, and no one can remember that first voice—except the one who stood up and said it and then afterward thinks, 'What made me do *that?*' for the next two hundred years."

"Well," Gabriel said, "anyway, I'll try not to do that again."

"Seriously, Gabriel," Enda said, "do not push your vision around. It has reasons for where it wants to go."

He got up. Whatever her chai might be like, his was now cold, and he needed a refill. "All right," he said, "but now I see that you do, too."

She glanced at him as she finished her braiding, uncertain what he meant.

" 'We were trapped, and you helped us find a way out,' " Gabriel said quietly, his back to her: " 'We were alone and hungry, and you fed us and bore us company.' " He reached up for the sugar bowl.

Enda chuckled and said, "Yes, well, an old sentiment, much quoted, though sometimes the universe will quote you back at yourself with particular force. So what if it did, one day when I was on Phorcys and heard a story of a young Concord Marine who, it seemed, had a great deal more hidden in his depths? What if it did occur to me that such 'quotations' are never without purpose and that sometimes timing is crucial? It became obvious to me that I had been purposely put in your path to be of help to you. Do not ask me how. I am as hazy on the details as anyone else might be, but if one who claims to listen to the universe as a lifeguide starts to do so only on certain occasions or when it is convenient, things will not turn out well." She drank her chai. "If I have enjoyed myself since, well, you cannot blame me for *that*. Only the powers of evil claim that doing good is boring."

"Gabriel," Helm's voice suddenly came over comms, "are you guys ready yet? We're hot to trot over here. The doctor wants to go sightseeing."

Gabriel grinned and said, "Ten minutes." He started finishing his chai. Enda finished her braiding and slipped into the corridor, making for her room.

"Enda . . ." Gabriel said. She looked at him. "Even if you did have fun, thanks anyway."

She bowed to him, a deeper bow than he had ever seen her use to anyone, and then she went off to get dressed.

* * * * *

About half an hour later they were in the air, heading in the general direction of Ohmel's north pole. They had left a sketchy flight plan with the port authorities, because no matter how secret you're trying to be, it's never wise to head off into mostly unknown territory without leaving at least the news that you've gone. Helm would have preferred to keep it all secret, but Gabriel refused. All of Void-Corp could have been hot on his trail, and he still would have insisted on what Helm jovially started referring to as "the suicide note." He did, however, let the port authorities think that the party was only going up to see the known, secured site.

"As for that," Helm had said, "why do we have to wander all over the landscape in atmosphere? I could be up in orbit until you find what you need, and then come down again."

"Helm, I can't get a decent fix from up high. I need to be down low for any kind of precision."

"You should get a better stone. Somebody stuck you with the monkey model."

Gabriel could think of no immediate response to this, and Helm had gone off chuckling.

Now that they were actually in the air, Gabriel was paying less attention to Helm's commentary on the landscape and more to the stone. Since they took to the air it had been warming steadily in his hands, and Gabriel was leaving the actual piloting to Enda at the moment. The warmth was not unbearable, but the stone was beginning to generate a peculiar buzz, a vibration that Gabriel was not entirely sure wasn't in his own mind or muscles. He would have liked to check this with Enda, but on no account would she touch the stone, and she seemed at the moment not even to like to look at it.

As they headed north over the red-brown terrain, Gabriel's mind kept harking back to last night's experience—he wasn't entirely sure it was wise to call these things "dreams"—and thinking there was more to Enda's departure from her people than merely the old disagreement between Wanderers and Builders. Maybe, as she had said, she had merely articulated something that many fraal had been feeling, yet in her case, as Gabriel remembered it from her "tone of mind" in the dream, something else had been going on inside her as well. She had a sense of something wrong with the way her people had been conducting their lives, a fatal flaw slowly expressing itself. Enda still had no idea what that flaw might be, though plainly the search for it had driven her for the first part of her life. Now Gabriel thought Enda suspected that the force or presence that had looked into her soul through the edanwe child had seen something of what she felt was wrong and could not understand. If it understood, it was not revealing what it knew.

She might be right about the connection between us, Gabriel thought, and it having something to do with our judgment on Danwell, but I really don't want to push her on this.

He glanced over at her. Enda was looking through the side viewport as she flew, gazing down at the ground. "The very beginnings of summer," she said to Gabriel. "Can you see it? Just the faintest haze of violet and blue over things—lichens and the simplest of the plants waking up. In a month this place will be ablaze with color as everything awakens and makes use of the water and the air while they are available." She glanced at him. "How is our direction?"

"We're all right," said Gabriel. "North still."

They went on northward in formation with *Longshot* and *Lalique*. Only twice did they pass any settlements. This came as no surprise, for Ohmel was still very sparsely settled—maybe forty thousand people on the whole planet, and fifteen thousand of those were in Charlotte. The rest were divided among thirty or forty hamlets, villages, or towns, little domed communities all of them, for there was no use building a place to live that was unliveable for half the year. In fall and winter when the atmosphere froze and became snow, and water was just another kind of stone, all human and other life retreated into the domes and tended the underground hydroponics farms and greenhouses that kept everyone alive.

The secured site was at a place called Boxcar, which was about thirty degrees south of Ohmel's arctic circle. It was cold enough that they would all probably add a layer or two under their coats, and one of those layers would be armor. While Boxcar had long since been scoured by the archaeologists and declared empty of the dangers associated with the Glassmakers or any of the other Precursor races, Gabriel preferred to be cautious.

If things went well, shortly after that they would come to the unsecured site, and that would be another matter entirely. The Ohmel government, insofar as it paid attention to such matters, did not encourage citizens or visitors to explore unsecured sites. It made sure that such access was expensive and difficult for anyone who didn't own a long range ship or other transport that would make access possible. Otherwise, it was assumed that you might do as you pleased, and that the reputation of the sites would help them to police themselves.

There were numerous cases every year, both on Ohmel and on High Mojave, the other best-known home of Glassmaker sites, of explorers going out and not coming back again. Some of these, admittedly, were half-witted tourists who insisted on making their way out to the sites, and their failure to return was variously considered by the locals as merely the universe "culling the herd." There were plenty of ways to come to grief on Ohmel that did not involve anything unusual: the terrain, the fierce weather—during the cold season, the most volatile gases had a tendency to freeze and condense out of the air, a particularly emphatic kind of snow—and what was left of Ohmel's biosphere could also be deadly enough for the unprepared or incautious. At the same time, there were explorers who went out well-equipped, well-prepared, people expert in their fields, steady, sensible old hands, who also did not come back. About those deaths, the rumors were rampant.

Some of the rumors were plainly ghost stories, products of an information vacuum. Others were possible enough, if unsubstantiated. The Glassmakers had dabbled in the creation of sentient and semisentient life with varying levels of success. Some of their creations, like the werewisp, had been possibly too successful. They had no natural enemies and roamed the empty places in the long nights, looking for energy to drain. Explorers, typically (and necessarily) well supplied with powered equipment to hold off the terrible cold and do their other work, might as well have stood out in the frigid darkness and banged dinner gongs. Then there were other lifeforms, like the arachnons, less scattershot in their tactics but far more deadly and much more specifically associated with the old Glassmaker sites. They were guardians, some said. Others said they were simply engineered creatures that had lost their programming. In either case, they could be deadly. Numerous people had gone out to study them and had sent no data back nor come back themselves.

Gabriel had no desire to become one of these. Even though Boxcar was supposed to be safe, he would be wearing his armor, and everyone else would too.

"How close are we?" he asked Helm over comms.

"About fifty kilometers," Helm said. "Ten minutes at this speed."

Gabriel sat with the stone in his hands and felt the "buzzing" in it increase. It was in a tiny way like the experience of hearing all those fraal minds had been in the dream, but somehow this was more like hearing a recording of the minds. A sense of immediacy was missing, though the other content and "meaning" was still there. Now if only I could figure out exactly what the content meant . . .

"Coming up on it now," Helm said after a few minutes.

Enda, piloting, swooped down lower and dropped much of her speed. The others came in on either side, matching Enda's reduced acceleration. They all looked down.

There was very little there. Gabriel had read some time back, while investigating Glassmaker matters, that the ruins on Ohmel had suffered badly and were not nearly as spectacular as those on High Mojave. "Ruins" was a poor word for the buildings left on High Mojave. Delicate spires and domes of a glasslike material, they were so tough that nothing could break them. Even a subsidence of land under one of the more spectacular sites had done nothing but spill the glittering minarets on the ground below the cliff where they had stood, and now they lay there undamaged but drastically relocated.

Here, though, little or none of the original glasswork remained above ground. There was apparently some of it under the surface still, but the archaeologists, having found nothing remarkable enough to get their patron organizations to fund them any further, had left it all mostly buried. As their ships circled the site in the advancing morning, Gabriel could just make out the occasional buried glint of "glass," low shapes of opaque white or pale translucent green in the sun.

Enda shook her head, looking down on the site as she brought the ship around. "Think of how old that is," she said. "How many millions of years . . ."

"Lots," Gabriel said and concentrated on the stone. He was rather shocked to find that the buzzing was dying off slightly.

"Where do you want us to land, Gabe?" Helm said.

Gabriel thought about that for a moment. "I don't."

"What?"

"This isn't it," Gabriel said, clenching the stone in one fist and trying to maximize the contact. "The stone's calming down. Swing north again and see what we get."

They turned north and headed slowly away from the Boxcar ruins. Gabriel closed his eyes.

Stronger, yes. The buzz was increasing. A little more to the left . . .

"A little farther to the west," Gabriel said.

Enda angled *Sunshine* a little that way. The "signal" got stronger.

"Whatever it is that the stone's been homing on," Gabriel said, "it's not that. That site's dead."

"So we're going unsecured right away?" Helm said. "Joy."

"Oh, come on, Helm," Gabriel said. "You know you love it. Think of all the weapons we can bring along with us."

"Think how little use they're going to be," Helm muttered, "against arachnons, for example."

"I thought you said you were ready for anything, Helm," said Enda, chuckling softly. "What a bastion of caution and conservatism you become at times like this."

"Mmf," Helm said.

They made their way northward. Gabriel stopped looking at the scenery, which at this point was pretty much red-brown rocks, outcroppings, and canyons. Instead he concentrated on the output he was getting from the stone.

"We're pretty close," he said, with some surprise. "In fact, we're very close."

"Query: how *very* 'very'?" Delde Sota asked.

"I almost understood that," said Angela from *Lalique*.

"Me, too," Gabriel answered. "Delde Sota, I'd say no more than two or three kilometers. Helm, don't overshoot it. Slow down!"

Enda slowed *Sunshine* still more. "Straight on?" she asked.

Gabriel tried to feel what the stone was trying to show him. "A little more to the west," he said.

"A canyon here, Gabe," Helm said, watching him from the center display.

"Right," Gabriel said. "Drop down a bit."

"Into it?"

"Yeah."

"How far?"

"I'll tell you."

Gabriel cupped the stone in his hands and tried to shut everything else out. Inside his mind he could just faintly see a kind of glow, like the glow from the stone, growing slowly stronger.

"Down more," Gabriel said as he watched that faint pearly light. It was hard to keep track of exactly what it was doing. The effect was like the light inside your own eyelids when you've been looking at the sun—very vague and diffuse.

"This is quite a deep canyon, Gabriel," Enda said. "I am not sure where we will find a place to land, except at the bottom."

"That might have to be it," Gabriel muttered. "Farther down."

Down the three ships dropped on their system drives, very gently, nearly hovering. Gabriel felt the glow growing stronger and then suddenly paling off again. "No," he said. "Stop and back up a little."

Enda coaxed the ship up again. Gabriel was more aware of this by the slight inroads he now had into her mind than by any feeling of the ship's movement. "Right here," he said.

"Gabe," said Helm's voice, "that's pretty nearly a sheer cliff face. A few little skinny ledges on it are about wide enough to take one of you. I might have trouble, and nowhere to land close by but a ledge about ten meters up. I wouldn't be sanguine about the ships' ability to stay there for long without the whole thing falling out from under them."

Gabriel opened his eyes and looked at the cliff face. It was striated beautifully in cream, brown, and red. It was very weathered, and with very few exceptions—mostly the little ledges Helm had mentioned—it was as vertical as anyone could hope. There was no sign of anything in the neighborhood even remotely glassy. There were, however, some deep cracks, wide enough for even Grawl to get through.

"The whole thing must be buried," Gabriel said. "Helm, tell me you have a grav belt or two in the Awful Room."

"I had one once, but I never used the damned thing. Sold it off. *Now* I wish I hadn't!"

"Too late. I guess we'll have to climb. What about ledges underneath us?"

"There's a couple," Helm said. He paused a moment then said, "Follow me."

About another twenty meters down were two separate parts of a big outcropping with room enough for the three ships. "I wouldn't go out late at night to take a leak," Helm said as he landed, and the others came down on either side of him.

Gabriel could see his point. *Longshot* was sitting right by the edge of the outcropping, and there was a thirty-meter drop directly beside her.

"Surely if you did that," Grawl said, "it would freeze in midair."

"For a poet," Helm said, "you can sure be pragmatic sometimes."

"What's the temperature now?" Gabriel asked.

"About three degrees C," replied Helm. "Heat getting

trapped down here a little, seems like. It might stay warmer at nights, too."

"Or it might get colder," Angela said. "You'll want to keep an eye on that."

Gabriel looked out the front viewports at the canyon wall. The stone twinged and sizzled in his hand.

"This is it," he said. "Let's get out there and look around."

* * * * *

It took perhaps half an hour for everyone else to get kitted out—cold weather gear, breathers, armor, weapons. They met at the edge of the outcropping and looked over the terrain.

It was a very confined, restricted kind of place. The canyon walls seemed almost to lean in over the viewer, a claustrophobic and unsettling effect. Beyond that, there was nothing overtly threatening about the place. Chilly wind whined down the canyon, making it seem more like negative ten C or so. Here and there a pebble tinkled downslope when someone put his foot down incautiously. There was no other sound.

Helm was looking down from the outcropping. "Actually," he said, "this isn't too bad. We climb down there then climb up the far side."

"One of us could always hover and drop the others on one of those little ledges," said Angela.

Helm snorted genially. "Not to run down your piloting, Ange, but you want to try that with that big barge of yours here? In this wind? You're braver than me. Then the one doing the flying gets to stay behind."

"No chance," Angela said hastily.

Gabriel looked up at the cliff on the far side. "It's a little less vertical than it looks," Gabriel said, "and it looks like there's plenty of handholds."

Helm grunted. "Good thing," he said. "Well, I have

climbing gear and a couple of harnesses. We can go up two at a time."

"Where exactly are we going?" asked Grawl.

Gabriel was still gazing at the cliff face. "See that big crack there," he said, "where it looks like the strata shifted? That's big enough for us to squeeze through."

"Better hope there's something on the far side," Helm said.

"Oh, there's something there all right," Gabriel said. "If we can only get at it. . . ."

Helm went to fetch the climbing gear. These, too, Gabriel realized, had been packed away in the Awful Cabin, and once more he became determined to find time to go through that place from top to bottom and see what else Helm might have stuffed in there.

It took another twenty minutes or so to get the first two, Angela and Enda, into the harnesses. Enda was quickest. "I have used these before," she said as she was buckled into the harness.

Helm looked at her curiously. "Didn't know you went in for climbing."

"I do not," Enda replied, "but in the Wanderers' cities, there is so much to be serviced, and not all of it can be handled by machines."

Gabriel laughed inwardly at the image of Enda as a window washer, but he remembered that she had worked her way up through a lot of jobs to city manager. Maybe it's like hotel work. They say the best way to become a manager is to learn all the jobs from the bottom up.

"All right," Helm said. "You're on belay now. Down you go."

Down the two of them went, alternately clinging to handholds and footholds or spinning like spiders briefly when no holds were available. At the bottom, Enda slipped out of the harness and called up to Helm, "It will not be hard coming up. The cliff does not shelve significantly, and there is plenty of support for an upward climb."

"Right," Helm said. He and Grawl started pulling the harnesses up, and Grawl finished making fast to *Lalique*'s skids the rope that would remain in place for access when they climbed back up again. Helm came over to check the knots, while Gabriel and Grawl harnessed themselves.

"Looking thoughtful," Gabriel said to Grawl as she gazed across the way at the cavern wall.

"I am making notes," Grawl said. "This will make a fine song some day."

"Assuming we find something."

"We have already found something," Grawl said, "or so you say."

Gabriel nodded. "That's not it, though."

Grawl glanced at him, an odd expression. "Your meaning is dark to me."

He tried not to smile, mostly because he could feel the tension in her gut and recognized it. He had it, too. "You don't like heights either."

Grawl bared her fangs . . . then let the look relax into a smile. Gabriel would not have thought it was possible for a weren to look sheepish.

"I did not care to mention," she said. "It makes poor reading in the tales later."

"I wouldn't have mentioned it either," Gabriel said, "but if I throw up on the way down, I just wanted you to know that it's nothing personal."

"Spew," Grawl said, "is normally about as personal as it is possible to get. Nonetheless, warrior, I take your meaning."

Together they went on belay and made their way down. Gabriel was much relieved by knowing Helm and Delde Sota were up there keeping an eye on the ropes, but the tension remained, and he concentrated on controlling his stomach as he descended. It was no more than a minute or so before he was on the rocks and sand and gravel at the bottom of the canyon, shrugging out of the harness and feeling profound relief. Climbing would not be as bad as descending, but he still wished he could do without it entirely. The thought of standing on that narrow ledge across the way was making his stomach flipflop again.

While he was waiting for Helm and Delde Sota to come down, Gabriel took out the stone and walked a little way up the canyon, trying to see if he could find any other indication of a way in. In his hand, even through gloves, he could feel the stone buzzing and stinging in a generalized kind of way.

The going was difficult, strewn with boulders and jagged rocks of every kind, some rounded as if water had passed there, and some sharp, the cracked remnants of rockfall. Gabriel picked his footing carefully, tried to keep his attention on the stone—

It stung him. At the same moment he tripped and whacked his shin against the sharp edge of a fallen shelf of stone in front of him.

"*Ow,* ow, ow, ow, ow," Gabriel said, in too much pain for the moment to even swear properly. When he had recovered a little, he looked at the stone in his hand. It was pulsing softly, the light hard to see in the bright day here. He looked around, trying to make out what it might have been reacting to.

Off to his right on the far side of the canyon, a glint of light reflected off something polished. Not stone.

Glass?

"Gabriel," Helm shouted at him, the sound thin in the frigid air, "come on!"

"No," he yelled back, "over here!"

Gabriel made his way over to the bright spot through the boulder-tumble and the cracked rocks, and finally came up to it. It was about three meters above the lowest level of the canyon and barely visible, just a ragged, partially obscured patch of glassy stuff about a meter across, more or less the shape of an oval laid on its side and pale green in color. It was perfectly smooth and unscratched, like a mirror.

The others came along. Helm, fully armored and looking like an aggressive mobile gun rack, brought up the rear. The big gun in his hands was a Ric ZI stutter cannon, and Gabriel felt much better and also started wondering where he had been keeping *that* one.

"Look at this," Gabriel said.

They gathered around the patch of glass. Those tall enough to reach it touched it.

"That's something," Helm muttered, "but how did *that* get inside all *this?*"

Delde Sota looked around her. "Analysis: all sedimentary," she said. "Original stone. Not later accretion."

"You mean," Angela said, "that someone built this facility here, and then the seas rose and deposited all this silt here, and the silt settled out into these layers and turned to stone, and then the sea dried up, and all this got carved away over time. . . ?"

"Open-ended assessment: fifty or sixty million years total, give or take a million," Delde Sota replied.

They all were quiet for a moment or so, thinking about that. "Well," Angela said at last, "can we get in through this?"

"No telling," Gabriel said. "This might be just a wall. I remember them having to shock the glass at High Mojave, trying to make it flow or create an opening. Sometimes it took them months to find the way in."

He stood up on a nearby boulder, took the stone in his hand, and laid it against the glass.

Nothing.

"Well, come on," he said irritably.

Nothing happened.

Gabriel closed his eyes, concentrated on the stone, thinking opening thoughts as hard as he could.

He opened his eyes again.

Nothing whatsoever had happened.

"Perhaps electricity would work better," Enda said, "since that was what they were using at High Mojave. . . ?"

"Or maybe . . ." Helm said. He started to sling the stutter rifle over his shoulder and go for the other piece of heavy armament he was carrying.

"No!" Gabriel shouted. The forcefulness of the objection surprised even him. Is the stone starting to get into the act now? he wondered.

"No," Gabriel said, as the others all looked at him. "I don't think that's it. Come on," he said, "let's look up and down the canyon at this level. We may find another piece that is an access."

"One we do not have to climb to," Grawl said enthusiastically.

They spent the rest of the morning and all that afternoon walking up and down the canyon, trying to find more glass or an access to the northern cliff, but there was none. Gabriel spent the second half of the afternoon simply sitting with the stone, trying to coax some more useful response out of it, but he had no luck. The canyon had fallen entirely into shadow when he finally looked up at Helm and Enda, who were coming back up the canyon toward him.

"Getting kind of late, Gabe," Helm said, looking around him. Above the canyon, twilight was beginning to fall, and the darkness would follow fast. Helm always wore a distrustful look at times like this, but with the evening drawing on, that look was now more distrustful than usual.

"Yeah," Gabriel said and looked down at the stone. "This thing isn't helping me much at the moment. Maybe we should call it a night."

Helm looked around. "I'll check the instrumentation when I go back in," he said, "but I don't think anything alive or mechanical has come near us all day, and I don't think anything's going to. Enda?"

She paused a moment then shrugged. "We may as well stay here," she said, "as leave and have to go through this whole operation again tomorrow. Additionally, I would dislike to attract too much attention to our goings and comings."

"Right," Helm said. "We can leave the cliff for tomorrow. Come on, folks, let's get ourselves back up to the ships and have some dinner."

* * * * *

Half an hour later, it was dark, and they were all inside *Lalique,* having dinner there—nothing fancy, just hot-packs shoved into the little galley oven. Everyone's appetites were sharp. Whether it was the cold, the exercise or the excitement that was responsible, they all ate twice what they normally would have, so that dinner took a good while. Some of them got sleepy afterward, out of all proportion to the exertion.

"Gonna go back and have my nap now," Helm said. "I'll take the late watch. Doctor?"

"Status: not weary at the moment," Delde Sota said. "Will stand this watch until 0200?"

"0300 would do better," Helm said. "Gabe, leave your comms on when you go back." He headed off, taking his various guns, and Delde Sota went after him.

"I will stand watch over on our side of things," Enda said. "There is no sleep in me tonight, I am afraid."

Gabriel nodded, for he knew why. He was all too able to hear how Enda heard the stone's buzzing as a tiny endless nagging noise, annoying like some little singing night insect singing a note specifically designed to drive you and no one else crazy.

He went back to *Lalique*'s galley and got himself another cup of chai, not wanting anything stronger tonight. Gabriel wanted all his senses undulled, though he wasn't sure what he hoped would happen.

Angela was cleaning up the dining area when he got back. "This is so frustrating," Gabriel said, sitting down on one of the sofas. "The whole thing was supposed to just pop open and spill its guts when I arrived."

She laughed at that, taking the last of the plates and bowls away. "Might be you have to go up that cliff, whether you want to or not," she said from the galley.

"Grawl won't thank you for that assessment."

"Probably she won't," Angela said. She came back in

and sat down on the lounger that was cattycorner to
Gabriel's. She looked at the wall display, which was showing a view of the canyon, centered on the "glass spot," and
augmented for IR and movement. Nothing was happening
out there. Starlight shone. The wind blew. Nothing more.

Angela looked at the uneventful darkness and blew out
an annoyed breath.

"You ought to get some sleep," Gabriel said.

"Hah," Angela said, "but so should you, if it comes to
that."

"No chance," Gabriel said. "Not in this situation."

"Me either," said Angela. "It's like getting shot at."

"Now when have you ever been shot at?" he said.

"Oh, it's happened once or twice," Angela said. "Mostly
I try to avoid it. It has unfortunate side effects, like causing
you to develop big holes in your body."

Gabriel's mind, however, was on another unfortunate
side effect that males sometimes experienced upon being
shot at, and from which he was also suffering at the
moment. Not that anyone had shot at him, but the excitement of being here on the planet in potentially dangerous
circumstances was now producing the same result. A good
meal and a slight rest, especially in the presence of Angela,
were all making it worse rather than better. He was
presently thinking hard about how he was going to stand up
without one particular embarrassing symptom of the side
effect showing. The singlesuit tended to rather unfortunately emphasize the presence of the symptom. Now if I
can just turn a little this way, Gabriel thought, and started
to get up.

Then he stopped himself. Why am I doing this? I don't
want to get up. I know perfectly well what I want, except I
must be nuts, and she'll kill me if I ask her.

"Something on your mind?" Angela asked.

"Uh—" Gabriel swallowed. "Now that you mention—"

"Yes," Angela said.

"Huh?"

"Me, too," Angela said with a knowing smile.

He looked at her.

"It affects me like that, too," she said, enunciating clearly, as if for someone who was hard of thinking. "For cripes sake," she added, "just this once . . . could it hurt?"

Put that way, Gabriel thought, she may have a point.

"Well?" she said softly.

He widened his eyes a little. She nodded once, waiting.

Gabriel very slowly pulled her close and kissed her very slowly. It was surprisingly easy. After a moment, he said so.

Angela looked at him in heavy-lidded amusement. "Did you think it was going to be hard?"

"I hope it is," Gabriel said.

Angela smacked him in the head, not very emphatically.

"I'm sorry," Gabriel said. "Earlier it would never have occurred to me. In fact, exactly the opposite."

He had an idea that he was possibly making an error. He remembered Hal, a long time ago now, saying, "Never admit to any woman that you would never have considered sleeping with her. This is a sure way to have someone wind up on charges for assault—her, not you. No jury in the military would convict either."

But Angela was decidedly un-military.

"Which just goes to show you," Angela said, reaching out, "that brains, too, can grow suddenly and without warning."

She turned out the light.

*　*　*　*　*

Some hours later, Gabriel slipped quietly back into *Sunshine*. His feelings were more than complex at the moment, especially since he knew that Enda would be sitting up keeping watch.

She simply looked at him from the pilot's couch and said, "Did you want some chai? I made an extra supply. In the pot."

He went back to get some. Normally he wouldn't have bothered this late at night, but he much doubted at the moment that mere chai would be able to do anything to keep him awake once he lay down again.

With his mug, he leaned over the free pilot's couch and looked out the front ports at the cliff on the other side of the canyon, into which a little starlight filtered. "If they wanted to hide that," Gabriel said, "I'd guess it worked."

Enda nodded. "Is everyone all right over there?" she said.

"More than all right," Gabriel said idly.

Enda gave him a sidelong look. "Grawl?"

"She was on watch when I left."

She nodded again and said, "A pleasant night."

"Yes, it was," Gabriel said and drank his chai.

"Gabriel."

He looked at her.

Enda was wearing one of those small demure smiles in which fraal specialize. "Perhaps you would do me a favor."

"Mmm?"

"I realize that you probably took this particular action out of consideration for me, but the next time by your favor . . . leave the stone *here*."

Gabriel stared at her . . . and then turned, very quickly, very quietly, and went to bed.

Grinning . . .

Chapter Twelve

IT WAS MORE of a doze than a sleep, and much later he had trouble remembering the details, but the dream itself was straightforward enough.

Eyes were looking at him.

At first this unnerved him, then Gabriel decided he had nothing to lose and looked back. *I have a right to be here,* he cried into the echoing darkness. *I'm the one who was sent. Give me what I came for!*

What would that be?

What exactly *am* I here for? He considered for a moment, then said, *My people are in trouble. There are forces coming from outside that mean to wipe us out. It's wrong to let that happen!*

A long silence, while the presence over there in the darkness considered that. It was not the one with which Gabriel had been communicating before, but it was possibly related to it somehow, but then probably all these Precursor races knew each other, he thought. I mean, a hundred million years ago, who else would they have had to talk to but each other?

He had a clear sense that this conversation was passing through some kind of a translator, that whatever was on the other side was stranger than he could possibly imagine, yet at the same time, he was related to it somehow, for the stone had been changing him. It, too, had been learning to perform this translation by being in his company for so long. Changing . . .

It suddenly occurred to Gabriel to be sorry for the stone. He had been complaining about the changes in *him* that it had been causing. Now the idea presented itself, not as a possibility but as a certainty, that it was changing too. A nature as unchanging as, well, as stone, was being forced to shift into a new one. For a purpose . . .

The change of viewpoint so staggered Gabriel that he hardly knew what to do or say for a moment. Finally he just kept quiet.

This has happened before, said whatever was on the other side of the translation.

This? Gabriel asked.

The ones from outside, said the one who had been listening. *The Externals. Their presence in this galaxy is nothing new.*

Well, that's a relief! Gabriel said. *Or I guess it is. So what did you do about them?*

We died, said the other.

Gabriel swallowed.

I'd like to avoid that if possible, he said after a moment. *I mean, in the short term.*

It may not be avoidable, said that voice sorrowfully, *in any term. Much depends on whether the new enemy is more powerful or wiser than the old one . . . and whether the new antagonists are capable of doing better than we did.*

Gabriel could see the point of that, but it didn't make him any less tense. He could see—or *feel*—all those eyes looking at him, a long unblinking regard, made worse by the sense that some of them had no eyelids to blink with anyway. No one had ever had anything but theories about what the Glassmakers or Precursors looked like. It was the merest guesswork that they were human-sized or human-shaped, all based upon the size of some doors that had been found in sites on High Mojave. There was something about those eyes that made Gabriel very uncertain about the theories, no matter how many university qualifications their propounders might possess.

This enemy is powerful enough, Gabriel said into the darkness, remembering the tremendous ships that had come slipping up out of drivespace just off Danwell. Nor did power mean just ships. He thought of the kroath, the terrible strength and savagery of them and of what their existence said about the creatures who willingly created them.

As for the rest of it, Gabriel said, *you will have to let us have the technology and see for yourself whether we will do better than you did. We cannot do worse.*

You can, said that old voice—or voices. *You can* fail *to die. You can survive to be their slaves, their creatures, without hope of ever being freed. Death would be preferable. At least they cannot reach you there. Should you succeed as we succeeded, there would at least be a chance for those who come after you—as we made one for you. . . .*

Then give us what we need to fight! Gabriel said. *Our present technology is behind theirs at the moment, and that's where the difference must be made.*

Assessment must be completed, said the voice.

All right, Gabriel said. *Go ahead. I'll wait.*

It has been in progress for some time, said whatever was listening. There was a choral quality to this presence Gabriel started to realize. Not just one voice but many, and an odd sense that some of it was here now and some in some other time. The past? The future? No telling.

Then let's get finished, Gabriel said.

All the eyes looked at him. There was a shifting, a rustling in the darkness.

* * * * *

Shifting, a rumbling through the fabric of things . . . the low, slow rumble, the sound of shifting stone . . .

Gabriel's eyes snapped open. All around him, *Sunshine* was shaking. Over comms from *Lalique* he heard Angela yell, "My *God!*"

Gabriel hurled himself out of bed, ran to the front viewports, looked out . . .

Outside, above the canyon, dawn was beginning. In

front of them, he saw the cliff sliding away. As Gabriel watched, he could see the stripes and layers of stone moving, shattering, sloughing away from something underneath them. Surely it was an illusion that the "something underneath" was actually shrugging them off, as a buried creature shrugs away the mud or silt that has settled over it since it came to rest . . . oh, fifty or sixty million years total, give or take a million . . .

The whole front of the cliff slipped away, gently and with little fuss, though a great deal of dust went up, and here and there some flake of stone under pressure snapped off and went flying through the air with great force, pinging into one or another of the ships. Over comms, Helm swore loudly at a deep impact mark left on *Longshot*'s hull, as if the ship had not already had more than enough micrometeorite strikes in its time to take the sheen off the factory finish. When the dust cleared, they were all standing in their ships and staring out at a canyon nearly filled with rubble almost up to the level of the little outcropping on which they were parked. When the light got better, they would be able to walk straight across to what was now a single unbroken wall of gleaming green glass.

"Gabriel, did you trigger something? A time lock?" Angela asked, looking a little unnerved.

"I don't know," Gabriel said. "Somehow I doubt it. Other things may have been involved." The conversation he had just finished, for example.

If it was in fact finished, Gabriel wondered. Somehow, I don't think so.

* * * * *

They waited until the sun was properly risen before suiting up and going outside. It was still shadowed in the canyon and would be until Coulomb got some more height. Slowly and with care, they made their way across the tumble of fallen and shattered rock until they came to the foot of the wall.

The top level of the canyon wall opposite still lay atop the "glass" wall, hinting at a structure that supported it and ran in. The wall itself towered up at least ten meters high in front of them, all perfect, seamless, and while not opaque, still far too thick to see though. Delde Sota ran her hands and her braid over the surface, shaking her head in wonder.

"Mensuration: perfectly flat within tolerance of point zero-zero-zero-zero-zero one millimeters," she said.

Helm, too, was running his hands over the material. "You think they ever built ships out of this?" he said. "They would have been somethin'."

"It's an interesting image," Gabriel said. He stood there with his hands on his hips, looking up at the wall.

"So what now?" Helm said. "You said they shocked their way in on High Mojave."

Gabriel stood there. "I wouldn't like to do that," he said. "There's always the possibility that someone here might get annoyed. Anyway, I've got this. I'm supposed to use it."

He had the stone in his hand. He moved up to the wall and stroked the stone along it.

Nothing.

"This may take a while," Gabriel said. "Maybe you should all sit down and make yourselves comfortable."

They did, and Gabriel for a while simply walked up and down that wall, touching the stone to one spot, then another, seeing what he felt. The stone showed nothing at all visually, no glow or pulse. After a while he stopped looking at it and simply walked along with the stone against the wall, his other hand laid against the glass a little ahead of it, eyes closed, trying to see what he could feel. That slight buzz or sting from the stone was still there, a constant low-level sensation like a tremor in the muscles. Slowly, though, Gabriel began to feel a variation. A slight increase in the "buzz" down toward the eastern end of the wall, a slight paling or brightening of a faint glow in his mind.

He followed it down, moving slowly, watching that glow behind his eyelids for any increase. It was a very subtle, faint effect, liable to be lost right away if he opened his eyes for any reason. It was maddening in its way. The stone had been shouting at him all this while, and now he was required to hear it whisper.

Gabriel grinned suddenly at that, realizing what was going on. Testing . . . he had been being tested for a long while now, and this was just another test.

He leaned against the glass and did his best to let his mind go empty and dark. This was not normally the kind of thing a young man Gabriel's age was good at, but hours in drivespace, sitting for days in the silence of a ship where the sound of the drives tended to fade into nothing, taught him more than he needed to know about the art of letting his mind unfocus, of letting time pass unhindered. The outside noises ceased to matter. The wind faded away, and the others' conversation faded with it. Darkness, silence, as if the inside of the mind was featureless as drivespace.

. . . nothing . . .

. . . nothing . . .

. . . and a little spear or curious pinprick of light, of energy looking curiously at him from the wall, from very close by.

Without opening his eyes, Gabriel reached out and put the stone directly on it.

Everything flowed . . .

"Holy Thor on a pogo stick," Helm whispered.

Gabriel opened his eyes. All around him the glass was moving, drawing away from him, not as if it was afraid, but almost with a flourish, as if it had been waiting for the chance to do this and had only been waiting for the right kind of invitation. Helm, Angela, Grawl, and Delde Sota came slowly closer. Enda hesitated.

"It's all right," Gabriel said, peering into the darkness behind the glass. There was a large space leading into the body of the cliff, all faced and floored with the same kind of glass, all glowing faintly.

He stepped in, pausing only to look at the edge of the doorway that had opened for them. Surprised, he reached out to touch it. "This can't be more than a centimeter thick," he said, yet leaning back to look at it the stuff from outside again, he could not see through. The optical effect was as if the glass was several meters thick.

"Come on," Gabriel said.

They all went in, Enda last, looking around with curiosity. The space in which they found themselves was perhaps a hundred meters by a hundred, all smooth glass except toward the far side of it, the side leading into the cliff. There a meter-high tangle of delicate rods and threads of glass or metal lay scattered all across the floor and piled against the wall.

Gabriel glanced at it, then at Helm. "Razor filament?"

"Yup," Helm said as he unslung the stutter cannon again, clicking off the safety.

Angela and Grawl glanced at each other then unshipped their weapons as well. Gabriel pulled out his mass pistol— a Nova 6 that Helm had given him—and transferred the stone to his left hand. If there was razor filament here, then there were arachnons here as well . . . or had been. Gabriel was not willing to take the chance that they were gone.

Slowly they made their way forward, Gabriel taking point and disliking it intensely but not having much choice. Helm and Delde Sota were behind him, Grawl and Enda and Angela behind them. A soft sound as they walked made Gabriel pause and turn to see the outer wall quietly sealing itself behind them. The others glanced at this too.

"I do not much like that," Enda said. "The glass is more like steel when it comes to trying to shoot your way out of it. Should we become trapped here . . ."

Gabriel shook his head. "It wouldn't be accidental, I think," he said. "We're either going to get out of here with what we came for, or I don't think we're going to get out at all."

Delde Sota gave him a look. Her braid peeked around from behind her back and began knotting itself into intricate designs. "Opinion: game disturbingly zero-sum," she said.

"That may be," Gabriel said, "but I have a feeling it's the only game in town."

They made their way on toward the razor filament. "Why pile it up against the wall?" Helm said.

"Unless there's a passage behind it," Angela said.

"Or unless there's not," Gabriel said. He paused and looked at it. The stuff would slice to ribbons anyone who tried to force their way through. They could shoot it up, but the flying fragments would probably do them as much damage as a flechette pistol. He put the stone in his pocket for a moment, pulled off his glove with his teeth, pushed it into his breast pocket, and came out with the stone again. He went over to the wall on the left side, and cupping the stone, laid his hand against it.

"Nothing here," he said after a moment. He then crossed over to the wall on the right, reached up, and laid the stone against it.

A tiny sense of movement in the wall, molecules shivering together a little farther down. "Here," Gabriel said and put the stone against that spot.

The glass flowed away from him, revealing a long corridor, glowing slightly, which led around the large hall they were in and onward into the cliff.

"What was that?" Helm said, glancing back at the razor filaments. "A DO NOT DISTURB sign?"

"BEWARE THE CROG more likely," Angela said.

"Could be either," Gabriel said. "Well, shall we?"

He led them inward, not hurrying. Soon that corridor dead-ended. Gabriel stood before it, briefly confused . . . then, on a hunch, he reached forward. The dead end drew aside as the outer wall had done, leaving a space exactly ten centimeters taller than he was and twenty centimeters wider.

"Thank you," he said and stepped through. Helm came

through behind him—but not before the door had contracted itself to a lower height and a broader width.

"Uh-huh," Gabriel said softly, continuing forward and starting to think with mild derision about all the theories about the shapes of the Precursors, theories based on the shapes of their doors. When a door could flow like water, who knew what shape its builder would normally be? Who knew whether the shape the door held as you approached was not one it had assumed from looking at you and working out what you needed?

He put the thought aside for the moment as he walked. The corridor they were in was shortly joined by others, some winding into it from the sides, some seeming to come from inside the cliff, and all sloping gently downward. Gabriel paused at the first large junction and looked down the three other corridors joining it. They were all of the same smooth green glass, all of hemispherical cross-section, some of them quite low, some taller. Gabriel gestured at one of the lower ones with his hand and saw it draw away and grow taller. All down the length of the corridor its roof stretched upward, and its cross-section narrowed slightly.

"I still want to know where those arachnons are," Helm said softly.

"Maybe down one of those," Gabriel said, "if they were the last to use it half an hour ago—"

"Or half a million years," Angela said.

"No telling."

"Attention," Delde Sota said, gesturing down one of the right-hand corridors with her braid. "More filament."

It was finer than the last batch, so much so that it was hard to see, strung across the whole breadth of the corridor. Delde Sota advanced slowly, the corridor reshaping itself to her height, and the sticky filament stretched effortlessly with the movement of the clear green-tinged glass.

"Could be unfortunate to run into this at speed," Delde Sota said. "Nearly as much so as the razor filament."

Gabriel nodded and said, "I wish there was a way to tell how old this stuff is." But there was none, at least not that he knew.

He turned back to the main junction and closed his eyes briefly, consulting the stone for some kind of advice on which way to turn. Where the most power is, he thought, the main part of the facility . . . the most important part . . .

Assuming the two had anything to do with one another.

The stone gave him an indication to his left and down.

"All right," he said softly. "Delde Sota, my eyes aren't as good as yours in this light. Maybe you'd come walk behind me and look over my shoulder so I don't run into any of those things all of a sudden."

He went forward with Delde Sota behind him and followed the stone's hints inward and downward. Once or twice he stopped and consulted the stone at places where corridors joined, and it nudged him left or right. Gabriel went the way it indicated, listening hard as he went, but he heard nothing but the others' footsteps behind him, the occasional chirp or ping of a weapon announcing its load status or charge level, a mutter from Angela, a growl from Grawl. Sometimes he could hear Enda's mind much more plainly than usual, as if the walls reflected her thoughts and concentrated them like sound. She was fascinated but cautious, and always nibbling at the edge of her consciousness was the constant awareness of the faintly malign regard of the stone, watching her.

Malign? I need to have a talk with this thing, Gabriel thought as he consulted it one more time and was told to turn a corner into another corridor. Gabriel did and then stopped immediately.

"Uh-oh," he said. "More razor filament." The corridor was completely blocked with it and did not stretch up and out when Gabriel entered. He eyed the stuff from a meter away.

Delde Sota's braid snaked past him and poked delicately at the blockage, its thinnest strands weaving themselves gingerly among the outermost filaments for a moment. "Assessment: strong filament," she said. "Hard to judge thickness. Helm?"

"My pleasure," he said, stepping forward as Delde Sota backed out of the tunnel, followed by Gabriel.

A second later the roar of the stutter cannon filled everything. It went on for what seemed like ages, and Gabriel was half-deaf when Helm finally lowered the gun and peered into the tunnel.

"Tough, that," he said, and let loose with another twenty-second burst of mobile thunder.

After that he straightened up and said, "Clear."

Gabriel shook his head at the thought of anything that could withstand a stutter cannon at that range for that length of time, and he went carefully back into the tunnel again—for it stayed tunnel-like, declining to stretch itself as the earlier corridors had done.

Bent half over, down Gabriel went with the others following him in varying degrees of discomfort. Helm probably had the least trouble, followed by Enda, who was more or less of a height with him. Down at the far end of the tunnel, Gabriel could see a difference in the light. It was brighter there. He came down to the end and put his head out.

"Great gods," he whispered.

Slowly he stepped into the great echoing open space that lay at this end of the tunnel. It was as if the builders of this place had set out to make a tribute to some great natural cave, but with less accidental formation and more grace. Formations of every kind hung from the ceiling and grew up from the glassy floor.

"What a wonder the world is," Enda breathed as she came out to stand near Gabriel.

He had to agree with her. This was nothing like the straightforward geometrical precision of the facility on Danwell—so little like it that Gabriel started wondering if the same species had created both these places. At this end of time, judging from just the evidence, there was no way to tell, but these people, whoever they had been, were most definitely artists. This might be a weapons depot or energy-manufacturing center, but it was also a work of art.

Endless spires and spines of crystal reared up here, acre-broad sheets of reflecting glass as polished as water lay scattered beneath the glittering sky. Glass cascaded down from ceiling and walls in a hundred shapes—curtains, spears, ropes, liquid flows caught as if frozen in the act of splashing, some with drops actually still hanging in midair as if caught by a fast imager. In reality, the drops were held in place by hair-thin threads of glass as strong and hard as steel. There were stalactites and stalagmites of the glass, but not simply dripping straight down. No, nothing so commonplace. They were mock chandeliers, swags, and twisted and braided cables of glass woven through one another, wound around pillars and posts of glass in cream and green and glowing rose. There were streams of cabling on the floor, like frozen serpents, which he looked at and had trouble swearing hadn't just moved. Up high near the shining ceiling, in shadows that dwelled there despite the softly glowing surroundings, there were tiny glints of light, and Gabriel looked up and couldn't swear that they weren't eyes, watching. He found he was having trouble just standing still and being there, for he didn't think he had ever seen a place more beautiful or more terrible. The beauty spoke for itself; the terror was because the makers were all gone.

The same thing will happen to us, Gabriel thought. No matter how successful we may be as a species, sooner or later time comes for us all. Your sun goes nova or dies of old age. Your planet goes cold and loses its atmosphere. Things run out of steam, give up, kill each other off . . .

All around him he thought he could hear a faint sound in the air, like chimes, sad notes colluding in a minor key, melancholy and melodious, endlessly resigned. Deep they made the resting place. Subtle they wrought it, strong to bear the years, wise to do their work, but they are gone, all gone. Gone a long time now . . .

In the middle of the sad song, Gabriel's head turned as he heard the delicate tickle-tickle-tickle sound of little feet running on glass.

Those *were* eyes, he thought.

The source of the sound came out from behind a pillar of glass and looked at them. Then another one came out, and another. And another, and another . . .

They stood about a meter high. The bodies had thirteen segments, each one legged in triplicate, the legs staggered at one-hundred-twenty degree intervals so that when they moved they gave the impression that glittering crowns were coming toward you. The central segment had a ring of six glowing eyes and huge mandibles that worked together softly all the time. Slowly they surrounded the group.

Arachnons.

"Gather together and don't do anything sudden," Gabriel said softly. "We haven't damaged anything. Even if they're controlled, they may let us pass."

"If they're *not* controlled?" Helm asked through clenched teeth.

There was no answer to that. Gabriel shook his head and for the moment just watched the arachnons circling them.

Slowly they began to press in. Helm cocked the stutter cannon.

"Don't, if you can help it," Gabriel said. "Don't! *Really*, Grawl, I mean it!"

The weren glared at him, growling. "This is a not a time for misplaced sentiment!"

"Whatever it is, it's not misplaced. Just trust me on this!"

They were pushed together as the arachnons pressed in closer. Some of the creatures were already lifting those razory claws, raking at the group as they were pushed closer together still.

"Don't let them hit you," Gabriel said, "especially with the acid, but stay out of their way! It matters."

Then one of them leaped at Gabriel, all its claws outstretched.

Shit! There was nothing to do. Gabriel lifted the pistol, let the creature have it right between the eyes, then threw himself to one side. From behind him, a roar of other shots broke out. There was nothing left when Gabriel scrambled to his feet but a scattering of dry shards and glittering broken bits.

He stared at the remnants then looked down the long corridor reaching into the darkness of the cliff.

"Well, so much for not breaking anything," he said softly. "Now what?"

The other arachnons stood still and watched them. Gabriel clutched the stone, trying to feel about for some hint as to what to do next.

Nothing . . .

Come on, he said. *I don't want to hurt you or any of these. I was told to come here. I came. Now what?*

A little shuffling movement came from the arachnons. All those eyes were dwelling on Gabriel now. Is it just me, he thought, or is the expression changing?

Two of the arachnons standing between Gabriel and the far end of the cavern drew aside, slowly, leaving a gap.

"That looks like a hint," Gabriel said.

He stepped forward slowly, watching the arachnons. They watched him, but they made no move to hinder him. "All right," Gabriel said. "Let's go this way."

"I'll just play rear guard," Helm said, looking at the arachnons less than kindly as the others went on behind Gabriel.

They continued through the cavern, the arachnons coming close behind but never nearer than a meter or so. The ambient lighting of the place began to trail off in this part of the cavern, and increasingly Gabriel had to slow down, choosing his path between the glass constructs standing up from the floor. Twilight fell around him until only the upstanding slabs and twisted pillars of glass glowed . . . and he suddenly caught sight of a dark shadow reflected in one slab of crystalline glass as he passed it. Human once, the figure was now green-hided, armored in glowing-veined armor, clawed, and hunchbacked. Kroath! Kroath here in the darkness—!

Gabriel lifted his pistol, horrified, then caught a motion from another side in another slab of glass. A smaller kroath this time, thin-armed, frail, small, but twisted and terrible. Something about the way the head armor was constructed raised the hair on his neck.

Then Gabriel suddenly knew what he was seeing: that strange image that had occurred to him long ago, of Enda as a kroath. He had rejected it violently then. He did the same now, realizing that this moment was the origin of the image, and that a shattered fragment of it had somehow reflected back into the past, into his mind.

"Cut it out," Gabriel said under his breath, trying to calm his breathing down. "I'm not interested."

But someone was. Suddenly the place was full of reflected images, moments of old fear, old pain. The dripping, glassy cold of the glacier on Epsedra, battle after battle with the little ball-bearing kroath fighters, the Void-Corp cruisers bearing down on them at Danwell, the horror of the tangle inside Major Norrik. Again and again, the terrible flower of fire as the shuttle blew up, taking the ambassador and Gabriel's friends with it.

Stop it! Gabriel cried inside him, clutching the stone as all around him in the crystalline interfaces old dreads and new ones played themselves out. *I'm not interested.* They're all gone, all over with. These are illusions!

The reflections surged toward him, faces twisting with pain and rage, fire and smoke and energy bolts rising around them, and Gabriel lost his temper. *"Stop it!"* he yelled.

The stone flared in his hand, not with heat but light. The light pierced right through his hand, too bright to see. The images flamed in the fire of it, impossible radiance filtered through flesh and blood and shattered. A great cry like half the windchimes of a world being murdered went up, and all the light and the terror went out of the air before him and fell ringing and glittering to the ground in bright shards.

Gabriel stood there in the darkness, shaking with fury and astonishment, and looked around him, completely confused. Pillars and slabs of glass lay everywhere, broken, ruined.

Slowly the others scuffed through the splinters and fragments, gazing around. "Boy," Helm said as he looked around with some satisfaction, "when you chuck your toys out of the pram, you do it proper."

"I'll do it again, too," Gabriel growled. He turned toward the deeper darkness and yelled, "It's me! It's *me,* for gods' sakes! Will you cut it out?"

The others looked around them, waiting for some response. None came. "Maybe they're just checking," Angela said quietly.

"Maybe they are. Well, they can *stop checking!*" Gabriel yelled.

The echoes said *checking! checking! checking!* . . . and died away. All around them glass and crystal chimed in peculiar harmonies to the words. Enda began to shiver.

Gabriel looked at her with some concern then turned away, for the harmonics he was hearing were beginning to bother him, too. All around him, the crystalline structures of the cavern shivered with sound, partly of his own making, partly rogue harmonies generated by his shout. Slowly the sound died away.

Behind them, the arachnons moved forward, pushing Gabriel and the others forward again.

Around them, to Gabriel's eyes anyway, the light was brighter now. How much of that did they see? he wondered. Must ask later . . . For the moment he concentrated on walking, while inside his hand the stone pulsed, pulsed stronger. They were going the right way. Up ahead was what he had come to see.

The cavern narrowed into a glassy thoroughfare about ten meters wide then suddenly widened out again. The light ahead was stronger. As they stepped through, Gabriel saw what it was coming from. He simply stopped and stared in amazement.

The whole place was full of great long glittering filaments of glass, interlaced, spun thin as silk or thick as cable, and all intricately interwoven in what Gabriel knew were patterns, though their symmetries were too subtle for him to grasp. Some of the strands shone with their own light, some with light reflected from the others. The immensity of this cavern dwarfed the last one, and everywhere it was hung with curtains and cables of glass running with light. Here and there, pathways through the great pattern were obvious, but Gabriel was chary of entering any of them. He wanted to be surer of his welcome.

At the same time, he was having to deal with the strange sensation of something inside his head. Well, something *different* inside my head, Gabriel thought, for there had been enough alien presences and voices and whatnot in him that he was beginning to feel like some kind of tourist attraction. This presence, though, was footing it very delicately among the strands of his thought, picking them up, matching them against each other, trying to make something of the color and the gauge. It seemed friendly. At least, nothing it was doing at the moment was precisely painful. That might be a misdirection, but Gabriel doubted that at the moment. Anything that could have killed him twenty minutes ago but had not would likely not be thinking seriously about it now.

"Uh, hello?" Gabriel said, a little more loudly than he might usually have spoken, like a guest announcing himself in the airlock. "I'm here now! Can we get on to specifics, please, before it gets dark? Really dark? *That* dark?"

He showed whatever was stepping carefully around in his mind that particular image, the strange one he had experienced in Charlotte. Falling into the abyss, not just a phys-

ical fall but an emotional and ethical and historical one as
well. All those things that made life worth living for
humans, fraal, weren, t'sa and all the rest of them, lost,
gone into the darkness, lost for millennia.

"I understand what we're playing for here," Gabriel said.
"Won't you come meet me, so we can talk about it?"

Out from among the shining, woven webwork, something came stepping on five, ten, fifteen legs. It looked at
Gabriel with about thirty hot blue eyes.

Its body was an oblate spheroid around which the many
legs were spaced, some of them in contact with the ground,
some of them held higher for manipulatory uses. The upper
limbs worked together busily, doing something delicate
that Gabriel could not easily see. The creature wore all
those eyes in a cluster atop its head and a belt of them
around the waist of the spheroid. All those eyes were blue.
The creature looked at Gabriel, inclining its body to help
the top eyes get a better view, and spoke to him in his mind
in a voice that glittered.

Identification, it said in his mind.

I am a man, Gabriel said replied, concentrating on
answering the same way. He was finding this communication hard to bear. He thought from his brief looks inside
Enda's mind that he knew what a dispassionate mind was
like, a cool assessment of the outer world. Now he saw that
he was much mistaken and that he and Enda were, from this
creature's standpoint, enough alike to be easily mistaken
for one another, all runny passions and wet biological
mindsets. Here was coolness apotheosized, the genuine
mineral mindset, rational, crystalline, organized, and curious. *Curious.* He would not have believed that anything so
mineral could have been so ravenously curious about its
surroundings, but then, it was perhaps crystals that had first
learned how to grow.

Man, the creature said, as if it was not the deeply defin-
ing term that Gabriel knew but just another name for just
another thing, yet the curiosity made that judgment less

painful than it might have been. The creature was genuinely
interested in him.

"Your species is known in the classifications," it said.

The thought now sounded like speech, at least to
Gabriel. Apparently, the creature had decided to directly
access Gabriel's speech center for communications.

"You look a little like the creature my people would call
an orbweaver," Gabriel said, "but very different, too."

"There are likenesses," replied the creature, "but I am not
one of the orbweavers. I began from the same design, but
many more features were added, tending toward a far more
sophisticated level of interaction, communications, and control. I am a prototype." Was that a touch of pride he heard in
that voice? "One of only three."

"How should I call you?" Gabriel said.

"I am the Patterner," the creature said.

He looked over his shoulder at the others. "Are you hearing this?" he said.

Enda said, "I hear whispers and chiming. Nothing else."

The others shook their heads.

Gabriel turned back to the Patterner. "I'm sorry we blew
up your arachnon," he said.

"That does not matter," the Patterner said. "Their func-
tion is to protect this facility." Its thought indicated the
webwork all around it, and Gabriel realized that this was all
one huge computer, which the Patterner had built and pro-
grammed to maintain this facility. "It was tasked to attack
you to observe your reaction."

"Oh?"

"You responded when it was appropriate to do so," said
the Patterner. "You did not overrespond. This has been
evaluated."

"Good," Gabriel said. He was enjoying the glitter and
the aural shimmer of its thought and voice twined together,
interwoven. It apparently did its weaving in more than one
idiom. "That other business back there . . . that was part of
the testing, too?"

"That last proving was the second-most important aspect being evaluated," the Patterner said. "Timebinding . . . What use in giving weaponry to one who cannot tell the past from the future, even under stress? Both are important. Discard one and the other is lost as well. One must be able to choose between the old and the new response and see which one will work better for the task at hand."

Gabriel thought about that for a moment. "And the first most important?"

It looked at him, and Gabriel now saw that with the very tips of the top legs it was knitting a strand of glass idly into something Gabriel could not make out.

"Passion," it said, "we lack, but the short-lived biologicals, so our builders instruct us, have in plenty. Again we now see that they were correct."

"They were correct about most things, it seems," Enda said.

The Patterner looked at her. "They are also dead," it said, "so we see, here at the end of things, how that benefited them." It gazed up at its knitting briefly. "No matter. If they are not alive, you are, and we were told that one would come seeking their legacy. It awaits you."

"Then take us to it," Gabriel said.

"We cannot do that," said the Patterner. "It is not here."

"What?"

"You seek the main facility. You shall come to it. That is now ordained, as it always was, but it is not here. The main stronghold of our makers is not in this system."

"Now you're going to tell me," Gabriel said, "that you don't have a map."

For a creature without access to human expression, the Patterner nonetheless managed to give him a very dry look. "On the contrary. That facility and this one are in constant communication, but you could not have come to that other facility without having come here first. This is . . ."

The concept that flooded into his mind was not one that would fit in a single word. It included parts of the concepts for "testbed," "research facility," and "place of judgment." This was courtroom and prison, exercise ground and play-room, school, examination room, and graveyard. Gabriel swallowed as he got a sense from the Patterner how rou-tinely it was expected that the examination room would lead directly to the graveyard in most cases.

"Having been here," it said, "you are now enabled for access to the other facility. You may proceed there. You will find there the basic equipment, in terms of technology, which will enable you to proceed with your plans."

"Uh," Gabriel said, "so you'll tell me where it is?"

"You have already been told," the Patterner said. "You will recognize the location. Meanwhile, I am authorized to tell you that they are coming."

Gabriel's head whipped around. "Who?"

"The enemy against whom our builders strove," it said, "and you strive now."

"The *Externals?*"

"They are coming in union and in force," it said. "They know of this site's activation and the successful processing of a facilitator. It has been expected. They will now move to take possession of the technology at that site."

"How would they know?"

"From *that,*" it said, indicating the stone.

Gabriel opened his mouth, closed it again.

"There are forms of broadcast emission that do not involve energy spectra with which you seem to be familiar, except anecdotally," the Patterner said. "Analysis of your vessels confirms this. You have little time. Estimation of some thousands of hours at best, some hundreds of hours at worst. No closer approximation is possible."

"Where are they headed?" Gabriel said.

"This region first," the Patterner said. "Here they failed before, though it took all the lives of all our builders to stop them. This area."

Gabriel saw in his mind a swirl of fire in the night, one which was still there, identifiable from the classic emission colors of the nebula, though the shape was much changed. "The Lightning Nebula!"

"Your evaluation would seem to be correct. They are creatures of habit, and their memories are long. They were driven out from there . . . from *here*. Therefore, they will take this part of space first and then move inward."

"In hundreds of hours," Gabriel whispered. "Oh, gods." He swallowed. His mouth was dry. "Where is this other site, the one with the weapons?"

Then he saw it in his mind, amid the streams of stars: a yellow sun, eleven planets, two of them habitable.

"Oh, no," Gabriel moaned. He turned to the others. "Algemron. *It's at Algemron!*"

Mouths fell open, and those whose pigmentation made it possible blanched.

"Gonna be kind of a problem going back there," Helm said.

"You have a gift for understatement," Gabriel said. "It's not just that they'll shoot us on sight. We've got to get the news to someone who can make use of it in time, and we have to do it *now*. We can't spend months and months getting back there!"

"Any suggestion as to *how?*" Angela asked.

Gabriel could only shake his head.

"That facility is now activating," said the Patterner, "pending your arrival. You must proceed there forthwith and make use of the enabling equipment before the Externals reach it."

"Or before someone else does," Gabriel muttered.

The thought of what would happen in that system if either the Galvinites or the Alitarins got their hands on the kind of Precursor technology that had been available at Danwell gave Gabriel the shakes. Things back there had been heating up enough as it was. If they found out about this . . .

"We've got to get back there right away," Gabriel said. How in the worlds would they reach it in time? Their small ships simply could not make the journey fast enough. He was ready to turn and run straight out the way he had come, but first he said to the Patterner, "Is there anything else you need to know?"

"Ideally we seek the totality of knowledge in the universe," the Patterner said. "Your contribution to this, however, is now complete."

Gabriel had to smile at that, terrified and upset as he was at the moment. "Thank you, then," he said. "We should go."

"Wait," said the Patterner.

Its top legs finished their knitting and brought the little object down for the eyes to look at again. Then one clawed limb hooked the thing, another one cut the thread that the Patterner had been spinning from, and a third limb took the object from the first one and flung it at Gabriel.

Startled, he nonetheless caught it one-handed with the hand that held the stone. The object prickled Gabriel's hand slightly. It was a little open latticework of Precursor glass, and it caught a dull glow from the stone, which ran down the filaments.

"Instruction: do not lose this object," said the Patterner. "It will complete the programming work at your destination."

"Which programming work?" Gabriel said.

"The programming that has been in progress on your facilitator," said the Patterner, "and on you."

He looked at the lattice thoughtfully and finally put it in his pocket. "Is there anything we can do for you?" Gabriel asked at last.

There was a pause, as if this had not been a question that the Patterner was expecting. Finally, it said, "Succeed where our builders failed."

It turned away and vanished into the veils and webs of glass. With the soft tinkling noise of their feet on the glassy floor, the arachnons followed.

Gabriel looked at the others. He was shaking with both anticipation and terror, and he was having trouble telling which of them was the stronger.

"Come on," he said. "Let's get out of here *right now.*"

Chapter Thirteen

THEY MADE THEIR way back toward Charlotte. Gabriel let Enda do the flying, for his mind was in turmoil over everything he had just been through.

There was other business going on as well. *To complete the programming,* the Patterner had said. Such a light act, to pitch him that little piece of glass . . . but a lot more was going on inside him. In his head he could feel the tickle-tickle-tickle of delicate glass claws on a glass floor, as things were rearranged, connections made or remade. Inside his mind, something was weaving together the strands of old thought and new thought—mind that was and mind that was about to be. It didn't hurt . . . yet, but he was beginning to be afraid in a way that he hadn't been before. Softly, in the back of his mind, he could hear the sound of chiming. Back there in the shadows, eluding him when he tried to look right at them, images were stirring, preparing themselves to be released.

I am being reprogrammed, he thought. More, I am being rebuilt into something else—a weapon—but whose finger is on the trigger?

If it's not mine, Gabriel thought, it's not going to be *anybody's.*

He reached into his pocket and could find nothing there by feel but the prickle of glasswork. Gabriel fished it out and then stared.

The stone was *inside* the delicate shell of glasswork now. How the devil did it get in there? Gabriel thought. It was too big to have fit through any of that latticework.

Regardless, it was in there now, and the whole business was glowing softly, pulsing with his heartbeat. As he watched, the latticework itself was fitting more and more snugly around the stone.

He shook his head and put the stone away. Enda was looking tense.

"Yes," she said. "Before you ask, I should tell you that I can feel it. It is changing you, and I fear that it will try to change anyone else who gets too close. Gabriel, it makes me very afraid."

"Not half as scared as it makes me," he said softly. "I'm really in it this time, Enda. Danwell was nothing to this. I'm afraid to go to sleep, now. Will I still be me when I wake up?"

She had no answer for him. For Enda, that was most unusual. Gabriel found himself becoming more frightened than ever.

There was nothing to do but cope with it, for there were other plans to be made. Gabriel reached out into the center display and triggered the comms link to *Longshot* and *Lalique*.

"Helm," he said, "Angela, this needs to be a short stop. We'll check the outgoing data manifest and be on our way."

"Right," Helm said. "Where to?"

"Aegis," Gabriel said. "Best bet, anyway. Lorand Kharls has been based there recently, and there's the drivesat relay to reach him if he's not. More to the point, the Concord's there in some force. I'll . . ." He had been feverishly doing math in his head over the many ways "several hundred hours" could be construed. "I'll have to turn myself in when we get there," he said. There was the admission, final. All the hopes of the last year came crashing down behind it. "Once I do, and tell them what's about to happen, all hell will break loose and Concord cruisers will head out for Algemron. I only hope it won't be too late. We'll . . . look, there's no need for you guys to get into the middle of this."

"Buddy," Helm said, "you need to get one thing

straight. Concord or not, we're staying with you. Haven't come this far with you with all this crap going on to lose sight of you now."

"Goes double for us," Angela said. "This is a poor time to expect us to run off and try to save our own skins. Someone has to be nearby who saw what you've been doing the last little while and makes sure you get credit for it. One of your witnesses might be dead, but not all of them."

He glanced at Enda. *You had to have known they would say that,* he clearly heard her think, *and you know my answer, too.*

Gabriel let out a long breath that was mostly unhappy, but not entirely. He really wished they would all take themselves somewhere safe.

"There is nowhere safe, Gabriel," Enda said aloud, partly for the others' benefit. "If the powers that have created the kroath and the powers that attempted to wipe us out at Danwell are now coming out in force, then nowhere from the Verge to the Stellar Ring will be safe for long. There is no point in running and hiding. Any hiding place would be at best temporary. Better to be at the sharp end of things. That way, if death comes head on, at least it can be clearly perceived and prepared for."

There was no arguing with that.

"I'm not wild about the death part," Angela said, "but Enda's right about the rest of it. Charlotte then for about an hour, and as soon as your transfer's done, let's go to ground and sit tight until our drives finish charging, then straight out of here and make for Aegis."

It was all they could do at the moment. It would be late afternoon in Charlotte when they landed there, and Gabriel's stomach, making its own bid for attention through the tinkling and buzzing going on in Gabriel's head, growled expressively and said something to him about dinner.

He let out a breath's worth of amusement and reached into the display to activate comms again, running one finger down the rolling list of text and lighting on the one

for the port infotrading officer at Charlotte. "Tabin," he
said, "you have that outgoing manifest for me?"

There was a pause. "Forward it over to you in a moment,
Sunshine," said a male voice, not Tabin's.

Gabriel sat and drummed his fingers on the arm of the
pilot's couch and let out a sigh. That was when the shadow
passed over his mind . . .

He groped at the image, got a grip on it, pulled it close and
clear. Oh, gods, he thought. Big, bulky, long and sleek,
weapon ports opening as it dropped down through the upper
layers of atmosphere . . . He had seen that shape before,
awash in drivespace, heading toward Danwell. There was
only one of them this time, but in the present circumstances,
one was no improvement on three or more. One VoidCorp
cruiser was more than enough to make their lives annoying,
and it was heading straight for them.

He thrust his hand into the display again and pulled the
fighting field down over him while Enda stared at him in
astonishment. She then caught the tenor of his mind and
started to do the same.

"Helm," Gabriel yelled down comms, "we've got company! Get out of here!"

"What?" Helm said. "Nothing showing on—"

He fell silent for an instant and then started to curse.

"Dammit, Gabriel, how'd you see that thing coming?"
Angela yelled at him. "Grawl, hurry up!"

"Don't try it!" Gabriel cried. "You idiots, forget it! It's
me they're after! What are you going to try to do, fight a
cruiser?"

"Watch me," Helm said. There was considerable enjoyment in his tone of voice. "I have a cherry bomb or so in the
hold that I've been waiting for a special occasion to use."

"Helm, *no!*" Gabriel yelled. "This isn't the time! Think
about the people down there in Charlotte. You'll toast the
whole lot of them!"

Helm swore again. Gabriel was in swearing mode himself, but he could at least try to get away. "Split up!" he

yelled, "Get out of atmosphere and make yourselves scarce in the system fringes. When your drives are charged, make starfall, and we'll see you at the place we agreed!"

Where the Marines will arrest me, right in my father's back yard, Gabriel thought, feeling completely heartsick as he reached over his shoulder for the controls for the rail gun. When fighting in the field he didn't need the virtual aids any more, but sometimes they were comforting. In the field he saw the gridwork of Charlotte laid down underneath him at the edge of the horizon, overlaid on the green and red lines of planet latitude and longitude. Above him, the sleek-shaped mass of the VoidCorp cruiser was coming down fast on system drive, its weapons hot and ready.

Tracked again! They tracked us again! There was no point in swearing now. It was too frustrating. The only ones who could afford starfall/starrise detection equipment were the very ones you would typically be running away from. They have to have been following us from Algemron, Gabriel thought, or even Aegis. The idea made the hair stand up all over him. This VoidCorp ship had been following them through those long jumps into the darkness, into places where it could have caught *Sunshine* and the other two ships, and no one else would ever have been the wiser. Then a thought still worse occurred. They should have been able to catch up with us easily, Gabriel thought. Why didn't they?

He hated uncertainties like that as much as the certainty presently hanging over their heads. The cruiser was here now. There was no way to fend it off, certainly no way for the Ohmel government to do anything. They had no force sufficient to deal with the likes of the great dark overweaponed monster that was falling toward them.

Then the call came that he was fearing. "*Sunshine*," the cool voice said over comms, "This is VoidCorp vessel CL 7119. Land or be destroyed."

"Not real wild about threats at the moment, VoidCorp cruiser," Gabriel growled.

"That hardly matters. If we can't have you, *they* won't." Of course he knew that "they" meant the Concord. "With us you stand a chance of staying free. We know you were set up. Let us get you out of here, and they'll never get their hands on you."

To his horror, *that* struck home. The image of his father, bewildered and shamed as his son was arrested in Aegis, very likely tried there . . . he would never recover from it. Never. It was all too likely that Gabriel would have another life on his conscience, later if not sooner.

The temptation was considerable.

Gabriel swore.

Helm cut in over the secure channel. "If we keep that thing busy for just a few moments, Gabe, *you* can slip by and run for it."

Gabriel toyed with the idea, but he couldn't take the chances of the effect it might have on the city. "Helm," he said, "nice try, but the present version of 'keeping them busy' involves you and Angela being blown straight to hell while I escape. That's not an option." He took a deep breath. "Enda, give me control."

She looked over at him, unnerved again. "You have control," she said.

"They're not going to take potshots at Charlotte," Gabriel said, leaving his virtual gun hovering in fieldspace off to one side in case he needed it. "The Ngongwes still have *some* pull—not enough to get rid of *them* maybe, but if they're going to take us, there are going to be witnesses." He opened the frequency to an open channel in the hopes that someone out there might be recording this. "VoidCorp vessel CL 7119, we are landing. Repeat: we are landing."

With that, Gabriel streaked straight at the huge shadow that was falling at them from the sky. He had entirely too good a view of the terror of it, the gunports open and their conduits glowing, ready to fire. Suicide was not in the plan, if it ever had been—not knowing what he knew, not knowing where the news had to go now if the Verge was to be saved. Gabriel threw *Sunshine* aside at the last moment and dropped swiftly toward Charlotte Port.

He understood now the cause of that silence from the port infotrade office. They *did* have starfall/starrise detectors. They had known that VoidCorp ship was coming. When the cruiser had come out of drivespace, Charlotte had been warned by VoidCorp not to alert Gabriel in any way to its presence. He had had a little warning but not enough.

If I hadn't been resisting this process, Gabriel thought, this rewiring, reprogramming . . . would I have had more warning?

It was a thought he hated to entertain, but now he had other problems. If VoidCorp got hold of him, and he didn't tell them what he had found, soon enough they would turn to other methods to get what they wanted. They had not turned from the worlds' biggest company into the worlds' biggest corporate stellar nation by being nice to their competitors, and as far as they were concerned, *everybody* was VoidCorp's competitor. They would turn Gabriel's mind inside out and find out everything they needed to know about the Precursor site on Ohmel and the one in the Algemron system.

Except, said that silent commentator inside him, *that you do not yet know exactly where that facility* is.

Gabriel blinked.

It added, *they might find that your mind has much more than it used to. Accessing it in an unfriendly manner might make them very, very sorry.*

There was something odd about that voice at the moment. Gabriel puzzled at it and then realized what it was. It was becoming more human.

Change, it said, *is rarely all one-sided. Physics militates against it. When even observation affects both observer and observed, how much more will interaction do?*

Gabriel swallowed, trying hard to keep from crashing and doing his best to lose the thread of this conversation. *You're the Patterner,* he thought.

Yes, and the programmer, the cool voice replied. *While a program is being first run after being newly rewritten, or while still being rewritten, it behooves the programmer to oversee the process.*

That's nice of you, he thought. *Is there anything you can do about* that? In his mind, he indicated the VoidCorp cruiser now following close behind him.

Here and now, it said, *no, but you have little to fear from them.*

Great, Gabriel thought. On my own again.

The port swelled below them. Gabriel was taking aim for his usual spot and wondering whether it would be possible to make a run into the city from there. But no, that might start them shooting at the place. No point in that.

"Not near the buildings, *Sunshine*," said the voice from the VoidCorp cruiser. "Out in mid field. It wouldn't be a good idea to try anything sudden."

They're in a rush, it occurred to him. Why are they in a rush?

In the back of Gabriel's mind, the chiming was briefly becoming noisy again. *Can you hold that* down *a little back there?* Gabriel thought in some annoyance, not knowing whether it would make any difference. The "program" was running at its own speed and with its own imperatives. Things were knitting together, reshaping themselves . . .

As he dropped toward the landing spot in the middle of the field, suddenly one particular set of connections completed themselves, and Gabriel shivered all over and groaned, *"Uh—!"* with the force of it. Enda looked at him in concern, ready to take control if she needed to. Gabriel throttled back and settled *Sunshine* toward the spotty, cracked tarmac, trying to keep his vision straight over the one that was now overlaying it.

The shadow, the second shadow falling over him and the third in company with it, shapes both desperately feared and very welcome, dropping toward the planet in a hurry.

"Take over!" he whispered to Enda as he struggled with

his swirling vision and the twinkling cacophony in this mind. "I need a moment. Stall them, Enda! Don't let them hurt us, but stall every way you can!"

The VoidCorp ship was landing a few hundred meters from them, settling its vast bulk down. Dust flew in all directions as it did, and the sky around the port, normally buzzing with a modicum of light air transport, suddenly became very quiet. A moment's pause, and then a couple of small armed shuttles came out of a bay near the cruiser's rear and flew toward *Sunshine*.

Off behind them, Gabriel could see in the fighting field where *Longshot* and *Lalique* were coming down fairly close to *Sunshine*.

"Helm," Gabriel said over closed comms, "if you ever saw sense before, see it now. Don't come out!"

"If you think I'm going to let them—"

Gabriel closed his eyes and felt the shadow dropping lower. "They're not," he said. "Someone else will, though. Don't overreact, Helm. That's the big danger in this particular game."

The two VoidCorp shuttles landed close to *Sunshine*. About thirty heavily armed men poured out of them, surrounding her.

"*Sunshine*," said another voice over comms, "open up right now and come out, unarmed, with your hands up."

Gabriel got up, looking at Enda. His vision seemed to have a light, hazy pulse to it, but at least the world had stopped spinning.

"Gabriel," Enda said, "if you go with them, you know they will kill you sooner or later. Probably sooner."

"They'll try," he said, "but Enda, we've got to play this out for the moment. Trust me."

She sat very still for a moment, regarding him with those luminous blue eyes. "Of course I will go first," she said finally, then unstrapped herself and went over to the lift column. She touched the cycling control to unlimber it from inflight status and enable it for ground use, then reached for her breather gear, hanging nearby. The door in front of her slipped open. "What are you planning?" she asked.

Gabriel shook his head.

"Then I will wait for you," she said, and the door closed.

The lift went down. Gabriel put on his own breather gear, then stood there with his eyes closed, his hands against the lift column, just breathing, feeling the tickle-tickle-tickle going on in the back of his head. Hurry up, he thought. There was so much more at stake now that he was willing to let the question of his humanity go by the boards. There are more important things.

Assuming that I get out of this alive.

Through his hands he felt the lift slip into locked position down at the bottom of the column, felt the column shiver slightly as the door slid open down there. He could faintly hear voices as Enda was taken, as armored men got in and closed the door. There came the faint rumble of the lift starting back up again.

He clenched his hand around the stone and saw the image more clearly than ever. The shadows were down in the atmosphere now and coming closer. Only a minute or so.

The lift door opened, and the armored men spilled into *Sunshine*, saw Gabriel, and grabbed him. Two of them hustled him immediately into the lift. The others went down the corridor to see if anyone else was inside.

Gabriel stood silent, looking at the faceless, helmeted, armor-shelled men who were squeezed into the lift with him. One way or another, he knew this was the end of his free time. From now well into the foreseeable future, he would be a prisoner of one kind or another. At the same time, those shadows dropped closer, blocking out the sun for a moment.

The door opened. The cold hit his exposed skin like a hammer, and his ears popped painfully as he was suddenly exposed to the low pressure of the atmosphere.

The soldiers hustled him out . . . and paused.

Even in the thin air, the sound of klaxons and alarms was noisy. Over everything, between them and the lazy orange-red light of Coulomb, a great shadow fell, burying them in darkness. Then came a moment of light and another shadow, this one bigger and lower. The VoidCorp troops stood and stared above them as the two Concord cruisers dropped low. One of them held station, hovering. The other landed between *Sunshine* and the VoidCorp vessel.

That moment was all Gabriel needed. He sagged as if he was fainting and reached into his waist pocket as he did so. The trooper on his right looked down at him in shock and mild annoyance. Gabriel didn't even bother to pull the pistol out from his pocket. He grabbed the handle, aimed the barrel in the direction of the guard, and squeezed. There was a loud *pop*, a smoldering hole appeared in Gabriel's pocket, and the guard took the round from Gabriel's little gun right in the faceplate. As Gabriel pulled away, the other trooper who had been holding him whirled and aimed his own weapon, but Gabriel was already rolling under *Sunshine*'s skids and away to the far side of her. Over on that side, a Concord shuttle was landing, and before it was even down, Marines were spilling out of it.

Running as fast as he could, Gabriel fired a few shots under *Sunshine*'s belly—more to discourage pursuit than in an attempt to harm anyone.

The Marines grabbed Gabriel roughly as he plowed into them, but he found it impossible to care. One armored soldier, whom Gabriel thought might have been a woman, disarmed him and led him toward the shuttle as her comrades took up a defensive position around the shuttle. As he was pulled into the shuttle, he saw another group of Marines from another shuttle storming toward *Sunshine*.

It's over, he thought. The limited freedom he had enjoyed these past several months was now gone. Once again, his life was about to change irrevocably. Well, then, he thought, let it begin.

The female Marine—whom Gabriel now saw as a sergeant by the insignia on her armor—and two other guards hustled him into the shuttle.

"Glad to see you," he said. He waited for what he knew would follow, and he didn't have to wait long.

The sergeant grabbed both his wrists and roughly snapped on a pair of sturdy handcuffs. "Gabriel Connor, I hereby arrest you on charges of murder, criminal manslaughter, sabotage, terrorist acts . . ."

Gabriel tuned her out as the list continued. He would hear it all again soon enough, probably in excruciating detail. After the sergeant finished reiterating his rights, she secured Gabriel onto a rough metal bench and ordered him to sit tight. The sergeant departed, but the guards sat down across from Gabriel. They held their weapons with casual confidence and said nothing.

The shuttle door slid shut behind the sergeant. Moments later, Gabriel felt the familiar tremor as the shuttle lifted off the ground.

It was a matter of some moments before the field was secured again. Gabriel could not hear the comms conversations that he knew were going on, but in this particular case he knew what the gist of them would be. Two Concord cruisers outgunned the one VoidCorp vessel. VoidCorp would withdraw, though with ill grace. If they did ever catch him again . . .

At the moment, the odds of that seemed small, since there were so many other things that were likely to happen first. Gabriel sighed.

Enda? He whispered tremulously in his mind.

A pause. *I am all right. I am with the Marines.*

You acted fast, he said.

When the universe sends one such a splendid distraction, she said, *it is a shame not to use it, but you anticipated that, did you not?*

I had a hint. I wasn't sure, but I'm glad it paid off.

You must let me know in future, came the reply, *when*

*you have such hints. They will lower my blood pressure
somewhat.* There was a touch of asperity there, and
Gabriel laughed. It sounded much more like the normal
Enda. *The Marines took* Sunshine, *Gabriel. I saw most of
it from the shuttle. I fear we may have a mess to clean up
when we go home.*

I'll look forward to it, he replied. *We're landing now. See
you shortly . . . I hope.*

Be very careful, Gabriel.

A few moments later someone opened the door and
stuck in a gun barrel so broad that Gabriel thought he might
have been able to wear it as a hat.

"Nice Aggie," Gabriel said.

There was always something reassuring about a
flechette gun, though at the moment, pointing the way it
was, he would have preferred reassurance that it wasn't
going to go off.

"Yeah," the man holding it muttered. "Come on, bud.
Out. Now."

He went out the narrow central aisle of the shuttle, past
other armed Marines and down the side stairs into the
ship's shuttle bay. Elsewhere in the bay, other shuttles were
landing and decanting more Marines. Gabriel had half-
hoped that coming aboard a Star Force cruiser would feel
like a sort of homecoming—albeit a rather dreaded one—
but strangely enough, it didn't. He felt like an unwanted
trespasser, and the Marines and Star Force personnel surrounding him did nothing to disabuse him of that notion.

Gabriel stood still, unwilling to make any many sudden
moves that might annoy the numerous Marines standing
around with their weapons trained on him. Some of them
ahead parted to the left and right in order to let someone
come through. Two uniformed figures approached.

Gabriel stood there and gave each of them a small bow
as they stopped a couple of meters away. "Captain Dareyev," he said, "and . . . it's *Commander* Delonghi now, isn't
it? See, I *told* you he wouldn't be vindictive."

The two women glanced at one another then back at
Gabriel. Elinke, he thought. That ice-hard blonde hand-
someness of hers had not changed in the slightest in the
past few years. It had occurred to Gabriel more than once
that Elinke Dareyev was one of those women who would
wear her age lightly well into her one-sixties or -seventies,
and then it would all come crashing down on her with no
warning, leaving her merely distinguished instead of beautiful. There was no point in thinking of her like that any
more though. Any friendship was all over between them.

Delonghi, with that dark hair of hers and those big
brown eyes, looked less happy to see him than Dareyev did.

"I'm a little surprised to see you two working together,"
Gabriel said.

"It became time to share data," Delonghi answered.
"Things have been going on that require cooperation
between our forces." She gave him a look.

He gave it right back to her in spades, for he knew that
she knew about the Externals. "Cooperation is important,"
Gabriel said. "More so now than usual, so listen to me,
because this is vital. We have to get to Algemron."

"After the way you left recently," Dareyev said, "I would
hardly have thought it was a priority."

Gabriel swallowed and said, "Yes, well, that can't be
helped right now, but we have to go back. I'm sure you'll
insist on taking me there in custody. That's just fine, but
let's get on with it."

"You might give me a sense first of why I should listen
to anything you have to say," Elinke said. "You've already
betrayed every thing you should have stood for, and Star
Force is not in the habit of letting her prisoners dictate
ships' destinations."

"I'm sure it looks that way to you," Gabriel said, "but
let's go see Lorand Kharls. He'll explain once I tell him
what I know."

"You're not going to see anything but the inside of a
cell for a while." She motioned to Gabriel's guards.

"Hand him over to security, then accompany them to his cell."

Elinke began to turn away as two of his guards grabbed his forearms and began pushing him forward. Gabriel shrugged them off fiercely.

"Elinke! Elinke, you've got to listen to—"

"Quiet, you!" The guards grabbed him, more fiercely this time. They began to drag him to a nearby corridor.

Elinke and Delonghi disappeared into a pack of officers and technicians who were quickly rushing off toward another corridor—probably to finish dealing with the small matter of the VoidCorp ship. The captain had already turned her attention elsewhere, shutting Gabriel out of her world for the time being. Gabriel struggled, but the Marines were prepared this time, and he couldn't break free.

"Captain!" he shouted above the din of a docking shuttle. "Captain, you've got to listen to me!" One of the guards jabbed the butt of his rifle into Gabriel's kidney. His knees collapsed, and he would have fallen had the guards not held him so tightly. "Elinke! Call Kharls! Tell Kharls we have to get to Algemron! Elinke!"

Chapter Fourteen

GABRIEL WAS TAKEN to a temporary holding cell lit by harsh ceiling lights that gave no warmth. The tiny room, no more than two meters square, had a cold metal bench set into the wall across from a large window that looked out onto the main cell block. He sat down and was about to try contacting Enda again when Captain Dareyev appeared before the window. He couldn't be sure under the harsh light of the cell, but he thought he could see the silhouette of someone else a few paces behind her.

"All right, Connor," Dareyev said tersely, "you have two minutes to say your piece. Out with it."

It all came out in a rush: the stone, Ohmel, the rockslide, the Glassmaker site, the arachnons, the Patterner. Gabriel left out the more intimate details, but he must have told it all inside of two minutes because the captain stood motionless, not saying a word, but listening intently. When he had finished, she said nothing, just stood there looking at him.

At a loss for words but desperate to convince her, he asked, "Did you tell Kharls I'm here?"

She ignored the question and simply said, "How did VoidCorp know where to find you?"

He was taken aback by the sudden change of subject, but it was something that had been on Gabriel's mind as well. He thought of that inner voice saying, *The stone . . . There are forms of broadcast emission with which you are not familiar.*

"Well?"

"I don't know," he answered truthfully. "If I did, don't you think I would have done my best to stop it?"

"That," Dareyev replied through a tight smile, *"I* don't know. I know you're a traitor to the Concord, but exactly where your loyalties lie, I'm still not sure. You tell me."

"You think *I'm* VoidCorp!" Gabriel was genuinely shocked, but he pushed his rising anger down. He didn't have time for this. "I am *not* VoidCorp, nor have I ever been. Would they have chased me across half the Verge, forced my ship down, and grabbed me with armed soldiers if I was one of them? If you can't believe that, if you won't even listen to me, *then call Lorand Kharls.* Please. You have no idea how important this is."

"You're not going to see anyone without *my* approval," Dareyev replied, "though it is amusing that you should ask for him, since he's been in the neighborhood recently."

"I should think so," Gabriel said. *"Schmetterling's* been his base for a while now."

"He's not aboard," she said. "It seems your information is outdated. He's at Algemron."

Gabriel blinked. A chill went over him, for he had long since had the sense that Lorand Kharls did not often go to planets unless they were literally or figuratively ready to blow up.

"It really *is* heating up over there, then," he said.

"The other Concord Administrator there called him in for emergency consultations," Dareyev replied. "They've got their heads together now, but they're both sure that another Galvinite offensive is about to start, and not just some little skirmish—another big one. We're going to be in the middle of a war unless something can be done to stop it."

"Offensives," Gabriel said. "You have no idea how offensive things are about to get, and *they* have nothing to do with it. Elinke, please—"

She gave him a cold look.

"Captain." Gabriel corrected himself. "They're coming. More trouble than you've ever seen in one place."

"Who is coming?"

Gabriel glanced around and dropped his voice. "Do you know what kind of—" He stopped himself. *Hundreds of hours,* the Patterner had said. There was no time for this. "Please, we've got to get to Algemron!"

She looked at him. Her voice took on a quiet coolness. "What exactly were you doing on Galvin, Connor?"

Gabriel clutched his head and moaned. "I went there to *shop,* but someone else was shopping, too—for me. I found Jacob Ricel there, Captain."

She stared at him. "He's *dead.*"

"A couple of him are," Gabriel said, "but the one you think was dead didn't die until a few weeks ago. Unfortunately he died without making a confession in front of anyone but me."

Elinke smiled slightly. "Convenient, that."

The fury flared up in Gabriel. He took a couple of steps toward the window until he was centimeters from the thick glass and said, very softly, "I am tired of being thought a liar when I'm not lying and a traitor when I've never been one. Some of that at least will come out at the trial, but if you don't get me back to Algemron now, there will never *be* a trial, and your sorry little vendetta is going to be swallowed up in the destruction of all human life in the Verge! You are going to be up to your chest rivets in the biggest war you ever saw, and everything you have—every weapon, every ship—is going to be worth no more than a bucket of warm spit against what's coming for you. You are all going to die. *We* are all going to die, unless you *get moving now!*"

A brief silence. "Without proof," Dareyev said after a moment, "all your ranting is going to get you nowhere."

"Proof," Gabriel said. "Damn it, Elinke! What kind of proof will you accept?" She started to object to his use of her name again, but he slammed the flat of his hand against the glass, silencing her. "In a few days you'll have all the proof you need when everyone and everything in Algemron is nothing but a smoking ruin!"

Shaking her head in quiet exasperation, Dareyev started to turn away. Gabriel was about to scream at her again when the dark silhouette behind her stepped forward into the light.

"A moment, Captain." It was Aleen Delonghi. Elinke stopped and faced Gabriel again, but she stepped no closer.

"What are *you* doing here?" Gabriel asked.

"Haven't we already been over this?" Delonghi replied. "For the time being, Captain Dareyev and I are working together. Now you can answer my questions, or we can both leave and you can await your permanent cell."

Still furious but left with no other choice, Gabriel sat down again.

"What were you doing on Ohmel?"

"I already answered that when you came in."

"Indeed," she smiled. He could tell she was enjoying this, and it only made him more furious. "You said that you were 'led' there by your little rock. This 'Pattern' creature—"

"Patterner," he corrected her.

"Patterner," she emphasized with a gracious nod, "told you that a similar facility exists somewhere in the Algemron system, and only you can activate it. Is that correct?"

"Yes."

"That's absurd."

Gabriel clenched his jaw. He had hoped to be able to convince Elinke. As stubborn and narrow-minded as she could be, she was still no fool, but Delonghi was prolonging this just for the sheer joy of it. I should have shot her on Danwell when I had the chance, Gabriel thought bitterly. Kharls would have probably even thanked me.

"However," Delonghi broke his reverie, "we still have a good many hours until our drives are charged, and if there is indeed a newly-discovered Precursor site on Ohmel, we would do well to have a look before the Ngongwes swarm into it."

"You're suggesting that we actually go see this site?"

Dareyev said. She seemed as genuinely stunned as Gabriel
was. "You actually believe him?"

"I believe that there may indeed be a Glassmaker site
down there," Delonghi said. "Whether or not the rest of his
tale is true remains to be seen, but it wouldn't hurt to find
out. Would it, Captain Dareyev? It would give us the proof
we need—or lack thereof. If by some chance what he says
is true, we would be fools to ignore it."

There was a long, painful silence as the two women
faced each other.

"Very well." Dareyev finally conceded. "I'll have the
site secured. It shouldn't take long."

She turned to go, but Delonghi stopped her. "Captain, I
suggest that you go and that you take Connor with you. *If*
what he says is true, you will certainly need him to access
the facility and escort you safely through. I would go
myself, but with this VoidCorp business so recently settled,
I have other duties which I must attend to immediately."

"As you wish." Dareyev nodded. She seemed resigned
but was still obviously unhappy about the whole thing.

Delonghi walked away, leaving Gabriel's field of vision.
When she was out of earshot, the captain approached his
cell again.

"I'm doing this in the slim chance that you might be
right, Connor, but don't think for a moment that you can
use this as a chance to escape. We're going down with
Marines who won't hesitate to decorate that site with your
insides, and I'll see to it that *Schmetterling* keeps a close
eye on things, so *watch your step.*"

Before he could think of a reply, Elinke Dareyev turned
and was gone.

*   *   *   *   *

Even though no other incoming ships were showing on
their starfall/starrise indicators, *Darwin*, *Schmetterling*'s
sister-ship, stayed on watch a few million kilometers

beyond Ohmel. Meanwhile, *Schmetterling* dropped into a low orbit above Ohmel so that they could keep a close eye on the goings-on below and be ready to offer any assistance. A scarce half-hour after the VoidCorp ship departed the system, *Schmetterling*'s bay doors opened and disgorged a large troop transport. The bulky gray craft quickly burned through the atmosphere and landed with great delicacy some half-kilometer from a large canyon, where it was now early evening. A few minutes later, Gabriel, Captain Dareyev, and an assortment of armed guards were standing outside the glasslike surface of the canyon wall. Gabriel held back, watching the Marines and Elinke touch it, walk up and down it, and peer through it. It lay before them flat, shining, and unmoving in the darkness.

Gabriel walked up to it with the stone in his hand. He didn't even have to do anything. The wall drew open for him, and he led them inside.

"Don't shoot at anything," he warned the guards. "The arachnons in here may not all be controlled."

The armored soldiers looked at each other. Elinke nodded to them then went after Gabriel down the shining corridor.

They saw no one else until they came into the second cavern, the great one, the museum of pillars and slabs of crystal. Gabriel was seeing this place rather differently now, as a kind of imaging facility, a room full of windows. Right now, to him, the windows were all clear. He had seen what he needed to see for the moment.

At the place where the cavern narrowed before heading into the main computing facility, the arachnons were waiting for them. They stood there, all those oblique, cool eyes trained on the Marines, their mandibles working thoughtfully. The Marines fingered their weapons and were thoughtful right back.

"Don't," Gabriel said. "Really. I don't know if I could stop them." He headed toward the arachnons, and they made way for him to pass.

Carefully Elinke came behind him, glancing around the passageway. The Marines came after, looking as uneasy as their captain was refusing to.

The inner cavern was full of light, glittering and streaking along the lines of the vast webwork.

"Patterner?" Gabriel said softly. His voice fell strangely silent into the chamber. No echoes.

Elinke unholstered her weapon.

"Don't," Gabriel said. *"Please*, Captain."

Already, after his last brush with the Patterner in mind, he was getting a clearer sense of what this place could do. It was not primarily a weapons facility, but there were things here that could be put to terrible uses if the right (or wrong) people got their hands on them. Because of this, the Patterner was prepared to do everything it could in order to prevent that.

"They know I'm friendly to them." Gabriel grinned. "They don't know about you."

"You seem to be friendly with all kinds of people," Elinke said, glancing around her. "Amazing you haven't got more of them killed."

Gabriel breathed out in guilt and annoyance.

The webwork shivered a little, and the Patterner stepped out through the glimmer and sheen of it. Elinke's pistol snapped up, training on it.

"Why are you still here?" the Patterner said, looking from Gabriel to Elinke. "The danger is great. I have explained this to you."

"This lady," Gabriel said to the Patterner, "will be taking me back to the other facility, but first she wanted to be convinced of why she should do it."

"Utmost necessity," said the Patterner, and silently it added, *The program implementation continues smoothly?*

Gabriel wasn't sure if "smooth" was the word he would have chosen. *I am suffering no ill effects,* he said. *So far.*

"I am under no obligation to make explanations to you," the Patterner told Elinke, who had slowly lowered her

sidearm. "This being has been expected for some time."
Elinke looked at Gabriel very strangely. "His presence is
necessary for the implementation of the main facility."

"That's at Algemron," Gabriel said.

"The Externals, whom I see you know, have been
alerted to his status and will attempt to obtain him and use
him to access that facility," said the Patterner. "This must
be prevented."

At the mention of the Externals, Gabriel saw Elinke's
eyes widen slightly.

"Delonghi mentioned them, did she?" Gabriel said. "Or
maybe Kharls? Well, it took long enough."

"What do you mean he had been 'expected for some
time'?" Elinke asked.

The Patterner looked at her. "The assessment object,
which was prepared for him alone and which he carries, has
been in circulation for approximately a tenth of a galactic
rotation. It was known that a being of the correct structure
and qualifications would eventually manifest itself. This is
the being."

Elinke stared at him. "Are you trying to tell me that
you've been waiting for *Gabriel Connor* for—what? Five
thousand years?"

"Fifty thousand," the Patterner replied.

"It wasn't me specifically that they were waiting for,"
Gabriel said. "I think I just sort of won the lottery." Even as
he said it, he was not entirely sure that the Patterner hadn't
meant exactly what it said.

Elinke closed her mouth and looked around. "I don't see
why I shouldn't believe you're making all this up."

The Patterner looked at her in complete bemusement,
then, rather coolly, it said, "Do you mean 'falsehood'? That
is an invention of the younger races."

Elinke flushed.

"Listen," Gabriel said. "This is obviously a Precursor
facility, Captain. This"—he pointed at the Patterner—"is a
member of a species engineered by the Glassmakers—or

the Precursors—but it's a little late to fight over terminology. These people are in the literature. Explorers have run into them before and have been greatly assisted by them or greatly killed, depending on their behavior. I *know* you know all about it. Now here you are in the middle of a Patterner's interface, and you have the bald-faced gall to tell something ten million years old—"

"Fifty million," the Patterner interrupted.

"—*Fifty* million years old that you think maybe it's lying? Just to get *me* off some kind of hook?" He could read it in her clearly. In fact, the clarity of the notion shocked him.

Elinke flushed harder.

"Look," Gabriel said. "The proof is all around you. Now I tell you, as this good creature has told you, that the Externals are coming. It's going to be like it was at Danwell, but worse—much, much worse because we don't have the kind of weaponry that we had there . . . yet. If you don't want to be up to your nostrils in kroath and gods know what else, *we need to get to Algemron*."

Elinke looked at the Patterner.

"I would advise this course of action," it said.

After a brief silence, Elinke nodded. "All right. My people will have been questioning your friends, and unless they've found some evidence of wrongdoing on their part, there's no need for us to hold them. After you've said your good-byes to them, they can go about their business . . . and then we have a journey to make."

"Oh, no." Gabriel said. "They go, too, or *I* don't go."

Dareyev glared at him and said, "You don't have a lot of choice in the matter."

"I have more than you think," Gabriel said.

Even now he could feel the slow strength swelling up inside this place, reacting to the greater threat that was coming. He had been drawn into synch with this facility so that the strength of the link between him and it could be tested and evaluated for the needed links of the next facility,

the one at Algemron. Now it occurred to Gabriel that the
link went both ways.

Patterner, he said silently, *perhaps you might do me a
favor?*

The Patterner listened to the suggestion. *That can be
implemented.*

Then please do.

"Captain," Gabriel said, "you had better call your ship."

"What?"

"Call *Schmetterling,*" Gabriel said, "if you'd be so kind."

She looked at him as if he was out of his head. Then she
reached down to her belt and unclipped the comms unit.
"Schmetterling. Ops officer."

"Captain," the voice said urgently, "we've been trying to
raise you. You're in a blackout area."

"Not at the moment," Dareyev said. "What's the situation?"

"We've just lost ship's lighting."

She blinked. "What do you mean?"

"The lights are out. Also, the engines are down, though
they shouldn't be. Their systems and all the others check
out fine. There is *no* fault that we can find, but they are still
inoperative. We can't budge."

Elinke shook her head and then saw the look on
Gabriel's face.

"Stand by," she said and killed the audio.

"Your ship is not going anywhere," Gabriel said, "until
you agree to this."

The Marines looked decidedly nervous. They had the
discipline to remain perfectly still, but every one of them
was looking at the captain for direction.

"You can't be doing this!"

Gabriel sighed and sat down with his back against a
glass pillar, while from its shrouding of webwork the Patterner watched. "Tell me when you would like me to turn it
back on."

"You are so full of—"

Gabriel sat there quietly in communication with the

Patterner, mentally looking to see what it was doing with the power management field that underlay and affected the whole canyon area, and incidentally, *Schmetterling*. Then he said silently, *Here, let me do something.*

Captain Dareyev's comm unit chirped. She pulled it out. "Yes?"

"Ma'am," said her comms officer, sounding rather confused. "Now ship's lights are blinking on and off."

"Well, find out why they—"

"They're blinking in code, ma'am."

"What?"

"They're blinking the code pattern for the letters G and C. Repeating: G, C . . . G, C . . ."

Elinke turned to stare at Gabriel. Then, very softly, she said, "You always did have a tendency to rub it in when you were right about something. One of your more unlikeable traits."

"We're wasting time," Gabriel said as he stood up again. "Every minute you make me sit here waiting for you to get sensible is a minute lost in the defense of the Verge. Potentially the best part of that defense is waking up right now, waiting for me to show up and tell it what to do. If anyone else gets near it, I can't vouch for what will happen next. The place has its own safeguards, and until I enable a level of response that's a little more flexible, it could do almost anything if approached by the wrong people."

"All this is going to happen if *you* don't get there?" she said. "Gabriel Connor, a couple of years ago, you were just another Marine, and then you turned traitor. Now you think you're the center of the universe—"

"Very occasionally," the Patterner interrupted, "someone who thinks that is right, whether it suits those around him or not."

There was a silence at that. Elinke looked from the Patterner to Gabriel.

"I can wait," he said, "but when we get to Algemron and find the system in flames, it won't take long for the word to get out as to whose action—or inaction—caused it to fall. You think *my* court-martial's going to be an event? I wish I could get the concession to sell the tickets to *yours* . . . except that we'll all be dead by then, and half the Verge will be a memory, which sort of cuts in on the number of spectators."

She looked at Gabriel, then let out a long breath. "All right," she said. "Your friends will ride inboard where I can keep an eye on them. I don't want them sitting outside *Schmetterling* in their ships, making who-knows-what mischief."

"I'm sure they'll find that entirely satisfactory," Gabriel said.

Elinke's comms unit cheeped again. "Ma'am," said the comms officer, "it's stopped. We have the lights back, and they're behaving normally."

"The engines?"

There was a moment's pause, then, "All systems are functioning normally, Captain."

"Good. Secure the ship," Elinke told the officer. "We'll be leaving immediately upon recharge"—a long pause—"for Algemron."

"Thank you." Gabriel sighed.

"Let's go." She nodded to the Patterner. "A pleasure to meet you," she said, for all the world as if she had been invited along to tea and was now returning home. Then she turned and marched out, gesturing to a couple of the Marines to bring Gabriel along.

He went in the middle of the group, trying not to let his amusement show. *I wish this had occurred to me an hour ago,* Gabriel said silently to the Patterner. *It would have been fun pulling all the power out of that VoidCorp cruiser and watching it crash.*

You would have been out of range, the Patterner said. *This facility is not made for long-range operations.*

And the other one?

It is the chief long-range facility, the Patterner answered.

That was useful information, but it scared Gabriel even more. It was imperative to get there before VoidCorp found out it was operational . . . or the Galvinites, or the Alitarins . . .

Then there was the problem of the Externals, who *knew* the place was operational.

I do not fully understand the reason for your desired intervention, however, the Patterner said.

I was bluffing, Gabriel replied.

The Patterner understood the term from Gabriel's mind. *I do not understand the mechanism by which it works,* the Patterner said. *The captain acted as if under compulsion.*

She believed, Gabriel said, *that what has happened once will happen again.*

An unusual religion, the Patterner said.

We call it logic, Gabriel said. *It doesn't always work, but I wasn't going to tell her that. I wanted her to do something, and now she's doing it. We're getting to where we need to be.*

Bluffing, the Patterner said, musing over the implications. *Exploring this phenomenon might be useful.*

After this is all over, Gabriel said, *we'll sit down and play poker with Helm. You'll get more than enough exploration out of that.*

Assuming we live to do it, he thought as he went out with the Marines to rejoin *Schmetterling.*

* * * * *

The crews of *Sunshine,* *Longshot,* and *Lalique* were reunited inside *Schmetterling* after the ship finished her recharge and made starfall. After searching them and removing all their weapons, the Marines had treated Gabriel's friends with all courtesy, giving them comfortable if cramped quarters on a deck that had rooms set aside for visitors.

Gabriel, being a prisoner, had a cell in the brig, which, being on ship, was no more luxurious than his cell on

Phorcys had been. There was a small snug meeting area down at the bottom of the cellblock, just the other side of the main Marine security post that guarded the cells. The others could come and see him there at mealtime.

Quite soon after his installation in his new cell, Gabriel was brought down to the meeting area where he had a visitation from a Marine legal officer who came to see him. He was accompanied by a recording officer, also a Marine. Shortly thereafter, an expressionless Elinke Dareyev joined them.

The legal officer read out Gabriel's arrest warrant. It went on for some pages, and finally the man asked, "How do you plead?"

"Not guilty," Gabriel replied.

Elinke looked away.

"So entered," said the legal officer. "Counsel will be appointed for you when we reach Algemron, and the case will go forward before the Concord Administrator at his earliest convenience."

The legal officer and his assistant got up and left.

Gabriel turned to Elinke and said softly, "He had better hurry, Captain. Time is going to be very short."

She looked at Gabriel coolly and said, "I had thought that you might have taken this quiet time to reassess your position."

He wanted very much to laugh, but it would have been counterproductive. "About what happened on *Falada?* Captain, I *know* what happened there. I think you know more about it than you've been letting on, too, but I am in no position to press you on that. Nor do I intend to say anything or do anything that might harm the progress of the trial. I intend to clear myself, though at the moment my options in that regard seem very limited." He looked up at her. "The status of testimony and evidence telepathically acquired is a very fuzzy area. We may wind up redefining it somewhat."

She raised her eyebrows, an unconcerned look. It did not fool Gabriel. He felt her unease.

And there's an idea, he thought. There was the way he

had "pressed" on Ricel before he died. He had been in no position to resist that. *She* would not be, either. It would finally lay to rest the question of whether or not she had she lied about Ricel's association with Concord Intel, and if she had, *why* had she lied?

Elinke had been his friend. He resisted the idea of doing anything like that to her—for the moment anyway. But when it comes down to it, when it looks like the case is going to go against me at last, will I still be so noble?

The other question came up at the back of his mind. Will I even care then? The reprogramming will surely be finished then. What will I be? How will I feel?

He shook his head and said, "Captain, please. Let's put the question of the trial aside for the moment. There are more important issues. The Externals . . ."

Elinke leaned back on the couch, looking at her folded hands. "When my Intel contact first told me about them," she said slowly, "I thought it was some new distillation of the paranoid rumors that you always get out here in the Verge. You would have heard them as often as anyone else aboard ship. Conspiracy theories, secret plots and threats . . . there's something about this part of space that breeds them in people. Whispering campaigns, crazy ideas, or so I would have thought."

Gabriel nodded. "After Delonghi told you what the Concord knew about some of the alien attacks—the kroath, for example—you found it difficult to believe, and Lorand Kharls called you in."

She looked at him strangely. Gabriel let her, for he had caught a glimpse in her mind of it happening exactly that way. "Yes," she said. "He was persuasive."

"He showed you the pictures."

She looked at him more strangely still.

"Someone had to get some eventually," Gabriel said. "Kroath and other things. Is there any record of a kind of communal telepathic worm colony that lives inside people?"

"Teln?" Elinke said, sounding uneasy.

"Is that what they're called? Teln, yes. Well, there are teln on Bluefall and on Algemron." Gabriel shied away somewhat from the memory—the stroking, writhing warmth, the quiet subversion of a mind from the inside, the incessant pressure on the vulnerable human will until it grew into a new shape that better suited that pressure, bent to it, served it. "I met one of them up close a couple of times there—if it's actually possible to meet *one* of them."

Elinke's look was shadowed.

"There are a lot more of them, aren't there?" Gabriel said. "Not that this is something that would be widely advertised."

"The experts think so," Elinke said after a moment. "There have only been a few tangles actually found. It's the usual theory, though. For every one you find in a situation like this, expect a hundred."

"More like a thousand," Gabriel said. "The people of Algemron hate each other so that it's possible to believe any amount of irrational behavior from them. It's a terrific hiding place for what's actually underneath."

"If you're trying to suggest that the whole war between Galvin and Alitar was *caused* by the teln . . ."

"Oh, no," Gabriel said, "but it's a great place to take cover while you're working on something else. When the others arrive in the system, the teln will be ideally placed to cause the maximum amount of trouble and confusion among the humans in whom they're emplaced."

Elinke frowned. "Do you have any better fix on 'when they arrive'?"

Gabriel shook his head. "The Patterner's implication was that they were no more than a few starfalls away."

The captain got up and started to pace. "That's another problem," she announced. "I wish we had had one more ship with us at Coulomb. I was unwilling to leave *Darwin* alone there to cope with whatever might happen in another hundred and twenty-one hours."

"For the moment," Gabriel said, "no one's going to be able to get in there without me. The Patterner will see to that, but the place shouldn't be left unguarded for long, for the sake of the people living on Ohmel. As soon as we get to Algemron, ships should be detailed to go there and set up some kind of constant presence. I'll work out arrangements with the Patterner to let the researchers inside and so forth. The Ngongwe family may not like the presence of Concord, but considering the status of the facility—and the threat from the Externals, who'll want to get in there too if possible—they're going to have to deal with the increased attention the best they can."

Gabriel leaned back and rubbed his eyes. Assuming he lived through the next couple of weeks, there was still going to be a lot of work to do.

Elinke watched him quietly. After a moment, she said, "Why *you?*"

Gabriel shook his head again and said, "I was standing in the right place at the right time, and someone gave me this." He reached into his pocket and came up with the stone. It was now tightly held within the lattice of Precursor glass, and its glow was muted. "Just as I was once standing in the wrong place at the wrong time, and Jacob Ricel handed me a chip."

Gabriel didn't look at her. He just closed his eyes and waited to see what would happen.

A flurry of images went by, all with a strange cast to them. He had not yet before looked very far into Elinke's mind. Gabriel wobbled a little as he looked at himself from *Falada*'s bridge, standing there rigid with fear and confusion, young and scared. The image was so tinged with fury and grief that the rigidity looked like anger, like some cold hostility held carefully in check. He saw himself again through Elinke's eyes, that fury gone cold during the trial as her voice said, *Jacob Ricel is not known to me as a Concord intelligence operative.*

In the next heartbeat, the back of her mind said,

perfectly audibly, *But as a* VoidCorp *Intelligence operative
. . . yes.*

Gabriel's eyes snapped open.

What a nasty way, he thought, to tell the truth and still
manage to send me away.

You're quite sure? the prosecutor had said.

Quite sure.

They asked her no further questions, because it suited
them to leave the matter right there.

One more question could have saved me . . . assuming
she would have answered it truthfully, but she would not
have, not then.

The fury had whited everything out for her. Her grief for
Lem had made it all seem all right. Later, when her judgment was cooler, months cooler, she had found herself
wondering what she should have done, how she could have
handled matters better.

Gabriel opened his eyes, unwilling to look any further
into this right now, but one good thing had come of this
meeting: he had an answer to the question that had haunted
him for the past year. Now if he had to die, he could do it
with his mind concentrated on the business at hand.

"That incident on *Falada* destroyed a lot," Gabriel said.
"The innocence of youth . . . maybe it's overrated these
days. How many of us have an 'innocent' childhood, when
we're exposed to the Grid from before the time we can talk?
If something in me was killed, it was the sense that I *was* at
the center of things, that the things happening to me would
necessarily be fair, or good." The words came with some
pain. It was the kind of thing he might have said to Elinke
Dareyev a long time ago, when she was still his friend.
"Maybe having that die wasn't a bad thing. It was a shame
it happened the way it did, but it left me open for other
things, maybe for fate to operate, if there is such a thing."

Elinke got up to leave.

"I have to say this to you," Gabriel said. "If I had known
what that one errand done for Ricel was going to do, I

would have shot myself sooner. Stone or no stone, fate or no fate, I would not have passed on that chip."

He knew he might be damaging his case by speaking to her so, but he had to do it. Possibly it was by way of apology to her for seeing, in her mind, what he had no permission to see.

The captain of *Schmetterling,* once the captain of *Falada,* looked at him and said, "I could almost believe you."

Gabriel could find nothing to say to that.

"You did pass it on," she said, "and for that, you are going to have to pay."

"And you," Gabriel said. "You, too, may have one payment to make before all this is over."

Her eyes were uncomprehending. "I don't know what you're talking about."

There was nothing strange about that, for Gabriel himself was uncertain what shape the payment would take. "It may not matter," Gabriel said. "Let's worry about it in a few weeks. If we still have the leisure to do that, then it will be an issue. Otherwise we're just wasting your time and mine."

She looked at him oddly and said, "Spending so much time with a fraal has been turning you into a mystic."

Gabriel laughed. "Captain, if anything it's made me a lot more pragmatic than I used to be. You learn not to ask for answers before they're ready, not to understand the ones you get, and when you finally get them, to check them after a month or so, because the answer has usually begun to mean something else."

She raised her eyebrows and went out.

Chapter Fifteen

FOR A PRISONER on a Star Force vessel, fifteen days in drive-space and the nine days spent between starrises and starfalls waiting to recharge could have been desperately boring, but Gabriel had no intention of letting them pass idly. In particular, he had Algemron on his mind. In between sharing meals with Enda, Helm, Angela, Grawl, and Delde Sota and socializing with them during the limited hours during which this was allowed him, Gabriel spent a lot of time on those parts of *Schmetterling*'s Grid to which he was permitted access via the display in his cell. Mostly he wanted news of what had been happening in the Algemron system, and there was entirely too much of it. One whole day he spent reading, blitzing himself with data. The second and third days he spent resurrecting the old art he had learned while in service with Ambassador Delvecchio: guessing or predicting what was really going on behind the public reports.

The simple fact that there were two Concord Administrators in one system at the moment was enough to suggest a level of trouble much more serious than just a war. Mara DeVrona had been stationed there for some years now, ostensibly as the head of the Neutrality Patrol in charge of organizing convoys and managing Pariah Station, but Gabriel immediately recognized this for the blind it was. No one sent Concord Administrators to run a single facility of any kind. They were emplaced to manage whole areas and to make those areas run as well as they could. Their methods might be unorthodox, but they tended to work.

DeVrona had a reputation of her own. A fierce little woman with close-cropped gray hair and an athletic build, she was quick, decisive, and sometimes abrupt, but not the "mean little cop" that her detractors sometimes tried to make her out to be. She had briefly been a study of Gabriel's while he was working with Delvecchio, for the situation at Algemron had borne some superficial similarities to the one at Thalaassa. It was not widely known outside Concord diplomatic circles, but DeVrona was quietly working to bring this war to an end by boosting the ability of the Alitarin government and people to resist their stronger neighbor. She was also trying to gently leverage the situation into that position best characterized by the statement, "Fighting is no fun any more. We're not winning." The situation might, of course, blow up, but then this one had been blowing up periodically for many years. There was much to play for and a good deal to lose, but not enough so as to make playing unviable.

Mention of her was made in the news, but her usual description as "Concord meddler" had for the moment been usurped by Lorand Kharls, of whom some passing note had been taken in the major news services. For his own part, Kharls had posed for the obligatory shots in his impressive formal uniform, holding the tri-staff. This served to emphasize his presence as an ambassador of goodwill from the Concord. Then he had retired to *Olnant,* the Concord cruiser to which he had transferred from *Schmetterling*, and had gone into "consultations with his advisers."

Gabriel snorted softly at that. Kharls's advisers might be anyone, even cashiered exiled Marines when the occasion demanded it. But at the moment, he had his feeling that Kharls and DeVrona had their heads together, working out a strategy for handling the upcoming close approach of Galvin and Alitar.

Meanwhile, both planets' news was otherwise about very little else, though the Galvinite and Alitarin news services were filled with a great deal of contradictory content.

The respectable services, especially on the Alitarin side, talked about "restraint," "not repeating the mistakes of the past," and "measured response." Gabriel took this to mean that the military was broke. The government was trying try to avert the whole campaign this year by convincing the Galvinites that while they had plenty of money, they had better things to spend it on. The "respectable" levels of the Galvinite media were shouting about "honor," "patriotism," and "righteous anger." The tabloid levels were yelling about "revenge" and "we'll get our own back" and "protecting our husbands, wives, and children from the ravages of a mindless, valueless enemy." Gabriel took these stories and announcements, all concocted at one level or another by the FSA, to mean that the Galvinites were well-budgeted, restive, annoyed at the presence of the Concord, and eager for a push that would leave them with more of their enemies' territory.

The Galvinite side bothered Gabriel rather more than the Alitarin, possibly because of the monotone quality of it—one voice, one hymnal, all voices singing on one note and scaling slowly up to a shriek. While the Supreme Commander was an excellent speaker, her rallies that Gabriel repeatedly watched were getting very good at that particular sound: more than a cheer, not quite a shriek but getting there, with a sort of rumble or growl on the edge of it.

One of Gabriel's instructors in Group Psychology had once said, "There are lots of noises mobs make—confused, angry, cheerful, annoyed—but there's one in particular, and when you hear it, you'll know it. When you hear it, *leave*. You'll want to anyway. It gets right down under your skin. If you're going to stick around, be in armor, and don't let that sound spoil your aim."

Gabriel was convinced that the sound of the crowds in these clips was a close match to what his instructor had meant. The other side was doing at least as much haranguing, but it felt weaker. They knew they were losing, but no one was going to breathe a word, lest the Galvinites find out. The problem was that the Galvinites knew it already and were preparing for what they thought would be the first of several pushes that would end it all in their favor.

They may not have time, Gabriel thought. Nonetheless, he kept wading through the news, everything that *Schmetterling* had downloaded until she left Algemron for Coulomb. He had nothing better to do with his time, and it was the kind of activity that Delvecchio would have described as "character building."

Sometimes he paused to consider the source of the information that had sent *Schmetterling* to Coulomb in the first place. Gabriel had long suspected that Concord Intel, Star Force Intel, Marine Intel, and VoidCorp Intel were all digging holes in one another's security. He had also suspected that all of them, or almost all of them, had planted agents inside all the others. Gabriel was equally sure that some of the players in the game knew where their opponents' pieces were placed and were intent on leaving the pieces exactly where they were for the purpose of feeding them bad data, which would come out at the other end and betray its origin. The whole business made his head hurt, but somehow Concord Intel had come up with the goods this time. Either they have a mole in VoidCorp Intel, he thought, or they extracted a mole in their own system and squeezed it until it bled.

Either way, if I ever find out who it was, I owe him a favor.

Meantime there was still plenty of news to work with. The tension in Algemron had dissuaded most infotraders from establishing regular hauls—one of the reasons why Gabriel and Enda had had so little trouble running in there to start with. The local governments knew that those to whom such things mattered—specifically the Concord— would read some of their news. They were trying to make it look as if this upcoming Close Approach was going to be nothing special, and that meant that one way or another, it was going to be.

Gabriel, lying there on the bed and staring at the display hanging from the wall, went back to one scrap that had caught his attention in passing. Later he found himself coming back to the story repeatedly—a sure sign, as the ambassador would have said, that it meant something that Gabriel hadn't yet understood. Now the little piece was beginning to obsess him.

"Display," Gabriel said. "Run 'weirdbit.' "

It ran it again for him.

The clip proceeded. It was a tailoff of some kind of advertising for the war effort, the martial music that the Galvinite Grid used for transitions between pieces, and then the image.

Outside at the military port of Fort Drum, craft were taking off and landing, but the shot had been taken from outside the port walls so that anything really interesting was hidden.

"A major step forward today for the forces of truth and justice," the voice said matter of factly, "the capture and return to the FSA of the wanted terrorist, Erik Mahon."

The view shifted to a close angle of a man in forearm and leg shackles being bundled out of a Galvinite Army shuttle and onto the tarmac. He was short, red-haired, and stocky, with a broad open face—an expressionless face at the moment, one apparently determined to show nothing to the slightly smiling men with the very big guns that surrounded him. Gabriel could see the slightly bigger smiles in the background, the gloating looks, the side-wise glances that suggested that, while no one might be hitting this guy now, they would be later. The man found his footing and started to walk, closely surrounded by the soldiers and the officers from the Galvinite Intelligence Directorate.

"This notorious assassin and bomber had eluded capture for nineteen months after the atrocities at Wayrene and Duithurt, where more than four hundred FSA citizens died. Mahon, thought to be a disciple of the rogue Churgalt

insurrectionist Bender Davis, was captured on Alitar and
turned over to FSA forces with the aid of an independent
diplomatic initiative backed by the ISA."

That was all.

Gabriel stopped the image of the man's retreating back as
the soldiers hurried him into one of the port buildings. He
stared at it. The Churgalt Insurgency was based down in the
jungles of the equatorial region of Galvin, an inaccessible
area that might have been designed for the successful con-
cealment of a rebel operation. The Churgalt Insurgents were
a nasty little secret that the FSA tried to keep quiet, but word
about them had leaked out while Gabriel was still serving on
Falada. At the time, he had found slightly amusing their
claim that the FSA government was in league with some
kind of unknown alien. Now, having met Major Norrik, he
wasn't laughing any more.

Even though the premise had sounded amusing at the
time, Gabriel hadn't had any doubt that there were a good
number of people on Galvin who found the government
desperately oppressive and would have liked to overthrow
it. Unfortunately, the Churgalt people were in no condition,
operationally or in terms of popularity, to do any such
thing. Nevertheless, the Insurgents remained a thorn in the
Galvinite Army's side, an uncomfortable indication that not
all Galvinites loved the war or the government.

This story by itself, therefore, was no great surprise.
Whenever Churgalt agents came out into the cities or
exposed themselves in any other way, the government
hunted them down mercilessly, but this particular terrorist
had been caught and turned over to them by the ISA.

The ISA was the Imperial State of Algemron . . . otherwise known as Alitar.

Now why did they do *that?* Gabriel wondered.

The two planets, for all the reasons that come with cen-
turies of war and atrocity, hated each other desperately. The
two worlds would normally do anything to prevent one
another from receiving normal trade or even normal flow of

data. It was something of an indication of Gabriel's good luck that their three little ships hadn't been descended on and blown out of the sky by an Alitarin task force.

Why then this odd little bit of sudden cooperation? A "terrorist" wanted by one side, suddenly handed to it by another? The "responsible" news services made a big deal of it, saying that it showed how little need there was for an outside presence in the system, that responsible behavior of adult states working through a process to gradually resolve their differences, blah, blah, blah . . .

Gabriel caught the word "outside" in that one journalistic piece and immediately became alert. "Outside" meant "Concord." He knew that from the bad old days monitoring Phorcys and Ino, another pair of planets stuck in the same star system with each other and equally stuck with a hate/hate relationship, though one of slightly different provenance. This was a message of sorts, and it was addressed to the Concord . . . though not directly. They were meant to see it, comment on it, and (if possible) to draw the wrong conclusion from it.

Now it was just a matter of working out what the right conclusion was.

Gabriel went back to studying that frozen image. " . . . with the aid of an independent diplomatic initiative backed by the ISA." The phrase was vague enough to make anyone attempting to answer the "who" part of a news question fairly turn around in their skin with frustration. No attribution. Almost as if no real person had been responsible at all. "An initiative." As if you might step out one morning and see an initiative walking down the street and scratching itself. Naturally, the FSA government was unwilling enough to make any reference to Alitar, but that they should do so in a news story like this and suggest, even admit, that their enemy had helped them . . .

Gabriel sat up on the bed, leaned over, and rubbed his eyes. He was tired. He very much wanted to lie down and rest a while, no matter what might happen to him while he was asleep.

The government, said Delvecchio's remembered voice in his head, *that's just code for "a whole lot of people." Your job, when someone mentions "the government," is to find out which person they mean. Then you can work out who just did what to who.*

That was the question here. Who on Alitar would willingly help Galvin? What did this mean? Who had spoken to whom and done what deal. . . ?

It would continue to bother Gabriel until they reached Algemron. *I need more data.*

There were plenty of other things to bother him anyway. Likely enough the other set of problems awaiting him at Algemron would drive the first batch out. He reached into his pocket and pulled out the stone. The glass latticework had actually melted into it now . . . or maybe melded was a better word, since heat had thankfully not been involved.

Still twanging at the edges of his consciousness was the Patterner's remark, *You still do not know where that facility is.* Gabriel was hoping vehemently that the Precursor facility now preparing itself for his arrival was not on one of the two inhabited planets, or matters would immediately become a lot more complex than they already were. Then again, he thought half in despair, why shouldn't it be on one of them? *Things are already about as bad as they can be at the moment. Why shouldn't they be worse?*

He had no idea where the site might be. His reasoning was hampered by the fact that Precursor facilities were *old.* If the whole system wasn't old—and it had been suspected for some time that there were star systems in which not all the planets had "formed out" at the same time—then the planet itself might need to be.

Algemron, to judge by its stellar type and general behavior, was nowhere nearly as old as Mantebron or Coulomb and their various planets. It appeared to be a respectable G star in its stable middle years, but appearances could be deceiving. It could, for all he knew, be cooling more slowly than was usual for stars of its type, possibly one of those atypical "former Os," blue-white a long time ago but balanced at exactly the right ratio of size-to-heat to slide much more slowly down the main sequence than usual.

Gabriel didn't have enough data to support that theory: *Schmetterling* carried a lot of gazetteer and hard info on her Grid, but not so much theoretical or detailed astronomical data. He was going to have to let that lie for the moment. If he was right, and the star was older than it looked and had experienced flares or luminosity, then maybe he had reason to be most suspicious of Calderon and Ilmater, the two innermost planets of the Algemron system. They might be more of an age with the star and might have suffered the consequences of whatever irregularities it went through in its earlier stages.

They were seared bare, both of them, too close to the present Algemron to be inhabited. Ilmater was mostly rock, Calderon a wilderness of molten metal with here and there a seasonal outcrop of solids. Early in the system's development, there had been frequent attempts to set up bases to mine metals and other strategic elements on Calderon. Many of them failed, betrayed by the vulnerability of such installations to attack—first in the colonial period disagreements between the Austrins and Thuldans, then later when the Alitarins and Galvinites became involved. Presently five Austrin metals extractions plants were operational on Calderon, but their positions were as precarious as those of any other installations built there. If war broke out in earnest, Gabriel was willing to believe that these would be among the first casualties.

Then there's Ilmater . . . that planet presented its own problems. At closest approach, it was only about 0.4 AU from Galvin, and the Alitarins had often attempted to establish a base there, while the Galvinites had done everything they could to block it. After the cease-fire some years back, the Alitarins had finally given up on these attempts, probably preferring to devote the needed funds to rebuilding the shattered infrastructure of the homeworld. Gabriel had a feeling that it had never entirely left either side's minds, and activity on Ilmater would immediately produce a lot of hostile interest.

He shook his head. The whole age question was insoluble without a lot more data, and he was unlikely to be able to find what he needed in time to do him any good. Besides, he thought then, what about Danwell? That would seem to throw the "age" theory out the window. Danwell was a youngish planet, as far as he knew, with a lot of active mountain building.

"Damn it," Gabriel muttered. The best he would be able to manage would be to use the stone to sense directly for location when they came out at Algemron.

He laughed briefly then, for as they had all sat at dinner the night before, Helm had once again fired the question at him. "We were *at* Algemron! Why didn't that damned stone set off its little warning bells *then,* for Thor's sake, instead of dragging us all the way to Coulomb?"

Gabriel could only shake his head. The Patterner had spoken of "ongoing programming." It was possible that the right "circuitry" simply had not been in place in Gabriel's head either to sense the facility in Algemron or to do anything with it if he had sensed it. That was all theory, too, at the moment, and he could only laugh and say to Helm, "We wouldn't have been able to get near it then anyway on our own—not with the Galvinites all over us as soon as we turned up. Now at least we have a chance."

"The only problem," Angela said, "is that then we were driving our ships, and we're *not* driving this one. What happens when we get to Algemron?"

"You'll all be free," Gabriel said, "so the captain says. I don't see why she would change her mind about that between now and then. If they'd seen cause to keep you when they first laid hands on you, they'd have said as much, but as to what else happens when we arrive . . ." He shook his head. "It's a mess over there."

They had been reading the news too. They agreed with

him, and dinner broke up in rather somber mood. Only
Delde Sota paused just before going out and slipped her
braid around his wrist to touch the medchip embedded
there and assess his condition for herself.

The look that crossed her face had struck Gabriel as
unusual.

"What?" Gabriel asked.

Delde Sota's face could be difficult to decipher at times.
The slightly slanted eyes and the high cheekbones always
made her look slightly haughty, and her thoughtful expressions sometimes could be misread as unduly cool, but now
she glanced up at Gabriel as the microfibrils interwoven
with the prehensile end of the braid interfaced with the
chip, and the look in her eyes was actually faintly envious.

"Possibly not as bad an outcome as expected," she said
quietly.

"What makes you think that?" Gabriel said.

He had been nervous enough about going to sleep just
the night before. This morning he had awakened feeling not
much different than yesterday—but such were the events of
the recent days that he mistrusted that judgment.

"Great increases in brain connectivity," she said, "as if
hardware 'bandwidth' was increasing. Myelination in
corpus callosum increasing."

"Is that good?"

"Assessment: it's impossible," she said. "Baseline: you
are long past period for active brain growth. Good thing,
head probably big enough already."

"Hmf."

"Nonetheless growth occurs but not in mass. *Quality* of
brain tissue shifting somewhat. Balance shifting somewhat
toward white matter, away from gray. Interconnectivity
among neurons increasing considerably over early base-
lines. Considerable opportunity here for study, research.
Possible useful spinoffs for various scholia of medical
treatment. May get to write that paper after all."

"You'll get to be famous, finally."

Delde Sota drew her statuesque self up and gave him a lordly look. "Fact: fame fleeting. *Service* lasts. Nice to get the occasional citation out of it, however." She undid her braid from around his wrist, gave him a curious little half-nod, and went out.

Now, as usual, he sat wondering what she'd meant. His mind still felt as if it were his own. The nervousness he had felt the other day was easing off a little. Maybe it was just all so new . . .

He would have given a great deal to be able to live in a time, oh, a year ago say, when sleep was just that, something you could depend on, something that happened at a fairly regular time, and after which you did not wake up and find out that your corpus callosum—whatever that was—was bigger or smaller or missing. That was another world, he thought as he lay down, and who knows what it'll all turn into tomorrow . . .

Chapter Sixteen

THE NEXT EVENING they were all at dinner in the common room of the brig when the door opened, and Elinke Dareyev came in.

She stood there looking cool and captainly. Bearing the timing in mind, she was almost certainly on her way to dinner in the officers' mess, and Gabriel's insides seized a little at the thought of the last time he could remember seeing her at such a time. It had been the party after the peace agreement between Phorcys and Ino was sealed, the night before it was signed, the night that that other Marine, long gone home now, Big Mil, had given him the stone.

The night before it all had changed . . .

Everyone looked up at her. Gabriel rose to greet her, a sudden access of the old reflex from his Marine days, and rather oddly, to Gabriel's turn of mind, so did Helm. Enda bowed her head a little to the captain, and Angela—

She looked up at Dareyev, and there was an unusual flicker in her eyes. Gabriel saw the look pass between them, saw Dareyev turn away, frowning, and saw Angela do the same.

Jealousy was his immediate assumption.

Then he made a face. Come on, Gabriel thought. Elinke was right. This thinking you're the center of the universe can really get in the way of rationality sometimes. You may be a primed weapon, but that doesn't mean that every woman you see has her eyes on you.

"Captain," Gabriel said.

Elinke looked around at all of them. "I just wanted to let you know," she said, "that we'll be making starrise at

Algemron in seventeen and a half hours. All of your ships will be returned to you, and you'll be free to pursue your business in the system once we make position and are secured. If I were you, I'd leave the area with all due speed. The indications are not good."

Gabriel looked at her. "Starrise indications?" he said.

"I did not feel it was fair to make this starrise without telling you," Dareyev said. "Before we left, the starfall indicators gave us positive indications of an indeterminate number of incoming vessels making for Algemron space. Most of them will arrive within the next hundred hours. Some will arrive sooner. Many of our own vessels and those of other friendly stellar nations are incoming as well, per orders from the Concord Administrators in the system, but that space is about to become a battleground, and you would be well advised to take yourself to safe haven immediately."

Helm looked at her and said, "Space around Algemron is not entirely controlled by Galvin and Alitar, or by the Concord either, for that matter."

She nodded. "I agree, but when the Concord passes this information on to the planetary governments, it will almost certainly cause both governments to go to their highest states of alert. They will both send their fleets out as soon as logistics enable them to do so, and they will start shooting at anything not identifiable as their own—as well as at one another, of course."

"They would have started this anyway," Gabriel said.

"I think you're right," Elinke replied. "The upcoming close approach was already appearing to be more active than the last. Now it *is* starting, and we are very unsure what will happen when their war—almost certain to be a rather smaller war—brushes up against the beginning of this big one."

She looked at them one by one, though not at Gabriel. "Those of you who are not under durance here, I say again that you're free to go. Please do so." She turned to leave.

"Captain," Helm said.

She paused and looked at him.

"We've come a long way with Gabriel," he said. "We're not going to drop him off in the middle of anybody's war and run away. I do not hire myself out to the military, but I have a suspicion which side in this war Gabe's going to wind up on . . . and I'll fight on that side and take my chances. After that, I want a chance to testify at his trial."

Grawl looked up at Dareyev as well and said, "Warriorleader, he speaks for us as well. To our capacity, we will fight, but I reserve the right to make the songs afterwards."

Elinke produced a very dry expression. "In the middle of a major fleet engagement, I intend to decline the invitation to get involved in a copyright dispute. You'll have to handle that yourself. As for the rest of you . . . don't say I didn't warn you."

She nodded to them all and went out.

Enda looked over at Gabriel. "Not a lot of information there for you, was there?"

He shook his head. "I didn't expect there to be. I don't think she's entirely made up her mind what tack to take. There's always the question of what orders she may find waiting for her when she gets there. She may be reluctant to commit herself and then find herself having to do something else entirely."

Enda looked at him. "If things become hectic, this may be the last chance we all have to be together before having to take the ships out and decide what to do next."

"We'll stay close to *Schmetterling* if they let us," Helm said. "Otherwise we may need to get on out to Pariah Station so we have a quiet place to make plans."

Gabriel nodded.

They did not linger over it. They made their good-byes casually—purposefully so, Gabriel thought, as if they would all be meeting again after the next starfall/starrise cycle. Except the symmetry was wrong here. They were in

starfall already and about to come out. Everything was
inverted. Nothing was going to be the same again.

Finally Gabriel was left alone in the common room, and
from there he made his way back to his cell and waited to
be secured there. For the next couple of hours he watched
the news from Algemron again, heard again that crowd-roar
with the shriek at the edges, and could only feel very sorry
for the people who were wasting their breath. Quite soon,
they were going to discover what Gabriel already knew too
well: that wars are not won by shouting.

Several hours along in this process, he blinked and
realized that there was a now-familiar noise that he had
not heard an hour or two previously, when he should
have: the sound of the solenoid clicking shut in the door
to his cell.

Gabriel stood up, bemused, and went over to the door . .
. then paused. He hated to look foolish by trying the lock
and finding himself shut in.

He tried it, and the door slipped open.

Gabriel stepped out into the hall. It was dimmed down
to almost-dark and empty—he was the only prisoner at
the moment. Down in the meeting area, he could see a
faint light.

He made his way quietly down there, every moment
expecting to come across a Marine guard who would order
him back the way he came. None such appeared, and the
door to the outer guard post was closed.

Gabriel stood in the doorway of the meeting area. It
was dim in there too, and the couches had been folded
down from the wall. The display against the wall was on,
faintly lighting the room, and someone indistinct was sitting on one of the couches watching *Verge Hunter,* for as
he came in he heard the traditional cry, "Not for myself,
but *for the Force!*" He didn't quite know whether to
laugh or burst out crying. Too many memories of hearing
Elinke Dareyev shouting that at the end of a boozy officers' mess, too many memories of watching it during late

stardrive nights on *Sunshine*. All gone now. All over, those parts of his life . . . both of them.

Gabriel looked at the figure sitting curled up on the couch and waited for his night vision to kick in. After a moment, he saw that it was Angela.

"Uh," Gabriel said and went and sat down near her. "My door seems to have been left unlocked."

"I know," Angela said. "I asked the captain."

Gabriel looked at her, opened his mouth, and closed again. Angela Valiz and Elinke Dareyev . . . together in the same room, alone. He realized suddenly that *that* was a conversation he would have paid the intelligence organization of his choice a lot to record for him.

"When?"

"A couple of days ago. She only said yes a little while ago. I didn't really have a chance to tell you."

"You didn't . . ." Gabriel paused. "You didn't tell her you were social services, did you?"

She gave Gabriel a very annoyed look. "I told her I was worried about you, and that I thought you might possibly feel like some company tonight, under the circumstances."

"What circumstances would those be?"

"That tomorrow we were coming out at Algemron," Angela replied, "and no matter what she decided to do with you when you got there, you were probably going to be in a lot of trouble. With a battle this size about to occur, anything might happen."

"Mmm," Gabriel said.

"And frankly," Angela said, "I thought I might be able to use a little company myself."

He looked at her and smiled just slightly.

"Well," Gabriel said, "just this once."

"Just this once."

Gabriel pulled Angela close and buried his face in her neck. He held her to him, hard.

* * * * *

Much later, in the near darkness, still holding her, Gabriel's eyes opened. He stared at the ceiling, but that was not what he saw or heard.

Somewhere on the other side of the darkness, light was stirring inside the stone. Something was breathing. Something knew he was coming, and it was waking up.

The initial indication had come four days ago, a flicker of sensation along nerve-lines that were the strings in space and the less palpable ones in drivespace, the gossamer threads of subdimensional energy that held everything together. Something had plucked one particular string, a very central one, and slowly the resonance was spreading throughout the unseen structure. One note, making the string next to it vibrate and then the next one and the one after that. One long harmony, dissonant at first, then resolving . . .

This is the time. . . .

The time is here. . . .

The time is here, but not the *man* . . . so the harmony, the knowledge, had said several days ago. One ship was moving closer to the place appointed, through the night that stretched between and under the realities, and the harmonies were shifting, the note was changing.

Soon the one waited for, the *man,* would be there, and then it would be the time. Everything would be ready.

They would come back.

He would be there. The two sets of circumstances, both set in order so long ago, would come together at last.

Then maybe . . . maybe . . .

Gabriel lay there looking into that plangent darkness and felt himself about ready to lose his temper again.

They will come back, he thought. *Who's that?*

No response.

All right, he thought, *be cryptic, but "maybe?" All this power, all this preparation, and the best you can do is "maybe?"*

A pause while the silence parsed his statement and composed a reply.

Yes or no, it came back after a while, cool and unconcerned, *rests only with you.*

"Wha—" said a soft voice in the darkness.

"Just a dream," Gabriel said, desperately hoping that this was true.

"Well, go back to sleep."

That being all Gabriel could do, he did.

Chapter Seventeen

THE SHIP'S GRID carried the starfall, a great wash of pale blue fire running down over everything and revealing Algemron's yellow star again. The imager showed little more than that before shutting down, and Gabriel turned away from it and started putting his things back into the little bag that Enda had brought over from *Sunshine*. He was about to be moved again, he felt sure.

When the Marines came for him to escort him to the bridge, Gabriel was ready for them. They took him away without a word, escorting him down the long white corridors to a lift. Gabriel did not need to speak to them to know the level of tension in the ship. He could have felt it in the air even before the stone had started doing things to his head, and now the place seemed to be positively singing with it—the feel of taut nerves and racing minds, adrenaline rushing. His back actually started to hurt from it.

The bridge itself, when Gabriel got there, was darkened down to alert lighting, cubic displays and screens alight everywhere, and over it all ran a cacophonous babble of incoming comms. Gabriel had not been on many cruiser bridges in his time. His last memory of one, *Falada's* bridge, was terrible enough for him mostly to have stifled it—or rather, he had little left of it except for the frozen look on Elinke Dareyev's face as she stood there on the big central dais gazing down on him, friend turned enemy and accuser. Now she was striding around from station to station around that big star-backed space and looking over her people's shoulders angrily.

She swung on Gabriel as he was ushered in. "Do you know what's going on out there?"

He looked past her toward the great main viewports. Stars shone untroubled through them. There was nothing to see.

"The only thing I'm sure of," he replied, "is that the Precursor facility out there is awake."

"You bet it is!" she said. "I don't believe anyone in the system appreciates your little joke!"

"Excuse me, Captain?" Gabriel asked.

"You know what you pulled in that other facility back on Ohmel."

"I'm not doing it here."

"Connor," said the captain, "both Alitar and Galvin comms are reporting sporadic power losses, transmission losses, broadcast power interruption, you name it. Ships in flight have crashed. People are dying down there."

"Captain, I'm not doing it! *That's* doing it." He waved his hand at the darkness, at the Precursor facility. Gabriel could feel it clearly through the skin of the ship, now, like sun on his bare body or an energy bolt going by too close through lightly rated armor. It stung, an unsettling sensation.

"Well, you'd better start talking it out of doing it, because the war is starting *right now*. Galvin and Alitar both think that their systems failures are some kind of attack from the other side, and they're sending their fleets up right now—those that are ready to move. Too damned many of them, in Galvin's case. They're going to be all over local space in a little while, shooting at anything that moves—"

"Crap," Gabriel said softly. Against what was coming, a united defense was going to be the only hope. Even a few ships one way or another might make a difference against the vast fleet incoming. Numbers weren't everything, you couldn't always tell . . .

"That includes *us,* you might remember," Elinke said. "So if you have any way to affect *this* facility, this is the time to do it."

Gabriel put his hand in his pocket and closed his eyes for a moment. The stone was throbbing—that stinging, insistent pulse, wanting something but not being able to do it for the moment.

"I can't affect it remotely," he said, "and I don't know for sure what needs to be done, anyway. If we can find the place, I can get into it and start figuring out how to make it behave."

She stared at him. "What do you mean 'find it'? I thought you knew where it was!"

"It's here in the system, all right," Gabriel told her. "I can feel it. What's *that* way?" He pointed down toward the floor of the ship and to the right.

"Talk to the navs officer," Elinke said. She made her way up to the dais and to her control seat, smacking its arm. The local 3-D representation of local space came to life all around her, so that she was suddenly a black-clad figure seemingly surrounded by a great globe of stars. Elinke gathered the representation in around her with a gesture of her arms and pulled one part of it closer to study. The noise of the comms all around was getting louder, angry voices elsewhere in the system shouting commands, screaming entreaties for help, confused babble coming from every quarter . . .

Gabriel made his way up to the navs officer, a short fair young man with a long nose and very blue eyes, which were wearing a coolness at the moment all out of joint with the way he was feeling inside. The name Viipunen was stitched onto his uniform. Gabriel got a sudden flash of the man's fear as he looked over to one side at the starrise/starfall detector, a most unusual piece of equipment for a ship as small as a cruiser to have, but this cruiser had been Lorand Kharls's base of operations, which had caused it to be rather better equipped than might have been expected. The display, about a meter high and a meter deep, showed space out to about fifty light-years, a bit more room than could be covered by *Schmetterling*'s normal starfall of thirty-five. The display was littered with tiny sparks. Gabriel had trouble judging how many at a quick glance. Hundreds would not have been too high an estimate.

"Listen," he said to the officer, "before we get started— where are my shipmates?"

The officer glanced at him, then looked over his shoulder at Captain Dareyev. She had heard the question. She nodded and waved a hand at him. "They're down in the bay, getting their ships ready. Let him talk to them if he wants to." She turned her back and got back to assessing the strategic situation.

"Right. My ship," he sad. "*Sunshine.*"

"Is that the little one?"

Gabriel gave him a look. Most private ships looked small next to *Lalique,* even Helm's. "Don't rub it in."

The nav officer smiled very slightly, touched his controls, and nodded at Gabriel.

"Enda?" Gabriel said.

"Here, Gabriel. Getting the systems up and running."

"What's the plan?"

"All of us will make for Pariah Station," she said, "unless you can provide something better."

"I'm looking at things right now," Gabriel said. "I'll tell you that they don't look great."

He was aware of the navs officer watching him intently. He didn't want to say anything that the man would take as compromising *Schmetterling*'s security.

"Well, we knew that before," Enda said, "but I am glad you were able to contact me, Gabriel. Two things. First, seeing that battle may ensue, I have left your suit for you. It is in the shuttle bay, and the Marines said they would see that you got it. Second, when I came in I turned on the info-trading system to load the local Grid. I got rather more than that, however. There is a drivespace relay in the system."

Gabriel looked over his shoulder at the tactical display in the midst of which Captain Dareyev stood. It was so cluttered with ships of all kinds, little red and blue and yellow

blips that he could hardly make out the real stars that
formed its background, but there was one very large blue
one that stood out.

"*Lighthouse* is here," Gabriel said.

"That would make sense. I did not see the system heralds come up. I was attending to other things." He was
almost certain she meant the weapons. "The system has
picked up some mail for you."

His eyebrows went up. "What is it?"

"I cannot tell. It is password-locked."

He sighed, leaned close to the pickup, and whispered his
password.

"Thank you," she said. There was a moment's silence.
"Shall I read it?"

"Yes. Who's it from?"

"I cannot tell. The headers are encrypted."

Not my father . . . Gabriel blinked hard a few times.
"Read it."

She paused. "It says, 'Message received. Contents noted.' "

"No other comment?"

"And no signature," Enda said. "The origin nodes and
transit path have been disguised."

"All right," Gabriel said, deciding to let it lie there.

Captain Dareyev said to him, rather pointedly, "Where
exactly are we supposed to be *going*, Connor?"

The nav officer turned to glare at him.

"Later, Enda," Gabriel said. "Feel for the stone."

"Ah," she said. "I will do that."

"Tell the others I said good luck. Keep them posted."

I will, he heard her think, quite clearly. There was a flash
of fear of the situation behind that, fear of the stone, but she
was managing them both.

Can we stay in touch this way? he asked silently.

*Difficult to say. I believe the effect may not propagate
well over distance when one or more of the parties are
under stress.*

Stress, Gabriel thought. Wonderful . . .

"Connor!"

"Yes, Captain," he said. He nodded to the navs officer. "All right, this is going to look weird . . . so bear with me." He pulled out the stone and closed his eyes, feeling for the source of the sensation that he had only been sensing bluntly and generally until now. "I'm going to point, and I want you to take a bearing identical to the direction in which I'm pointing. Then we're going to have to go in that direction at best speed."

"No problem," said the young man's voice. "Tell me when you're ready."

Gabriel concentrated on the stone, on the source of the stinging sensation, that feeling of something out there alive . . . and angry. That was a new one on him. If he had gotten any emotional effect from the facility on Ohmel, it had been one of patience, cool waiting, calm evaluation, and utmost logic with no passion or emotion of any kind. This place, though, felt as if it had woken up enraged. It was running power through conduits that had not been used for a long while, systems that had been offline for ages . . . and now it was having to compensate for a whole new set of baseline energy readings in its area. Gabriel was shown, in a flash, a great sheaf of criteria and qualities of this system that had changed and to which the place was now having to adapt.

People, he thought. There was no one living here when it was last active a few minutes ago . . . or a hundred years . . .

He shook his head.

"There," he said to the navs officer, pointing as exactly as he could toward the heart of that awakening, testy energy. "Can you work with that, Mr. Viipunen?"

"I think so."

He opened his eyes again and watched the young man work briefly at his console. The starrise/starfall indicator next to him went briefly dark, then filled with a system schematic for Algemron. One small white light, slow-moving, indicated *Schmetterling*. From it, a white line ran outward, down into the plane of the ecliptic and into the space between the little white globes marking the small gas giant Dalius and the icy planet Reliance. Between the two worlds, a faint band of representative glitter lay.

"The asteroid belt," Gabriel said . . . and suddenly smiled slightly, for things were now starting to make sense. "Can you go higher definition on this?"

"Yes, sir, I can," replied Viipunen, doing it, "but there's hardly any need, because I know what you're pointing at already." The tank shimmered, and the white line now ran in through its top, out through its bottom, and very nearly speared a small irregular shape tumbling through the sparks of light that represented the rest of the belt.

"Argolos," Viipunen said. "Is that what you're after?"

"Has to be," Gabriel said. "Has to."

Argolos was one of two big fragments left over from the destruction of the planet that had once occupied this orbit. The astronomers said that another star with its own system of planets had come straight through this system, millions of years back. One of the planets of the other star had managed somehow to collide with Havryn. Havryn had nearly been torn apart but had managed to resettle itself, though at the price of the loss of most of its kinetic energy. It was now just about the slowest-rotating gas giant known. After the dust settled—literally and figuratively—the space between Dalius and Reliance had filled up with the wreckage of the collision, the remains of the other planet. Two big pieces remained: Wreathe and Argolos, both of them rich in heavy metals and big enough to be mined.

How old was the star that passed through here? Gabriel thought. How old were its planets? He grinned more broadly. Accidents did happen in space, but not accidents like this, and not where the Precursors were concerned.

"That's it," Gabriel said.

"Argolos, Captain," said the navs officer.

"Damnation!" Elinke said. "You mean we're going to have to run all the way out there, when right here we've got—"

Alarms began to go off, and people changed stations in a hurry. Gabriel heard several of them say to one another, "Casting gunnery loose. I have your weapon. I confirm it hot—"

Captain Dareyev pointed at part of the starry display englobing her and beckoned it bigger. It ballooned until she was in the midst of a three-meter globe of stars and tiny globes, the globes moving in a pattern, each tagged with a small letter-and-number label that followed it.

"We have a Galvinite fleet coming at us, fifteen vessels in quarter-englobe. Six corvettes, six cutters, three frigates, no problem."

Gabriel swallowed. He had heard reports of this kind from Elinke before, but the numbers had been smaller.

"Navs, shape us one thirteen on the ecliptic, best solution for Dalius. I'm going to go in low and shake up our little friends' gravity grids a little, and then we'll consider our options. Comms, warn that fleet off and tell them my rules of engagement now allow their destruction, and I think that would be a real pity. Then get me *Namur*—my compliments to Captain Estevan. I think we should get together and have a little shooting match right now. Give her the coordinates—"

"Captain!" Gabriel interrupted.

"It's kind of a shame, since there are other things we're all probably going to be shooting at," Elinke said, wheeling in her display to bring the neighborhood of Dalius up big, "but I have a job to do, and if these people put themselves in my way, too bad."

"Captain!"

She looked at him with annoyance that for once was not directed at him. "Sorry, Connor," she said. "No time for your side trip at the moment. We're going to be busy."

"If I don't get out there, Captain, it's going to be disastrous for everyone. You *know* why. Please let me."

She frowned at him through that cloak of stars, while she touched one after another of the enemy ships with a finger, targeting them for her gunnery crew in one color, marking those for *Namur* in another. "If you think I am going to let you depart custody at this point, Connor, you had better think again."

He was getting desperate. "Look, I'm glad to give you parole, but you've got to let me get out there, or there won't be any trial."

"Let *me* take him out, if there's a problem," said a soft voice from one side.

Gabriel turned. Aleen Delonghi was standing there, not in Intel uniform to Gabriel's surprise, but kitted out as a Star Force commander. She looked over at Dareyev, who raised her eyebrows.

"If you lose him . . ." Dareyev warned her.

"Oh, no," said Delonghi, "not at this point. Our people have too many questions they want to ask him."

Captain Dareyev studied both of them. "Kharls trusts you," she said after a moment. "That's good enough for me." She turned to Gabriel. "Go with her. Comms, have a small detachment of Marines go with them—a shuttle's worth."

"Thank you, Captain." Gabriel said.

"Don't thank me yet," said Elinke with a dry look, "and don't get killed. You're needed for that trial you seem so eager to save us all for."

"I'll keep him safe for you," Delonghi said, "never fear."

They headed off the bridge together, on the egde of another blast of klaxons.

"They're really coming this time, aren't they?" she said as they ran down the corridor toward the lift for the shuttle bay.

"They really are."

*   *   *   *   *

In the bay, half a dozen Marines joined them.

"Get him suited, and give him some armor," said Delonghi. "He's going to need it where we're going."

"Eighteen on the chiton, forty-four inseam on the

greaves," Gabriel said, and the other Marines looked at him in brief surprise . . . then some faces changed as they remembered who he was.

He blinked. The wash of discomfort and distrust that came to him from them was very hard to take. This gift of mindwalking, he thought, if it is a gift, is not all it's cracked up to be. There was no time to waste wishing it gone. He needed it now, and anyway, Gabriel thought, it's too late. I'm hardwired.

One of them, a young woman with a mass cannon slung over her back, returned from an armory cabinet at the side of the shuttle bay with a breastplate, apron and leg pieces, and Gabriel's suit. Gabriel suited up and strapped on the armor with the speed of long practice, noticing the names on the chitons around him. Lacey, Dirigent, Rathbone, MacLain, and on the young woman's chiton, Bertin. It sounded familiar.

"You were on *Falada*," Gabriel said, very quietly.

She looked at Gabriel. "Yes."

"Well met, shipmate," Gabriel said, knowing all too well what response he was likely to get.

He got it. Bertin turned away without a word. Gabriel finished checking his armor then looked up at Delonghi, who had been watching this. She had a gun. Everyone else had a gun.

"Well?" he said.

Delonghi looked at him then shook her head.

"I gave parole."

"Don't know if my trust extends that far," Delonghi said. "Let it lie for now. We'll see how you behave. Get in."

They piled into the shuttle.

"Captain's done us a favor," Delonghi said as she slipped into the pilot's seat and started heating the shuttle up. "When she swings past Dalius, she'll have brought us a lot of the way we needed to go anyway. Time to Argolos won't be more than, oh, twenty minutes from there."

Gabriel nodded and gulped. He could feel some kind of

large shadow moving over him, and he wasn't sure he liked
the feel of it, for he didn't know what it was.

Yes I do, he thought then. It was like this on Ohmel
when the VoidCorp cruisers turned up.

Something coming out of drivespace. Something *big* . . .

But it hadn't happened yet. It would happen soon,
though. He wished he was somewhere that he could see, but
soon enough they would be on Argolos, and he ought to be
able to get a glimpse from there.

He closed his eyes for a moment. *Enda?*

Nothing.

Enda?

Very faintly he heard the answer. *I hear.*

Argolos, Enda!

*So I thought. I am glad, Gabriel! I thought I caught an
image, a white line—*

That was me. Can you feel the stone?

It is faint. There is an anger that interferes—

That's on Argolos, Gabriel told her. *This facility doesn't
feel like the other one. This may not be as easy—*

I did not think that *one was particularly easy,* she
replied. *The stone was like a live thing then—and an angry
one. What it may become like now . . .*

Gabriel started to shake his head then stopped himself.
Gods only knew what the Marines would think. *Got to
make some conversation here, Enda,* he said. *Tell the
others—*

Helm knows. We follow.

*Tell him I'm with a bunch of Marines. He's not to try
anything dumb, like a snatch. I need to work with these
people. Some of them are friends.* Gabriel felt like laughing
at the next thing he needed to tell her and had to stifle that
too. *Delonghi is here.*

Is she indeed?

She's the one who pried me out of there, Gabriel said. *I
tell you, I don't know what to think of my fellow human
beings any more. You think you know them, and then. . . !*

Ironic laughter from the other end of the tenuous thread of communication. *If you—*

Snapped. Gone, as Delonghi lifted the shuttle out of the bay, and all around him Bertin and Lacey and the other Marines sat and fingered their weapons.

"Cent for your thoughts, Connor," said Delonghi. She brought the shuttle around in a big curve away from *Schmetterling,* and once again Gabriel got to appreciate the big deadly curves of her from underneath, the gunports open and hot, Algemron's light on her sleek sides. Good luck, he thought.

A sudden sense of shock from a mind very ordered, very excited, very ready inside *Schmetterling* . . . but not ready for this, not for *hearing* him when he wasn't even there, like a sudden pang of a overactive or overburdened conscience.

Elinke—

Gabriel shied away from that contact. He had already learned too much from his first one. He didn't want any more right now.

"Wouldn't know that they're worth that much at the moment," he replied.

She glanced at him from the pilot's couch, bringing the shuttle around expertly and bringing up the navigation display. Argolos showed in it, tumbling gently some ten thousand kilometers away. Delonghi locked the ship onto it and touched the autopilot to life.

"Keep an eye on it," she said to Rathbone, who was co-piloting.

"Yes, ma'am."

They rode in silence for a while, as Delonghi checked her own weapons and slung them about her. Then she looked over at Gabriel.

"I suppose," she said, "that all this comes as a surprise to you."

He nodded.

"Look," she said, "if I was wrong the last time we met, maybe this is my chance to put it all right."

"All of it?" Gabriel said. "You were going to blow my ship up. You were going to shoot me."

"You threw *me* in a meat locker," she said, "and assaulted me telepathically."

The other Marines were looking at her in some bemusement as she said this.

"All right," Gabriel conceded, "it's true about the meat locker."

Lacey, Dirigent and even Bertin turned their faces away from Gabriel, but this did nothing to hide their smiles. He could "hear" them from the inside in perfect clarity. He was not going to say anything about the telepathic "assault."

Well, it *was* assault, maybe, he thought, but she was lying to me. I had no choice.

She was hiding something. She was working with someone else . . . gods know who. I never did find out.

Just for that moment the thought tempted him. He might have refrained from using this technique on Elinke, but Delonghi was no friend of his, and whatever favors she did him, Gabriel was sure she was doing for her own reasons.

The stone was inside his suit glove. That had seemed the simplest way to stay in contact with it. Now he considered how best to proceed. Reach out very carefully and—

"Ma'am," said Rathbone, "we've got company."

Delonghi looked away from Gabriel and said, "What?"

"Three ships. Looks like the ones we were carrying in *Schmetterling*."

She looked at the tactical display and saw the ships' IDs displayed.

"Yes indeed," Delonghi said. "I was wondering if they would turn up. Thought they would have cut and run."

Gabriel opened his mouth to say, "You don't know them very well," and then closed it again. For the moment he put aside the thought of "leaning" on her and merely said, "Look, Commander, I've told them they're not to try anything dumb. I have no desire to leave custody at the moment, no matter what you might think."

"If they come near you," she said, "if they try to come near me, I will personally fry them. Do you hear me? Even if I believed your bona fides, which is a moot point right now, I don't believe in theirs. I promised the captain I would bring you back for trial in good condition, and I will." She smiled slightly.

Gabriel fell quiet for a moment. *Enda,* he thought.

A faint response. *Query?*

Stay out of sight. She's not going to be reasonable. She'll shoot if she sees you come near.

Noted.

Feel for the stone.

Yes. A shiver. Gabriel felt slightly guilty making her expose herself to it, but it was the only way for her to be sure where he was.

They skimmed low over Argolos. It was a good-sized fragment of rock that was a little embedded ice. Several small domed mining facilities were scattered here and there over the moonlet's surface. Along with the scratches and gouges of many abandoned attempts and many more scars caused by crashed ships were several destroyed facilities dating back to earlier times—places that had been wiped out by attacks.

"All right, Connor," said Delonghi, looking down at the scarred surface of the place with a skeptical expression. "Where's what you're looking for?"

"Can I get Mr. Rathbone to hover for a bit," Gabriel said, "so I can get a directional fix?"

Rathbone reached into the central display and made a couple of adjustments. A few moments later, the shuttle was proceeding in a path identical to the moonlet's, nearly stationary above it, as the moonlet tumbled very slightly below.

"Good," Gabriel said. "Hold that, please."

He closed his eyes and felt down below him. At first he expected a stronger-weaker-stronger pattern, like the one he had gotten from the site at Ohmel, but this time it seemed less straightforwardly directional, more diffuse.

He opened his eyes again, startled by the conclusion. Nearly the whole moonlet was full of this particular Precursor facility.

In fact, he thought, that might be what held the thing together when it hit the gas giant all that while ago. He swallowed and had hard work of it; his mouth had gone dry at the thought of how much Precursor material might be buried in such a place. It also amazed him slightly that no mining operations here had managed to come up against any Glassmaker material.

Maybe not, Gabriel thought. Increasingly he was beginning to believe that nothing associated with these places was accidental.

"All right," he said after a moment. "Just land anywhere."

Delonghi gave him a cockeyed look. *"Anywhere?"*

"Probably somewhere away from one of the domes would be better," Gabriel replied. "See if you can find something like a cliff face or a ravine."

They found one after a few minutes—the remnant of some rocky hillsides up near the "pointy" end of the moonlet, mined once or twice and then abandoned. The pilot landed the shuttle there, and Gabriel and all the others checked their suit gaskets and then stepped out into the light gravity of the moonlet's surface.

All this while Delonghi was watching Gabriel like someone she expected to catch in a trick. He walked over to one of the nearer hillsides with all the Marines and their weapons in tow and stood there with his fist clenched on the stone, deep in concentration.

It was all over. It was under his feet. It was buried in the hill. Gabriel could feel it under him, alive, breathing like some gigantic beast. He felt like a character in one of those ancient pre-space stories of a mariner who lands on what he thinks is an island. Everything is fine until he builds a fire. Then the "island" arches its back, rolls him and the fire and everything else off into the endless sea, and the great maw opens to devour him. . . .

I don't care much for the first part of that image, Gabriel thought, but the "great maw" is useful. He closed his eyes again, tried to feel where the most likely contour was . . .

There. Just off to the left, down and in.

I'm here, he said to the facility. *Let me in.*

Nothing. Nothing at all.

Then just the slightest tremor . . . growing stronger so that the ground began to rattle, unheard but plainly felt under the Marines' feet. Delonghi found herself bouncing in place in shock. Little rocks danced around, and big boulders jumped and bumped in their sockets. Dust was jolted up into the hard vacuum and floated like a siliceous fog a meter or so above the surface, twinkling and jittering with the transmitted energy in Algemron's light. Lacey and Bertin lost their footing, fell down, and got up again with annoyed expressions. Gabriel shook, too, but he shook in harmony with what was shaking underneath him. He didn't fall . . . not even when the hill stood up.

It hunched up slowly, shrugging away the dust and the stones that had overlaid it. The first thing to emerge was the spire, which Gabriel had hardly expected. He had thought this would be like Ohmel, all subterranean, but this one apparently felt no need to hide. The glass grew while they watched, spinning itself up into five slim minarets, one off to the side, and a sixth one taller than all the others. This last was a towering spike, past which the silent stars slid, their light catching in it, running down it in a way that suggested the facility buried underneath here would let not even that energy be wasted. The place glittered, for this glass was less greenish than what Gabriel had seen on Ohmel, more like crystal. It grew up spikily through the ground, pushing upward, flowing as if molten, but the glass looked cold as ice, clearer than any ice Gabriel had ever seen. After the spires came the roof of the facility—or its roof for the moment. Gabriel had the feeling that this whole structure could and would resorb itself into the greater mass below if there was need. The personality of the place was

definitely more active, more aggressive than the one on
Ohmel, and even though he and it had obviously been built
or rebuilt for one another, Gabriel shivered a little at the
touch of the presence inside it, waiting impatiently for him.
It had been waiting for a long, long time. . . .

Delonghi and the Marines were staring at this in awe.
"How does it do that?" she whispered.

"Will," Gabriel answered. "The glass moves when the
will moves it . . . and until it does, unless it does, nothing
else can make the slightest impression on it. Come on."

He led them toward the broad domed wall, crowned with
spikes and spines, that now stood thirty meters high against
the hard starry dark. The wall drew aside for him.

Gabriel paused on the threshold. *Enda?*

Nothing.

It's open, he said into the silent dark. *It's perfectly visible. We're going in. You can see their shuttle parked outside.*

No answer. He would only have to hope she had
heard him.

Gabriel rested the gloved hand containing the stone
against the doorsill as he went in. As he did, he felt the
whole place shiver around him, almost flinching away from
his touch. It had been waiting for a long while, but even
now it might have to wait longer.

Lacey and Bertin went in first, at point, then stepped
aside for the others to follow them into the great central hall
that lay open before them. They all looked down and
around at the long corridors, six of them, which led from
the central hall, downward into the heart of Argolos. From
the inside, the glass was full of light, though none of this
showed on the outside. Delonghi went over to one of the
walls and touched it thoughtfully . . . then took her gloved
hand back quickly.

"It's alive!"

"It's a vessel for life," Gabriel said. "I don't know if it's
necessarily the same thing." He looked around, clenching
his fist on the stone again, saying, *Which way?*

No immediate answer.

Well, I'm here. Get on with it!

Nothing, though. Gabriel frowned. It was strange . . .

Dirigent, Rathbone and MacLain were now quartering the area, examining the openings into the long, smooth, shining corridors and looking up at the great dome that now rose above them.

"There's atmosphere in here," Dirigent said.

"Is there?" said Delonghi. She went over to look down one of the corridors.

MacLain was looking at a gauge on the outside of his sleeve. "It's inside the green zone for humans," he said. "Pressure's good."

"I'd just like to know how it's staying in here," said Lacey.

"It's some kind of invisible barrier," Gabriel replied. "Go back there to where the wall was, where it let us in. You can feel it a little as you pass through."

Delonghi looked curiously up at the dome. It appeared clear, but no stars were visible through it, only darkness. She shook her head. "Okay, people. Go ahead and reconnoiter. Check these tunnels to five hundred meters, see what you can see, then report back."

Bertin and Lacey led the way again, heading inward. The others followed.

"We really ought to stay together," Gabriel said.

"Well," she said, "I'd prefer to do the first part of this by the book, anyway." She walked over to examine the nearby wall again.

Gabriel closed his eyes for the moment and stood still, concentrating on the stone, trying to find out what the problem was. Where was the direction he was expecting?

Nothing . . .

He swore. Suddenly it was as if the crystal had gone opaque, as if there were a glass wall in his mind, and a blank one. He opened himself out as wide as he knew how and listened with everything in him.

Nothing.

"Connor."

Still listening, he opened his eyes, looked at Delonghi, and felt what he had not been open enough to feel before.

Curl. The green warmth, the writhing and stroking. It pressed, pressed on her mind, and there was no way she could fight it, none at all. It had been there too long. The only question was how much Delonghi there was in there anymore.

All this in a single moment of absolute shock and horror. Gabriel opened his mouth to say he didn't know what—

Everything whited out.

Gabriel crumpled. What was that? What—

The stone in his glove seared him. Then he knew. The teln in her had attacked him, tried some kind of psionic blast on him. The stone had protected him, but the protection wasn't enough. The blow hit him again, and everything whited out in pain again. Slowly, after a few moments, the world came back.

It came back to show her straddling him. Her helmet was off. She was wrestling *his* off. Her face was terrible, a complete study in serenity, pleasure, the warm stroking and writhing tangle inside her quite invisible, but its influence showing in her eyes. Those big, beautiful brown eyes . . . The windows of the soul, they called them. So they might be, but from out of those windows, there was nothing looking but teln.

". . . had enough of you," the voice was saying softly, invitingly. "Now we'll see what use you can really be. Come now, lover. Give us a kiss."

Her hands grabbed his head. Blank-eyed, smiling, she lowered her face to his, ready to cough out the larval tangle that would climb into Gabriel's mouth and possess him.

Gabriel moaned . . . and his fist, with the stone in it, came up and hit her full in the side of the head.

Delonghi screamed as the force of the blow knocked her sideways off Gabriel. He staggered to his feet.

She did too, screaming, "How can you? You can't—!"

She was fumbling around for her gun, which had gone skittering away when Gabriel hit her. Gabriel thought about going for it, too, then discarded the idea. *Just blowing her apart isn't going to be enough,* he thought, *I don't want those things crawling around in here. Everybody in the place could wind up infected.* He had no idea whether you needed a "threshold" number of larval teln for an infection to take place. Right now, he didn't care.

She spotted the gun a few meters away and made for it. Gabriel staggered after her, swung, and missed. His body was suffering from the after effects of the mindblast. Nothing was working right. He was seeing three of everything. *It could be worse,* Gabriel thought. *I should be completely immobile, but the stone spared me that.*

She was in better shape. She turned, kicked out, and caught Gabriel in the solar plexus. The stone couldn't help him with that. He went down, rolling and retching. She jumped onto him again, grabbing for his head.

Can't just lie here! Can't! Can't—!

He thrashed and writhed as best he could, rolled again, threw her off, pushed himself up to hands and knees. She came down on top of him again. He rolled, trying to get rid of her, all the while weakly cursing himself inside. Now he knew why she had been so willing to blow up his ship and nearly everything else in the area when they had first met at Danwell. Delonghi herself might not have wanted to be quite so thorough, but the teln inside her had been willing to take such action, letting her take the heat for them as an inexperienced officer overreacting to the situations with which she was presented. It was a good enough disguise.

But I was in her mind. Why didn't I hear them?

There were too many answers to bother with right now.

Gabriel rolled and struggled to keep her face away from his. *I was too inexpert,* he thought, *too new to this. Too attuned to humans and the edanweir at that point to successfully* hear *what I heard—or to hear it as separate*

thought rather than something of her own. Gabriel remembered pressing on her mind while interrogating her and
hearing the flashes of fear/terror/fear/anguish. He had
thought they were *her.* . . .

They were not. They had been half-heard thoughts from
the teln, trying to protect themselves, desperate not to be
detected.

Then Norrik, the man looking at him . . . was Delonghi
in the Algemron system then? Was Norrik's tangle in contact with hers? Had they identified Gabriel to her, alerting
her to his whereabouts, to his plans? Possibly they had
picked up some telepathic seepage from him—

Gabriel moaned and tried to shake her off. If he didn't,
those things would shortly be crawling down his own
throat. The stroking, writhing, creeping warmth would
grow inside him, until he would not be able to resist it, until
it would be all right, until they would own him.

That was the goal, of course. He had led her right to the
Precursor facility, had opened it for her and made it available. Now the Others would come, and they would know
what use to make of it. They would learn from Gabriel, too,
what more uses to make of it. For within six or eight
months, they would own him, body and soul. After that, he
would die, used up by the tangle, but by then it wouldn't
matter. They would have gained everything they needed
from him, and the Verge would be falling before them, with
the Stellar Ring to follow. Everything would go. Bluefall,
Grith, Danwell, all of it . . .

No. *No.*

It would be so nice, not to have to think any more, not to
have to worry, to be taken care of. They will take the best
care of you, and you won't worry forever. You'll learn how
to stop. We will teach you. Slowly you'll learn not to worry,
not to think, so restful, so peaceful, no more troubles, think
how lovely . . . let it happen, just let it happen, rest . . .

The wave of peace, rest and the promise of a mind emp-
tied of all its troubles washed over Gabriel. He didn't want

to move. He didn't need to move. Just rest, just let it happen
. . . rest . . . lie still and rest, and let . . . it . . . happen . . .

No.

No, I won't! STOP IT!

The answering pain in his glove was like a knife driven
through his hand. Gabriel screamed and rolled out of Delonghi's grasp one last time. It was all he had in him. He
pushed himself up to his hands and knees again. He could
hear the sound of footsteps. He tried hard to stand up, knowing that the Marines would assume that Gabriel had attacked
Delonghi. They would restrain him, and after she had recovered, when she had more privacy, she would move in on him
again, and this time she would succeed.

He got up, watched Delonghi come slowly toward
him—

A deafening roar souddenly shook the ground, and a
stream of flechettes came from the direction of the front
door, ripping her right arm off.

She staggered back, shrieking, but it was not just her
voice in the shriek. *They* were screaming, too, both in mind
and through her throat, horrified, furious at their plans
being interrupted.

Gabriel reeled back, startled out of his balance. In the
doorway, Helm stood in his ancient battered armor, holding
flechette guns in both gauntleted hands. Delonghi clutched
the bleeding ragged stump where her arm had been and
somehow, horribly, managed to lurch forward, making for
the gun on the floor.

The next stream of flechettes took her left leg off
between hip and knee. She fell over sideways and should
not have gotten up again . . . except she did, hauling herself
up, actually bearing weight right on the shattered, bleeding
bone, reaching out for the gun—

The flechettes ripped out one last time and tore her
right in two.

When he recovered, he saw Helm still standing in the
doorway, holstering the flechette guns. Delde Sota,

Grawl, Enda, and Angela were immediately behind him, all suited and all armed sufficiently to storm some unsuspecting city.

Bertin, Lacey and the other Marines came out of the tunnels, saw Helm and the others, and lifted their weapons.

"No, *don't!*" Gabriel shouted. "It's not what it looks like!"

Helm lifted what he was now bracing with his other hand, the back end of the long stock tucked under his armpit, and all of them froze. None of them had anything to match a plasma gun, and the big open bell looked more than ominous.

"Helm, *don't do it!*" Gabriel yelled at him. "They're on our side!"

"Of course they are," Helm said, though his tone was faintly ironic. "I'd never do such a thing. However . . ."

He took a few steps forward, looking at the two halves of Delonghi. "Huh," he said and poked at one half of the shredded corpse with his foot. "Lookit that. You," he said, pointing at Bertin, "and you"—pointing at Rathbone—"come here and look at this."

They came over slowly, regarding the assortment of restricted but nonetheless present firepower that was being concentrated on them.

"Look at those," Helm said.

They looked down at the writhing remnants of the teln tangle, spilled out and writhing, all green and wet in the red wetness on the floor.

"Your boss there," Helm said, "assuming she is your boss—is nobody you want to be working for. Anybody *you* know have stuff like that in them?"

Rathbone and Bertin looked at each other. Rathbone turned away and began having difficulty controlling his stomach.

"Yeah," Helm said. "Delde Sota?"

She handed him the flamer.

"Whatever she may have been before," Helm said, "she wasn't human anymore. Think a little housecleaning's in order."

He turned the flamer on Delonghi's remains until the

ragged, oozing meat and green writhing worms scorched down to bubbling juices and finally to smoking black tar. Gabriel winced, hearing the death-shriek of the teln tangle and hearing it echoed elsewhere around the system, twice, twenty times, fifty times, a hundred, more . . .

To his astonishment, the others, both Marines and Gabriel's friends were wincing, too.

"You heard that?" Gabriel managed to croak.

Plainly they had. Enda turned off to one side and began discreetly and genteelly to retch.

"Absolutely." Gabriel rubbed his face and went to get his helmet. "Helm, what's the story out there?"

"Gettin' hot," Helm said. "Everybody's gone completely bufu. Galvinites shootin' up Alitarins everywhere in sight and attacking the Concord vessels as well, but you saw that. You think *these* things are to blame?"

Gabriel shook his head. "Maybe some of them, but Helm, they were getting ready for this war anyway. This is a nice excuse." Still . . . Gabriel found himself thinking of the slightly dazed-looking man who had been sent back to Galvin by the Alitarins. Does he have a tangle inside him? He thought. Is there someone in particular they're trying to affect? Or some other plan—

His head was spinning. He put the thought aside for the moment, for it was too easy just now to let paranoia overwhelm common sense.

"The system is filling up with ships, Gabriel," Enda said. "The drivesat relay does indeed belong to the *Lighthouse*. They have been broadcasting to everyone who will listen about the incoming alien vessels—not that the Galvinites or Alitarins seem to care at the moment." Her expression was rueful. "There have been some peculiar arrivals as well. VoidCorps vessels, many of them . . ."

"Doing what?"

"Nothing. That is the great mystery. Waiting, it seems, but for what? It seems as if everything else in near space is on its way here to fight."

"It may not be enough," Gabriel said. "Oh, gods, come on. We've lost too much time already!"

He got back into his helmet, not knowing for sure what might be farther inside the facility. He was afraid. Delonghi and her tangle might be dead, but that didn't mean that he was now safe—or by extension, the others with him. How exactly does telepathy travel? he wondered. How fast, and how far? Does being in drivespace stop it? Or speed it up? For even before *Schmetterling* had made starrise, Gabriel had felt the Precursor facility here waking up. Who knew what could be heard from what distance?

He thought of the teln and shivered briefly at the memory of the stroking, writhing thought buried inside Major Norrik, how it had looked at him. Are those things sensitive to the stone? Gabriel wondered. They were all in contact with one another to a greater or lesser extent . . . at least that was what Delonghi's had intimated. Was word passed about that a "facilitator" was on the move, that something was happening?

There was no more time for to spend up here. He turned to the Marines, who were looking dubiously at Helm and Delde Sota.

"Who's CO now?" Gabriel asked.

"Me," Bertin said.

"Well, cousins," Gabriel said, using the old Marine affectionate name—and he meant it and didn't care what they thought about him using it, "you know what we were coming for, what the captain sent me to do. Do you want to come along? If you can't, if your oaths won't take the strain, my friends will hold you here." He looked at Bertin. "If you—"

He staggered and went to his knees, the stone flaming in his palm again, the vision overcoming him.

The shadow, the overarching shadow. Here. Now.

"Oh, gods," he whispered, "they're here."

Delde Sota and Enda went to him. "What?"

"Helmets," Gabriel said. "Quick. I need to have a look outside."

Everyone helmeted up again. Gabriel managed to get back to his feet and go after Helm, assisted by Delde Sota with Enda on his other side. He was weak. The shadow was in his heart as well as his mind—the cold of it, the pain struck him deep.

As they came near the exit, all of them slowed a little. The moonlet tumbled as usual, but it did so very slowly. This had been the bright end when they came in. It still should be, yet it was oddly twilit outside.

Followed by the Marines, they made their way hurriedly through the barrier and looked toward Algemron.

It was speckled and patched with many hundreds of little dark shapes, far into the system . . . a sick sun, a paling sun, which should have cast all their shadows sharp and black behind them, but now was only dim.

"When she said 'indeterminate,'" Helm whispered, "she wasn't kidding."

As they watched, starrise fire erupted in sickly purple-blue around a huge shape that slowly extruded up and out of drivespace: a great spherical ship, dark green, blooming up out of the nowhere into the here, and coming between them and the sun to blot it out entirely.

It was nightfall, but a kind that Gabriel had never thought to see and didn't want to see now. Behind him the others fell silent, horrified.

It slipped away, coming out of direct alignment with Algemron. The sun shone again, if weakly, and that image lasted not much longer, for the great mass of ships producing it was already making toward the outer planets. Gabriel was grimly amused by their bearing. It was so arranged that they would come in past the two inner planets first. They had apparently shared Gabriel's suspicion that this facility might have been planted there.

"They'll wipe out everything else that gets within range of them on the way here," he said, "but it's here they want." He did not say, *And me.*

The Marines were staring up at all this in horror.

"Buddy," Bertin said, "if you can do something to stop this, we're with you." She looked around at her comrades. Heads nodded all around.

Gabriel swallowed hard. The emotion that seized his throat at her words had not been anything he had been prepared for. "Come on."

They went back inside. Gabriel stood in the midst of the front hall and once again clenched the stone in his fist, hissing at the pain. It had burned him when he screamed his rage and defiance. *Got to find a way to teach you not to do that,* he thought. Now stop stalling. *Which way now?*

This way . . .

He startled at that silent voice. *Patterner?*

One of the three. We are all one. Come! Be quick!

"Down here, troops," Gabriel said.

He went off down one of the left-hand tunnels without a moment's hesitation. After the first moment or so, the stone almost began pulling him along, as if someone's hand was in his, hurrying him. Enda went after Gabriel. The others and the five Marines brought up the rear.

"I heard you," Enda said softly as Gabriel paused at a turning and went right, "and with great clarity, greater all the time. If you are not a mindwalker now, I do not know what to call by such a name."

"I thought," Gabriel said, "you said you had little training in this art."

"No one ever has all they need of it," Enda said. "Gabriel, I told you the truth. I know enough to get by, but my family did not consider me much of a mindwalker. I was always the one who preferred to work with physical things—suits, ships and gardens. They despaired of me."

"I think you did just fine," Gabriel said. "Now all we have to do is stay alive through this so that we can hunt that old city of yours down and I can go in there and kick some fraals' rear ends for throwing you out of there. They have no idea what they lost."

She smiled as they went around a great curve, downward and downward, a spiral. "I take that very kindly, Gabriel. I too will kick some fundaments at your trial, if given the opportunity."

He laughed gently as they trotted down the long curve together.

"Here we are," he said, "acting as if we're going to survive this. You know as well as I do that that big ship is sending down smaller craft this minute, and this place is going to be full of bad guys shortly."

"Can you not seal the outer entry?"

"I tried," Gabriel said. "Seems like there are still some things to be done before my control here is complete."

"You had better get on with it, then."

Gabriel had to laugh. Silently, in his mind, he said to the silent presence that was listening, *Where* were *you?*

Waiting.

You might have let me know!

Not while that *was here.* It pointed through Gabriel's mind at the dry baked stain on the floor of the main hall. *One of the enemies . . .*

Your makers seem to have had a whole lot of them.

There are many, some surviving from the ancient days, some new ones. We have no power against them by ourselves. Only you can empower us.

Gabriel blinked and raced down the tunnel, Enda coming fast in his wake. "I thought we had a problem," he said, "and I was right. What's down here can't defend us against what's coming."

"They can't?"

"Not at the moment," Gabriel said. He had heard the qualification in what the Patterner was telling him. He could only hope that he had read rightly what it meant. "We have to defend *it* . . . for a while."

"Hope you got someplace good for us to hole up," Helm said, catching up with them from behind, "because that big ship . . ." He gulped. It wasn't a sound that filled Gabriel with any reassurance. "We've seen that one before, Gabe, one of those green warty veiny ones. We know what it means."

"Kroath sphere ships," Gabriel said, "and kroath."

"The ships can't hurt *this* stuff, though," Angela said, glancing around at the "glass" as she caught up with them.

"No," Gabriel agreed, "which is a slight advantage, because it means they can't just fire on it and bring it down and kill us all, but I can't close it up either—not right now anyway. That means that the kroath are going to come down here after us."

"Opinion: bad place to be trapped," said Delde Sota, bringing up the rear.

"You know any *good* places?" Helm remarked.

Delde Sota gave Helm a look that Gabriel found completely opaque. For the first time, he caught a clear flash of feeling from her, absolutely the essence of mischief—a bizarre feeling in the present circumstances, but one which nonetheless made him laugh out loud, just a short sharp bark of amusement.

"Several," Delde Sota said, "highly inappropriate for discussion now. Many more important matters to attend to. Will take this up again with you later."

They had been going around in increasing downward spirals for some short while. Now Gabriel, his friends, and the Marines came out at one side of a wide hemispherical space some hundred meters across. Empty, the glass of all its walls gleamed and glowed, the ceiling towering a hundred meters above them.

The Patterner grew up out of the flat glass of the floor.

"It's all right, it's with me," Gabriel said hurriedly, as Lacey and Bertin trained their weapons on the bizarre creature rising up out of the solid-seeming floor, or that was what it looked like at first glance. Gabriel thought of the way the Patterner at Ohmel had slipped in and out of hangings of what seemed impenetrable webwork. He knelt down to look more closely at the floor. This was not the

usual smooth glass, but rather the Patterner's typical webwork, here packed so closely together that it was a solid,
yet he could see the fibrous structure of it, all swirled
together and interknotted like delicate weed in water. If the
other facility had been a computer—and the other Patterner had said it was—then this was more like a brain.

While the Marines looked around apprehensively, Delde
Sota was on her knees, too, stroking the surface with her
braid. She glanced up at Gabriel. "Was discussing corpus
callosum earlier," she said. "Similarities to this material.
Pure neural fibril, packed side by side rather than end to
end. Maximized bandwidth . . ." *Such as has been forming
inside your own brain,* he heard her think.

From above, Gabriel could hear a mutter and rumble,
and the whole facility shook.

"What just landed on top of us?" asked Helm.

Delde Sota looked briefly distant look as she gazed out
at the upper world through the sensors of Helm's ship.
"Advice: neglect to ask."

The Patterner came gliding over to Gabriel on its many
legs, a graceful waltzing motion. *Harbinger, you are
awaited,* it said. *Immediate complete interface is required.
We are here to assist.*

"Then let's do it," Gabriel said.

At the edges of his mind, he could hear a faint wash of
cries and screams. Local space was becoming too full of
human, fraal, and other species' anguish. The terrible sound
would become more audible if something didn't happen
fast. What frightened Gabriel most was the possibility that,
if he failed, he would hear no more of those voices at all,
because they would all be gone.

"What needs to be done?" he asked.

Growth, replied the Patterner.

Then it started. There was a shivering in the substance
on which they stood. Fingers and tendrils of the crystalline
matter began to extrude slowly upwards around him where
he stood, some thin as hairs, some as thick around as his

wrist, all perfectly clear. They tangled around his feet and shins and knees, slowly climbing upward as if he were a tree being wrapped in vines.

He shivered at first, but then other sensations started that made it plain that merely being held in place by threads and ropes and cables of living glass was going to be the least of his troubles. Activated by the presence and nearness of the glass and moderated by the stone down in the fist of his spacesuit's glove, Gabriel could feel the new connections in his mind starting to awaken—an itching, fizzing feeling. His consciousness began to feel hot and tight inside, as if the brain growth of which Delde Sota spoken had actually started to push his skull out from the inside, pressure, an uncomfortable pressure, looking for release. It was not actively painful yet, but Gabriel thought that it soon would be. The sweat started out on him.

Unfortunately he could also feel other things happening. On the surface, a dark shadow lowered, and small dark-green shapes were pouring out of it and into the entrance hall high above them, making for the corridors . . .

"They're coming," Gabriel rasped.

"Can you not stop them?" Grawl asked.

"No."

"What do we do?" Angela said. There was only the slightest tremor to her voice.

Gabriel swallowed. "Keep them out."

"Do our best," Bertin said, then nodded to her companions. They started sorting themselves around the perimeter of the space.

"You got it," Helm said.

Helm began detaching weapons from the gun rack on his back. Gabriel found time for just one incredulous thought: to wonder where and how he had laid hands on some of those weapons. Half of them were strictly military and highly illegal. The others were only moderately illegal, depending on what jurisdiction you were in at the time, but Helm had never worried much about jurisdictions. The

Marines were giving him looks that were half envious and half admiring as Helm passed guns the size of small trees to Angela and Grawl and Enda, and finally, having handed another one to Delde Sota, he paused by Gabriel.

The webwork of glass had grown up around Gabriel to his waist and was swiftly extending upward.

"How do you get out of that?" Helm asked conversationally.

"Maybe I don't," Gabriel said.

No time to worry about it now. A memory surfaced of some old story his father had told him about a magician stuck in a rock—in some kind of crystal coffin. Now he was becoming the magician. Unfortunately, he was feeling painfully short of magic at the moment, and though he had known in his heart that this final battle would come eventually, it had never occurred to him that he might have to stand, immobile and imprisoned with empty hands while his friends fought . . . and won or lost it.

He was damned if he wouldn't fight. He turned to look down at the Patterner. It, too, was now anchored in place to the milky floor, the delicate legs wrapped about with the glass, the eyes set around the middle body now peering out between more cables of crystal as they grew and wound upward.

Patterner, Gabriel said to it, *we have other problems to deal with while this is going on. There's a war starting out there. We need the weapons.*

What weapons?

Gabriel stared at it. *Don't tell me that there aren't weapons here! Or some kind of defense! The other Patterner said—*

There are instrumentalities here that may serve you, said the Patterner before him, *but completion first.*

The tension and pressure, the hot prickling sense of connections knitting and awakening in his mind, was worsening. Memories began firing in his mind uncontrollably—not in order, nothing like the march of memory that you were supposed to suffer when you died. These came completely at random.

Childhood, fishing on the beach.

His father turning to his mother late one night as they sat in the sitting room.

A sunset over the ocean.

Gabriel's last day in school.

His first day in the Marines.

Glimpses of space.

The first time he had killed.

His first starfall.

The drip of water in the glaciers on Epsedra.

The frozen fury of Elinke Dareyev's face. Behind her, the recording of Ambassador Delvecchio's last shuttle trip played. . . .

Gabriel blinked, hot tears ran, but he could do nothing, couldn't move, couldn't speak—

Tramping, clattering noises came from the corridor entrance. The kroath—

His friends and the Marines were looking at each other. He could see them, feel their terror, their exhilaration. Bertin nodded at her people, and the safeties came off.

"I haven't killed anything at all today," Helm growled as he checked the charge on his weapon. "Good place to start."

"No ethical problem here," Delde Sota said, checking her weapon as well. "Cannot kill what is already dead. Simplifies matters. Oaths intact."

Enda stood there, small and frail in her little spacesuit, checking the charge on the mass rifle that Gabriel usually used. She glanced at the door then looked over toward him.

Inside, something kept rifling through Gabriel's memories, as if trying to see if everything was there. Ricel's memories were there, too. They were rifled as well, and Gabriel struggled against it, but the struggling was no use. In his palm, the stone burned fiercely as Gabriel watched that other life go by.

Then Gabriel suddenly realized what Ricel had been practice for. Yes, the stone had made all that happen, too.

Gods only knew how many years of tweaks and changes to what would otherwise have been history's normal course that the stone had made to make sure that Ricel was there for Gabriel, that his mission went forward, that the ambassador died, that Gabriel was semi-convicted by the Phorcyns and fled—always with the stone in hand. It had made sure that Ricel died in front of him so that those memories were laid out in front of Gabriel, utterly necessary, otherwise irretrievable. All unwittingly he had done his homework, further investigating those memories—digging, laying them bare, refining the connections to them, in his own interest, he'd thought at the time. Now Gabriel wondered.

Now the facility here knew that Gabriel had mastered the fine art of absorbing another's memories, sorting and compiling and filing them away for himself. As a result, now it had another set of memories for him. These were much bigger, much more complex, much more important. Some changes had been made in his own mind so that he would be ready to handle the new load. Everything was now ready.

The shriek brought his eyes open, distracting him. He saw the first few kroath come through the entrance. The noise had been Grawl, letting loose a warcry of her people, leveling her weapon, and firing. Gabriel got a first whiff of that terrible sour acid odor, the slime that surrounded the bodies of the undead inside their armor. The kroath went down, its abdomen torn into jagged strips of sizzling armor. It struggled up again. Enda was firing at it now, then Angela, and finally Lacey and Rathbone. Together they brought it down, only to see it struggle up one more time, aiming its dark plasma weapon, firing—

More kroath came. Their armor was too strong to make it a simple matter to take them out. Their shrieks and screams of rage and pain filled the air. Before Gabriel had not been equipped to realize that the kroath were not mere automata, reactivated corpses moving and fighting, but that there was also some semblance of consciousness inside them. They walked in anguish and fury that could never be quenched, a madness of mind degraded to programming. Memory was nearly lost. Even worse, memories were stripped of their associations so that old loves and familiar faces might pass in front of them and they would not know them, would kill them with unconcern, and then afterward never understand why the pain inside was even greater than it had been before. That endless anguish . . .

Gabriel wanted to weep for them, but there was no time for it now. It was kinder simply to mince them so small they could never be put back together again, burn them to ashes, blow them apart . . .

The Marines and Gabriel's friends were all doing a fair job of that at the moment. The kroath bodies were piling up so that the entry was somehat choked with them, but even as they were torn apart by the big caliber fire, the armor broke and let out that terrible acid slime. It ate bodies and armor alike so that the pile kept getting smaller, and more kroath came climbing in over it. It was like trying to stop the tide from coming in. Even as he watched, Dirigent went down with a dark plasma bolt through the chest. The others closed ranks over his body, still firing, and all Gabriel could think of was what would happen when his friends' guns ran out of ammunition, when their charges ran down . . .

All around him the facility waited. Gabriel stood shuddering and helpless, wholly imprisoned in the crystal now. Here they were, waiting, a vast set of memories in a glass matrix, preserved for him and only for him. It was the map. The master map of the other Glassmaker sites—*all* the other sites, all their secrets, everything they held. All this treasure of data was ready to pour into Gabriel, old wine into a new bottle. Ready for use at last.

If he accepted it.

If he didn't . . .

He could hear the whole facility listening to his thought.

Every fiber of it was alive, waiting, and desperate. Outside his crystalline prison, dark plasma bolts flew. Enda rolled out of the way of one and fired. Helm stood blasting away with the D6 tucked under one arm and a reloaded flechette gun in the other. Another kroath went down in the doorway and got up again, while another climbed over it and leaped into the room. Grawl's fire took them both down.

You must accept it!

Oh, must I? Gabriel asked.

It all came down, finally, to this: become the chosen vessel of this huge and terrible knowledge and make sure that humanity and its allies received it. For without it, they would not survive.

Refuse it, and it will all be destroyed now . . . for no one else is capable of handling it. The others who can handle it, too, are not worthy. They will take this information and use it. Within twenty years—thirty?—mankind and its allies will be gone.

The other choice was to take the knowledge, and . . .

Change. Irreversible, change impossible to describe, impossible to understand . . . from this side of the process. Knowledge was promised on the other side, but by then it will be too late. Accept the knowledge and become . . . more than human? Less? Or will there even be words that are capable of describing the difference?

Gabriel breathed in, breathed out. This was what the stone had been preparing him for. If he refused the change, he would never be complete, never know what might have been.

I get to keep my humanity.

For a little while, replied the Patterner, *until you die . . .*

Gabriel gasped for breath, struggled inside the crystal for a way to help his friends. They all had their backs turned, fighting the kroath: Helm, who had been made more than human to start with; Delde Sota, who had built herself that way, slowly, over time; Enda, who had never been human but knew more about it than some; Grawl, never human either, but involved with the species as her people had been for many years; Angela, as human as Gabriel was now—more so, for the stone had not changed her.

Yet, said the Patterner.

The choice is still mine?

Yours alone. Without your willing acceptance, all that has gone before is meaningless.

"Gabriel!" Angela shouted at him, looking over her shoulder while changing charge packs. The bodies were beginning to pile up in the doorway, but other kroath still were pushing in from behind. "Just this once, *could you hurry up and do whatever?*"

Just this once . . .

He closed his eyes, took one last deep breath, and said to the Patterner, *Do it.*

Chapter Eighteen

H<small>E HAD TRIED</small> to brace himself, but nothing could have prepared Gabriel for the incandescent stream of power that blasted into and through him, burning him from within. He tried to hang onto some sense of himself, but it was lost in moments, seared away in the access of light that completely inhabited him, filled him like liquid—

—then not just a flood of light, but billions of individual sparks of it, each gravitating to one particular spot, one cell, one strand of DNA, one atom, and etching itself there. Every spark meant something. He was a map. Here and there, as the blindness began to fade and the dazzlement passed, Gabriel caught glimpses of what was now written inside him, in every cell: a star here, a patch of nebula there, a planet indicated somewhere else, all the other Precursor sites, all that information was now stored in him. It had written itself in his genes, as it could not have done without his consent. For as long as he lived, that data could be used by him and his delegates, and should there ever be children, they too would carry it . . . and their children, and theirs after that.

Wonderful, he thought, dazed, *so now what?*

He opened his eyes to see a troop of bigger kroath forcing their way past the ones who had been coming in the first wave. Their armor was hugely broad across the shoulders, and their claws lanced out further. Grawl roared a terrible cry at the sight of them, realizing that as the other kroath had been made of men, sesheyans, or fraal, some of these were weren. With her scream, one of them launched itself at her—

Helm raised the D6, pulled the trigger, and the charge gave out. He dropped it, reached over his back, came up with something else, something squarish that he shook a handle out of.

An *axe?*

Gabriel stared as Helm, in that battered armor, threw himself at the kroath, slashing, the axe whirling, seemingly appearing in several places at once. One of the kroath's arms fell away at the elbow. The kroath struck Helm with the other, but the claws made only marks on his armor. Helm was set like a rock, as if he were anchored into the floor like Gabriel and the Patterner.

Helm struck it and struck again, slashing off the other arm. It staggered at him, went down, oozing acidic slime. There were no other weapons nearby, nothing more effective to grab, but Helm spread his legs and planted himself firm and yelled, "Anybody else?"

Lacey had gone down next to where Delde Sota lay firing. The doctor grabbed the poor kid's mass rifle, yelled, "Helm!" and threw it to him. Helm caught it out of the air one-handed as he was hitting the next kroath with the axe. He slapped the axe back into carry position over his shoulder and used the mass rifle to stitch along the middle of the kroath, trying to cut it in half as he had with Delonghi. Gabriel could not see his face through the armor, but he could imagine what it looked like—that crazy grin that went halfway around his face, the teeth bared, the fiercely crewcut hair bristling. The kroath went down. Helm fired two long bursts into it, severing its legs at the knees.

"Walk away from that," he yelled. *"Anybody else?"*

He was tiring. He couldn't possibly keep it up, and the others had to be running out of charge or ammo. And there were still more kroath coming.

Gabriel was struggling in the crystal again.

Let me out! Let me fight! Where are the weapons?

There are no weapons here. Only information—

He screamed in frustration. Like an echo came the sound

of screams and gunfire from farther up, echoing like thunder in the corridors above. We're all going to die, Gabriel thought, and I can't do anything. They're all going to die.

Confusion spread as the kroath blundered more quickly into the great room. Helm cut one more off at the legs, and then that mass rifle's change went out. MacLain went down but took another kroath with him. Helm snatched the axe from over his back and went for the next kroath, ducked the dark plasma blast that went past, and brought the axe down on arm and weapon together. The weapon exploded, throwing Helm backward and taking the kroath's arm off at the shoulder. With a crash of armor Helm went down, and kroath piled on top of him.

No! Gabriel cried. *Let me out! Let me help! They'll all—*

—and Helm rolled, plunged, and shook them off, clubbing them away, swinging the axe. He dragged himself to his feet again, the armor dented, his helmet half crushed against his face, blood running from it and from his shoulder. His arm hung limp.

With his one good hand, he pulled his axe again and roared, *"Anybody else?!?"*

—and the sound of gunfire echoed and roared in the access corridor.

Suddenly there were no more kroath in the corridor, only a pile of oozing, dissolving bodies and armor. More Marines had come.

A kind of gasping quiet fell as the two groups stood looking at each other in disbelief and joy, but the joy didn't last long.

Enda came to them, casting her gun aside. "You are from *Schmetterling?*"

"The captain sent us," said one of the Marines. "She didn't want you to get away." He was looking over at Gabriel as he said it. "Maybe that wasn't a problem."

Through the crystal, he gave the man a bemused look. "Without you guys," Gabriel said, "getting away would not have been even slightly on the cards." He looked around at

the fallen ones, Lacey, Dirigent and MacLain, their armor
and bodies half-eaten away already by the kroath slime.

"But you're supposed to save everything now," said the
young lieutenant. "That was the word."

"I'm so glad people tell me these things," Gabriel said.
"I just wish I knew how!"

You do know, said the Patterner, as calm as if a major
battle had not just taken place in front of her. *Look within.*

It took a little doing. Suddenly Gabriel found it much
easier to hear the rest of this facility. What he could mostly
hear at the moment was, *They have come back!* A terrible
sound of rejoicing, a crash of martial music in his mind,
guns and trumpets, drums beating.

They?

The makers. The creators.

Where?

You.

Gabriel would have looked over his shoulder, if he could
have moved.

*They said to us, "We will come back. We will use you
again. Where once we failed, we will rise up and succeed."*

Some kind of reincarnation belief, Gabriel thought, yet
the facility was deadly serious about it.

Well, fine, he said silently, *but meanwhile there's a space
battle going on out there, and my people's ships are being
chopped in pieces, and it needs to stop!*

There was not even a pause for access time. *The enemies' ship defense . . .*

Everything visual around him went away. In his mind,
Gabriel found himself looking at something that was like a
circuit diagram, but it was about a kilometer across. However, it was not a diagram; it was an equation. He could
understand the terms but wasn't sure how they fit together.

He puzzled over it. The symmetry of the equation was
strange. *I don't see what this does, or how it works,* Gabriel
said. *It looks like it makes something out of nothing!*

Exactly, replied the Patterner. *That is how everything*

was *made at the beginning, out of nothing . . .*

Gabriel knew as much about big bang theory as anyone else, but he had never thought of it in quite those terms before. If he was right, he was looking at some kind of intangible shield technology, and it seemed to have something to do with engines powered by darkmatter reactions, which every Concord and Star Force ship out there had.

Can we make this for our ships? he demanded.

Impossible, the answer came back. *Installation requires more reconfiguration and rebuilding than can be managed at this time.*

Gabriel felt like swearing, but it wouldn't have helped. It's not fair that they have this advantage as well as numbers! We're going to get slaughtered here!

The Others may be made to lose this advantage, the answer came back.

The imagery filling his mind was suddenly all directed toward one part of the equation. Gabriel realized abruptly that he was being shown its weak spot, the one part of the process of "making something out of nothing" that could feasibly be interfered with. A ship close enough to another one using this screen could just possibly generate the pulse of energy that would strike at this particular weak point and render the screen useless.

How do I get this to them in the middle of a battle? Gabriel thought in desperation. *Or in time for them to do anything with it?* There was no way to get the information where it was needed, and people were dying out there.

Implementation does not have to be carried out remotely. Local implementation is possible on a limited basis.

Gabriel gulped. *Define limited.*

One pulse of the power necessary to disable all such operations in local space can be produced. Time to recharge: eight to the eighth hours.

Gabriel did the first few multiplications in his head and then gave up. *Never mind that,* he said. *Get ready to do it!*

Then he paused. *What if it doesn't work?*

There is no other remedy, came that cool reply.

He swallowed. It's just going to have to do, he thought, but at the same time I can't take the chance that this information might be lost. This could make all the difference in fights yet to come. It might mean the difference between our side's survival and its extinction, but I don't even understand it. How am I supposed to store it, share it. . . ?

The idea came. "Delde Sota!" Gabriel shouted. "Are you still linked to *Longshot*'s comms?"

She tapped the remote transmitter at her belt. "Clear and operating."

That'll do it, Gabriel thought. This was a mechalus who had been able to sabotage Delonghi's ship by sliding her mind down into its computers via nothing but comms circuitry. At the time, it had seemed dangerously like magic. Now Gabriel was entirely happy to apply anything, up to and including magic, to the problem before him.

"How are you with figuring out schematics?"

She grinned, one of those slightly feral smiles she produced sometimes when someone asked her a question that was very much to her liking. "Admission: have been known to do such things every now and then."

"Do you think you can link up with me?"

She strode over to him, keeping the gun in her hands, and leaned up against the column of wrapped and woven crystal in which he now stood imprisoned. Her braid slipped in through the interstices and wrapped its finest tendrils around his wrist, sinking into the medchip there as it had so many times before.

"Not just hardware," Gabriel said. "Software . . ."

She looked at him. Just the barest spark of alarm in those eyes, but it was quickly gone. "Semantics," she said. "Rhetorical question: for a mechalus, is there a difference?"

"Are you sure?" he said. "I don't know if this—"

"Exhortation!" Delde Sota interrupted. "Try it and find out."

Gabriel closed his eyes and slipped into the webwork, into the crystal.

The connection, when it came, was overwhelming. Gabriel found himself looking across what seemed thousands of kilometers of space, all glittering with the constructs of thought, down to great depths, up to unguessed-at heights. Delde Sota had been a Grid pilot before she had been a doctor. Gabriel knew that, but he knew it casually. Now he looked down into her mind and saw that she was still a Grid pilot, for she carried huge amounts of the Grid inside her tailored memory, which she had had installed in herself, bit by bit over time. When she had come away from her medical work on Iphus Station, she had finished the last of that customization, feeling that she might need it sometime soon. All those trips back to Corrivale, he thought, " . . . to do some errands."

One has to do the shopping sometime, the answer came back, and Delde Sota laughed inside.

Gabriel gulped at the vastness within her. All minds were landscapes to some extent—at least that was the paradigm in which he found himself tending to think of them—but Delde Sota's was a landscape in more dimensions than most. It had directions and axes the existence of which he would never have suspected, stretching off through many star systems, encapsulating parts of their Grids down which she had run herself at one time or another. The textures were amazing. He saw the spit of electricity and the hot burn of nuclear particles as she came close to one power source or another, the caress of others' thoughts as she passed them in the Grid. Down the myriad networks she quested, hunting information about one subject or another that interested her . . . and nearly everything interested Delde Sota. Doctor she might be, but she was also technician, philosopher, and engineer—all necessary talents, since she had been building and rebuilding herself for years. The rebuilding, the redesigning of an existing design to some new and unexpected use was what chiefly delighted her.

What did you have in mind? She asked silently.

This, Gabriel said. He showed her the shield.

She slipped down into that schematic, wore it like a coat, looked at it all over, checked the fit, and then started to look closely at the fabric. A torrent of imagery flooded over Gabriel, picked up second-hand from her. Whirling virtual shell-structures of atoms that did not yet exist but could if conditions were correct, the probability clouds of their attendant particles even more subjective and uncertain than usual, and other particles, exotic but easily enough produced for short periods if you gave them a chance. Then came a flood of equivalencies between the symbology at which Gabriel had been looking and her own.

A long pause. Even Delde Sota was briefly confused by what she saw. Then suddenly Gabriel felt her suck her breath in, and he felt a great cry of astonishment and hope go up inside her.

Sides balance, she said silently to Gabriel.

Of the equation?

Possibly of the battle as well. Possibly a little imbalance . . .

Take all this information, Gabriel said. *Store it in every ship's computer in the fleet that you're able to reach. If even one survives to bring this home, we may lose this battle, but we'll have a better than even chance of winning the war.*

"After that?" she said aloud.

We'll see if we can make this little change in the Externals' ships, Gabriel said, *and even things up slightly.*

Query: chances of success? Delde Sota asked.

Gabriel shook his head. *We're rolling double or nothing on this one. Do what you need to and hurry. I won't move until you're done.*

He was afraid, afraid that the pulse he felt from the "mind" of the installation, considering so calmly, might burn him out in its passing. He was also afraid that using the information in this way, targeting the External ships with the pulse meant to burn out their protective screen, might also tempt them to destroy the facility itself, no matter how much they wanted it. Gabriel knew little or nothing about the psychology of his enemy, except that it was inimical to everything human. He was moving in an information vacuum and was very afraid to move in any direction at all, yet at the same time he didn't dare *not* move. People were dying.

Delde Sota had withdrawn from Gabriel, standing still for a moment, planning out how to handle her intervention, concentrating. Gabriel stood there and shivered, for the wash of terror and pain that he had picked up earlier was even stronger now. The battle was in full career, and it was not going well for the Concord. The External ships were slicing them up with great energy beams like blades, and the Star Force weapons were just sliding off them, unable to inflict any similar damage. Kroath were landing on Galvin and Alitar, killing people, stealing people. Here and there, bizarrely, were the VoidCorp ships, waiting, doing nothing, but everywhere else, local space was full of the silvery bloom of lost atmosphere as ships burst apart, spilling their crews into vacuum, exploding. One swung past with an External ship in pursuit as another ship akin to it blew not far away, and Gabriel got a sudden sense of familiarity.

"Schmetterling!" Gabriel cried.

"Schmetterling comms." There were screams in the background, sirens, a voice yelling "Get me that damage report! What the hell's happened to the main battery?"

"This is Gabriel Connor. Get me the captain. I think I can save her ship."

A pause. Then that fierce voice. "I thought I would have taken help from one of *them* sooner than from you, but the ruthlessness of the situation makes liars of us all. What have you got? Did you find what you were after?"

He had no immediate answer for that. "Listen, I think we can even up the odds a little. These guys have a shield—"

She swore. "Tell me about it. I hit them with everything I've got and it makes no difference!"

"I think I can do something about that. If it works, they're going to lose those shields shortly. They may not even realize it's happened at first."

"I'll pass the word, but you'd damned well better hurry up!"

Gabriel felt around inside the installation and was shocked to feel the wave of power growing in it, beating against him like a wind felt from behind.

"It won't be long. There's information we'll be dumping to *Schmetterling*'s computers—and to all the other ships in the fleet. It has to get back to the Concord. It's the hardware and software information for a similar shield."

"Well *do* it, then! We have a few problems up here at the moment, and I don't have—"

An explosion, and sudden silence. Gabriel frantically groped for the contact but couldn't get it back.

"Delde Sota, go!" he screamed.

In her mind, she fled down her contact with *Schmetterling,* still alive though her audio comms were gone. She had carrier; it was enough. Down into *Schmetterling*'s computers, which resisted her for ages—several seconds at least— Gabriel could hear the doctor's cry of frustration as she worried her way through course after course of firewall meant to prevent just this kind of attack. Then she found a chink, slipped through, and was in.

Now the tricky part. She was intent. She was also a doctor and was not distracted by the blood and screams that she could "hear" all around her. She was in the middle of a procedure. Doctor Sota ran down the circuitry and solids of the ship's computer, found memory empty there, and impressed the plans on it—the equations, the installation's own visualization of the hardware needed to manage the mass reactors and gravitic coils and all the other changes and tweaks that would be necessary to make the new shield work.

All around Gabriel, the power of the Precursor facility was building to its peak. He was still afraid, afraid that it wouldn't be enough and that all these ships full of brave and desperate people were going to die.

The power peaked.

"Delde Sota!" Gabriel shrieked.

She did not bother to answer with her voice. She knew he could feel her flashing out of the computers in *Schmetterling* and leaping to the computers of other ships in the fleet. In microsecond jumps, she printed the data in their computers' memories, firewalling them so they could not be accidentally overwritten or altered. A moment of approval and surprise, even for her, as she slipped into the *Lighthouse*'s Grid and planted the data there. The sheer size of it impressed her. Then on to the rest, packing the data down into every one of even the tiniest ships. Some exploded behind her, but she did not stop. She kept up the dance from machine mind to machine mind until every one still extant had the data.

The Precursor facility's power was beating harder against Gabriel, impatient to be let go, but he had to wait until Delde Sota had done what was needed. She was still in the midst of the dance, checking her work, making sure that none of the ships' computers had dumped the data.

"Done!" she cried.

With the power of the Precursor facility rushing through him like the great waterfall on Danwell, Gabriel picked up one image he had not intended to. The landscape inside Elinke Dareyev's mind, now suddenly flooded with horror and grief as she saw the huge spheroid ship swing away from cutting up *Tournant* not twenty kilometers from her, then come in with that great blade of energy ready to slice *Schmetterling* in two. *This is it,* he heard her think. *My people, my poor people, oh, my poor crew!* She got ready to die, but shouted, "One more time! All weapons, fire!"

"Go!" Gabriel said to the facility.

The force blasted out around him, through him, whiting out Gabriel's world in a torrent of power and pain. He had no idea what kind of pulse was being generated. It seemed to him to be running around under the crust of the planet as if under a skin, then pouring out of from every crack and crevice, blasting into all neighboring space and propagating at lightspeed, possibly faster. Were there tachyons and other faster-than-light particles involved in this? No way to tell for sure. All he could do was concentrate on bearing this, not losing himself in it, for there were more things he would need to do afterwards. The pulse tore through all local space, and he could feel it begin to impact the Externals' ships. Where it touched them, something happened that he was not sure how to define. As the pulse touched those shields, he could feel them. They seemed to be in the process of creating subatomic particles that did not actually exist. Fire from the Concord ships hit the enemy vessels, creating patches of these not-really-existing particles, and the patches turned the ships' fire away—until the firestorm stopped, at which time they vanished.

Except now, when the pulse hit the ships generating the screen. For a millisecond, the ships were completely screened—and then suddenly their screens could no longer generate the particles at all. The hulls of the Externals' ships were suddenly just so much metal and alloy.

Gabriel felt Elinke watching hopelessly as that External ship swung toward her, swung in close with that blade of energy.

A line of fire from *Schmetterling* struck the ship.

The great spherical monstrosity cracked open, spilled atmosphere and bodies out into the void, then cracked again, flaming wider, and blew up in a dazzling array.

"It works!" Delde Sota cried and burst out laughing.

Gabriel laughed, too. *It works!*

"Captain," Gabriel shouted down the comms link, "it worked! It worked!"

"What did you do?" Elinke yelled, and over her shoulder yelled again, "Where the devil are my front batteries, *someone's going to have their pay docked in a minute!*"

"I can't explain right now," said Gabriel.

"Well, what do I care? *Will it last?*"

"For these ships, yes," Gabriel said. "They'll never screen again."

"We'll find out in a moment," Elinke muttered. "Here comes another one. Forward batteries, are you up now? That one, there, hit him!"

The torpedoes and the forward energy weapons both let go together. The energy weapons took the big approaching sphere amidships, and the torpedoes followed, hitting slightly off to one side. It exploded brilliantly.

There was a long pause. "You're the devil himself," Elinke Dareyev's voice said. "I've always said so. Are you sure this will last?"

"It's permanent, Captain."

"Good. Then all we have to do is deal with two-to-one odds," she said. Her voice was grimly pleased. "We'll all just have to shoot twice, that's all."

Inside the facility of which Gabriel was now a part, the battle now seemed to have begun happening *inside* everyone who watched. They were all being drawn in as the power turned its attention away from Gabriel and began to focus outward, as the facility witnessed what it had been placed here for, a great stroke against the enemy that had destroyed its makers so many millions of years before. Through Delde Sota it flowed into them from a thousand viewpoints, for she was in the system Grid and the tactical sub-Grid connecting the Concord vessels. For his own part, Gabriel was struggling for control, unwilling to be forced permanently into this status. Limiting that power too strictly now could mean the end of everything for the Verge, and so Gabriel walked the edge of that glassy razor with care, trying to keep a steady course and not to let emotion tip him over one way or the other.

The fear was still there. He could see, as his friends could see through him, the terrible carnage that the Externals' ships were wreaking—great blasts of energy lancing out, flowers of fire blooming in the night, carving up Concord, Galvinite, and Alitarin ships. Already something was happening. Something was beginning to shift. Ships that had fired again and again at their enemies without result were now getting results—those of them that had survived that long—and were throwing themselves feverishly into the offensive, looking to make up lost time. The biggest Concord ships, which had been cautious not to throw themselves too hastily into battle with the very biggest External ships, now went after them with a vengeance. Even the *Lighthouse* slowly moved into the center of the battle, its terrible weaponry lancing out and wreaking the same kind of destruction on the Externals that they had been meting out to the Concord fleet. The odds were still bad, but the tone of the fight had changed. People were still dying, Gabriel knew, but at least they were now doing so with the hope that it might make some difference.

They watched for a while, knowing that there was no danger of attack to them at the moment. As the minutes passed, slowly at first, then more quickly, the tide of battle began turning. The Concord ships took the battle to the Externals in earnest, and now the ships that bloomed fire and breathed atmosphere into the vacuum were more often those of the invaders. There was a long hesitation, an uncertain period during which the fighting went on much as before—but then slowly the External ships gathered together and started to make for the outer reaches of the system as if to regroup. The Concord ships pursued them, and even more of the External vessels made starfall as minutes and tens of minutes and an hour and two hours went by.

The Marines inside the cavern were recouping themselves, dealing with their dead and binding up the wounded. Gabriel looked out of the pillar at where Grawl was working on Helm.

"What a song this will make," Grawl was saying as she bound up his face and eye with pressure tape. Gabriel sucked in breath as he watched her do it, for the eye clearly would never be the same, no matter what bionics could be installed in the ruined socket later. "Great was the slaughter. The kroath fell in heaps. Then Helm Ragnar's son strode forth with the axe and paid the price for wisdom: an eye—"

"The meter will need work," Enda said, "but you begin well."

Gabriel stretched, came up against the resistance of the crystal, and abruptly felt it bend in front of him. He *was* that crystal now. *No need for this,* he said silently, and slowly the glasslike substance started to retract, slipping back down into the fibril bed of the master facility.

The Patterner, too, was coming undone from its shackles and came over to Gabriel. *Harbinger,* it said, *your initiation is done.*

Gabriel stretched . . . then felt something odd in his glove. Or rather, something odd that was not in his glove. The stone was gone.

I *am* the stone now, Gabriel thought. Everything that it had been, directional source, ancient personality, power feed, information storage core, all of that was part of Gabriel now, wound into his DNA, engraved on his genes. I am what it was, he thought, a map . . . a guidepost. The harbinger. The one who shows the way. And if there were ever children at some point down the line, they would carry the same map in their genes. They would always know the way to wonder. . . .

He glanced idly at Angela.

She looked up at him from an injured Marine whose head she was holding in her lap. *Well, who knows?* He heard her think. *Maybe just once.*

Gabriel swallowed.

He turned his attention silently upward and outward. The battle had plainly reached that moment when the enemy says to itself, "This is not fun any more. We aren't winning." The system was almost empty of External ships now, except for the remnants of those that had been destroyed. A few of the great spherical ships still lingered in the outer regions of the system, but one by one they were vanishing into drive-space as the Concord vessels took control of the area, most massing over and around Argolos. The VoidCorp ships that had turned up also took themselves out into the darkness, vanishing into the darkness beyond the farthest fringes of the Algemron system.

"They're going to have some explaining to do about that," Gabriel said softly.

He would be interested in hearing them. Probably they would make the excuse that they had initially been as over-gunned as the Concord ships had been. He would have loved to hear how they explained leaving just as the Externals lost their shields and became vulnerable.

That would keep. He would probably have plenty of time to see their reaction in the Grid news to that . . . while spending all his time in custody, before the trial and afterward.

Helm came over to him, the dislocated left arm bound against his side at the moment. Delde Sota had done a field relocation but would want to do more work on it later.

"You know . . ." Helm rasped.

Gabriel looked at him quizzically.

Helm gave Gabriel a one-eyed look of amusement. "Aw, it didn't work. I thought we could all just sort of think at you now."

Enda came up beside him. "That is a sure way to give him a headache," she said, "assuming he doesn't have one already."

Gabriel smiled at her somberly. "I ache all over, and my head feels like it might fall off shortly, but there are other things to do first."

"Yeah," Helm said. "I was thinking . . ."

Gabriel heard the thought but said nothing about it for the moment. "We should get suited up," he said, "and get the hurt people out of here."

Helm looked at him a little strangely.

You know what he has in mind, Enda said silently.

I do, Gabriel said. *I won't do it.*

He turned to the Patterner, which stood nearby, watching the others prepare to leave. *This facility is too dangerous to leave open,* Gabriel told the creature. *There are inhabitants of this system who would attempt to make inappropriate usage of it.*

This facility has no further use, the Patterner said. *When you depart, it will be destroyed.*

That shocked Gabriel a little. *Don't you think it would be wise to keep a backup?*

It felt around in his mind for his meaning and then made a simple sense of negation in reply. *The data was not copied but transferred. It was always intended to be held inside a life form. It had been hoped that we might serve that purpose, but it seems life is more than intelligence and free will. When there were no more of our makers left and our prototype program was discontinued unfinished, that data was stored solid, but such storage is merely static and is seen as far more insecure than that in living beings.*

Oh?

That was their way, it said. *That is the way the programming was laid in. You must now see to the propagation of the data yourself.*

Gabriel laughed a little, seeing that what he was going to have to do with Jacob Ricel's memories for his testimony was the same thing he was going to have to do with the mapping information of which he was now the sole bearer. More homework, he thought. *Is the testing stage ever going to end?*

The Patterner gave him a dry look with all those eyes.

What about you, Patterner? Gabriel asked.

I and my other selves are done, it said. *We have fulfilled our programming and our purpose. Go well, Harbinger. Fulfill your programming as well.*

It fell silent. Gabriel felt for its mind . . . and found that it was gone.

He looked at Enda, sad and a little shocked. "That was sudden."

She shook her head and turned to look at the others.

The Marines, suited and waiting, stood a little distance away, regarding Gabriel with expressions of which he could make little. There was horror in some of them and awe in others. Some seemed afraid to look at him. Others seemed unable to take their eyes off him.

Gabriel could only shake his head and wonder what they saw. He had seen too much of the insides of others' minds for the moment. For the next little while, the only mind he wanted to see the inside of was his own. It would take a while to get a sense of what it looked like these days, but he would have plenty of time for that.

He turned to Enda again. "Let's get my cousins here into *Longshot* and *Lalique*."

Helm looked thoughtfully at Gabriel.

"Give them a ride back to *Schmetterling,* but you and I will go in first." He put his arm through Enda's, and they headed toward the corridor entrance. "I have an appointment to keep."

Chapter Nineteen

THEY WERE ABOARD *Schmetterling* for several days before anything significant happened. Mostly everyone in the system
was preoccupied with repairing damage done during the
battle, helping add their own information to the master report
that was being assembled, and simply recovering.

Gabriel was returned to the same cell where he had
previously been kept, and Enda and the crews of *Longshot* and *Lalique* were allowed to visit him pretty much
at will. Gabriel spent his first day aboard in collapse, and
the next couple of days trying to sort out what had happened to him. For one thing, he understood the strange
looks on the faces of Bertin and the other Marines. When
he had finally had strength to get up and have a shower
and a shave, the first look in the mirror shocked him. The
hair had a little ways yet to go before it became completely white, but the eyes, his eyes, were now silver-
pale, gone white as Precursor glass. That he had not
expected. Shaving had taken a long time that day.

Longer still would be the business of sorting out everything he now had in his head—a task Gabriel began to
despair of ever completing before he died of old age. *I was
so bloody worried about not being human at the end of this,*
he thought late one night, *and it turns out the problem was
the reverse. I'm still* too *human. I'm terrified of losing this
data . . .*

It seemed to be safely esconced inside him for the time
being, and by the third day he found himself able to start to
relax. That was his error, for he came out of the little head

down at the end of the cell corridor that evening to find the door to the living area open. Gabriel went toward it, smiling slightly.

Inside, sitting on one of the pulldown sofas and looking at the wall display, was Lorand Kharls.

He stood up to greet Gabriel, which he did not have to do, and saw him seated first, as he might have done with an honored guest. Then he sat down and looked at him for a while.

"Are you surprised to see me back here?" Gabriel asked at last.

"Oh, no," the administrator replied. "I was expecting you."

Gabriel looked at him. "I could have left."

"I didn't expect that," Kharls said, "but indeed, here you are back. So I came partly to ask whether you have the proof you went for."

"Not in any form that is likely to be useful," Gabriel said, "but I have it all."

Kharls looked at him strangely. "What form is it in?"

"Telepathic. Jacob Ricel dumped me the story of his life before he died."

Kharls blinked. "No, you *don't* make this easy, do you?"

"That doesn't seem to have been the story of *my* life recently," Gabriel said, "no."

Kharls nodded and said, "Well, I would imagine that we should be able to find someone in the Concord Legal Service who's also a mindwalker, one certified highly enough that he would be empowered to assess your evidence . . . seeing that this is the only form in which it can be provided."

Gabriel nodded. His main fear was that whatever mindwalker they found would either not be able to work out what had happened to the inside of his head and synchronize successfully with it or to clearly perceive all the nuances that Gabriel had acquired from Ricel while going over his memories. But it was a better outcome than he had hoped for, and all he could hope for, under the circumstances.

"Where will the trial be held?" Gabriel asked.

"On *Lighthouse,*" Kharls said. "It's here now, and I will be moving my administrative work there for a while. If I can, during my own part in these proceedings, I will suggest to the adjudicators that your sentence, for I assume there will be one, should be served on *Lighthouse* as well. It strikes me that we might be able to use your services should you be inclined to give them."

The man's presumption was amazing, Gabriel thought. "If you think that after everything I've been through, the way I was set up, that I would—"

Then he stopped himself, for he knew that he would do exactly that.

Damn it, Gabriel thought.

"Oaths," Kharls said, "are an annoyance sometimes, but once taken, they seem almost impossible to remove. I see you have been unable to remove yours."

"Kharls," Gabriel said, "are *you* a mindwalker?"

He shook his head. "Heavens, no, and I resist any attempt to turn me into one, so keep your distance."

"Then how do you always know what's going on around you?"

"I keep my eyes open. Most people don't, Connor. They look but don't see, listen but don't hear—the great fault of our age, I think, and probably of most ages before it. The mind that already is made up and sees only what reinforces its own beliefs, no matter what else it perceives . . . that's our greatest enemy. Me, I don't have any beliefs. I just look at people."

"And judge them."

"That's what I'm paid for, partly."

"There's something I want to talk to you about in that regard."

"Your friend Ragnarsson," said Kharls, "and Delonghi."

"Possibly I shouldn't say this without counsel present,"

Gabriel said, "but I very much wish I had killed her myself."

"If I understand the circumstances correctly, you were trying."

"And now Helm's going to take the blame for it."

"Well," Kharls said, "there are some aspects of this business with which I can involve myself without there being a conflict of interest. This was a battlefield situation . . ."

"But it—"

"Those who understand the issues," Kharls interrupted, "are already calling this not the Battle of Algemron, but the Battle of Argolos—with good reason, especially after we started to analyze the inbound data tracks on the External vessels. We realized that, excepting the sweep past Ilmater and Calderon, all of them were heading in your direction—right past Galvin or Alitar or anything else of interest in that part of the system, so a battlefield situation. Witnesses saw that Delonghi was infected with something clearly identifiable as not part of a normal human organism. Those witnesses will later be able to identify this as a teln, when we remove a tangle to show them from one of the sources we've acquired. Further investigation will, I believe, show that if the organism had succeeded in what it intended, then the whole battle would have been lost with tremendous equipment and personnel losses to the Concord and the associated stellar nations. I rather think all that will be set in the side of the scales containing acts to your friend's credit—not to mention his exploits later on down deeper in the facility, where he apparently bought you the time needed for reserves to arrive. An amazing feat, really. If he were in any of the services, I would have thought they would have decorated him so heavily he could barely stand, though plainly that would take a cartload of medals." Kharls stretched his legs out in front of him. "So I think you can put your mind to rest on that account."

Gabriel nodded.

"As for Delonghi . . ." Kharls said, then fell silent a moment. "You know, I think the standard treatment for a spy when you know that one has been placed in your organization is the fungal treatment. Keep them in the dark, feed them . . ." He smiled.

"Waste products," Gabriel said.

"It can be very difficult to do that," Kharls said. "I have suspected such emplacements in my own organization for a long while. It can be very hard to let them continue doing damage while trying to contain the larger damage they might do otherwise . . . or which might be done if they were forcefully removed. Off the record, I will thank you for doing me a favor. As for the others"—he shrugged—"there is no doing everything at once. These Externals are not a problem to be so lightly solved. We have won an engagement with them, but it will be many years, I think, before we have enough intelligence about them to know how major or minor an engagement it was. Meantime, good intel practice at my end involves leaving their present agents in place . . . and making sure I have a big enough bag of waste products handy."

Gabriel nodded at that, too.

"So," Kharls said. "I'll be moving over to *Lighthouse* for at least a few weeks. Meanwhile, you will be held here, in what I hope you will find reasonable comfort. I would have preferred something a little less spartan, but the Marines—"

"I just saved a whole lot of their asses," Gabriel said, rather more hotly than he had intended, *"and* half the Verge, as an incidental. You'd think that would count for something."

"Well, *I* would," Kharls said, "but you should know, as a former Marine yourself, that the lives of your own people count for more than anything else. If you don't take care of yourselves, who will? The deaths of the Marines from *Falada* and the pursuit of this trial remain important to the organization, and I am unwilling to do anything that might impair morale at this point . . . such as show undue favor to the accused."

Gabriel made a rueful face. "Well, yes, I do understand, even though at the moment I don't much care for it."

"That said," Kharls continued, "I am willing to listen to anything for which you might personally ask me."

Gabriel looked at him quietly for a few moments then shook his head.

"No," he said at last.

"Unusual," said Kharls, after a pause nearly as long.

"Maybe not," Gabriel said.

Kharls was quiet for a moment. "You have given us," he said, "perhaps the one tool that will turn this struggle in our favor. It may take years yet to tell, but this kind of defense leaves us freer than we would have thought possible to turn our attention to offense."

"Always my preferred mode," Gabriel said.

Kharls gave him a look. "I wonder. I was about to accuse you of mellowing, but possibly that's premature. It's probably just as well, for you have a lot more searching ahead of you after you serve your sentence . . . and that edge will help keep you alive."

Gabriel nodded. "One question, though."

"Certainly."

"VoidCorp."

"Yes," said Kharls. He stood and stretched again. "There is a situation that will want to be looked at closely in the coming weeks and months. It was interesting to note"—he looked sideways at Gabriel—"that during the battle, though there were a surprising number of them there, none of their vessels seemed willing to do anything on either side. It is . . . suggestive."

"Yes," Gabriel said. "Almost as if they were unwilling to annoy a potential ally, before they knew which way things seemed to be going."

Kharls nodded, then he seemed to stand indecisive for a moment. A strange sight, one which Gabriel had never seen. "Tell me something. You have apparently been through something . . . very strange. Who *were* they? The Precursors, I mean."

It was a question that had been on Gabriel's mind. "Administrator," he replied, "I wish I knew. The Patterners seem to have been built to be very like them, and the Patterners have almost no sense of self as such. In what I have inside me now, which is everything that was there—a great library of practical science material mostly, and directions to other facilities—there are no images of them. Either they had a religious injunction against it, or"—he laughed once, softly—"or we *are* them come back again after a great failure for another chance at success. Who knows? The Patterner seemed to think so, but even it was unsure."

Kharls nodded slowly.

"And you," Kharls said. "Who are you, now?"

"You mean, 'What are you?' " Gabriel said.

"No," Kharls said. "Who?"

Gabriel smiled slightly. "I am a man. Maybe not 'just another human,' but definitely a man, and very confused."

"And not guilty."

"Of murder," Gabriel said, "no. Not guilty."

Kharls made for the door, paused there. "After this is all over, I think I can tell you that, should your oaths guide you in that direction—as they seem to have done for the last year—the Concord would deeply appreciate your service."

"After this is over, Administrator," Gabriel said, "I would certainly meet you in the gym of your choosing and attempt to knock your block off for all the trouble you've caused me." He smiled, but it was one of those smiles he had borrowed from Grawl, with fangs showing. "After *that* we'll discuss service."

"Yes," Kharls said, "that I *did* expect. I would say we will certainly have some dealings outside the judicial process." He went down to the door at the end of the corridor, rapped on it, and the guard let him out.

* * * * *

The trial happened about a month and a half later and lasted for several weeks. They did not try to rush it. There was too much attention being paid to it in the media, for whom interest in Gabriel had greatly increased after news of the events at Argolos got out. Gabriel tried to contact his father during that period and got the expected response. Silence. It would be a while before that particular disjuncture in his personal universe would be healed, if ever.

There were few surprises at the trial, except that it took so long to actually happen. Finding someone to take Gabriel's testimony was the main difficulty, but finally the Concord authorities found a fraal working on Lucullus who was able to see into Gabriel's mind in enough detail to do the necessary documentation.

Gabriel's own written testimony, along with his elaboration of the material the fraal was able to elicit from him, was all entered into the record, and the evidence about Ricel was much argued.

"Everything Connor has given us independently," Gabriel's defense attorney argued, "matches exactly the records concerning the development and use of this clone group as we understand it. To earlier data, we have no access."

"It doesn't mean anything," countered the other prosecutor. "Just because this information is correct does not mean that the defendant is innocent of the actions of which he is accused. Indeed it could suggest, if looked at by an unfriendly eye, that the two were in even deeper collusion than the court originally thought."

"Nonetheless, the information is accurate, and this must be taken into account . . ."

It went on for days like that, and Gabriel knew where it was all going, even without telepathy. The judges' minds were all too open a book. Kharls himself was not adjudicating, much to Gabriel's disappointment, but it was precisely because of the contact between them that he had disqualified himself.

When the discovery stage was over and the nonevidentiary phase began, Enda was the first one to request the right to testify before the panel. After that came Helm, Delde Sota, Angela, Grawl, and the Marines who had been present at Delonghi's killing (of which Helm had been acquitted days before in a separate proceeding). This was the hardest part for Gabriel, for he knew that, while the judges were listening, they had their minds made up already. The pain his friends were in affected him directly, despite his attempts to shut it out. He wound up taking lessons with the fraal who had taken his testimony on how to erect personal barriers.

"You know," the fraal said, after the last of four wearying lessons was done, "that you cannot keep your friends out of your mind, anyway."

Gabriel sighed at that and lay awake that night, listening to the others worrying down in their ships attached to the *Lighthouse*'s spars. The next day was sentencing, and he knew what was going to happen. He had said nothing to them, because it would have depressed them. An extra day of hope is better . . .

The following morning he was brought in for the sentencing and received the only surprise of the proceeding. The judges announced that there was one more nonevidentiary statement to be made.

Elinke Dareyev walked in.

Gabriel sat there and, to his own astonishment, began to shake as Elinke spoke.

"Your honors," she said, "mental reservation does not protect one from charges of perjury. Maybe it would just be simpler to say that in the aftermath of the *Falada* shuttle disaster, I testified that Jacob Ricel was not working for Concord Intel in any capacity. That was true. However, I did know that he was VoidCorp . . . and I withheld this information from the court."

There were very few people in the courtroom, not enough for there to be a great ruckus of any kind, but the judges immediately retired to review all the evidence with an eye to this sudden new development.

Gabriel, for his own part, could only sit numbly as Elinke made her way out of the courtroom. The two of them would spend the next several days elaborating on the information behind that statement. She went past him, and Gabriel felt, like a cool draft, that terrible ambivalence in her, the division between kindness and cruelty, a line she always had trouble straddling. *I might have known this could happen,* he thought. There had been the matter of a door left open one night, without explanation, on *Schmetterling.* He had heard that awful, anguished thought, *my poor crew . . .* and later, *I always said you were the devil himself.* He had not done that favor for her. She would not have accepted it from him if he had, but for her crew . . .

She went by him, cool, composed, the uniform perfect, and glanced down as she passed. "Now all debts are paid," she said as she passed, and the security people went after her.

* * * * *

Four days later Gabriel stood up for the sentencing and heard the chief judge read the long statement that started out detailing the events on *Falada* and ended with those on *Schmetterling.* There was a brief dry mention of the extenuating circumstances and the great assistance the defendant had lent to the Concord forces at the Battle of Argolos.

"Of the first charge of murder and all subsequent charges relating thereto," the chief judge said, "we find the defendant not guilty. The circumstances require us, however, to find him guilty on twenty counts of manslaughter in the second degree. With mitigating circumstances considered, we sentence the defendant to ten years' confinement, to be served in the Marine confinement facility on the Galactic Concord vessel *Lighthouse,* beginning immediately and minus time served."

That was all. Everyone stood up, and the guards came for Gabriel. Enda, Helm, Delde Sota, Angela, and Grawl were waiting behind the bar separating court from spectators, and their faces were sad. Helm looked positiviely dour behind his new eyepatch.

"You knew it was going to happen," Gabriel told them.

"Well . . ." Enda said. "I think *Sunshine* will be riding with the *Lighthouse* for a while."

"We'll come and go," Helm said, "but we won't be far, not for long." He looked around. "This is a nice place . . . good facilities here. You could get used to not roughing it for ten years or so."

Gabriel smiled at him and Delde Sota and then turned to Angela and Grawl.

"We'll be here," Angela said.

"I know," Gabriel said. "Thanks . . . thank you all."

They took him away to the comfortable but windowless cell that would be his home for the next ten years.

Chapter Twenty

TWO EVENINGS LATER, Lorand Kharls came by to see him.

"So," Kharls said, "no surprises."

Gabriel lay on the bed in the small bare room. He nodded. This was Phorcys all over again, but at least there were Marines outside this cell. Also, Gabriel was not quite who he had been nearly three years before, and the walls seemed rather more transparent this time.

"None?" Gabriel said. "Not even Elinke?"

"Not at all," Kharls said. "When you have my job for long enough, you learn not to waste your time with platitudes or beliefs about human nature. Human beings in the specific, rather than the general are my study. Trends and large movements . . . yes, those, too, but separately. Lumping them all together, expecting human people to behave in a human way is always a mistake. We're much too, well, too personally Brownian a species to behave as expected. Great trends may move us. Great threats or inducements cause large groups of people to move one way or another, but there is always room for any particular particle to jiggle, and it tends to do so exactly in the way opposite from what one might reasonably expect. She jiggled, that's all."

Gabriel filed that away for later analysis, but said nothing in response.

Kharls sighed. "This will be my last visit for a while. I am moving on in a day or so."

"I suppose I should thank you," Gabriel said.

"For what?" Kharls said. "You must now spend ten years in confinement. Lives are longer than they used to be, but ten years is a long while for so young a man. Tools rust, talents go to hell." Kharls looked at him sharply. "I expect you not to let that happen."

And he was gone, just that suddenly, while Gabriel still was in the process of opening his mouth to say something cutting.

Too late. The door of the cell was shut. Gabriel looked at it and said silently, *I'll get you for that some day.*

*   *   *   *   *

Late that night something woke Gabriel up, a sense that he was being looked at. This happened often enough, especially now that a mere glance at his door by a passerby could cause Gabriel to come alert, but this time he genuinely *was* being looked at.

Blue eyes. Big blue eyes, almost luminous even in this near darkness.

Will you come with me? Enda asked.

Gabriel sat up in the bed, half confused by sleep. *How'd you get in here? Where's the guard?*

Gabriel, be still and come on!

They made their way swiftly out of the cell and through the dimmed corridors of the security area. Not a soul was to be seen. The one duty officer who routinely manned the desk down at the corridor's end was not there.

Gabriel came out at the end of the corridor, and someone slipped near him from around a corner and threw a cloak over him, the kind of thing an Orlamu based on the station might wear.

"Come on," said Delde Sota's voice as she fell into step beside him. "Window of opportunity only so wide. Put these on." She pushed a pair of shaded glasses into his hands, something like a vacationer might wear on a sunny Bluefall day. "Will help to hide your eyes."

They do attract attention. Enda smiled at him apologetically as he donned the shades.

Ten minutes later they were on the public transport that led down to the main lifts serving the docking spars. The transport was full of a group of people coming back from a party, laughing and joking. No one had time to spare a glance for a fraal, a mechalus, and a sleepy Orlamu, all clinging together like the punchline from some offcolor joke.

The three of them got off the lift and headed down spar five. As they passed a port, Gabriel could see four ships berthed together there. *Sunshine*, *Lalique*, *Longshot*, and another ship he didn't know. To his astonishment, Enda pushed him past the lock serving *Sunshine*'s tube and into the next one along, the one for the larger sleek ship he didn't know, the one as large as *Lalique*.

"But Enda—!"

"Grawl is handling *Sunshine* at the moment," she hissed. "Hurry!"

She pushed him into the new ship, shut the outer door and the inner door behind them, slapped the control to disconnect the tube, and headed forward to the pilot's cabin.

"Go, Helm!" she called.

"Grapples away," Helm said down comms, "starfall in one minute. Last one away gets to cook when we come out."

"Enda!" Gabriel raced after her, ditched the cloak and glasses in passing, and slid into the pilot's seat across from her. They were in a cabin that had to be three times the size of *Sunshine*'s. "How did we. . . ? *Helm?*"

"Someone died and left it to you," Helm answered.

"Who?"

"Bald guy with a funny staff. Just an opinion, of course. Can't swear to it. *I* didn't see anything. Can we get out of here before he changes his mind?"

"Where are we going?"

"Away out where you can look for all these other strange places you've been told about," Enda said, "and where we can use up all those staples you bought!" She tsked softly. "I really am going to have to find a way to get some more exercise. I shall put on weight, otherwise."

We will certainly have some dealings outside of the judicial process, Kharls had said.

The ships arrowed away from the docking spars, and Gabriel looked over his shoulder at the great bulk of *Lighthouse.* The side turned toward Algemron shone brilliantly. The battle scars from the battle had been thoroughly cleaned, though a few rents in the hull were still being repaired. The vast ship's darker half sparkled with dozens of lights, any one of which could have come from the viewport of the Concord Administrator's office. Perhaps . . .

You son of a bitch! Gabriel thought as loudly as he could.

Four vessels soared away briefly on system drive, then made starfall.

And all the starfalls were black.

* * * * *

Aboard the *Lighthouse,* a man in the act of packing his few belongings stood up straight, suddenly possessed of a roaring headache.

I've brought this on myself, he thought.

The Concord Administrator stood there with his head throbbing. The pain was probably only a harbinger of things to come. The events of the past weeks were going to take a good while to settle, and he expected a fair amount of recrimination from his superiors over exactly how his plans had worked out. It was the cross he routinely bore that they usually did not understand what he had been doing, even when he explained it in mind-shattering detail.

Results, though . . . those they understood . . . eventually. They would be weeks digesting the ones that had resulted from the events at Algemron. It would give him time to marshal his thoughts and recuperate a little. It never took him long, for completing any piece of work always lent him energy. Then he would start the next plan of action, which would also have to be explained to the people above him in the hierarchy, and which despite the explanation, they also would not understand.

He was used to that, though. Such situations often provided their own refreshments—such as beings who were not his superiors but did understand.

He paused, went out to the window, and looked out into the darkness. There was a greater darkness coming, one with its own terrible agenda and possessing power much greater than had recently been seen. Humanity and its cousins would need all the help they could find in the fight against that encroaching darkness.

If there was anything he was sure of, it was that bureaucracy and governments and armies and mighty weapons were not the force that would finally win that fight. Individuals would do it, people who walked their own road, lifting their single weapons against the night and refusing to be cowed by the darkness around them. They were his kindred spirits, the ones who understood the old saying, "The lifting of the single sword will keep the whole world in peace." He would help them as he could, knowing that their swords and his were lifted in the same cause. Eventually they or their successors would triumph. Months or lifetimes . . . it did not matter to him. Together they would get the job done, though some of them walked strange roads to do so.

In the meantime, Lorand Kharls smiled to himself, enjoying the headache, for he knew where it came from. Then he picked up his tri-staff and headed off toward his next job.

Glossary

Aegis - A G2 yellow star. The metropolitan center of the Verge.

AI - Artificial Intelligence. Sentient computer programming whose sophistication varies from model to model.

alaith - A tropical tree native to Bluefall.

Aleerin - see mechalus.

Algemron – A G5 yellow star.

Alitar – Fourth planet of the Algemron system, and home to the Imperial State of Algemron.

Argolos – A large asteroid of the Algemron system.

AU - Astronomical Unit. 150 million km

Austrin-Ontis Unlimited - A corporate stellar nation that is the strongest arms dealer in the Stellar Ring. Most Austrins view themselves as strong individualists with a deep sense of altruism.

Beronin – Once the largest and most beautiful city of Alitar, Beronin was nearly destroyed by the Galvinites in 2461. It has since been rebuilt as a fortress city.

Bluefall - Capital planet of the Aegis system. Ruled by the Regency government.

Builder - A segment of fraal society that believes in integration with other species and cultures.

Calderon - The innermost world of the Algemron system.

caulia - A red vegetable from the Stellar Ring noted for its rich flavor.

cerametal - An extremely strong alloy made from laminated ceramics and lightweight metals.

charge weapon - A firearm in which an electric firing pin ignites a
     chemical explosive into a white-hot plasma propellant, thus
     expelling a cerametallic slug at extremely high velocity.

Churgalt Insurgency - A force of rebels on Galvin who claim that
     the Federal State of Algemron is in league with unknown
     aliens.

Churgalt region - A densely forested area of Galvin's equatorial
     regions.

CM armor - cerametal armor.

Concord - see Galactic Concord.

Concord Survey Service - A division of Star Force dedicated to
     scouting, surveying, and first contacts.

Conker - A derogatory term for citizens of the Galactic Concord.

Connor, Gabriel - A former Concord marine lieutenant, now
     freelance explorer and infotrader.

Corpse - A derogatory term for a VoidCorp Employee.

Corrivale - An F2 yellow-white star.

Coulomb - A red dwarf star near the edge of the Verge.

CSS - see Concord Survey Service.

Dalius – A small gas giant and the fifth world of the Algemron
     system.

Danwell - The only hospitable world of the Eldala system;
     homeworld of the edanweir.

Dareyev, Elinke - Captain of Star Force vessel *Schmetterling*.

David, Lemke - A Star Force second lieutenant navigator, usually
     called "Lem." Now deceased.

Delonghi, Aleen - A member of Concord Intelligence.

DeVrona, Mara - A Concord Administrator currently assigned to the
     Algemron system.

drivecore - The central engine core of a stardrive.

drivesat - A communications satellite that drops into drivespace in
     order to transmit and receive messages.

driveship - Any spaceship that is equipped with a stardrive.

drivespace - The dimension into which starships enter through use
     of the stardrive. In this dimension, gravity works on a
     quantum level, thus enabling movement of a ship from one
     point in space to another in only 121 hours.

durasteel - Steel that has been strengthened at the molecular level.

edanwe (pl. edanweir) - A sentient species native to Danwell.

Eldala - A newly discovered system past Mantebron.

Enda - A fraal.

Erhardt Field - The main spaceport and airport of Galvin. Located about 20 kilometers from the city center in the Verdant Mountains.

e-suit - An environment suit intended to keep the wearer safe from vacuum, extreme temperatures, and radiation.

external - A term used to describe anything that originates beyond known space.

Falada - A Concord Star Force Heavy Cruiser.

flechette gun - Any firearm that utilizes bundles of tiny, razor-sharp aerofoils as projectiles.

Fort Drum – The capital city of the Federal State of Algemron on Galvin.

fraal - A non-Terran sentient species. Fraal are very slender, large-eyed humanoids.

Galactic Concord - The thirteenth stellar nation, formed by the Treaty of Concord. Concord law and administration rule in the Verge.

Galactic Standard - The lingua franca of known space.

Galvin – Home planet of the Federal State of Algemron.

gillie – A small gamefish native to Bluefall noted for its seventeen gill-slits.

gravity induction - A process whereby a cyclotron accelerates particles to near-light speeds, thereby creating gravitons between the particle and the surrounding mass. This process can be adjusted and redirected, thus allowing the force of gravity to be overcome. Most starships use a gravity induction engine for in-system travel.

Grawl - A weren poetess.

Grid - An interstellar computer network.

Grith - A moon of Hydrocus and the only habitable world in the Corrivale system.

gurnet - A quadripedal species native to Kurg favored for its meat.

Gyrofresia ondothalis fraalii - see "Ondothwait"

Halo – A small gas giant of the Algemron system.

Hammer's Star - A yellow G5 star. Site of the outermost Concord outpost in the Verge.

Hatire Community - A theocratic stellar nation founded on the founded on the general anti-technology religion of the same name.

Hatire faith - A religion that preaches ascendance through union with the spirit of the Cosimir, a Precursor deity that the Hatire adopted as their own. Most Hatire hold attitudes antagonistic to technology and abhor all forms of man-machine integration.

Havryn – A gas giant of Algemron and largest planet in the system.

High Mojave - The only inhabited world of the Mantebron system. Also the site of the best-preserved Glassmaker ruins.

holocomm - holographic communication.

holodisplay - The display of a holocomm that can be viewed in either one, two, or three dimensions.

Ilmater - A lifeless world of Algemron.

Inseer - A citizen of Insight.

Insight - A subsidiary of VoidCorp that broke away to form a separate stellar nation. Citizenry is dominated by freethinking Grid pilots who believe that humanity can reach its destiny only in Gridspace.

Iphus - A planet in the Corrivale system.

Iphus Collective - A mining facility run by StarMech Collective on Iphus.

JustWadeln - A software program developed by Insight that allows the user to learn space combat at ever-increasing levels of difficulty.

Kendai - A planet of the edge of the Stellar Ring that houses the drivespace relay that connects communications between the stellar nations and the Verge.

Kharls, Lorand - A Concord Administrator.

kroath - A hostile external species of unknown origin.

Lalique - Angela Valiz's driveship.

lanth cell - The standard lanthanide battery used to power most small electronic equipment and firearms.

Lighthouse - A huge space station, capable of 50 light-year starfalls, that roams the Verge.

Lightning Nebula - An unexplored region of space beyond Hammer's Star.

Longshot - Helm Ragnarsson's weapon-laden driveship.

Long Silence - That period of time when the Stellar Nations lost contact with the Verge because of the Second Galactic War.

Mantebron - One of the outermost star systems of the Verge.

mass weapon - A weapon that fires a ripple of intense gravity waves, striking its target like a massive physical blow.

mass reactor - The primary power source of a stardrive. The reactor collects, stores, and processes dark matter, thus producing massive amounts of energy.

mechalus - The most common term used for an Aleerin, a sentient humanoid symbiote species that has achieved a union between biological life and cybernetic enhancements.

mindwalker - Any being proficient with psionic powers.

Monitor Mandate - The mandate of 2497 that granted both Alitar and Galvin full independence from the Thuldan Empire and Austrin-Ontis Unlimited.

neurocircuitry - Cybernetic implants intended to fuse electronic or mechanical systems with a living biological entity.

Norrik, Garth - Deputy Chief of Field Operations for the Federal State of Algemron's Intelligence Directorate.

ondothwait - A plant. Scientific name: Gyrofresia ondothalis fraalii.

orbweaver - A sentient organism, whose body is made of living crystal and glass, believed to have been created by the Glassmakers. Though highly intelligent and curious, no orbweaver encountered thus far has ever displayed any inherent sense of self.

Orion League - A heterogenous stellar nation founded on principles of freedom and equal rights for all sentients.

Palshizon – A planet of Algemron on which the Concord keeps a permanent installation in order to enforce the *Monitor* Mandate.

Pariah Station – The Concord installation orbiting Palshizon whose job it is to enforce the *Montior* Mandate.

Phorcys - A planet of the Thalaassa system.

phymech - An automated emergency medical system with a fairly sophisticated AI system. Most phymechs come with fairly specialized medical supplies—skinfilms, bandages, antiseptics, painkillers, etc.

plasma weapon - A weapon that converts an electro-chemical mixture into white-hot plasma and then utilizes a magnetic accelerator to throw a blast of the plasma at the target. The super-heated plasma explodes upon striking its target.

prassith - A genetically enhanced sweet root first introduced in the Stellar Ring by the Orlamu.

Ragnarsson, Helm - A human mutant.

rail cannon - An electromagnetic accelerator that fires projectiles at extremely high velocities.

Rand - Lorand Kharls's assistant.

Red Rain - A bioweapon that converts any kind of organic matter into a lethal mycotoxin.

Reliance – A world of Algemron.

rhin - A weren lap-harp.

rlin noch'i - The common garb of the mechalus. Consists of a multi-pocketed smartsuit and soft boots.

RS201 67LEK - A VoidCorp intelligence officer.

sabot weapon - A firearm that uses electromagnetic pulses to accelerate a discarding-rocket slug at hypersonic speeds.

Schmetterling - A Concord Star Force Heavy Cruiser.

Sealed Knot, the - A mechalus symbol favored by medical practitioners of that species.

seeker - The formal term given to initiates of the Orlamu faith.

sesheyan - A bipedal sentient species possessing long, bulbous heads, large ears, and eight light-sensitive eyes. Most sesheyans are about 1.7 meters tall and have two leathery wings that span between 2.5 - 4 meters. Sheya, the sesheyan homeworld, has been subjugated by VoidCorp. However, a substantial population of "free sesheyans" live on Grith.

Silence, the - see the Long Silence.

skinfilm - An artifical polymer membrane, usually only a few molecules thick, that is often used for sanitary protection or containment.

Sota, Delde - A mechalus doctor and former Grid pilot.

spaceport - A planetary landing zone for driveships.

spee-g - short for specific gravity.

Standard - see Galactic Standard.

stardrive - The standard starship engine that combines a gravity induction coil and a mass reactor to open a temporary singularity in space and thus allow a ship to enter drivespace. All jumps take 121 hours, no matter the distance.

starfall - The term used to describe a ship entering drivespace.

Star Force - The naval branch of the Concord military.

starport - A zero-g, orbital docking zone for driveships.

starrise - The term used to describe a ship leaving drivespace.

stellar nations - The thirteeen sovereign governing the Stellar Ring, the center of which is Sol (Earth).

Stellar Ring - The systems that make up the thirteen stellar nations, the center of which is Sol.

STG shuttle - Space-To-Ground shuttle.

Stricken – A large island in Bluefall's northern hemisphere.

stutter cannon - A powerful but nonlethal weapon that uses blasts of compressed air to render targets unconscious without causing serious harm.

sunfish – A shallow water fish native to Bluefall.

Sunshine – Gabriel Connor and Enda's starship.

system drive - Any form of non-stardrive propulsion used for inner system traffic.

Thalaassa - An F2 yellow star. Also the name of the system.

Thuldan Empire - A militaristic, fiercely patriotic stellar nation that considers the unity of humanity under the Thuldan banner to be its manifest destiny. The largest of the stellar nations.

Tisane – A small settled island near Stricken.

Tlelai - An edanwe hunter.

Treaty of Concord, the - The Treaty that ended the Second Galactic War and formed the Galactic Concord.

tri-staff - The traditional weapon carried by Concord Administrators.

Valiz, Angela - A human freelance trader and explorer.

Verdant Mountains — A chain of small mountains near Fort Drum on Galvin.

Verge, the - A frontier region of space originally colonized by the stellar nations that was cut off during the Second Galactic War.

verjuice - A beverage made from the berry of the verrillia plant in the Borealis Republic.

VoidCorp - A corporate stellar nation. Citizens are referred to as Employees and all have an assigned number.

Wanderer - 1.) Fraal: A term used to describe that segment of fraal culture that prefers life aboard their wandering city-ships rather than settling down to mingle with other species. 2.) Sesheyan: Weyshe the Wanderer, a sesheyan deity.

Welsh, Rina — An officer of the Department of Hospitality at Erhardt Field.

weren - A sentient species native to the planet Kurg. Most weren stand well over 2 meters tall, are covered in thick fur, and have sharp claws. Male weren have large tusks protruding from the bottom jaw.

weren - A sentient species native to the planet Kurg in the Stellar Ring. Most weren stand well over two meters tall, are covered in thick fur, and have sharp claws. Male weren have large tusks protruding from the bottom jaw.

werewisp - An electromagnetic creature, usually aggressive, that is most often found on High Mojave.

whilom - A quadripedal species native to Kurg, favored for its meat.

whitetails — An arboreal bird native to Bluefall.

Wreathe — A large asteroid of Algemron. The planetoid possesses a thin but very toxic atmosphere.

STAR✦DRIVE®

Adventure beyond the stars with Diane Duane

The Harbinger Trilogy

Starrise at Corrivale
Volume One

Gabriel Connor is up against it. Expelled from the Concord
Marines and exiled in disgrace, he's offered one last chance by
the Concord to redeem himself. All it involves is gambling
his life in a vicious game of death.

Storm at Eldala
Volume Two

Gabriel and his fraal companion are scratching out a
living among the dangerous stars of the Verge when they
stumble onto new, unknown forces. Only their deaths seem
likely to avert disaster. But an astonishing revelation from the
depths of time makes the prospect of survival even
more terrible than a clean death.

Nightfall at Algemron
Volume Three

Gabriel Connor's quest to save the Verge and clear his
name leads him to a system ravaged by war and to the ruins of
a long-dead alien civilization. Along the way, he discovers that
to save himself and all he holds dear, his one salvation may
also be his ultimate destruction.

Available April 2000

S T A R • D R I V E®

To the edge of the galaxy and back!

Two of Minds
Williams H. Keith, Jr.

In the urban underground hell of Tribon on the planet Oberon, life in a street gang doesn't offer many possibilities. That is, until one day Kai St. Kyr robs the wrong man and finds himself in the middle of a power struggle that stretches beyond the stars.

Available July 2000

Gridrunner
Thomas M. Reid

When a black market courier journeys to the Verge, she must enter the virtual world of the mysterious Grid. Together with an undercover agent, she finds herself embroiled in a desperate conflict between a crime syndicate, terrorists, and her own boss. The solution lies in the Grid.

Available September 2000

Zero Point
Richard Baker

Peter Sokolov is a bounty hunter and killer for hire. Geille Monashi, a brilliant data engineer, is his quarry. After Sokolov and Monashi encounter an alien derelict in the farthest reaches of space, they have only one chance to survive. They've got to trust each other.

On the Verge
Roland J. Green

War erupts on Arist, a frozen world on the borders of known space. The Concord Marines charge in to prevent the conflict from escalating, but soon discover that an even darker threat awaits them.

R.A. Salvatore
Servant of the Shard

The exciting climax of the story of the Crystal Shard

In 1988 R.A. Salvatore burst onto the fantasy scene with a novel about a powerful magical artifact—the Crystal Shard. Now, more than a decade later, he brings the story of the Shard to its shattering conclusion.

From the dark, twisted streets of Calimport to the lofty passes of the Snowflake Mountains, from flashing swords to sizzling spells, this is R.A. Salvatore at his best.

Available October 2000

From the best-selling writing team of Weis and Hickman

Dragons of a Fallen Sun

The War of Souls • Volume One
Margaret Weis and Tracy Hickman

Change—for good or for ill—comes to the world of Krynn. A violent magical storm sweeps over Ansalon, bringing flood and fire, death and destruction. Out of the tumult rises a strange, mystical young woman. Her destiny is bound up with that of Krynn. For she alone knows the truth about the future, a future strangely and inextricably tied to the terrifying mystery in Krynn's past.

Sequel to
the best-selling *Dragons of Summer Flame*,
this is the first volume in a magnificent new epic trilogy
by the creators of the DRAGONLANCE saga,
Margaret Weis and Tracy Hickman.

Available March 2000